For The Ones
Who Prevail

R. Collins

Samsara Fleet | Book Five

Books By Riley Collins

To learn more about Riley Collins, see an updated list of titles, and join his mailing list go to his webpage at https://www.rileycollins.info.

Samsara Fleet Series

Book One: For the Ones Who Remain
Book Two: For the Ones Who Are Forgotten
Book Three: For the Ones Who Rebel
Book Four: For the Ones Who Liberate
Book Five: For the Ones Who Prevail

Central Worlds Series

Book One: Escape From the Fringe

Copyright © 2022
All rights reserved.
ISBN-13: 979-8-9872085-1-9
Print Edition

Cover Art by: 17 Studio Book Design
Editing by: Lisa Binion

For the men and women of the 54th EN BN (C)(M)

Chapter One
Nicole | Patagonia

"Ma'am, we've got a Nasi patrol entering the area."

Lieutenant Colonel Nicole Bergeron felt an icy sliver of fear down her spine as she turned to meet Staff Sergeant Koula Bhatt's green eyes.

"Damn it, they must've trailed us. How long?"

"Five minutes, maybe ten, tops."

Nicole turned back to the Patagonia Front rebel she'd been talking to. The man glanced around nervously at the pitted concrete walls of the small bunker they were in, his breath coming out in quick gulps.

"Okay, let's make this quick then," said Nicole, trying to keep her voice level. "What can you tell us that's not on this?" She held up the small chit he'd given to her.

"I don't know exactly what's on that thing, but I can tell you the Nasi have stepped up their training program. You should hear their soldiers complaining in the bars."

Nicole wasn't surprised. All soldiers, even Nasi ones, complained about training and missions.

She nodded. "How's the commander?" Sergeant Frederick Kinawadi was the leader of the Patagonia Front and a former member of Samsara Fleet. Despite his youth, he'd molded them into an effective intelligence apparatus and fighting force.

"The commander's good, ma'am. He said to let you know that we're ready when you are." The rebel gave a small grin.

"I can't believe we're so close."

Nicole returned the smile. "Just be ready." She turned to Sergeant Bhatt, who'd remained behind her. "Let's go."

They crawled through the dank, muck-filled tunnel and climbed the metal rungs of the ladder that led to the forest above. The facility they'd used for the meeting had been a former Earth Defense Force training site. Now that the EDF was gone, destroyed by the Nasi, the bunker had begun to fall into disrepair. Although she couldn't see them, Nicole knew there were two fire teams of Tac-I soldiers guarding the perimeter. After having conducted infiltration missions on Patagonia for the past nine months, they'd become experts at concealing themselves in the thick underbrush of the forest that covered much of the planet's single continent.

The rebel nodded to Nicole and Bhatt and crept into the trees, barely making a noise as he left. Sergeant Peng, Alpha Team leader, appeared a moment later and knelt next to Nicole and Bhatt.

"What do we got?" Nicole asked.

"Ma'am, we got two to four of 'em coming down from the northeast," replied Peng.

"That's our primary avenue of escape." Bhatt screwed up her mouth in annoyance. "We're going to need to head north and then circle around to the transport."

Nicole nodded. As the ranking NCO, Bhatt was the commander on the ground, and she'd follow her lead.

Bhatt rustled a nearby branch to catch the others' attention and circled her hand in the air in a rally sign.

6

Normally they could use their neural implants to communicate, but with the Nasi so close, there was a chance they might triangulate on the signal—especially in what *should* be a vacant former EDF training camp. The five other members of the Tac-I squad materialized from the brush around them, and Bhatt whispered quick words of instruction. The past several months had hardened the squad, and they needed little direction on what to do. Less than a minute later, they were headed south, creeping single-file through waist-high yellow plants.

As Nicole trod through the brush, carefully following the person in front of her, she listened for sounds of the enemy. Without her battle suit or a tacmap, she was blind to where they were. The forest was deathly quiet except for the small rustle of the soldiers in front of and behind her. Occasionally, she heard the faint sound of scurrying feet and saw a branch rustle over their heads. The reds, yellows, and oranges of the native flora were distracting and more than once something caught her eye, only for her to realize it was a small animal jumping between tree limbs.

Finally, they arrived at the small clearing where their transport rested on the decaying leaves of the forest floor. It was invisible to the naked eye, hidden by several optical projectors placed around the craft.

"They're close. Very close," Bhatt whispered. Nicole didn't bother to ask how the woman knew; she'd found that NCOs just did. "Sergeant Peng, get Alpha Team in the vehicle. Corporal Basu, pick up the optical projectors and have your team cover Alpha until I get the engines on."

The two privates in Bravo Team hastily started picking up the small projectors from the ground and shutting them off, revealing the luxury civilian transport the Bones had requisitioned for the mission. Nicole followed Sergeant Bhatt as she jumped into the side door of the vehicle. Plush couches completely lined the interior except for a small break where the original minibar had been converted to storage for ammunition. Originally, the vehicle had belonged to a local celebrity, but the Front had recovered it and added armor, energy shields, and a small complement of weapons.

Bhatt squeezed herself through the partition between the passenger compartment and the driver's area. Seconds later as Alpha Team rushed into the vehicle the deep vibrations of the engine started.

An explosion at the edge of the clearing rocked the transport. The three members of Bravo Team jumped from their positions, firing their weapons through the trees, and ran toward the transport. There wasn't a point in trying to hold their positions; they didn't stand a chance against a group of Nasi in battle suits. Even without the suits, the Nasi were stronger and faster than any Human could hope to be.

The hum of the vehicle's engine had turned into a full-throated roar as Bhatt lifted them off the forest floor. Corporal Basu, the Bravo Team leader, and one of his soldiers jumped into the passenger compartment. As soon as they landed, the corporal frantically looked around the interior.

"Where's Wilson?" he shouted.

Nicole felt her heart sink as she glanced around the compartment. There was nothing they could do though. The Nasi were almost at the transport and the entire mission was in jeopardy. She saw something out of the corner of her eye. A young woman was running toward the transport, the side of her blouse stained red. Private Wilson.

"There!" shouted one of the soldiers, pointing towards Wilson.

"Sergeant Bhatt, wait!" Basu screamed, his eyes wide.

The vehicle continued to lift from the ground, and the door closed with a soft click.

"I said wait!" The corporal rushed to the front of the transport, wedging the front of his body in the driver's compartment as he shouted.

"Get back and sit down," Bhatt shouted with a turn of her head. "They've got her."

"But—"

"Sit down!" Nicole could hear pain in the sergeant's voice.

Plasma bolts hit their energy shields as they reached the top of the forest canopy. Looking down, Nicole could see Private Wilson standing in the center of the clearing, looking up. Although she was too far away for Nicole to see her face, she imagined the look of terror that must be on it. She almost screamed herself as three black-suited Nasi leapt into the clearing and tackled the private.

We left her, Nicole thought to herself. We left her to them.

The transport shot over the trees and Corporal Basu dropped into a seat with a scream of frustration. He buried his head in lap, trying to conceal his tears as they headed back toward their ship.

❖

Nicole saw Chief Heather Ramos open her mouth then snap it closed it as she noticed the dark expressions of the Bones as they trudged up the *Chester's* cargo ramp. The entire flight from the abandoned EDF base to their ship had been deathly quiet. They'd been through rough times before, and Nicole had learned that it was best to let her soldiers process everything on their own. Some of them might talk to Sergeant Bhatt later, but they were still on a mission at that moment.

"Let's go," Nicole said quietly as she passed the chief. She could see the question in Ramos' eyes. *What had happened?* Nicole was too tired to provide an answer now; the chief would figure it out soon enough.

The past months had taken their toll on them. For almost a year, Not Bergeron's Boneheads, or the Bones, had been conducting regular scouting missions into each of the four Human colonies gathering intel or providing tech and arms to the varied rebel groups on each.

Minutes after they'd entered the *Chester*, the ship took off and left Patagonia's atmosphere. They needed to get far enough from the planet to activate their fold drive since the planet's gravitational field disrupted it. Too close to the planet, and the drive could cause their ship to implode—or worse. As they flew away, Nicole sat in the ship's cockpit and watched Patagonia shrink in her personal viewscreen. Its single continent, Pangea, was facing away from them, making the planet appear as a deep blue orb glowing in the darkness of space. From this distance, it was an image filled with beauty and light, but she'd seen more death on the blue planet than she could remember.

"So far, no evidence the Nasi have detected us," Ramos called out from the copilot's chair.

The fleet of five Nasi ships orbiting the planet was intended to prevent anyone or anything from entering or leaving. The *Chester* was designed for situations just like this and Nicole had faith in their optical cloak, which hid them from the Nasi sensors. Occasionally, one of the Nasi fighters strayed close and they had to change their course, but Nicole wasn't too worried. They'd gone through the Nasi blockade countless times without getting caught.

"We've got a few squadrons on maneuvers," said Captain Uhaa, their pilot. "I'm taking us around 'em."

"We're seeing more and more of them." Ramos sighed.

"The Nasi are preparing best they can," Nicole said. "We stopped them from building capital ships, but they're going to get as many fighters ready as they can before we attack."

For almost a year, Samsara Fleet had been at a stalemate with the Nasi. After losing half their fleet and their orbital shipbuilding facilities, the Nasi had pulled back to the four Human colonies: New America, Patagonia, Wudexingqiu and Mariga. Samsara Fleet couldn't attack the planets because of the Nasi plasma lances underneath each planet's surface. The lances were powerful weapons that fired beams of pure plasma that instantly destroyed any ship unlucky enough to be in their path. The enormous weapons were built underground or underwater, making them invulnerable to orbital fire.

Since they'd pushed the Nasi back, Samsara Fleet had been running recon missions on all four Human worlds. Their goal was to develop a strategy to take out the lances from the ground. It meant a lot of scouting missions and collaboration with local rebel groups to get schematics and locations of all the lances. All the while, Nicole knew the Nasi were planning something. But despite all the intel they'd gathered, neither she nor Samsara Fleet had a clue what it was.

Their missions had the secondary purpose of bolstering the local resistance forces on the planets. The Bones brought whatever equipment and resources they could provide on their missions and returned to the fleet with intel. It was a grind, constant life and death missions into enemy held territory. Anything outside the war was now a distant memory as real to her as a holo or book she'd read on her implant.

For the shipboard personnel, the last several months had been uneventful. The fleet remained in deep space except for resupply runs to allied planets.

The other species the Nasi had attacked—the Kurz, X'Ado, Qudoru, Tounous, and Z'Ta—had all been part of the fleet. But when the Nasi had been defeated, their ships had slowly attritted away to help rebuild their decimated planets.

Now they provided material support when they could but were otherwise completely out of the war. Nicole couldn't really blame them, but she still felt a sense of resentment.

Human soldiers were desperate to get into the fight, and there was a long list who'd expressed a desire to join Nicole's team. Being a part of the Bones was almost as prestigious as being a member of the Skulls, their sister team.

"We've got a squadron heading right towards us," Chief Ramos, the ship's copilot and chief engineer, called out.

Nicole's breath caught in her throat. "Have they seen us?"

Ramos grunted. "Not sure yet. Could be a regular exercise."

"We should be at the fold point in a few minutes," Uhaa said.

When they reached the fold point, they'd be able to engage their fold drive, creating a Minkowski wormhole and allowing them to change their location in space instantly. Through chaining together hundreds or thousands of these "folds" in space, they could travel between systems. The only problem was they needed to be completely free of gravitational disruptions before engaging the drive, which meant being clear of planets, capital ships, and anything else with a significant mass.

Nicole felt a familiar sense of dread. Dread for a situation where things could go horribly wrong and where she had no control. It was a constant that weighed on them all. Often, soldiers had to be rotated out of the Bones because they couldn't handle it anymore. Too many of them thought their missions would be assaulting an enemy position, guns blazing. More often than not, it was sneaking through enemy lines and hoping they didn't get caught.

"We can't go on like this much longer," she muttered to herself.

Captain Uhaa turned to look at her. "We'll be fine, ma'am." He pointed to the tacmap. "The Nasi fighters are turning already."

"Not that," Nicole said. "This stalemate. This entire thing." She thought of Private Wilson, standing in the clearing and looking up at them.

"We're almost ready," Ramos said. "We've located all the Nasi lances. The rebels are trained and armed. Hell, they even have some battle suits."

Nicole wished she shared their confidence. Nothing had ever been easy with the Nasi. Sure, it seemed like they had the advantage, but there was so much they didn't know yet. What did the Nasi's leader, Esma Baykara, have up her sleeves? Nicole was sure the woman hadn't been spending the past year sitting idly by.

"Maybe." Nicole said, unconvinced, idly tapping on her console. "Maybe."

"Once we take out the lances, they've got nothing else. We'll destroy their fleet and recapture the planets. Humanity will be restored, Nasi gone." Ramos held up her hands and gave a theatrical wave. "Ta da."

That was the plan. It was simple but direct. It hadn't been easy getting to this point, but Nicole couldn't help thinking they weren't nearly as close to winning as her soldiers thought.

"We're almost at eight-nines," Uhaa called out. The ship's computer let them know the probability of a successful fold based on the gravitational waves around them. There was always the chance that the drive would fail, but eight-nines or 99.999999 percent was enough they could activate the drive with near certain success.

"Okay, let's get out of here," Nicole ordered.

She zoomed in on the blue planet behind them on her viewscreen. Patagonia was *still* beautiful. Small lines of white clouds above a deep blue ocean. The hint of a green landmass on the edges. But it was a place Nicole never wanted to see again.

In a blink, the *Chester* folded, and the blue orb disappeared.

"How'd it go?" Colonel Irina Petrov asked.

Nicole looked at her across the conference table. "It went quick, ma'am. The Nasi were onto us almost as soon as we made contact." The image of Private Wilson, surrounded by Nasi soldiers, flashed through her head again. *That'll be one that'll stay for a while.*

"I heard you lost another soldier," said Junior Chief Atyakari, staring at her intently with his orange eyes. "I assume they didn't have any compromising information."

Atyakari was one of the Jadid advisors that had joined the crew of the *Ofira* and had become Colonel Petrov's shadow. Whether she liked it or not. Ostensibly, he was there to learn battle tactics from Petrov and provide her with information on the Nasi. But Nicole couldn't shake the feeling that he was also there to pass information to the Jadid's commander, Ancient Bao Wang. When Wang had asked to have some of his officers embedded into the rest of Samsara Fleet, Nicole doubted General Samaha felt she could say no.

"No, nothing that can affect the fleet or mission." Nicole always followed the strict protocols about what information Tac-I soldiers could know since the Bones were constantly behind enemy lines and capture was always a risk. "Still..."

Petrov laid her hand on Nicole's. She understood that the loss wasn't any easier to take because their secrets were safe. Normally, the colonel had what Nicole would describe as a severe face, defined cheekbones under a pair of intense brown eyes. Now those eyes were gazing into hers with a look of concern and understanding. "It's rough. Losing soldiers. Something you never get used to."

Nicole had lost six soldiers in the past few months, but Private Wilson was the first that had been captured and in front of her. Knowing the Nasi, Nicole was sure her fate would be worse than death. They would make her suffer.

"Thanks." She gently pulled her hand away. "At least it'll be for something."

The Nasi had entered the galaxy and lit it on fire. Despite proclaiming that they were there to lead Humanity forward, they'd destroyed Earth and the home worlds of several other species. While the defending militaries were scrambling to understand what had happened, the Nasi conquered their colonies and consolidated their grip. For the first months of the war, it had appeared that there was no hope. It was only because of Kal Norman, and what would become the Skulls, that anyone was willing to fight back. Then the Jadid had joined Samsara Fleet, and together they had pushed the Nasi out of every planet except the Human colonies. Now after almost a year of plotting and scouting, they were about ready to win the war.

"The Skulls are back from New America as well," Petrov said, her eyes focused on Nicole.

"And?"

"Minor casualties. They're on R&R right now."

That meant Kal would be in their stateroom. She hadn't seen him in two weeks because of the overlap in their missions. Whenever the Skulls returned, he went straight to the room, only leaving for meals or when it was time to go on another mission.

"I'll have to go see Kal." Nicole feigned a smile. "It's been a while."

Honestly, she wasn't looking forward to it. Talking to him was like trying to wring water from a stone. He'd seen and done too much during the war and was suffering from injuries that no medbot could treat.

"Tell him I said hello." Petrov returned Nicole's smile with a small one of her own. "The data chit you brought back is already in intel's hands."

"Yes, we should have enough information to begin the assault," Atyakari said curtly. Originally, when Nicole had first met the Jadid, they'd all been stiff and stilted. Talking with them had been like talking to a low-end bot. But over the past year, some of them had become more and more Human-like and less formal. Atyakari was one of the many that hadn't. "We shall see soon enough. Ancient Wang is going to speak to the fleet."

Colonel Petrov shot the junior chief an annoyed look. "Along with General Samaha."

Atyakari's mouth twisted in annoyance. "Yes, with your general as well."

Nicole knew Petrov hated having the Jadid officer on her staff. The junior chief wasn't the only one; there were Jadid officers embedded in every department of the *Ofira*. After a few too many drinks, Petrov had confided in Nicole that she loved their work but hated dealing with them. The colonel wasn't the only officer she'd heard complaining about their Jadid counterparts in the lounge either.

Nicole stood up from her seat. "I'm heading back to my stateroom. Let me know if you need anything."

"Enjoy the rest." Petrov stood and Atyakari was not far behind. "We'll know in the next day or so if we've got enough intelligence to move forward."

"Can't wait, ma'am," Nicole replied breezily as she stepped out the door. "About time the rest of you did something."

19

Chapter Two
Kal | Deep Space

Brigadier General Kal Norman stood up from his bunk and padded to his stateroom's bio recycler. He'd spent the last several hours lying on his covers, staring at the ceiling. When not on a mission, he found himself unable to do anything else. He knew he should go through training, speak with his soldiers, or do something other than lie there, but what was the point?

When she was around, Nicole tried her best to get him out of bed. Sometimes she'd force him to go to the lounge with her to grab a bite to eat. When he was outside the room and around others, Kal could fake it. He'd plaster on a smile, talk with the soldiers, and get through it. But he couldn't shake the melancholy that was always with him.

When the war had started, he thought he'd been at his worst. After having lost his family a decade earlier, he'd become a free merchant, traveling the galaxy with whatever cargo he could find between systems. The Nasi invasion had changed all that; he'd rejoined the Earth Defense Force, and then Samsara Fleet, and had found a sense of purpose: fighting for Humanity's survival. As the war had ground on, it had taken more and more from him until it took every bit of strength to leave his room and lead his team on missions.

Kal looked at the small paper photo of Nicole on the bulkhead. He'd wanted a reminder of her he could carry with him. In the image, she was smiling at the camera, her blue eyes twinkling. He stood with his arm around her, smiling as well. But it was a smile that didn't reach his eyes.

That had been months ago. Even she didn't smile as much anymore.

Trudging to the wardrobe, he reached in and grabbed one of his outfits—cargo pants and a loose blouse. One of the advantages of being on missions all the time was that he never had to wear the stiff blue uniform of Samsara Fleet. The free merchant outfit was the unofficial uniform of his team, Not Norman's Numbskulls, or the Skulls for short.

Their exploits had become legend within the fleet, which meant the stories were full of crap. They were filled with adventure and heroics, none of which he'd seen. Nicole had been a part of the Skulls, but their success had inspired General Samaha to divide them and create the Bones with Nicole as lead. Kal was proud to say the former diplomatic attaché had shined in her role as military commander.

"Hey!"

Nicole's greeting startled Kal, causing him to trip onto the floor, his pants halfway up his legs. He looked up to see Nicole laughing above him. "Sorry…I didn't mean to…surprise you." She had a hard time speaking between her snickers. She kneeled with her red-tinged face above his.

Kal had a hard time speaking as well. The absurdity of the situation was too much. He just lay back and laughed, his amusement genuine.

Their laughter petered out and Kal put his arm around her, pulling her close.

"Let's get out of here, go to the lounge, and then come back," Nicole whispered. "We haven't had a moment together for a long time." She winked.

"We could just stay here…" Kal trailed off.

"Food first. Then we'll see what happens." She stood with a mischievous smile still on her lips.

It ended up taking them longer than planned to leave the stateroom.

They found the *Ofira's* lounge was almost empty. Most of the tables were unoccupied, but there were a few where soldiers chatted quietly with each other, drinks in hand. Since it was night, at least according to the ship's duty cycle, the viewscreens that covered the walls displayed evening scenes from what Kal guessed was Wudexingqiu. Three of the planet's four moons were in the sky, their pale light reflecting over the still waters of a marsh. Occasionally, the ripple of a fish diving out of the water disturbed the tranquility.

Kal grabbed a table in the corner and waited for the attendant bot to reach them. He wanted to be as far out of sight as possible. Soldiers often approached him asking to join the Bones or trying to get inside information, not realizing that as a scout he had less info than they did.

"How was it?" Kal asked after the bot had taken their orders.

He could tell from Nicole's expression that her mission

hadn't gone to plan. Again. She watched the still waters on the viewscreen behind him and sighed.

"We lost Wilson. They captured her."

"Damn, I'm sorry." Kal couldn't picture the private in his head. But he remembered she'd been young. Hell, they all were young. "How'd they find you?"

"Not sure," Nicole said. "We did everything by the book. The Front had a vehicle waiting when we landed, and it was supposed to be a simple in and out. Maybe they devised a way to intercept communications. Maybe they have a spy on the inside. Who knows?" She ran her hands through her blonde hair.

Samsara Fleet had continued to develop new technology and adjust their tactics and so had the Nasi. Each time the scout teams went out on a mission, they encountered something new and had to adapt. Sometimes they were successful, sometime not. The fleet had ten scout teams like the Skulls and Bones. During the past few months, their casualty rates were around fifty percent. Thankfully, there was no shortage of volunteers eager to join their ranks.

"It's never simple."

"No, it—"

"Ma'am. Sir." Staff Sergeant Ekon Kimathi sauntered up to their table with his usual swagger. Despite the horrors of the war and everything they'd been through, Kimathi had maintained his self-assured jovial nature. Kal's Tac-1 squad leader was a man who'd seen more death than most in his twenty-odd years, but he always picked himself up, making a joke in the process.

"Sergeant Kimathi, enjoying your time off?" Nicole smiled easily.

"Yes, ma'am. You got some time for the trainers later?" When they were both back on the *Ofira*, Nicole and Sergeant Kimathi always found time to train together in the battle simulators. It had been months since Kal had joined them; he just couldn't work up the motivation. The Skulls ran enough real-world missions that he didn't need the training anyway.

Nicole nodded. "You bet."

Kimathi stood awkwardly, looking back and forth before giving the table a small rap with his knuckle. "Well then...I'll be on my way."

As the sergeant turned to leave, Chief Taisha Kanumba walked into the lounge and waved at them. She grinned as she headed toward their table, her pleasant expression marred by a pair of scars across her face. Her son, Jae-Ho was strapped across her chest; his large black eyes scanned the room, drinking in everything.

"Looks like we've got a little reunion," said Nicole as she stood up and embraced her friend gingerly.

"Just like old times," Kanumba replied, returning the hug.

"Not *exactly* like them." Kimathi grabbed Jae-Ho's tiny hand and tapped it against his own in a miniature high-five.

Chief Kanumba looked down at her son with a smile. She'd named him after his father, Captain Jae-Ho Park, a former pilot on the Skulls who'd been killed by the Nasi on Patagonia. He'd been a bit of an unexpected miracle, a ray of light in the darkness of the Nasi attack. Despite the war, or maybe because of it, Park and Kanumba had disabled their birth control. Although technically against regs, Kal couldn't blame them. It had turned out that they weren't the only ones; there was now a growing nursery on the ship.

While she had been pregnant, Chief Kanumba had worked on the fleet's R&D team but was back as the copilot and engineer for the Skulls despite Kal's protests.

Kal smiled at Jae-Ho, who gurgled happily as he stared back, a small streamer of drool making its way down his plump chin. As always, the sight of the beautiful child brought a mixture of emotions. He couldn't help thinking of the future the child represented while remembering the pain of Captain Jae-Ho's death.

"Sir, heads up that the *Cumae* will be out of service for a few hours. Bo's upgrading the fold drive again." The *Cumae* was the Skulls' ship, a heavily upgraded scout corvette. Kal would have bet all the credits he had, which wasn't many, that it was the most advanced ship in the fleet thanks to the efforts of Bowen Nguyen, a Jadid scientist the Skulls had freed from Nasi captivity.

Since then, he'd become an integral part of their team. As a Jadid, he had physical abilities beyond any human. More importantly though, he was the foremost expert in fold drives and avionics in the galaxy.

"Okay." Kal felt overwhelmed. He didn't want to talk about their ship or the war. He wanted a quiet dinner with the woman he loved. "Should be fine since we're not on rotation for another two days."

"Catch up later?" Kanumba asked, eying Nicole.

Nicole nodded. "Sounds good. I want to hear all about what Jae-Ho's been up to." She made a goofy face at the boy, who smiled back at her.

"Little bugger is a handful." Kanumba laughed. "Sergeant Kimathi, why don't you tell me about how you took down three Nasi with one shot again?" She gently guided the sergeant away from the table.

"You're popular," Nicole observed once the others were out of earshot.

"Commanders generally are. Though I think it's clear you're the one they really want to talk to." *And no surprise there*, thought Kal. "Can't go anywhere without hearing how great Lieutenant Colonel Nicole Bergeron is." He laughed.

"You disagree?"

"Not at all. I'm usually the one who says it first. I'm just jealous." Kal couldn't have been prouder of her.

"Well, everything I know, I learned from you." When they had first met, Nicole had been a civilian, a former diplomatic attaché. Since then, she'd remade herself into one of the most respected officers in the fleet.

"I doubt that," Kal replied. "I think you're—"

Welcome back. General Aamina Samaha's message sounded like a mechanical female voice in Kal's implant. *We need to talk. Bergeron with you?*

Yes, Kal replied. He didn't have to say the words; his implant could interpret his thoughts and send the message

26

without him speaking or moving his lips. Though some people never could shake the need to at least mouth the words as they talked through their implants.

Nicole waited patiently, watching the holo on the viewscreen next to them. She could tell he was talking on his implant. Although others couldn't hear the dialog, the vacant stares made it obvious when someone was using theirs.

I need to talk to both of you, Samaha said. *With the information we received during the Bones' last mission, we have all the pieces in place. We're finally ready.*

Kal smiled and a surge of excitement coursed through his body. All the sacrifice and loss may finally have a happy ending. He corrected himself. Maybe not happy, but at least an ending. Were they finally going to finish this?

Roger, on our way. Kal cut the connection.

"Looks like your mission was a success. Samaha let me know they're ready to proceed," he said, a smile on his face.

Nicole grabbed his hand and stood up. "What are we waiting for? Dinner can wait."

"I never thought this day would come." Colonel Irina Petrov waved to the seats next to her with a grin as Nicole and Kal entered the viewscreen-lined conference room.

She sat at the head of the large table that dominated the center of the room while her Jadid advisor, Junior Chief Atyakari, sat in the middle with a neutral expression on his gaunt violet face. Whenever Kal saw the officer, he felt a pang of anxiety. He wasn't sure why; he'd been working with the Jadid for over a year now.

"Well, it's not quite here yet," Kal said as he took one of the seats next to the commander. Despite his correction, he had to tamp down his own excitement about the news. It was a ray of very much needed hope.

"It is a step in the right direction though," Nicole said, taking a seat across from Kal. "A big one."

Kal didn't want to get his hopes up. But liberating one or more of the Human colonies would be a turning point in the war. Samsara Fleet, along with the Jadid, had decimated the Nasi. But their enemy still had half their fleet remaining, not to mention their plasma lances.

"Good to see you both," General Samaha said as she appeared on a viewscreen. She was sitting along the bench that ran along the wall of her conference room on her flagship, the *Gedorhan's Return*. "I thought about meeting in person, but it's your last R&R for a while, so I figured I'd save you the trouble."

Ancient Bao Wang appeared in the viewscreen next to her with General Frederick Zhou behind him. Although Bao was an Ancient and the leader of the Jadid fleet, he was Human.

The Jadid were the descendants of the Ancients; Humans who had been cast into another universe as part of the development of the fold drive hundreds of years ago. Earth had been overcrowded and dying, and governments were desperate to find a way to other systems. In order to perfect

28

the fold drive and reach other systems, the governments of the time had been willing to send prisoners and debtors into space as test subjects. Most of them had died, but the Ancients had been sent into another universe. One that was strange and inhospitable.

They had survived and learned to adapt to the strange physics of their new home, Altterra. Eventually, the Humans that survived, the Ancients, procreated. When their children were born, they were mutated by the universe. The Jadid were much taller and stronger than their Human parents, with gaunt features and an altered skin tone. After centuries, Bao was one of only four original Human Ancients still alive. Two others were still back on Altterra, and the fourth was Esma Baykara, the leader of the Nasi.

Despite Bao's advanced age, he only looked around forty years old. One of the side effects of the new universe was that it stopped the aging process once Humans or Jadid reached adulthood. Kal had a hard time remembering that many of the Jadid were hundreds of years old. He noticed the gray in the man's temples had grown since he saw him last; he'd begun aging again since returning to this universe.

"We felt you three would want to be the first to know," Wang said. "Along with General Zhou, you were the first to strike back at the Nasi. It seems…poetic that you would be here to see the beginning of the end."

"Before we get ahead of ourselves, let's talk about the mission," Samaha said. "As you know, the Nasi plasma lances have prevented us from getting close to their planets. With the information that your teams provided, we've been able to map out the lances on Patagonia and New America."

"And we also know exactly how to disable them," Zhou added.

A three-dimensional wireframe appeared over their table. At the top was a circular disc with lines that led down to two rectangles.

"The lances have three principal components—the cannon itself, the generator, and the harvester," General Zhou continued. "I can't tell you how the things work exactly, but I do know that all three components need to be online and connected in order for the cannon to fire."

"Why can't we just cut one of the connections?" Kal asked.

"That would be the easy solution," General Zhou agreed. "But they're almost all underground, tunneled through rock. There's only one place where the plasma and energy conduits are vulnerable, the Nexus. It's where the conduits meet, and the highly charged plasma is funneled to the cannon. Although it's pretty well protected, our engineering teams have developed a Triple-A shape charge that can take them out. We just need to get inside and place it on them."

Triple-A, or Azidoazide Azide Antimatter, was one of the most powerful explosives in the galaxy. Kal hated the thought of conducting a mission with it onboard his ship.

"There are six cannons spread across both planets," Samaha added. "We'll need to take out all of them ahead of our fleet's arrival. Since all the components are underground and heavily protected, we'll need to have six assault teams on each planet take them out simultaneously. Then we can bring in the fleet and take out their fleets in orbit."

"Why not just strike all four planets at once, ma'am?" asked Colonel Petrov. "If we need to wait an extra month to get more intel, it would be worth it to finish this war in one go."

"Resources," said General Zhou. "We can take on half the Nasi fleet. But even with our skip missiles, if we split into four then the Nasi have a good chance of defeating us. We can focus on the two planets where we have complete intel and then move to the other two—Wudexingqiu and Mariga."

The plan didn't surprise Kal; it was straightforward. It was also completely predictable, which made him nervous. Unfortunately, there wasn't a better way to get through the Nasi defenses. The skip missiles allowed Samsara Fleet to even the playing field with the Nasi by folding through their ship's point defenses and energy shields. But they wouldn't work against the subterranean plasma lances. They would need to use ground forces to take out those. He took some solace in the fact that the Nasi couldn't know which planets they'd strike or when.

"There's no way we can launch simultaneous assaults on six objectives scattered on each world," said Nicole. "We don't have the resources for it." She was right. They had twelve scout teams in the fleet, but they were never intended to be used to launch full-on assaults on heavily fortified positions. Perhaps they could find additional ships, soldiers, and battle suits. But they wouldn't be trained, and the Nasi would make quick work of them.

Although they'd never directly told him, Kal already had a good idea of what they were planning. "We're not going to be the ones doing the assaulting," said Kal. "The rebels will."

"You will be *leading* the assault," Zhou corrected, "but you'll have a lot of help. We've been supplying and training Patagonia Front and the rebels' forces on New America for over a year now. They have hundreds of thousands of fighters that have combat experience against the Nasi."

"We take out the cannons. The fleet swoops in and destroys the Nasi. Then what?" asked Kal. "They still have their Footholds." The Footholds were the enormous Nasi bases built on each planet. But they weren't just military bases. They contained workers, families, and children. Kal knew the Nasi had also started to spread out from their Footholds, building smaller garrisons and facilities. More targets they'd have to capture after the fleet came in.

General Zhou looked confused. "Well, then we demand their surrender."

"And if they don't?" Kal knew where this was going.

"We destroy the Footholds from orbit. Wipe them all out." The general's response was as matter-of-fact as could be.

The reply surprised him though he knew it shouldn't. Despite being a high-ranking officer, Zhou had never met a Nasi, never even seen one with his own eyes. He'd only heard stories, many of them untrue, about them. Kal had been in the Footholds and had spoken to Nasi artists and merchants. He'd even become friends, of a sort, with several of them. He hated the idea of just destroying an entire city—but he also understood it. What other choice did they have?

"If we do that, then what makes us different from them?" Nicole asked heatedly.

"We definitely hope it doesn't come to that," Wang said, holding his hands up placatingly. "We won't act without warning. I think when they see their situation, they'll stand down."

"And if they don't, we kill every last one of them." Nicole shot back with an arched eyebrow.

"Colonel Bergeron," Samaha's voice had a tired edge to it. "We're all well aware of your opinions on this. Unfortunately, the realities of modern warfare do not align with your morals."

Kal hesitated to say anything; this was a fight that had been going on for over a year. Since Nicole had discovered Samaha's sanctioning "enhanced interrogation" techniques on the Nasi, she'd questioned the morality of every decision the woman made. Kal knew that back in the EDF, Nicole would have been relieved of her position long ago for questioning orders and challenging the general. But under Samsara Fleet, General Samaha had to tolerate it, at least somewhat. Kal had come to appreciate and even agree with some of what Nicole said. If they would do anything to survive, then did they deserve to?

"Ma'am, all I am saying is that there are innocent civilians in that Foothold. Nasi that haven't harmed a fly. Children.

33

Families. I know this because I've seen it." She flung her hand toward Kal. "He's seen it too. While you're out here with the fleet." She took a breath and looked toward Ancient Wang's viewscreen. "These are your children. Surely, you're opposed to this. Or at least have doubts."

It was the kind of speech that would have ended an officer's career in the EDF. In Samsara Fleet, the only reactions were Zhou's and Samaha's flushed faces.

The Nasi were a cult—Kal could think of no better word—within the Jadid. They believed it was the duty of the Jadid to return to Humanity and lead them to a glorious new future using any means possible. Under their leader, Grand Ancient Esma Baykara, they'd twisted this mission in to one where they destroyed Earth and occupied the Human colonies.

The rest of the Jadid had tried to ignore them for as long as they could until the Nasi had attacked them, and Kal and the Skulls convinced them to join Samsara Fleet. The other two Ancients still referred to all the Jadid as their children, Nasi included. But Kal believed that Ancient Wang viewed the Nasi as something else and harbored a deep grudge, Kal would have even said hatred, toward their leader, Esma.

"Of course, I don't want to kill innocents," Ancient Wang replied with an edge of anger. "But sometimes things must be done. The Nasi in these Footholds all willingly came to this universe. They must bear the consequences of their decisions."

"Even if it means death?" The words escaped Kal's lips before he could stop them.

34

"Yes." Samaha's single-word response was emotionless. She took a deep breath. "I'd love to have the time to sit here and pontificate the morality of our actions, but I'm more focused on surviving. General Zhou, keep going." Nicole flushed and balled her hands in barely suppressed anger.

Zhou detailed the missions on both planets, outlining where the lances were, the forces on hand, and how they'd strike at each one. As he talked, a viewscreen cycled through holos and images of the planets and plasma lances. Kal focused on the faces around him; he knew these details would be readily available via his implant when the official order was distributed to the units.

Nicole seemed nervous and suspicious while Petrov seemed almost elated as she listened. Samaha appeared more tired than anything, a feeling Kal could relate to. It was Zhou and Wang that were strange to him. They were clinical and emotionless as they talked about the mission.

Shouldn't they be excited? Kal wondered. Shouldn't we all be?

Zhou brought his hands together. "Kal. Nicole. The bottom line is this. We'll be depending on you to be the relays between the fleets and the forces on the ground—both before the battle and after. There will be the other scout teams, but you're the two most experienced commanders. If our attack is swift and overwhelming, I think the Nasi Footholds will surrender. Then we can start rebuilding the UEG."

Kal almost fell out of his seat in surprise. Surely Zhou had

35

to be joking about rebuilding the United Earth Government. The UEG had been Humanity's interstellar government before the Nasi arrived. When the Nasi destroyed Earth, they destroyed the UEG and its military, the Earth Defense Force, at the same time. For many people, it was good riddance. Under the UEG, the colonies had a second-class status; they had been expected to provide cheap materials to Earth and be a captive audience for their manufactured goods. Nothing he'd seen in the past several years made Kal believe *anyone* wanted to the UEG to return.

"There's no Earth. How can there be a UEG?" Kal asked.

"Maybe we'll need to tinker with the name, but we need some sort of unifying government." Zhou waved his hand dismissively. "Humanity needs a common defense against all the other species in the galaxy. We need order and structure to thrive. The lessons the Nasi have taught us have been hard, but we must listen."

"I have my reservations about *another* UEG as well," Samaha admitted. "But we still haven't liberated a single planet, so I'd say any talk of what we do *after* we defeat the Nasi is premature."

"Ma'am, we need—" began General Zhou.

"Let's talk later," Ancient Wang said, placing a hand on Zhou's shoulder. "General Samaha is right. We need to focus on what's in front of us."

Zhou shook his head then continued. "We'll have the full briefing with the fleet's command team in three hours. We'll send the assault teams to Patagonia and New America in two days. You'll be on point to let the relay ships know when you're ready for the fleets to come."

"All we need to do is organize six simultaneous assaults on the most destructive weapons systems the galaxy has ever known?" Kal asked.

"Yes," General Samaha replied. She winked. "You've had harder assignments."

Kal sighed and nodded. Perhaps she was right. But they were the ones where his soldiers died.

Chapter Three
Nicole | Deep Space

The two days before the mission were a whirlwind for Nicole. She split her time between ensuring her team was prepared and spending as much time as she could with Kal. Everything felt different. They weren't just going to Patagonia to scout or provide weapons; the Bones were going to be leading an assault to dismantle the Nasi occupation.

She was pleasantly surprised to discover that Kal felt the same way and had become the man she'd first known. He'd stopped hiding in their stateroom and joined his Tac-I squad in the training rooms. At the briefing with the full fleet staff, Kal had been attentive and awake even stepping forward to give a quick rundown of the Nasi capabilities. She couldn't help noticing that everyone in the briefing stopped talking and paid full attention when he spoke. He might not realize it, but Kal had achieved the status of a living legend.

There were only a few hours left before the mission, and Nicole wanted to spend them with Kal. But before that, she needed to see her old teammates. Since General Samaha had split the Skulls and given Nicole her own scout team a year ago, there were few chances for her to talk with them. When she'd invited them to grab a drink in the lounge, she wasn't surprised they'd all agreed.

Nicole arrived in the lounge to find Bowen Nguyen and Sergeant Ekon Kimathi already seated. Taisha was supposed to come as well, but she had Jae-Ho to take care of. Nicole knew that a small child, even with the ship's nursery, could make anyone late.

"Ma'am," Bo pulled a seat from the table. "It's good to see you."

Despite not being a soldier or even fully Human, the Jadid had taken to calling her ma'am. If she were to guess, he subconsciously did it to fit in with the rest of the Skulls. When they'd first discovered the scientist imprisoned in a Nasi research facility, he'd been stiff and formal like the other Jadid. However, he'd quickly adapted Human mannerisms and slang like some of the Jadid and most of the Nasi she'd met. As a former anthropology student, it was a phenomenon that deeply intrigued her.

"Hey, Bo," Nicole said as she wrapped her arms around his body for a quick hug. Despite his slender frame, there was nothing but muscle underneath his loose clothing. "Long time, no see."

"Indeed." He smiled; it came so naturally to him now. "I ordered you a tea."

"You know what I like." She sat down. Surprisingly, Ekon looked to be having one as well. "Ekon, what are you drinking? Is that something"—she made a theatrical gasp—"nonalcoholic?"

"I'll make up for it when we get back," Ekon replied with a grin. He ran his hand over the smooth stubble that covered his head. "This is the big one. I need to be on point. Told my squad the same."

"How are they?"

"We're great. As always." He took a drink. But Nicole could see a flicker of uncertainty before he did. "We've had a few days to relax. It's about time to get back to work."

"It's the turning of a page," Bo said poetically. "I wonder what we'll find on the next one."

Nicole thought about Bo's comment. For everything they'd gone over in the briefings, very little they'd discussed was about what they'd do *when* they defeated the Nasi. She didn't know how many of them were in their universe, but it was enough that she couldn't see them just disappearing. They'd need to be integrated into society somehow.

Taisha walked into the room without Jae-Ho. Nicole figured she must have dropped him off at the nursery. The chief smiled and waved as she walked to their table and grabbed a seat.

"Sorry, had to do last-minute checks on the *Cumae*," Taisha said smiling. "General Norman has been living in the landing bay lately."

Even though it meant Kal was away from Nicole, she was glad to hear it. She knew him well enough to know that activity kept the doubt and depression away. If he was in the bay looking over his ship, he wasn't sitting in bed with his thoughts.

"Well, I get him back after this mission," Nicole said.

"Ugh." Taisha waved her hand. "You can have him."

"Seems a shame we're not gonna finish this together," said Ekon, looking around the table. "We started as a team—kinda—and we should finish as one."

When we started, I was your prisoner, Nicole thought to herself.

However, she felt the same way. Except for Bo, the three of them had been together since the beginning. Along with Kal, they'd created the Skulls. "Well, the war's not over yet. Even if we capture New America and Patagonia, there's still Wudexingqiu and Mariga."

"Perhaps," Bo said thoughtfully. "However, at the risk of being overly optimistic, I believe that the capture of the two planets will force the Nasi's hand. Their grip in this galaxy will be too tenuous at that point not to strike out."

"You think they'll come at us?" Nicole asked.

"Very likely," Bo said. "I never met Ancient Baykara, but from everything I've heard, she's not someone who waits for her enemy to attack."

"Well, if we destroy half their fleet, they won't have much of a chance," Taisha said.

Nicole looked at her friend. Right now, Taisha was at ease. Her kind face was open and radiated a warmth that Nicole had come to see as motherly. Nicole had never had a child, hadn't even considered it. *What was all this like for her friend?*

"You ready?" Nicole asked.

Taisha looked at her closely for a moment and seemed to understand the subtext to her question. "Yeah, you'd better believe it. I've got more to fight for than I ever had." Her smile disappeared and the warmth vanished, replaced with a steely resolve. She looked ready to take on the Nasi single-handedly. "I don't know if I'll survive, but I guarantee you Jae-

41

Ho will."

❖

Nicole walked around the *Chester*, drinking in the ship's sleek profile and matte gray hull. Even with the extra pieces bolted on the hull to camouflage the nacelles containing advanced equipment, she was a beauty. Her swept-back wings and smooth curves hinted at danger and excitement.

"We've got clearance to depart, ma'am," Chief Ramos said as she stepped next to Nicole. "The other scout teams have already left."

Nicole's mind turned to Kal and her other friends aboard the *Cumae*. The Skulls were already on their way to New America, and she wouldn't see them until this was all over—if she saw them again. She took solace in the fact that she'd had a chance to spend time with Kal before the mission—the *real* Kal. He'd been so optimistic and full of life before their missions. She smiled to herself; it had been a *good* night. There hadn't been many of them lately.

"Time to head out then." She gave a final, affectionate pat on the hull and walked up the cargo ramp.

Half the Tac-I squad was in the ship's cargo bay doing final checks. Their battle suits were in their docks against the bulkhead, and the crates of weapons for the rebels on Patagonia were fixed onto the floor.

"Get ready to go," Nicole called out.

She climbed to the second deck and entered the cockpit

42

with Chief Ramos trailing her. Captain Uhaa turned as she entered and gave a quick thumbs-up. "Ready to lift off, ma'am."

"Let's do this," Nicole said. "You're cleared to exit the bay."

Ramos slid into her seat next to Uhaa, and soon the low thrum of the ship's engines reverberated through the hull. The two pilots had been working together long enough that they didn't need to speak as they checked the ship's systems and prepared for takeoff. It was a routine they'd done hundreds of times before.

"*Chester*, you're cleared," the *Ofira's* control center called over the net.

"Give 'em hell!" The voice on the net was unmistakably Colonel Petrov's.

"Oh, we will, ma'am," said Uhaa before closing the connection.

The *Chester* rose from the landing bay floor and glided through the energy shield, keeping the atmosphere in. After fifteen minutes, they were far enough away for Uhaa to engage their fold drives.

"No turning back now," Nicole whispered to herself as she watched the stars blink in front of her.

The Bones had been traveling between Samsara Fleet and Patagonia regularly for months. It was a journey that had become rote in many ways. This time was different though. Sergeant Bhatt had the Tac-I squad training in the bays almost the entire journey while Nicole spent hours poring over old mission reports and reviewing everything she could about the Nasi forces on the planet.

When they had grown close to their destination, the flight crew had summoned Nicole to the cockpit.

"Ma'am, we're ready for our final fold," Captain Uhaa said.

"Good to hear." Nicole took a deep breath. *This was it.* "Do it."

Seconds later, Patagonia was in front of them with the continent of Pangea directly in the center, partially obscured by large cloud formations on the west portion.

"We've still got five Nasi ships in orbit," Ramos called out. "Haven't moved since we were last here."

The *Chester* headed straight for the western portion of Pangea. Small squadrons of Nasi fighters patrolled the area around them, but none were close enough for alarm. The ship's optical cloak seemed to be doing its job hiding them from the Nasi and allowing them to enter the atmosphere undetected.

As they entered the exosphere, Nicole studied the large ridge of mountains that split the continent in half. She could also make out the continents' major cities: Kasongo to the west, nestled in the foothills of the mountains, Foyleton to the north, and Chengdu to the south hugging the coastline.

The Bones were going to meet with Karl Garcia first. As

the leader of the Human government on the planet, he needed to know what they were doing to get his troops prepared. What the Nasi didn't know was that Garcia was a former member of the Skulls. Since he'd consolidated his control over the planet, he'd been working with Samsara Fleet, preparing to turn on the Nasi when the time was right. Garcia's government pretended to be at war with the Patagonia Front, but the leaders of both organizations were former members of the Skulls and working hand in hand to defeat the Nasi from the shadows.

They headed west of the capital, Kasongo, and landed in a small copse of trees surrounded by fields of crops that had been brought from Earth hundreds of years ago.

The Bones didn't need to be told what to do once the ship touched down. Before the engines had even shut off, Ramos was up and heading toward the rear of the ship to set up the optical projects outside. By the time Nicole reached the cargo bay, the Tac-I squad was waiting, already segregated into their two teams.

Over the past several months, the Bones had learned how to get around the planet while not being noticed. Unfortunately, the battle suits that lined the bay weren't an option for a clandestine mission like theirs. Instead, they wore their de facto uniform, loose-fitting pants and a billowing blouse that was common among free merchants. These outfits made it easier for them to conceal the blasters and advanced equipment that they brought with them.

"You're clear," Uhaa called over the ship's intercom. "No

activity in scanner range."

Nicole traded glances with Sergeant Bhatt and strode down the open ramp and into the trees. Immediately the familiar pungent smell of the native flora hit her. The Tac-1 squad followed, fanning out into separate teams as they hit the ground.

Nicole stayed with Sergeant Peng's Alpha Team as they made their way through the tree line and hurried through the rows of vines until they reached a corrugated metal barn. After peeking through the door, Peng motioned for Nicole and the others to get inside. The interior was filled with refuse and rusted farm equipment. Broken irrigation and cultivation bots were stacked in small piles on the dirt-covered floor. Stylus-sized rays of light came through the patchwork ceiling and glistened in the dust-filled air.

"Sampson, Fischer," Peng called out as he handed the tacmap to Private Sampson, "watch the area. We'll get the transport spun up."

The two soldiers had already pulled out their pistols and were headed to two small gaps in the wall.

"Ma'am, can you help me with this?" asked Peng, standing next to a cloth-covered mound.

Nicole walked next to the Sergeant and helped him pull a tarp off a large transport. The cargo hauler was almost as rusty as the barn itself. The vehicle had a large rectangular cabin in front, which looked to be able to seat three in front, and a dirt-encrusted bed in the back.

Peng jumped into the cabin and Nicole could hear a string

of profanities as he tried to get the vehicle working. The thrusters emitted small coughs as the engine turned over but failed to start.

"Bravo Team's approaching," announced Sampson. "They're...wait, we've got three, no four, Nasi patrollers in the area." He licked his lips.

Nicole ran over to look at the tacmap. Sure enough, there were four dots, indicating Bravo Team was heading their direction as well as another line of four red dots heading straight for the barn.

Nicole remained calm. Even if the Nasi discovered Bravo Team, there was no guarantee that they'd know they were Samsara Fleet soldiers. They had false identity chits, and their implants shouldn't be on any of the local databases.

"Hold tight," Nicole said. "We attack only if we need to."

She walked to the cargo hauler and looked Sergeant Peng in the eye. "Don't start that thing up unless I say so."

Peng nodded.

Nicole walked back to the wall and pressed her eye against a rusted hole in the metal wall. At first, all she could see were the tops of the vines. Harvest was still months away, and clusters of tiny white flowers hung among the broad leaves.

Nicole moved her head against the wall, trying to see anything. Based on what she'd grasped from the tacmap, Bravo Team should be visible. The problem was she couldn't see anything through the vines. She looked around the room. She needed to find a way to see over the vines.

She spotted another hole, near the top of a pile of drones and carefully climbed the pile of discarded equipment, testing each one of the boxy machines before stepping on it. Privates Fischer and Sampson nervously glanced at her as she climbed. The Nasi were close enough that they would certainly hear it if she fell or knocked one of the drones loose.

She reached the top of the pile and placed her head against the hole in the wall. The vineyard spread before her, and she could see Bhatt and Bravo Team facing a group of four Nasi, thankfully not in battle suits. They appeared to be arguing for some reason though Nicole couldn't imagine Sergeant Bhatt was dumb enough to argue with a Nasi patrol while on a mission.

One of the Nasi suddenly slapped Bhatt across the face, his arm moving so fast that Nicole only realized what had happened when she saw the woman fly back and land on the ground in a heap. From a Nasi, a blow like that could be fatal.

Nicole felt one of the bots she was standing on suddenly give way. She looked down at her feet as it teetered precariously before bouncing down the pile, making a loud metallic clang every step of the way.

Before the bot hit the ground, the cargo hauler's engine roared to life, its thrusters blowing a dense cloud of dirt through the building. The other team forgotten, the Nasi turned and looked directly at the barn. Two of them started to sprint toward the building at superhuman speed.

"Get in the back!" Peng shouted as he navigated the hauler forward so the front was touching the large barn door.

Both Sampson and Fischer crawled over the side of the bed in back. Nicole's feet slipped out from under her as she tried to jump from the pile of drones. The side of her torso hit the edge of the hauler bed, knocking the wind out of her and sending a debilitating wave of pain up her side. Sampson reached at her with both hands and pulled her inside just as a hail of plasma bolts seared through the thin metal cladding of the building.

The transport lurched forward, crashing through the large door with a shriek and sending Nicole and the two privates slamming into the back of the bed.

Nicole pulled herself up and looked out the side of the transport. Two Nasi lay on the ground behind them, slowly pulling themselves up. The vehicle slammed to a stop and Corporal Basu's team leapt over the side of the bed. The vehicle took off as soon as they hit the dirt-encrusted bottom.

As they sped away, two of the Nasi chased them, firing their small plasma pistols wildly. Their lithe figures ran gracefully behind the vehicle, keeping up for a few seconds before they gave up and stopped.

"You okay, ma'am?" Sampson asked in a concerned voice.

"Yeah." Nicole lay still on the bottom of the hauler bed. "I need a second. We've got to get out of here. They'll call for reinforcements."

"Doubt that," said Corporal Basu as he pushed himself into a sitting position. "They were trying to shake us down for credits."

"Thieves?" Nicole was in disbelief. When the Nasi had come to this universe to *help* Humanity—at least in their minds—they'd been emotionless and completely driven by their mission. Now there were bands of them trying to rob people in the countryside?

They sped over the packed-dirt road for another few minutes and then stopped under the shade of a small empty rest station. The simple pavilion consisted of a sloped roof covering parking spots, a fabricator kiosk, and a bio recycler.

After they'd touched down Nicole clambered over the side of the bed with a groan of pain. It appeared only she and Bhatt were worse for wear from the experience; an angry-looking bruise had already formed on the side of the sergeant's face. Nicole wouldn't be surprised if her jaw was broken, from the look of it.

"We"—Bhatt gasped and paused for a moment, clearly in pain—"should keep...going. Bandits." Her words came out with a painful slur.

"Basu said they were trying to rob you," Nicole said, trying to spare the sergeant from talking. Bhatt nodded. "Then we keep going with the mission as planned. I'll go ahead and ride in the cabin. But before we do anything, can we get some bandages?" She motioned toward her injured side.

The new private—Private Renata Saad—stepped forward and pulled two bandages from a pocket in her trousers. She handed one to Nicole and gently applied the other to Bhatt's face. The bandage was coated in a cocktail of nanobots, medicine, and topical anesthesia that would promote healing and reduce the pain and swelling. Nicole climbed next to Sergeant Peng in the front cabin while the rest of the Bones climbed back into the bed and leaned against the metal sides.

The rest of the journey into Kasongo was uneventful. None of the few people they saw paid much attention to the dilapidated cargo hauler filled with what looked to be field techs. When on a mission, Nicole sometimes found herself looking around and appreciating the scenery. She wouldn't admit it to others, but she couldn't help it. They knew what they needed to do and obsessing about what may or may not happen wasn't going to help anyone. There sky was clear, and the sun beat down on them as they sped across the paved road, which widened as they neared the capital. Orchards and vineyards covered the billowing hills around them in neat rows. It was the kind of landscape she'd imagined growing up as a kid in Earth's communes.

All of the other vehicles on the road were either agricultural or large freight haulers. Most were driven by AI, but occasionally, they'd see another person as they coasted along.

They reached the top of a particularly large hill to find Kasongo laid out before them. From this vantage point, the city looked like someone had dumped a container of unsorted parts across the valley and hillsides. There was no rhyme or reason to the city's layout, and the buildings shared no common design element other than their eccentricity. Ornate old-earth homes stood next to ultra-sleek glass spheres. In the far distance, Nicole could make out the dim jagged profile of the mountain range that split Pangea in two.

The Nasi foothold sat in the center of the city like a cancer. Roughly circular in shape and surrounded by a large wall, it was a city unto itself. At its center was a large twisted tower that soared into the sky. Shorter buildings radiated out from the tower in circles, broken only by a large sphere—the gateway. Before the Jadid had closed it, the gateway had served as a portal between the Nasi in the Human universe and their home planet of Altterra. It had allowed them to bring people and supplies to Patagonia in order to build their fleet and consolidate their hold on the planet.

The hauler crested the hill and turned onto one of the main roads, joining the stream of industrial and civilian vehicles entering the city.

"What a city," Peng said with a note of distain as they entered the city proper.

"You get used to it after a while," Nicole replied with a smile. She remembered her first time seeing Kasongo. She'd learned to appreciate the eccentric nature of the city and its people.

There was no other word to describe Kasongo other than chaotic. Crowds rushed through the winding streets while transports floated above them, stopping frequently as traffic jammed up on itself. Peng was forced to stop their vehicle several times to avoid crashing into another vehicle or pedestrian. The buildings only added to the chaos. They were a juxtaposition of colors, styles, and sizes; enormous glass towers stood next to small earthen huts and angular metallic estates next to classical-style shops.

When they neared the center of the city, the hauler turned down a small alley and landed, the thrusters blowing small bits of glass and trash against the adjacent walls.

"How's the jaw?" Nicole asked Bhatt.

The sergeant gingerly pulled the bandage from her face. It had reduced the swelling and bruising somewhat though she still looked like she'd fallen off a building and landed face first.

"It's better"—she moaned in pain—"ma'am. Not a hundred percent, though."

Nicole's bandage had worked as well. The pain in her side had faded to a dull throb. Luckily, she could keep it on underneath her loose fitting blouse and let the painkillers continue to work their magic.

After ensuring that there was nothing left in the vehicle that could tie them to it, the Bones set off in two teams for their rendezvous. The governor's mansion sat in the center of a complex of government buildings. A well-manicured garden filled with earthen plants and civilians strolling along surrounded the sprawling old-Earth style structure.

"Look," Sampson hissed. Nicole followed his gaze and saw pairs of Nasi soldiers standing outside each entrance to the building. The creatures scanned the civilians strolling along the gravel paths, their faces hidden behind the black helmets of their battle suits.

"What's going on?" Nicole asked a couple walking by.

The woman shrugged. "No idea. They've been here since the morning."

"I'll say there's definitely *something* up," added the man conspiratorially. "The Nasi never come to the governor's mansion."

Nicole tried to keep her face calm despite the icy fear that had gripped her. There was only one reason she could think of. The Nasi had discovered that Garcia was working with them.

The plan was shot.

Chapter Four
Kal | Deep Space

Ever since General Samaha had told Kal they were finally going to recapture New America and Patagonia, he'd felt reinvigorated. The cloudy haze that had enveloped him had lifted. Before the Skulls' departure to New America, he'd been more focused than he had in months, perhaps ever.

The *Cumae* was only a day out from the planet and every soldier aboard was ready. Sergeant Kimathi had been working the Tac-I squad the entire voyage, taking over the cargo bay and going through every single training scenario he had. Bo spent his time in the galley, inspecting and fine-tuning the arsenal of advanced devices he'd built over the past year. Kal split his time between studying the most recent reports of the Nasi forces on the planet and speaking to each member of his team.

When his haze lifted, Kal had a stark realization that he hadn't been the leader he should have been for the past several months. His most important duty was to care about the soldiers under his command, and he'd failed miserably. While on the *Ofira*, Kal had to be focused on making sure they were ready for the mission.

Now that they were traveling to New America, he tried to make up for lost time by talking—and more importantly listening—to the soldiers. He listened to Private Zeineb Diaz tell him about her life growing up in the countryside of South America back on Earth and her worries about her boyfriend, who'd been an EDF soldier when the Nasi attacked. Sergeant Gabriel Popov talked about his wife and small daughter who were on Wudexingqiu. He hadn't heard from them for years but was *sure* they were okay—no matter what. Corporal Elinore Sato told him about her time living on the streets in North America and her husband, who'd died along with the rest of the planet, when the Nasi attacked. His conversations were a stark reminder that everyone in the fleet had their own issues and ghosts. He was no different, not anymore.

Kal had one final person he needed to speak with. He waited until he saw Staff Sergeant Kimathi step into the galley alone. Kal had known and served with the man since the beginning of the war. Their relationship was, in Kal's opinion, conflicted at best.

"Sir." Ekon nodded at Kal as he stepped in the room and made his way to the food fabricator on the wall.

Kal grabbed a coffee from the machine and sat down across from the sergeant. "How's it going, Sergeant Kimathi?"

"Good," Kimathi took a small bite of the food in front of him. Kal thought it was pan-fried tofu, but it was always hard to tell with the fabricated food. "Soldiers are ready to go. We've been going through our drills nonstop."

"I've been watching. They're ready."

"Ready as they'll ever be." Kimathi nodded. He took another bite.

Their conversations were always like this, brief and cordial. When the Nasi had first attacked Earth, Kal had been a merchant living on his ship, mourning his family and wallowing in his own depression. That's when he'd met Ekon, a kid who'd been traveling with friends after graduation. He'd held a lot of resentment against Kal at first. It seemed to have faded, but they never had the easy relationship they had with others.

"How are *you*?" Kal asked, emphasizing the last word.

Kimathi looked up from his meal to meet Kal's gaze. "I'm motivated," he said. "I'm ready to take back New America." The planet was his home. "I'm ready to stop going from mission to mission."

There was a weariness in the man's words. Something Kal didn't often hear from him.

"We're close. Soon your family will be free." Kal had met them on one of their first missions when Kimathi had ignored orders and led the team right to his family. He'd been a private at the time and still wet behind the ears. But he'd developed quickly. When Staff Sergeant Jones, the Skulls' first Tac-I Squad leader had died, it had taken Kimathi a while to adjust to the new role. Now he was a well-practiced hand and a seasoned leader. Jones would have been proud.

"I try not to think about it." Kimathi paused. "Right now, all I can focus on is what we're going to do next. What we're asking these kids to do." He motioned towards the cargo bay. "If I think about my family, it just gets to be…"

"Too much?" Kal asked.

Kimathi nodded again. "Yeah."

"Look, if you need anything, if the soldiers need anything, I'm here."

"For now." Ekon pushed his bowl away.

Kal felt the heat rise in his face. "Why does every one of our conversations end up this way? What do you want?"

"I don't want anything, sir," Ekon remained calm and unruffled. "The soldiers look up to you. They need a leader who's always present, not just some of the time. *Always.*" He pointed his fork at Kal for emphasis.

"I get it," Kal said. "I was wrong. I've got my own issues."

"Oh, I know you've got issues, sir." Kimathi breathed deeply as if trying to control himself. "All I'm saying is that they respect you. Hell, so do I. I know you care. The others who've been on the Skulls for a while know you do too. But these new soldiers, you've got to remember what it's like for them."

"I know. I get it." Kal had never met anyone who was able to throw him off so quickly. "Look, we've got a mission in front of us that might end this whole war. I'm focused on that."

"I know. The soldiers know it too. But that's the case *right now*. We need you here, with us, until this war is over. No one's talking about it, but there's still two planets left to liberate after this is over."

"You got it." Kal smiled, trying to shove his anger and annoyance to the side. "I'll be there for all of you. I'll be the commander you deserve."

"Just be the one we need," said Kimathi quietly. "Sir."

❖

New America had become all too familiar to Kal in the past year. The Skulls had conducted multiple missions on each of the planet's three main continents. Each landmass was the same well-laid out patchwork of zones that had been meticulously planned by the original settlers. As they descended into one of the nature reserves, Kal could see the clean-cut patchwork of zones stretching across the horizon to Tiradentes, the capital, in the distance.

Tiradentes was really multiple cities, grouped into one enormous urban conglomeration. From a distance, it looked like a mountain range with buildings rising at each city center and falling in-between. The tallest building of all was the grotesque central tower of the Nasi Foothold, nestled directly in the center. Every time Kal saw it, he felt a surge of anger; it was a sign of the Nasi arrogance, a sign they'd ripped away the Human homes and businesses and replaced them with something they saw as superior. He didn't want innocents to die—even Nasi ones—but he couldn't wait to see the Foothold reduced to a crater in the ground.

Once *the Cumae* touched down in a small clearing in the nature preserve, Kal made his way to the cargo hold to find the Tac-1 already formed up with Sergeant Kimathi in front of them giving final instructions for the mission.

"—what we can. Remember, we will come back for you if we can, but the mission must always come first." He gave a nod to Kal. "Okay, general's here. Let's move out. Popov, you've got lead."

Sergeant Popov walked down the ramp with the rest of Bravo Team. They wore the black uniform of New America's Domestic Patrol or Domespat, goons that enforced the hold of the New American Empire on the planet. The New American Empire was the Human government that ruled the planet at the Nasi's behest. They were corrupt, ruthless, and had even fewer morals than their masters. Kal thought the Domespat might be the only force he'd seen in the galaxy that could match the Nasi for cruelty.

"Good luck, sir," Bo said, slapping Kal on the back. The Jadid scientist was staying behind. Although he sometimes came with them on missions, he usually remained on the ship; his presence would be a dead giveaway.

Corporal Sato led Alpha Team off the ramp with Kal and Sergeant Kimathi in the middle and Bravo Team trailing. As they walked through the dense underbrush, Kal could hear the rustle of small creatures scurrying around them. One of the privates held the portable tacmap, checking for Nasi or Domespat patrols as they made their way. The thick bushes made progress difficult, and the rifles slung over their shoulders often caught on branches as they made their way.

Kal noticed small pieces of refuse stuck in the bushes around them. Small containers with vines growing around them, piles of rock that were clearly not natural, and rusted equipment half-buried in the red soil. They were nearing their objective.

He began to make out the straight lines and sharp corners of the abandoned factory that had become a base for the

Tiradentes Liberation Front, or TLF, between the wide leaves of the forest. The building had been decommissioned when the government had rezoned the area from industrial to natural uses. In the intervening decades the forest had swallowed it whole, making it an ideal place to avoid the Domespat and Nasi patrols.

Kal knew they were being watched by sensors the TLF had placed around the base. He'd been there enough times that he'd seen their operations center and the enormous viewscreen that contained a complete register of everything that happened outside. For anyone who stumbled across the area, it would seem like an abandoned complex of buildings with rust covering most of the rectangular structures. Vines crawled up the sides and discarded equipment littered the ground.

They stepped through a pair of multistory rusted doors that hung off the side of the largest building and entered an enormous chamber. Giant furnaces and industrial machines covered in dust and oxidation towered above them. The metal floor was also covered in the same thick layer of dust that looked to have been the result of years of neglect.

A rectangular column, as wide as a single-family dwelling, with smoothed edges stood in the center of the room. A dented set of half-open doors faced them with a lift car resting at an odd angle inside. As they approached, the broken car rose, revealing a nondescript interior with an amber-tinged light flickering on the ceiling.

Kal nervously glanced around the room. He had been

there several times before, and each time, he couldn't shake the feeling of malevolence that seemed to permeate the decrepit base.

They climbed inside and the car descended several meters into the ground. The doors opened to reveal a large operations center buzzing with activity. People scurried between makeshift workstations and small meeting areas. Viewscreens hung on the wall or were placed atop tables, lending an eerie blue tint to the yellow light streaming from the naked bulbs hung from the ceiling.

"General Norman, good to see you." Li Wei Santos gave Kal a friendly nod then turned to Sergeant Kimathi with open arms. "Ekon, you bastard, you're still alive."

"Yup," Kimathi embraced his childhood friend. "For now."

Li Wei and Ekon had grown up together in Tiradentes. Li Wei had been one of the friends Kimathi had been traveling through the galaxy with after graduation. Then the Nasi had attacked New America, and Kimathi had barely escaped with Kal while Li Wei had been stranded on the planet. When the Domespat took control of New America, he joined the resistance, fighting against them and the Nasi occupiers.

"Come with me," Li Wei said. "We're in the command room. We're running a raid on one of the Domespat stations." Li Wei led them towards a large reinforced door on the other side of the room.

Kal raised an eyebrow. "Isn't that risky? What's the payoff?"

"Two things. One, they captured one of our patrols during

62

a routine scavenging mission. With everything going on, we want to get them back. Two, we've seen an uptick in Nasi activity. Based on the movements of their leadership, it seems like it's being run out of this station."

Just months ago, a mission like that wouldn't have even been considered except in the direst circumstances. But the tide was not only turning against the Nasi but their Domespat lackies as well. It was gratifying for Kal to know that the Skulls had played some part in it.

Kal guessed that the command room had been used to store some sort of volatile material when the factory had been working. The walls were lined with a metal alloy, and the door was at least a half-meter thick. These characteristics also made it perfect for monitoring extremely sensitive operations.

A viewscreen displaying a live feed from a battle suit took up an entire wall of the room. Kal and the other Skulls stepped into the back and joined the others watching the feed. Several rows of consoles, occupied by TLF fighters whispering in hushed tones to each other as they watched the action unfold, filled the room.

"General," Chief Rafaela Pham whispered, giving Kal a nod. Her blue eyes seemed to gleam in the dim light from the viewscreen.

"Chief." Kal returned the nod. Rafaela was the chief of this cell of the TLF and their primary contact with the group. He'd come to trust her implicitly over the past months.

She angled her head toward the viewscreen. "Big mission. We've got three companies encircling the station. Time to see if all that tech you've been bringing us works."

The feed was being recorded from a position outside the ten-story Domespat base in Tiradentes. Guards were posted on the doors at the base while patrol vehicles landed and took off from the roof.

A tacmap was on the viewscreen next to the live feed. Kal could see the three TLF companies surrounding the base, having taken positions in or on the buildings around it. Their icons created an almost solid circle of green around the white outline of the facility on the tacmap. It was the largest operation Kal had seen the TLF perform. He guessed it was nearly every fighter in their cell.

Chief, we're ready to proceed. The synthetic voice from a neural implant echoed around the chamber.

"Go ahead," Pham called out.

Rockets streaked from the soldier's point of view and impacted the side of the building seconds later. Other explosions peppered the building, most of them hitting the roof and top floors. The TLF were clearly trying to funnel the Domespat to the bottom floors; they were there to free the prisoners and capture intel, not capture the station.

The helmet-mounted cam suddenly lifted in the air and streaked towards the building—the soldier was using their thrusters. They landed on the rooftop, where the landing pads for the patrol transports were.

Top floor clear.

"Proceed to the objective," Pham ordered.

The soldier moved to the back of the landing bay. Kal saw

glimpses of other fighters in battle suits moving forward with their railguns pressed to their shoulders as they searched through the bay. The smoke from the explosions still hung in the air, obscuring the far corners of the area. Kal felt a pang of nervousness, imagining a Domespat patroller leaping out and attacking despite knowing that the soldier's battle-suit's sensors could pick up anything through the smoke.

Other fighters, without battle suits, had taken positions on the ground outside the main doors to the building. They'd quickly created defensive positions using vehicles and portable barricades and had small mortar teams behind them. Only a trickle of Domespat patrollers ran out the doors; the rest must have realized what was going on and remained on the bottom floors.

"Looks like they're not running," Kal observed.

Pham nodded. "Yeah, I'm surprised. The Domespat are normally cowards, running at the first sign of a real fight." She sighed. "Guess they're toughening up."

At the worst time, thought Kal.

He watched the viewscreen with rapt attention as the fighters made their way down the stairs at the corner of the building. So far, they'd come against no resistance. The patrollers at the top of the building had turned and ran, the only ones remaining were too injured to move or dead.

Proceeding to the next level. They threw a grenade down the stairwell and rushed in. It was empty.

"The detention cells are on the center floors of the building," Pham whispered to Kal. He felt a pang of nervousness. The assault team would need to clear several more levels before they got to the objective.

The entire control room watched silently as the TLF assault team made their way through the building. Despite the Domespat's horrific reputation, their station looked like any civilian office. Rows of consoles lined the room with small areas for breaks and conference rooms to the sides. Kal noticed a few differences: bars on the windows of the rooms, small lights on the ceiling, and red panic buttons dotting the walls every few meters.

"Shit!" Kal yelled. "Get them out!"

"What! Why?" Pham cried out in shock.

"It's a trap. They knew you were coming." Kal flung out his arm and pointed to the screen. "They never pressed the panic buttons."

Pham turned back to study the viewscreen. The alert lights on the ceiling of the station remained off. There was no alarm going off to signal an emergency.

"All teams exit the building, immediately!" Pham shouted. "Cover team, light that building up to cover their escape."

The interior team turned around and began to run toward the stairwell while the teams outside began firing at all four sides of the building.

The assault team made it up one flight before an explosion rocked the building and rubble began to rain down on their heads. At the same time a hail of plasma bolts erupted from the middle floors of the station towards the defenders on the ground. A second later, the ground beneath them erupted in gouts of fire.

"We've got fighters inbound," shouted one of the techs.

"Tell them to get out of there. Whatever they can do!" Pham instructed.

"No, ma'am. *We* have fighters inbound," the tech shouted. "Here. On *our* position."

The room erupted into chaos, but all Kal could see was the video feed. The soldier avoided the worst of the explosions in the stairwell and ran back through the building. He was trying to pull the reinforced metal bars from the windows when he spun and fell on the ground, his camera facing up towards the ceiling. The last thing Kal saw was the black boot of a Nasi battle suit as it slammed onto the soldier's head and cut off the feed.

Chapter Five
Nicole | Kasongo, Patagonia

"What the hell do we do now?" Sergeant Peng asked, nervously running his hand through his black hair.

After finding the governor's mansion's grounds swarming with Nasi, Nicole and the rest of Alpha Team had taken refuge at a rally point near the edge of the city. They'd picked a small logistics facility since the automated cargo drones carrying material in and out helped obscure any vehicles coming into the area, and since it was at the edge of the city, there were several escape routes into the surrounding forest.

"We'll need to decide when Sergeant Bhatt gets here," Nicole replied calmly. She was as nervous as the sergeant, but she couldn't let it show. Either way, Bhatt was the squad leader, and they needed to decide as a team. Nicole just hoped that Bravo Team hadn't done anything stupid like getting caught.

Nicole wondered what had happened to Major Karl Garcia. He'd been one of the original members of the Skulls and Nicole considered him a friend. Since taking over his family's syndicate and then the entire planet, he'd been working behind the scenes to set the stage for this very day, appearing to collaborate with the Nasi while aiding the Patagonian Front.

If the Nasi were there at the palace, Nicole feared it could mean only one thing; Karl had been found out. The worse part was she didn't know if the Nasi had killed him or were holding him to extract information. Probably the latter, the Nasi were pragmatic and would see value in trying to extract as much information as possible. Unfortunately, the Bones were in no position to launch a rescue.

"Do you think—"

"Stop talking," Nicole snapped. She pointed to several empty bins scattered against the walls around them. "Take cover and wait."

She had no desire to talk to anyone. Instead, she crouched against the wall, pistol pointed at the large gap between the buildings and tried her best not to think about what might be happening to Karl or what it might mean for them and the mission.

A quarter of an hour later, the Bravo Team arrived with Sergeant Bhatt in the lead.

"This is shit," Bhatt announced as Nicole stepped away from her hiding spot.

"Yeah," Nicole agreed. "But what do we do about it?"

"We need to go to the Patagonian Front. Maybe they know what happened."

"What if the Nasi got them as well?" Sergeant Peng looked around nervously. "I mean, they clearly realize that Foyleton was up to something."

"Well, then we're already screwed." Bhatt shrugged. "But we're here to meet with them next anyway."

"What about the Alliance?" Nicole asked. The interstellar organization had been assisting Samsara Fleet where they could. The Nasi had seen them as a threat and closed many of the fronts they operated out of, but they still had the ability to get information and materials.

"Ishmael?" Bhatt scoffed. "The guy's nuts."

Nicole couldn't disagree with that. The Alliance leader on Patagonia was eccentric, for sure. "Perhaps, but he's been helpful. You know as well as I that we wouldn't be where we are without him."

"Where's that exactly, ma'am?" Bhatt looked around. "In an alley?"

Nicole was about to reply when Corporal Basu cleared his throat loudly. "Sergeant, let's split up," suggested the corporal. "My team can go with the commander to meet up with the Alliance, and you can go with Corporal Basu to meet with the Front."

"I'm not sure I like the idea of splitting up," Peng said. He cleared his throat. "The Nasi are already onto us."

"That's exactly why we *should* split up," Basu said. "We can't risk the whole squad."

Nicole wondered about the other five scout teams. Each one of them had landed at a different point on the planet and had contacts that they were meeting up with. Each one also had the Triple-A charges that could destroy the plasma lances' nexuses. The Bones were supposed to be the central command and control, establishing contact with the government and the PF. So far, things were not looking good for them. However, Nicole had to do whatever maximized their chances of success. Peng was right, splitting up the squad ensured the Nasi wouldn't be able to take them out all at once.

"Basu's right We need to split up," Nicole said with resignation. Sergeant Peng grunted in frustration. "We have one chance at this. If the Nasi have discovered the Alliance or the Front, then we'll be walking into a trap."

"Use the net only when necessary," Nicole continued. The planet's neural net allowed them to communicate through their implants even if they were on opposite sides of the planet. Unfortunately, even though the traffic was encrypted, there was the potential for the Nasi to break through the encryption and intercept their communication. Additionally, each time they used their implants to communicate, there was the risk of the Nasi triangulating the signal to find their location.

"Yes, ma'am," Bhatt said, rounding on her two team leaders. "We'll only use our neural implants to communicate in life-or-death situations. Otherwise, we rendezvous here in a day. You heard the commander. Get your soldiers ready. We're out in five. Corporal Basu, we'll leave first."

The two NCOs nodded in acknowledgement then walked back to their teams to explain the plan.

"You sure about this, ma'am?" Bhatt asked once they were out of earshot.

"No." Nicole chuckled bitterly. "But we're going to do it anyway."

The Alliance front on Patagonia was in the city of Foyleton on the eastern half of Pangea. Nicole and Alpha Team made their way through Kasongo's crowded street to where the *Cumae* was hidden. A certain sense of danger permeated the air, and the citizens eyed her nervously as she made her way through the streets.

"Back so soon, ma'am?" asked Chief Ramos as she walked down the cargo ramp to greet them.

"The Nasi have swarmed the governor's mansion." Nicole trudged up the ramp with the rest of Alpha Team. "We're heading to Foyleton to meet with the Alliance. We need to figure out what's happening, and fast."

"Where're the others?" Ramos looked out the end of the ramp.

"Bhatt and Bravo Team are heading to one of the Front's encampments to see if they know anything," Nicole said tiredly. "Get us out of here. The plan's gone to crap and we need to figure out how to salvage it."

Ramos nodded and followed her to the cockpit. A few minutes later, the *Chester* was soaring across the green Patagonian landscape. The mountain range between Foyleton and Kasongo jutted out in front of them, clawing toward the sky.

Nicole wasn't sure what she'd do if the Alliance had been compromised as well. She'd never had so much responsibility on her shoulders. A few years ago, she'd been a low-level paper pusher and now the entire fleet was counting on her to somehow recapture a planet. Worst part was, she couldn't even communicate with the other assault teams since she didn't know exactly what was happening yet and didn't want to risk exposing herself.

Less than an hour later, they landed in a small field outside of Foyleton. Rows of what Nicole suspected was corn stretched across the gently sloping hillock around them.

Nicole entered the cargo bay to find Sergeant Peng's squad already in battle suits. The gray augmented armor not only gave them access to an arsenal of weapons but also allowed them to fly across the landscape and enter Foyleton without being tracked by the planetary defenses. Once they were close, they'd have to ditch the suits and enter on foot though.

Nicole activated her suit with her implant, and the back spread open, allowing her to step inside. Once she was inside, it sealed around her, closing along the arms, legs, and finally the back. Nicole grabbed the helmet and placed it over her head, hearing a small click and hiss as the suit's airtight seal took hold. The battle suit, which had felt so strange and bulky only a year ago, now made her feel almost invincible.

Be ready to leave at a moment's notice, Nicole instructed Chief Ramos through her implant. She activated her external speaker and turned towards Peng. "Your team ready?"

"Yes, ma'am."

They departed the *Chester* in a staggered formation. The four battle suits soared above the knee-high stalks of corn towards the faint skyline of Foyleton. As they got closer, Nicole was able to make out individual buildings. Like

Kasongo, they were a mishmash of different styles, both ancient and modern with a few alien architectural features thrown in. It reminded her of a junkyard, buildings of all types seemingly thrown around by a careless giant.

Sergeant Peng touched down in a small copse of trees at the edge of the town, and they exited their suits and activated the security protocols. As Nicole stepped out of her suit, she felt suddenly vulnerable. The icy terror that had gripped her outside the presidential palace had only grown. She dreaded what they would find inside the city.

"Whatever happens, do not go back for anyone," Nicole ordered, looking at each of the soldiers in the eyes.

"But—"

"I get it, Sergeant Peng. Honor and all that. But this is too important. Do. Not. Stop. Keep going."

The Tac-I soldiers looked at each other uncertainly and then reluctantly nodded. Nicole got it. The idea of leaving a comrade behind was heretical to their very being, but in this case, the mission was too important.

Private Sampson took lead as they walked through a maze of warehouses, heading toward the center of the city. The former pilot had blossomed in his time as a lowly foot soldier and deftly navigated through the area, barely making a sound as he guided them between buildings and equipment.

As the warehouses turned into squat homes then mid-level buildings more and more people filled the streets. Soon they were surrounded by a crush of people and chaotic transport traffic. They distanced themselves from one another but made sure to keep close enough that they maintained visual contact.

Sampson took them on a circuitous route through the city, doubling back more than once before finally turning down a forgotten street filled with debris and hedged in by dilapidated buildings.

Take your positions, Nicole instructed through her implant. I'll go inside and make contact.

The three Tac-I soldiers disappeared into the cityscape, leaving Nicole standing alone on the grimy street. They'd been there enough times that the soldiers knew exactly where to position themselves while she was talking with the Alliance. She walked into a neglected building covered in a faded green paint. Floor-to-ceiling display cases covered the walls, while other waist-high ones made a rectangle in the center of the room. Nicole walked between the center cases and placed her Alliance chit against a gutted bot lying on the floor.

Metal shutters snapped down over the entrance and windows, and the floor beneath her began to descend. The platform glided several meters beneath the shop floor. It stopped with a small hiss and a door in the wall opened, revealing a small man dressed in rags, his arms spread wide in greeting.

"Colonel Bergeron," he said warmly.

"Ishmael." Nicole smiled and gave a small nod, not wanting to get close to him. If he smelled anything like he looked, she wanted no part of it.

"It's always good to see a member of Samsara Fleet."
Ishmael winked playfully. "Don't worry. I was doing some
recon before you got here." He waved her in. "I've been
expecting you." The Alliance leader was often dressed as a
beggar, saying that seeming poor and in need of help was
one of the easiest ways to get people not to notice him.

Nicole followed the man through the door, down a bright
hallway, and into a green-walled room filled with expensive
furniture. "Take a seat," said Ishmael, pointing to a gilded
chair.

"Where's Ava?" Nicole always enjoyed seeing Ishmael's
companion. She was a former Domespat that had been
captured by the Skulls. Ishmael had been her jailor, but in the
intervening months, their relationship had become practically
domestic.

"She's out scouting." Ishmael replied breezily. "We need
all hands on deck, so I've got her out checking on what the
Nasi are doing in the city." He frowned. "They've really been
picking up their operations in the past few days. Used to be
rare, but now I see them every time I leave here."

"What are they up to?" asked Nicole.

"Ain't that the question of the day," said Ishmael, tapping
a finger against the ornate goblet in his hand. "My guess?"
He leaned forward. "They're getting ready for you. Ready for
us I guess I should say since I'm part of all this."

"They took over the governor's residence."

"I'd heard. Seems like your friend Karl is in a boatload of

trouble. Along with them taking out the Patagonia Front stronghold, there's not much left on the planet that *isn't* directly under those bastards' thumbs." His face twisted into an expression of distaste.

"They captured the Front's headquarters?" asked Nicole, almost jumping out of her chair. She'd sent Sergeant Bhatt and Bravo Team to meet with them.

"Not just the headquarters, the entire thing." Ishmael shook his head ruefully. "The Nasi must have known about the Front and Foyleton colluding for a while. Question is whether the timing is a coincidence or intentional." He raised an eyebrow.

Clearly Ishmael knew, or at least suspected, that Nicole's mission was not an ordinary one. *How much did the Nasi know of their plans?* she wondered. *How much could they know?*

Samsara Fleet and the Front went through extraordinary precautions to make sure that even if they were captured, agents couldn't divulge information. But to have the entire Front rounded up at one time meant there was almost no question the Nasi knew exactly what they were up to. But Nicole had no idea how that was possible since even she hadn't known before coming to the planet hours ago.

"Whatever you've got planned, it's gonna have to wait," said Ishmael. "The Nasi are tracking anything and everything entering the planet."

"I need to understand what's going on."

"You've got to get out of here." Ishmael's grin vanished.

Nicole paused. How much should she tell the man? He wasn't part of Samsara Fleet, but he was an ally.

"We're starting our assault," said Nicole. "We've got teams on the planet to take out their plasma lances."

"They obviously know what you're doing," said Ishmael, unfazed. "This is all a trap."

"Probably," said Nicole. Of course it was. "But we've got a relay ship in deep orbit. The fleet isn't coming without our signal."

Ishmael sighed and looked at the ceiling. "Ugh. I would have thought *you'd* be more reasonable. Seems like palling around with a bunch of Tac-I's has warped your common sense as well."

Nicole took it as a compliment.

"If you're going—"

Ishmael was interrupted by the earsplitting screech of an alarm. One of the pictures on the wall disappeared, revealing a video feed from outside the building. Nicole could see Peng's team was arrayed around the building, their dim silhouettes highlighted with green reticles from the Alliance's security system. Several red boxes, highlighting the enemy, were slowly moving towards them.

Peng, you've got company, Nicole called out. Get out of here.

"If you're trying to communicate with them, it won't work," said Ishmael. "This place is designed to prevent outgoing communications."

Nicole looked at him in surprise. *Had he betrayed them?*

"It's not against you, damn it," Ishmael said, seeming to read her mind. "It's standard security protocol for an Alliance front, especially in the current environment." He stood up. "Follow me, we've gotta get out of here."

Nicole stood, but her eyes remain fixed on the viewscreen. The red Nasi squares were almost touching the Tac-I squad's position. Three bright flashes caused the screen to white out for a moment and the green squares turned to yellow—status unknown.

"Enough!" Ishmael grabbed her arm. "There's nothing you can do for them. Let's focus on what we can actually control."

He pulled her through a door and down a narrow metal-lined corridor. Nicole snapped back and focused on what was in front of her. Whatever happened, she needed to get out of there. As far as she knew, she was the assault teams' last hope. She needed to let the other five teams know the mission was fully compromised and to retreat. Ishmael sprinted through the winding passageway and almost ran directly into a closed door.

He slapped his palm against a nearby sensor plate and the enormous door swung open, revealing a small pod barely able to fit two people.

"Well, I always figured this day would come," Ishmael said begrudgingly under his breath. He shrugged, then turned to Nicole. "Hop in. We're goin' for a ride."

The pod was even more cramped than it had appeared from the outside. For them to both fit in, Nicole had to tuck her legs to her chest while Ishmael wrapped himself around her. The interior was empty except for a glowing button on the ceiling.

"I've never used this before," said Ishmael lightly as the door closed behind them. "But I've heard it's not the most fun. Guess we'll be friends by the time this is over."

The pod's door clicked shut, immersing them in darkness. Nicole could make out the contours of the Alliance leader's face in the dim light and thought she saw a small tear work its way down his face. He slammed his hand against the button on the ceiling and they both yelped as the pod instantly shot away from the building.

Seconds later an enormous thump came from the direction of the Alliance base, and the shockwave of an explosion rocked the pod, slamming them into each other and the pod walls.

"Where're we going?" asked Nicole as she pulled Ishmael's foot off her head.

"Away," Ishmael said. His voice sounded tired, defeated. A contrast to the light tone just minutes earlier. "We're in an underground river and following the current. Eventually we'll wash up somewhere."

They bobbed along in complete darkness for the next hour. Both of them remained silent, lost in their thoughts. Occasionally, the pod bounced—likely against the sides of the subterranean cavern they were floating through—causing Nicole's legs to groan in pain. They ached at first, and then grew numb as the pod continued its journey. Finally, a loud grating sound filled the interior, and they were pitched forward as the pod came to a halt.

"Looks like we're here," said Ishmael. "Wherever here is." He pushed the button again and the door to the pod popped off, landing in water with a splash. Light streamed through the opening, forcing Nicole to shield her eyes.

Ishmael slowly crawled out of the pod and flopped down. Nicole followed, her legs screaming as she climbed out of the tiny opening and landed with a thunk on soft wet ground. For a moment she couldn't see a thing as she slammed her eyes shut against the overpowering light.

They were lying on the muddy riverbank of a small stream. The water burbled by, clear and sparkling in the bright light. She could hear insects humming nearby. She would have considered it peaceful at any other moment.

"Well, la di da, we're alive," Ishmael said, pushing himself up using his hands and knees.

Nicole started to get up as well when she heard movement in the clump of bushes next to them and dove back to the ground. A second later a small scaled creature darted out and dove into the stream, ignoring the two Human interlopers.

Nicole couldn't help it. She laughed. Laughed until she cried. Everything was lost and she was diving to the ground because of an animal no bigger than her hand. "Any idea on what to do next?" she asked when she'd recovered.

"Not a clue," said Ishmael, eying her wearily.

Chapter Six
Nicole | Patagonia

After inspecting the area near the riverbank, Nicole and Ishmael guessed there were in one of the planet's wildlife preserves. Like other colonized worlds, Patagonia had several protected areas dedicated to conserving the native flora and fauna of the planet.

After spending a few minutes resting and stretching their legs, the two set off toward the nearest town. Although they didn't dare transmit with their implants, they could still use them to track where they were. Nicole estimated it would be a couple hours until they reached the small town they'd picked out.

Since they were in a preserve, there were no trails or paths. Instead they had to tramp through waist-high grasses and pry themselves through walls of iridescent shrubs. Nicole had been born and raised in the city, and the strange noises, the small animals rustling around them, and the gusts of wind causing the branches above them to sway caused her already fraught nerves to scream in terror. She jumped in terror every few seconds only to realize it was a small wide-eyed creature or two branches rubbing against each other.

Ishmael led them through the area with curt gestures and his eyes focused on the ground in front. Finally, he stopped in a small clearing covered from above by the interlocking branches of several large trees. He knelt down, grabbed a fist-sized round fungus from the ground, and held it out to Nicole.

"Hungry?"

She eyed the grayish mass. "What is it?"

"I've always called 'em dragon eggs. Don't know it's real name. Tastes like smoke and dirt."

Nicole was intrigued. She took the fungus from Ishmael's hand and turned it around, examining it. Why? She didn't know. It was a completely uniform sphere. Interestingly, there was no sign of a root or stem. It was as if it had just grown from air. Finally, she took a small nibble. Ishmael was right, the flavor was decidedly earthy with a hint of smoke. To her, it tasted like forest, like wilderness.

Ishmael picked another dragon egg from the ground and took a deep bite, wiping his mouth with a bedraggled sleeve. "Ya know, these things are interesting. They're the only lifeform that occurs across multiple planets. At some point, millions of years ago, their spores somehow traveled through the void of space, landing and surviving on multiple planets." Ishmael took another deep bite. "Some people say they're proof of an interstellar race that died out before Humans and others came along."

Nicole looked down at the fungi in her hand appreciatively. It was interesting to think about another species, or several, that had existed before them, the only evidence of their existence being a simple spore that grew in the woods.

"Makes you wonder how important all of this is," said Nicole. "Are we just rearranging a few things before an inevitable decline?"

"Maybe." Ishmael placed several of the eggs inside folds in his clothing and stood up. "To me, it doesn't much matter. What happens now is what I care about." He started walking toward the edge of the clearing. "Come on, we got another hour at least."

The dense brush and trees of the preserve gave way to rolling farmland almost identical to where the Bones had landed the *Chester*. Nicole desperately wanted to contact her ship to see if the Nasi had captured it but didn't dare. At this point she had to assume any call that they made over the planetwide neural net would alert the Nasi to her location. She took solace in the fact that Chief Ramos was an excellent pilot and wouldn't be an easy target.

Nicole and Ishmael dropped to the ground when they heard the whine of a transport thruster on their left. A hedge of broad-leafed vines blocked them from view but also prevented Nicole from seeing what had made the noise. Instead, she had to wait, her hand clasped around the grip of her pistol as the sound grew louder. Questions raced through her mind as she waited.

"Screw this," Ishmael whispered. He stood up and looked around, brushing the dirt and clay from the front of his outfit. He gave a small snort. "It's fine. You can get up. It's a farming drone."

"You insane?" Nicole asked incredulously as she stood.

"That's all the running I'm going to do today. If they're gonna capture or kill me, then I wanna be standing when they do it. I'll die like a Human before I live like an animal."

"Are you kiddin' me with that?" Nicole had no idea where the sudden wave of bravado was coming from.

Ishmael's mouth screwed up in annoyance. "Can you just give me this?" He huffed. "Fine. I was tired of flopping on the ground and snapped. Is that better?"

"More honest."

"Whatever. Let's go." Ishmael waved her forward.

The town they were heading to was called Trokar. It occupied a small depression in the middle of several large farms. As they rounded a hill, the small town lay nestled in a valley below them. It wasn't much to look at: a few houses, some small apartment blocks, shops, and a grain warehouse that was larger than the rest of the town combined. Small skiffs, loaded with canisters, floated between the buildings alongside people dressed in the rough blouses and breeches of farm workers.

They tromped through the field and made their way to one of the roads leading into town without any of the inhabitants paying them a second glance.

"I happen to know someone here," said Ishmael as they reached the edge of town.

They ended up in front of a small house, its umber paint faded and cracked from years in the sun. Ishmael pressed the call button near the door and looked into the camera positioned above with a broad smile.

After a few seconds, the door cracked open, and a woman peered out with narrowed eyes. A hard life spent outdoors was written in the crow's feet and wrinkles of her leathery face. She frowned slightly as she studied Ishmael.

"Yorick, what are you doing here?" She looked at Nicole. "Our business was finished *years* ago."

Ishmael gave a slight nod. "Hello, Deepta," he said jovially. "Bet you thought you'd never see me again. I'm here regarding something else though. Apologies for appearing out of nowhere, but I'm in a bit of a bind as you can imagine. Can we come inside?"

Deepta considered the request for a moment before opening the door and stepping to the side to allow them in. "Can't say I'm not curious."

The house's spartan interior matched the outside. A tarnished food fabricator stood in a corner with a prep table and dining area nearby. On the other side, a small seating area was arranged around an ancient holo projector.

"We've got a bit of a problem," said Ishmael after they'd sat down. "My client here"—he gestured to Nicole—"needs a transport. No questions asked."

Deepta chuckled and leaned back. "Yorick. You're gonna need to do better than that. You want me to *what*? Give you my transport? No questions asked? I've gotta lot of 'em, and I need answers before I'm willing to do anything."

"You know how I operate," said Ishmael. "How *we* operate. I'm willing to give you more credits than you'll earn in a year."

The woman scoffed. "You know I can't spend the credits I got already. Not with all the Nasi embargos and tributes and such. Nah, the only payment I'll accept is answers." She looked at Nicole. "I don't know what he's got you mixed up in. But remember, there's always a price to pay."

"We'll tell you whatever you want to know," said Nicole desperately. "But we *need* a transport."

"I can tell she ain't one of yours," said Deepta wryly, looking at Ishmael. She turned back to Nicole. "Okay, so spill it. Why do you need my transport so badly?"

Nicole considered her options and realized she had none. She needed help and had no option but the truth. She explained her mission and what had happened since the Bones had arrived on Patagonia. The woman listened without saying a word, her eyes fixed on a point somewhere behind Nicole's head. Once Nicole had finished, the woman stood up and grabbed a small bag hanging near the door.

"I'm in," said Deepta, her hand hovering over the plate next to the door. "Where we goin'?"

"Wait," said Ishmael, "you're not going with us."

"Damn straight I am," said Deepta. "Now *where* are we going?"

Deepta's transport wasn't the most modern, but she clearly took good care of it. The green hull was polished, free from nicks and scratches, and the interior almost spotless.

Nicole could only think of one place to go, where the Skulls had first met the Patagonia Front over a year ago. They headed to an old base that had been destroyed in the civil war and had gripped Patagonia before Foyleton under Karl Garcia's control had gained control.

An hour later, they descended through a dense canopy of trees and landed outside a decrepit series of bunkers. In one of his darker moments, Kal had told her about the abandoned Front camp and how bodies had littered the ground. Someone had cleaned the area up.

"What is this place?" asked Deepta.

"An old Front base," said Nicole. "Before that, it was used by the EDF. During the civil war, Foyleton cleared it out." She hoped that some of the Patagonia Front members still remembered its location. There was a good chance at least a few of them would come here if that was the case.

"You're hoping the Nasi won't have surveillance here," said Ishmael as he looked around. "That's a big risk."

"Eh," Nicole said indifferently. "Maybe. As far as we know, they never discovered this camp. Either way, it's a calculated risk since we don't have a better idea."

Deepta strode toward one of the squat gray bunkers at the edge of the clearing. "We're here now. Let's look around."

They walked through the camp, pistols in hand, trying to find any sign of occupation. The first small structures they came across were all empty, stripped clean of any equipment. Even the wiring had been pulled out of the walls.

Finally they came to a large bunker that Nicole guessed had been used as a hangar or command center based on its size. Their footsteps made grinding noises on the coating of dust that coated the metal floor. Each of them had a small light out, casting small portals of brightness against the pitch-black of the cavernous building.

"This one's different," said Ishmael. "Someone's been here."

Nicole didn't see anything different but didn't doubt him. The man hadn't become the head of an Alliance front for no reason. If he said that someone had been in the building, she believed him. She checked her pistol for what felt like the millionth time. The plasma weapon had plenty of charges, and the safety was off.

Ishmael bent down and studied the floor, duck-walking around the room with his light focused in front of him. Deepta and Nicole walked behind, trying to shine their lights ahead to give him additional visibility. Finally, he stopped at a wall and began to run his hand against its rough metal surface.

"There's some tracks," said Ishmael. "They're faint but they're still there."

Nicole bent down and studied the floor. She couldn't see anything different. Perhaps there were a few lines, but she wouldn't have thought they were an indication of anyone having been there. "You sure?"

"Yeah, pretty damn sure," said Ishmael.

"I *think* I see what you're talking about," said Deepta. She motioned at a small irregularity in the thin coating of dust.

"Nope, that's not it." Ishmael shook his head. "Focus on where the floor and wall meet. Whatever went through the room, came to or from here." He rapped the wall with his knuckle. "And I'll wager my Alliance retirement that there's a way in."

"You get a retirement?" asked Nicole in surprise.

Ishmael guffawed, the laughs reverberating through the chamber. "No, we do not."

They spent another ten minutes studying the area, looking for seams, buttons, or panels that might allow them access. Ishmael claimed he could see razor thin lines where there was a door though neither Deepta nor Nicole could verify. They split up and worked their way along the walls, shining their lights and pressing their splayed fingers against the surface.

With a curse, Ishmael shined his light at Deepta and Nicole. "Follow me," he said.

He strode through the hallways of the building reaching dead end after dead end. Then he led them outside and circled the entire structure twice before walking into a small copse of bushes and kneeling.

"The door may be opened by implant," said Ishmael. "But there's only one way in or out of this building. Let's take positions and wait for whoever's in there to come to us."

"You sure there's someone in there?" asked Deepta.

"As sure as I regret inviting you along." Ishmael flashed a pearly white smile. He turned to Nicole. "You're the hardened battle leader. Where do we go to watch for people coming in or out without getting shot at?"

I guess I am, Nicole thought to herself in surprise. She still thought of herself as a paper-pushing diplomat, but that hadn't been true for a while.

Nicole directed Ishmael and Deepta to covered positions on either side of the door, while she took one in a clump of bushes almost directly in front. As she crouched down holding her pistol, she hoped that the Alliance leader knew what he was talking about. Otherwise, they were wasting time they didn't have.

The light faded as the sun dropped beneath the horizon and an eerie amber glow filled the sky, trickling through the branches above. The very nature of the forest changed as small iridescent creatures swung through the branches above them. The leaves around her changed hues, trading in their subdued daytime colors for more colorful ones for the night.

He'd better be right, thought Nicole. Not only because they were wasting a lot of time but because she didn't know what to do if they weren't. The mission had started with six elite Tac-1 teams spread throughout the planet. And now as far as she knew, she was all that was left. She wondered what had happened to the other members of the Skulls. She knew Alpha Team was apprehended, but she clung on to the hope that Sergeant Bhatt and Bravo Team had escaped the Nasi. Nicole thought about trying to contact Bhatt and the other assault teams over the net then discarded the idea. Trying to communicate at this point would be like sending up a flare. It was a last resort.

A small flicker of movement caught Nicole's eye. She held her breath and stared into the inky black entrance of the former Front bunker. An elderly man, clutching a bag strapped across his chest, tottered through the opening. He stopped, adjusted the bag, and then pulled himself up to his full height.

"I know you're out there!" The man quivered as he shouted. "Come where I can see you."

The elderly face and the slight frame looked familiar to Nicole. She squinted.

"Kinkaid?" asked Nicole.

"Step out where I can see you!"

Nicole put her pistol back in its holster and strode into the opening with her hands in the air. "It's me, Nicole Bergeron."

"Nicole?" Bohai Kinkaid shuffled toward her, his feet sliding across the ground. "What are you doing here?"

"Are there any others?" asked Nicole.

"Aye, there's a few of us left." He motioned toward the large bunker behind him. "They killed or captured everyone else. Come on in."

Chapter Seven
Kal | Tiradentes, New America

Explosions rattled the Tiradentes Liberation Front base as the Nasi fighters streaked overhead. Rafaela Pham pulled Kal and the other Skulls out of the room and led them down a utility corridor as the Nasi bombardment continued to pound the building.

"Come on," shouted Pham over the din. "We've got another way out."

The end of the hallway was filled with junk—empty equipment containers, rusted equipment, and ammo boxes. As they approached, the pile cracked apart, revealing a small door barely big enough for them to fit through.

"We knew we were on borrowed time," Pham explained. "When we took over this base, we suspected the Nasi may find it one day. I was beginning to believe that day would never come."

She opened the door, revealing a small tunnel and what Kal could only describe as a cart. It consisted of a single metal sheet on wheels and what appeared to be a transport thruster attached to one end of it. The makeshift sled looked ready to fall apart at any moment.

"Is this what I think it is?" Sergeant Kimathi asked, eying the contraption.

"If you mean a way to get of here, then yes."

"I was thinking more that it's the way that I'll die."

"It's either this or the Nasi." The chief gestured at the

sled. "This will take you into the center of Tiradentes. From there, you can disappear. The tunnel is old, and no one knows about it."

"Get on," Kal ordered.

The eight Skulls barely fit on the sled's metal bottom. As the last person on, half of Kal's body was hanging over the side of the vehicle. He grabbed one of the loops of fabric that dotted the sled's bottom and pulled to keep himself from falling off.

"Thanks," said Kal.

"Just get out of here and make this worth it," Pham said, turning as the sound of an explosion rattled down the hall behind her. The Nasi had breached the building.

The chief pressed a button on the engine, and a faint whine emanated from the tarnished cylinder. Just as Kal wondered if the device worked, the sled shot forward, almost throwing him off. The glow of the engine's exhaust illuminated the tunnel for a few meters in front of them as they streaked along. The rush of the wind—and a few screams—filled Kal's ears. He cautiously looked to the side, careful to keep a tight grip on the sled's fabric loop. The others were all still there, their faces locked in either terror or disbelief.

A wall appeared in the glow ahead of them. Kal didn't have time to yell before the front of the sled pierced through it and he felt himself falling. The next thing his senses registered was the shock of being thrown into ice-cold water. For a moment, all was quiet, and Kal felt a calm before his head broke the water's surface.

"That was a rush," said Private Chadha with a grin.

Kal couldn't understand exactly what the private was grinning about, and judging from the looks on the others' faces, he wasn't the only one who felt that way.

"Where the hell are we?" Kal asked as he swam to the side of the small pool they'd landed in. They were in some sort of manmade cavern, and light streamed from slits in the ceiling above. They were in a drainage area, and water flowed into the ultracrete-lined room through several large pipes jutting out from the walls.

"The center of Tiradentes," replied Kimathi. The sergeant had his sidearm out and was scanning the room.

Cumae, can you hear me? Kal asked through his implant. The Nasi might be able to lock onto his signal, but it was a risk he was willing to take.

Roger. It was Sergeant Chedjou. *We're here.*

Glad to hear it. A small bit of relief flooded through Kal. At least they could get off the planet. Nasi forces have attacked the TLF. We've escaped and are heading back to your location. You see anything, you get out of there.

Sergeant Chedjou acknowledged, and Kal cut the line. They had a way off planet if needed. The next question was if what was happening was what he suspected: that the Nasi knew all about their mission and had been waiting for them. If so, it meant there was a mole somewhere in Samsara Fleet.

He sent out a general hail to the other five assault teams. If the Skulls had been attacked by the Nasi, there was a good chance the others had as well. For a moment, there was no response. Finally Colonel Roberts, commander of Assault Team Delta, responded.

Glad to hear your voice—so to speak—sir, said Roberts. The Nasi bastards were waiting for us.

Kal's mind immediately went Nicole and the Bones. If the Nasi knew of the invasion on New America, there was a good chance they'd be waiting on Patagonia as well. He tried to stuff the thought away. There was nothing he could do about it, and she was more than capable.

What's your status?

I lost half my team. Although Roberts' message came through the implant flat and synthetic, Kal could imagine the emotion in the man's words. *My squad leader, one team leader, and three soldiers all killed within minutes of landing.*

What about your ship?

A pause. The man must be choked up, which was understandable. The fold drive's been destroyed. It can still fly though. We've got to assume the other teams are compromised. I suggest we regroup.

Kal thought about it. Their entire mission had relied on them operating independently. But the mission had already spectacularly failed. They had to focus on getting off the planet and limiting their losses.

Agreed. Meet us outside of Tiradentes. Kal sent the coordinates for the *Cumae* and closed the connection.

"Sir, you ready?" asked Sergeant Kimathi.

While Kal had been talking over the long-range net, the

sergeant had been checking on the team. Surprisingly, all of them had made it through the ordeal unharmed and were crouched against the walls of the room, their weapons unholstered, looking to him to give the order to move.

Kal nodded. "Yeah, let's head back to the ship. The mission's scrapped."

As one of the largest—*the* largest with Earth destroyed—Human cities, Tiradentes was a mass of vehicles and people hemmed in by enormous glass towers. The city stretched for kilometers in every direction, not that Kal could tell walking the streets. As they made their way to the outskirts, the glistening towers of the city centers turned into mid-rises and apartment blocks.

Kal had grown used to clandestine missions. Meeting contacts in remote locations. Always watching over his shoulder for Nasi or Domespat security forces to attack. But he never got used to walking the streets after these missions and realizing that for the billions of other Humans on the planet, life was normal. Kids walked to school. Businessmen and women hopped onto public transports and headed to their offices. All of them blissfully unaware that an enormous fleet was waiting just a few folds away to liberate their planet.

Per their standard operating procedure, Kimathi had split the Skulls into small groups to avoid notice, putting Kal was with Sergeant Popov and Private Xie. The other groups weren't in sight but remained close enough they could speak through a direct link using their implants.

They reached the *Cumae* without issue and found the engine already spun up, ready for takeoff. As Kal walked up the ramp into the ship's cargo bay, Chief Kanumba came down the ladder from the cockpit.

"Sir," Kanumba said with a grave face. "We tried to contact the other ships without any luck."

"Even Delta's?" Kal asked.

"No, sir, the *Thebe* hasn't responded. I'm guessing whatever took out their fold drive also got their comms as well."

Bowen stepped out from the galley, placing a small tablet into his pants' cargo pocket. "I've been checking the planetary net for any reports or news. Nothing. The Nasi have managed to keep their entire operation under wraps."

"Ugh." Kal clapped his hands together in frustration. The entire past year had been wasted. "This entire year of planning and plotting, gone. We're right back where we started."

Sergeant Kimathi was already barking orders at the Tac-I squad, commanding them to get into their battle suits and prepare for anything. They moved with the grace of a well-oiled machine, stepping from one high-stress scenario to another as if it was all perfectly normal. Which for them, Kal realized, was somewhat true. He couldn't remember how many times they'd had a mission go off the rails.

"Stay inside the ship," Kal said to the squad leader.

"Hopefully Delta Team will be here and can just jump on board."

"We'll be ready either way, sir." Kimathi stepped into his battle suit.

They waited inside the *Cumae* for the better part of an hour. Kal made his way to the cockpit, sat down in the commander's chair behind the two pilots, and watched the tacmap, looking for the green icon of Delta Team's ship, the *Thebes.*

"What the hell?" Chief Kanumba cursed, slapping her hand on the console in front of her.

"What?" Kal asked.

"I've been trying to send a message to the fleet letting them know what happened, but the relay ship is down."

"Of course." Taking out the relay ship was probably the first thing the Nasi did. Kal was still surprised they'd managed it. The fleet often used relays on their missions and not a single one had ever been taken out or even discovered.

"We haven't seen any signs of battle in orbit," said Sergeant Chedjou. "Whatever the Nasi did to take out the ship must have been quick and small."

"Small?"

"Yes, sir," Chedjou nodded her head and looked back at him. "Small. We would have detected any large explosions or firefights."

"They have some sort of stealth ship-destroying technology?" asked Kal.

"That or the ship left of its own accord."

"Great." Kal slumped back in his chair, reminding himself of his son Stephen. He'd slunk in his chair in the same way when he was disappointed or annoyed. Kal felt the familiar pang of loss still there over a decade later.

"We've got something on approach," Kanumba said.

Kal looked at the tacmap. Something *was* heading their way. The icon was gray, meaning the ship's computer couldn't identify whether it was friend or foe.

"Can you get a visual on it?" Kal asked.

"Not yet," Kanumba said. "It's flying too low to see anything. You want to hail it?"

Kal considered the question. They were far enough outside the city that a random ship coming at their location was unlikely. But opening up a general comms channel would be suicidal if it was a Nasi or Domespat ship.

"No, hold tight."

General Norman, you there? It was Colonel Roberts over a local net.

What happened to your ship? asked Kal. *Where's the Thebes?*

Damage was worse than expected. Please turn off your camouflage, and we'll land near your ship.

Something in the request made Kal nervous. He had only talked to Roberts a couple of times. The man had an easygoing manner about him, not the straightforward, almost stilted talk that Kal was hearing now. It might be because they were on a mission, and communication through implants removed any inflection or tone in words. But still, something didn't feel right.

"There's something off here." Kal whispered the words to himself, but he noticed that both Chedjou and Kanumba nodded.

"This all stinks, sir," Chedjou agreed. "What'd they say?"

Kal quickly relayed the colonel's message.

"It'd be insane to drop our camo," said Kanumba.

Kal agreed with Kanumba's assessment. But still the communication was definitely coming from Colonel Roberts. *Land the ship and dismount,* said Kal. *We'll come and pick you up.*

Roberts' response was quick. We don't have time for that. We need to get out of here. Now.

Either do as I say, or we leave without you.

Fine. We're landing. Get your people out here to retrieve us. The connection went dead.

"They're landing about a kilo south of here," said Kanumba.

Kal contacted Sergeant Kimathi and explained the situation. After the expected protests that it was clearly a trap, the Tac-I squad headed toward the other ship.

"If you're so sure this is a trap, why are you doing it, sir?" asked Chedjou.

"Simple," said Kal. "There's a chance it's not. I can live with myself if it's a trap. I can't if I thought we left our own people here. If there's a chance to recover them, I've gotta take it."

Kimathi had his two fire teams approach the ship from

opposite sides and kept his suit's mic hot so they could hear his breathing as the squad approached the ship. A live feed from a camera on Sergeant Popov's suit played on a cockpit viewscreen.

"Still no sign of anyone," said Kimathi uneasily.

The ship was a former EDF assault craft with stubby wings and chipped gray paint. It was a model that had been in service when Kal had joined the EDF some thirty years ago. Now it was a relic of a bygone era. Ships like it were only to be found in local planetary forces, museums, and with the occasional collector. The rear door was open, but the interior was pitch-black.

"Hold there," Kal ordered.

Kimathi and the Tac-I squad held their positions, arrayed in two teams that bracketed the open door.

Delta Team, you need to exit the vehicle now, Kal instructed. He could see shapes inside the ship, one of them holding something to its side.

A second later, several missiles shot out of the ship's rear door. Plasma cannons on the stubby wings rained fire at the two Tac-I teams, splattering around them and igniting fires in the brush around them.

Private Xie's status indicator turned red as a missile slammed into her suit, sending pieces of it and her flying backwards into the brush.

"Get back to the ship," Kal shouted. "We're taking off! Fly up and meet us."

Chedjou and Kanumba lifted off and flew over the trees.

Moments later, the spot where they'd been standing erupted in a ball of fire.

"What the hell was that?" asked Chedjou.

"Orbital fire," said Kal. "Small caliber though. They seem to be trying to avoid hitting their own personnel."

"That's unusual for the Nasi," said Kanumba. "Normally they're all about whatever means necessary."

The Tac-I squad had lifted off at the same time as the *Cumae* and used their suits to catch up and land inside the ship's open cargo door as plasma fire and missiles streaked past them.

"We're in," shouted Kimathi over the intercom. "Get us out of here."

"Gladly." Chedjou maxed out the accelerator and Kal felt himself pressed back in his seat as the *Cumae's* inertial dampeners struggled to keep up.

An alarm blared and several red icons appeared on the tacmap.

"We've got multiple Nasi fighters," Kanumba called out. "They're moving to intercept."

"Of course they are," Kal said, annoyed. "Can you get us away?"

"Kinda hard, sir." Chedjou wiped her forehead with her sleeve. "They're tracking us from orbit, and their fighters almost have us surrounded. Even if we use our optical cloak, they'll be able to track us."

"Do what you can to evade them, and maybe we can figure out a way out of this."

"Not much else to do," said Chedjou.

They flew across the landscape, tracing along the tops of the trees. The *Cumae* was the height of Human technological achievement, a ship that just a year ago would have been unthinkable. It contained equipment that the fleet had reverse engineered from the Nasi as well as contributions from allies like the Tounous and Kurz. Despite all that, the Nasi fighters were just as fast and continued their pursuit.

Chedjou maneuvered *the Cumae* as two Nasi fighters streaked past them, expertly dodging their plasma bolts and missile fire. One of the bolts splashed against the ship's front energy shield, reducing its power by half.

"I can't keep doing this," Chedjou shouted. "It's just going to be a matter of time."

"Head to Tiradentes," said Kanumba. "We can lose them in the buildings and traffic."

Chedjou evaded the Nasi fire while gradually shifting their course. Kal expected orbital fire, but none came. He guessed they must be moving too fast for the Nasi capital ships in orbit to get a solid bead on them.

The trees of the nature reserve ended abruptly and were replaced with squat industrial buildings that covered areas the size of small towns. The skyline of Tiradentes loomed in front of them, a purple-black outline that looked like mountains.

"Keep it up; we're almost there," Kal said as he watched the tacmap.

"Thanks, sir," said Chedjou sarcastically. "Appreciate the pep talk."

Five Nasi fighters remained on their tail, maintaining a distance that allowed the best chance for their weapons to lock on. Kal knew Chedjou was right: the question wasn't if but when would they be shot down.

The sky in front of them was filled with small drone ships hauling cargo between the various factories. Chedjou used them for cover, weaving as she continued to head toward the capital city. Several Nasi plasma bolts struck the drones, sending them crashing to the ground in flaming heaps.

"Seems like Tiradentes air control doesn't like how you're flying," Kanumba said, pointing to an icon on the console indicating an incoming transmission.

"Please give them my apologies." Chedjou sucked in her breath as a missile streaked past them.

As they neared the city, Kanumba activated the ship's optical cloak. It would hide them from sight as well as disguise most of their electrical and thermal signature. If they could get enough distance, it *might* be enough to lose the Nasi.

They reached the first downtown of Tiradentes and weaved through the towers with Nasi fire on their tail. Missiles and plasma fire struck the buildings, sending debris raining down on the people below. The Nasi clearly weren't concerned about Human collateral damage.

"How low can you take this thing?" Kal asked. The *Cumae* was more than halfway through the downtown area, and if they didn't drop altitude, they'd be completely exposed.

"Let's find out," Chedjou grunted.

The pilot sent the ship diving toward the surface, barely

missing an elevated roadway as she leveled off less than a meter from the ground. Transports streamed past them and several peeled off the road, careening into the sidewalk as the *Cumae* thundered through the crowded streets. Chedjou dove around corners, using every single ounce of the ships lateral thrusters to avoid smashing into buildings as she evaded the Nasi fighters.

The fighters had split up and were soaring above the buildings, maintaining a constant velocity and direction. Kal wasn't sure if they weren't willing to risk crashing into the buildings or if they had lost the *Cumae*.

"I think they lost us," said Kanumba. "They're in a search formation."

Chedjou slammed on the reverse thrusters, bringing them to a metal-shrieking stop and then pivoted the ship in place. A moment later they were flying back the way they had come at a *slightly* higher elevation.

"Now we just need to pray they don't see us," said Kanumba hopefully.

The *Cumae* sailed over the busy streets and passed underneath the Nasi ships. Kal let out a small sigh as the Nasi continued forward, clearly not realizing that their quarry had turned around.

The enormous towers of the downtown were in their rear and the Nasi fighters were almost off the tacmap when Chedjou turned around in her seat with a smile, "Where to?"

Kal had no idea. The mission was scrapped; it'd clearly been doomed before it'd even started. Was he okay with just leaving the rest of the assault teams on the planet? Were any of them still alive?

The ship's proximity alarm blared and Chedjou didn't have time to react before an explosion rocked the front of the ship. The status console became a mass of red lights, and Kal felt a sudden sensation of weightlessness as the thrusters sputtered out. He belatedly realized that the Nasi had left a ship waiting for them.

Chedjou cursed as she tried to get the *Cumae* back under control. They flew past the Nasi ship, a second missile barely missing them as they streaked toward the ground. Flat industrial buildings loomed below them in the main viewscreen as the *Cumae* continued to drop.

"Brace yourselves," Kal shouted over the ship's intercom.

Chedjou had been able to gain some control, but they were still heading directly at an enormous building within the industrial zone in the city's outskirts. She fired an unending torrent of plasma rounds at the building's side, melting a hole in the metal exterior, and the *Cumae* crashed through seconds later, bouncing against the building's floor in an ear-shattering screech.

Kal felt lightheaded as Chedjou applied the reverse thrusters, and he slammed against his restraints. The ship's frame groaned, and a grinding noise filled the air as they skidded through the factory floor, bouncing large pieces of equipment off the ship's hull.

With a small groan, the ship finally stopped with its nose resting against a machine that stretched from the floor to the ceiling. An overpowering stench of burned electronics and melted metal filled the cockpit. Kal was exhausted. He wanted nothing more than to remain in his console and let the Nasi take them. Instead, he released his restraints and stood up with a small groan as he felt tendrils of pain sweep across his torso where the straps had dug in.

"You okay?" asked Chedjou, already up.

Kal nodded.

Kanumba pulled herself out of the pilot's chair. "It's a total loss," she said.

"You think?" asked Chedjou, eyeing a small fire that had erupted near the base of the control console.

"Let's get out of here." Kal rushed out of the cockpit with an unsteady gait.

The Tac-I squad were still in their battle suits and standing in the cargo bay with the door already open. Bo stood next to them, a small rifle slung across his back. The same stench of destruction that was in the cockpit filled the bay.

"Let's go," Kal ordered. "No time to grab anything."

They rushed down the ramp and onto the factory floor. The brightly lit room was a mess. A trail of destruction led from their ship to the enormous hole Chedjou had blasted in the building's side with the *Cumae's* plasma cannons. Thankfully, the factory appeared to be fully automated; bots hummed along the floor, seemingly oblivious to the devastation that the Skulls' ship had wrought.

"Look for a transport of some sort," Kal instructed. "I'm sure they didn't miss our landing."

The Tac-I squad took off from the floor and hovered near the ceiling, looking down to find any sort of means of escape. Kal dodged drones and ran around machines to an exit at the edge of the room. After several attempts he was able to push the heavy double doors open with a creak, letting in a blast of light.

He stopped in his tracks as he saw a group of four Nasi outside. He couldn't believe he'd been so stupid as to not have his weapon ready. He jumped back, diving behind the door and grabbed his pistol from its holster.

There's already four by the door, Kal said over the net. He'd have to hold them off until the Tac-I squad could get into position. Kal waited, weapon held close, for the Nasi to stream in with their weapons blazing.

"You need to come with us," shouted one of the Nasi from outside. "We can help you."

Chapter Eight
Kal | Tiradentes, New America

Kal struggled with his confusion. Whatever tactic the Nasi were using, it was new and—in his assessment—completely unnecessary. The Skulls were trapped in the factory, and the Nasi were probably reorienting their ships and orbital cannons to wipe them out. They were completely helpless.

They must want us as prisoners, Kal thought to himself.

Whatever the reason, he might be able to use it to their advantage. To buy some time.

Don't fire, he instructed over the net, but get to my location and be ready to get the hell out on my command.

"How do I know we can trust you?" Kal shouted through the open doorway.

What the hell is going on? Kimathi asked.

Not sure. They're offering help. They must be trying to take us prisoner.

Unlikely. It was Bowen. The Nasi don't think that way. This is—he paused—uncharacteristic.

"We could have already killed you," shouted the Nasi outside the door. "Please," there was real emotion in the word, "we're trying to help. We're risking everything."

Kal thought back to what he'd seen when he'd looked out the door. The four Nasi hadn't been holding weapons. They hadn't been in battle suits. They weren't the warriors and soldiers. They were workers and caretakers.

They may actually be trying to help us, Kal admitted.

Several transmissions—each expression incredulity or concerns about his sanity—came rapid fire over the net. He could understand where the soldiers were coming from. Not too long ago, he would have thought the idea insane as well, but the Skulls had been saved by Nasi before.

Get over here now.

"I'm coming out," Kal shouted as he stepped in front of the open doorway and faced the four Nasi with his hands in the air.

They didn't appear to be soldiers, at least none like Kal had ever seen. They wore the baggy workers coveralls. None of them had Shishen, the scrolling ceremonial tattoo's that indicated someone of high rank.

"Who are you?" asked Kal.

A tall man stepped forward. "If we make it out of here, we'll give you our names. For now, follow us."

Bo rushed out the door and stood next to Kal. His appearance clearly surprised the Nasi, who took a step back, fear in their eyes. A second later the Tac-1 squad, weapons at the ready, barreled through the opening, followed by Kanumba and Chedjou.

"You'll need to exit your suits," said the one Kal assumed was the leader, still eying Bo.

"Like hell we will," Kimathi shot back.

"The only way you escape here alive is by getting out of those suits," said a small female evenly. "Now either you get out of 'em or we leave."

"Ditch the suits," Kal ordered. "They won't do any good

against orbital fire anyways."

The Tac-I squad exited their suits, their faces locked in identical expressions of disbelief and anger. Kal could read entire paragraphs of outrage in Kimathi's eyes as the sergeant stepped out of his suit and pulled his rifle from its holster.

The four Nasi turned and began rushing through a paved yard stacked with piles of sheet metal and machine parts with the Skulls on their heels. As they rounded a large bin filled with scrap metal, the factory exploded behind them in a mushroom cloud of fire, sending the Skulls to the ground. The shockwave radiated out across the yard, turning much of the material into deadly projectiles. Thankfully the bin blocked most of the shockwave, but small pieces of metal still rained down from the sky and landed around them.

"Well, I guess they found us," said Kanumba matter-of-factly.

"I can't believe we lost *another* ship." Ekon shook his head ruefully.

The Nasi had already stood back up and started moving again. The small female turned and motioned for them to follow. "Keep up!"

With a start, the Skulls jumped up and ran towards the waiting Nasi. When they were close, the Nasi turned around and continued to run through the now destroyed yard. Although Kal felt like his lungs were going to explode from exertion, the four Nasi—and Bo—looked like they were barely trying.

They entered a small shed at the far end of the yard where

a large cargo transport hovered inside, its engine humming.

One of the Nasi placed their hand on the security plate near the back cargo bay, and it opened with a small hiss. The interior looked like a checkerboard, divided into a four-by-four array of square tubes that appeared to stretch the length of the bay.

"Get inside," ordered the small female. "Sensors can't penetrate the tubes. You should be safe."

"*Should* be?" asked Private Diaz.

The woman nodded. "Yes. Do you want some sort of guarantee?"

Kal reluctantly motioned for everyone to get in. "Just do it."

Kal helped the others as they climbed into the tubes, filling the top rows first. Once everyone else was in, he climbed in himself.

"We installed an atmospheric system in the back. So you *shouldn't*"—the woman smiled in a less-than-reassuring manner—"suffocate during transit. Once we get to our destination, we can tell you more."

With another hiss, the back door closed, plunging Kal in darkness.

The transport lifted off and smoothly glided along. Without any sensation from the outside, Kal tried not to imagine what was going on around him. Instead, he focused on what to do next. Their plan was in the garbage, but at least they were alive—mostly. Private Xie was another name on the long list of people who'd died trying to liberate Humanity from the Nasi.

The biggest question Kal had was why *these* Nasi would help them escape. He had been around enough Nasi to know that they were not monolithic. They might have all originally joined the—cult, he guessed was the appropriate word— because of a passion to return to what they considered their ancestral universe, but many of them had balked at what had happened since. A large portion of them had gone native, adapting Human mannerisms and values. Still, it was surprising to see Nasi who would challenge their own soldiers like this.

Finally, the transport touched down and the back door opened a minute later. Kal squinted as he pushed himself out of the square cargo tube and climbed to the ground. What he'd thought was sunlight was actually large panels of ultrabright lights hung from the ceiling of an enormous motor pool. Transports, identical to the one they'd been in, were parked haphazardly throughout the area. Although the parking appeared random, Kal was sure there was some sort of order to it. He'd come to appreciate that although the Nasi thought differently, they didn't do anything randomly or chaotically. There was always a "method to their madness" as his father used to say.

The four Nasi stood around the transport, waiting for the Skulls to recover from the trip. Kal could instantly tell they were much more relaxed based on their posture and the almost Human-like way they chatted quietly with each other.

"We finally did it," said one of the men in triumph. "I knew if we upped the oxygen intake they wouldn't suffocate."

"*Finally?*" Chedjou looked at the transport with a look of disgust.

"Don't worry about it." The leader placed his thin arms around Kal. "Suffice it to say, we're successful now. That's all that matters. Right?"

Kal wasn't sure about that, but he wasn't going to argue with people who'd just saved his life.

"Who *are* you?" Kal asked, looking around the room.

"Transport and Storage Unit Forty-One Delta," said the leader.

"I meant your names."

The man flushed and drew himself up to his full height. "Ah, yes. I'm Duke." Kal immediately recognized it as what the Nasi called a "friend name," another way in which they'd begun to mimic—albeit in a twisted way—the Human ancestors they'd almost wiped out.

Duke pointed at the others as he said their names, starting with the petite woman. "These are Daggs, Trip, and Fry."

"Fry?" asked Sergeant Sato. "Like frying someone with Plasma?"

"Like fried food," replied the Nasi. He patted his flat midsection. "I never knew that oil had such amazing culinary properties."

"Thanks for saving our asses back there," said Kal, holding

out his hand. "We owe you."

Duke looked at the proffered hand for a moment and then hesitatingly shook it. "It's the least we could do," he said, his face darkening. "We followed the Grand Ancient to this universe, thinking we'd be welcomed. Then we watched as our fleet destroyed the planet we'd supposedly come to help. Our true home world." His voice shook with emotion. "As Jadid, we understand that sacrifices must be made. It's what kept our people alive in such a hostile universe. But this has become too much, especially after we saw how you Humans resisted our help."

"You call it help?" snapped Kanumba.

Duke looked away. "No. Not anymore. But many of our people still see it that way."

"Also, there's the rumors," whispered Trip.

"What rumors?" Kal asked.

"About the Ancients. About all of them. Strange things." The Nasi looked around carefully as he spoke as if afraid someone would burst in on them at any second.

"Esma is as crazy as they come," said Kimathi. "You're just realizing this?"

"Crazy? No." Daggs shook her head. "The Grand Ancient is ruthless and unforgiving. But not crazy," she paused, "until recently."

"How so?" asked Kal.

"She's lost her way," said Daggs, her angular face looking sad for a moment. "We didn't come here to kill; we came to help. We knew there would be some resistance. But not like this. We're here to stand beside our ancestors and lead them to glory. But the Grand Ancient seems to have forgotten this."

"And now with the gateways blocked, we're stuck here," added Fry. "Even if we wanted to return to Altterra, we cannot and are forced to be a part of this." He motioned around the room.

Kal looked at the walls again, noticing their organic and alien design for the first time. It was not a Human building; it was a Nasi one built from the weaves that they had fabricated on their home world, Altterra.

"Where are we?" asked Kal hesitantly. He already knew the answer.

"We're in a secondary receiving bay inside our logistics cell," replied Duke.

"Inside the Foothold," added Fry.

"What?" Kimathi's voice echoed through the chamber.

The Foothold was a fort that was their center of Nasi power on the planet. There wasn't a worse place for the Skulls to be at that moment—or ever. Kal tugged at his collar as he thought about the soldiers and ships that must be just outside the building.

"Where else were we to take you?" asked Hal. "We aren't able to deviate from our work route."

"Can you get us out of here?" asked Kal.

"We'll make every attempt to do so," said Fry in what Kal was guessing was his version of a calming voice. However, it had the opposite effect.

"Make every attempt?" asked Kanumba. "Did you just

save us from death in order to get us captured?"

"We had two options," Duke's voice grew cold and toneless. Kal had learned this was common among the Nasi and Jadid; it was a sign or nervousness or excitement. "We could leave you where you were which meant almost certain death. Or we could risk our own lives to bring you here where there is at least a non-zero chance of survival."

"Thanks," said Kal. He held out a hand to silence the others. There was no need to further insult the people who'd saved their lives. "Honestly, thank you. But do you have a plan to get us out of here?"

"Not yet," said Duke, cheering up slightly. "But we'll start work on it immediately."

❖

At first, Kal had tried to be part of Delta Unit's—as he had started calling them in his head—conversation as they discussed how to get the Skulls out of the Foothold. But too many of the terms they used went right over Kal's head. After the tenth time he asked them to explain something, Daggs bluntly asked him to wait on the opposite side of the bay.

The rest of the Skulls had already given up and taken seats near a cluster of transports. They leaned back, using the vehicles as backrests, and chatted as they cleaned their weapons.

Sergeant Kimathi stood and wiped his hands on his pants as Kal approached. "Sir, you got a moment?"

Kal nodded.

"Bo, you got a sec?" Kimathi asked.

Bowen nodded and stood. Kimathi led them behind a cluster of transports on the other side of the room.

"There's something I saw that I think you should know about." Kimathi frowned. Kal had noticed the man was doing that more and more lately.

"What?" asked Kal.

"When we were approaching that transport and the Nasi started firing, I saw something." Kimathi cleared his throat. "You wonder how they were able to pretend to be Colonel Roberts?"

Kal *had* wondered that. Quite a bit. Neural implants had a host of safeguards to ensure they couldn't be tampered with. Not to mention the fact that the method that allowed them to integrate with a person's nervous system was basically inimitable. Kal had asked Bo a year ago if he thought the Nasi could hack their neural implants, and he'd seemed pretty sure it wasn't possible.

"I've been thinking about it," said Bo. "I've studied your implants and there shouldn't be a way to hack into them. Even for the Nasi. My assumption was that Colonel Roberts had assisted the enemy."

"What makes you say they pretended to be him?" asked Kal.

"When the Nasi fired at us, I saw inside that ship. One of them was holding…" Kimathi took a deep breath, "a head."

"A head? Like a *Human* head?" Kal asked. He

remembered seeing one of the figures in the ship holding something.

"Yeah. There were things coming out of it." Kimathi shuddered.

Kal's stomach turned at the thought.

"Interesting," Bo said, tapping a finger to his chin, seemingly unbothered by the grisly detail. "That still shouldn't allow them to access his implant. It would have shut down when the head was removed."

"There were...tubes and machines attached," said Kimathi with a shudder. "I don't think—I don't think he was dead."

Kal felt a pain in his stomach and swallowed, trying to keep down the bile.

"This *is* interesting," said Bo. He noticed the others' expressions and blinked. "Horrible of course, but the ramifications are not good. If what Ekon saw is true, then we must assume our entire operation's communications are compromised."

Kal pushed away the image of Colonel Roberts' head away. A thought, a horrible one, occurred to him. "It means that the relay may have already been contacted. That would be why they weren't there when we tried to contact them earlier."

"Which means the fleet is on its way to a trap," finished Kimathi.

All three of them jumped as a light over one of the doors to the large bay flashed, and it dilated open.

"Hide!" shouted Duke from across the room.

Chapter Nine
Nicole | Patagonia

Bohai Kinkaid gingerly led Nicole and the others back through the former EDF base and into the large room they'd spent so much time searching. The man had clearly been injured, but Nicole couldn't tell how recently. Either way, he was a far cry from the man she'd first met almost a year prior. As they cleared the entrance, a door in the wall swung open. Ishmael turned to smirk at Deepta and Nicole. It had been right where he'd said.

"Implant?" asked Ishmael, pointing at the opening.

"Yup." Kinkaid nodded.

"Damn it, I knew it."

A steep ramp led them into a low-ceilinged room with a few low-grade consoles scattered throughout. The dozen or so Front members were either sitting at a console or slouched against the wall. A cloud of depression and defeat hung over the room.

Kinkaid led them to a far corner of the room and sat down on the patterned metal floor, using the wall to steady himself.

"How many are here?" asked Nicole.

"I don't know," said Kinkaid, "a hundred, maybe. The Nasi struck quickly and completely. Took out almost everything. Only the people who were out on mission stood a chance, and even then, many of them were killed."

"Kinawadi?" asked Ishmael.

"The commander's presumed dead. Nasi struck the facility

he was in hard and quick. I doubt he made it out." Kinkaid shook his head. "He was a great leader. I don't know what you Samsara Fleet folks do but…"

No one spoke after Kinkaid trailed off. It had been one hell of a day, and already their plan had fallen apart.

"Lovin' this self-propelled misery, but we've got a lot of work ahead of us," said Ishmael. He turned to Nicole. "We've got to get you off planet to warn the fleet. The rest of us need to rebuild. Even *more* carefully this time."

"I'll need to get back to the *Chester*," said Nicole. She didn't like the idea of just turning tail and running. But what else could she do at that point? The fleet had to know what had happened.

"What about scouts or recon?" asked Ishmael with a strange tilt to his voice. "We need to find some of the missing people."

Ava. Nicole realized that he had no idea where his companion—or perhaps wife was the more appropriate word—was or even if she was alive. He hadn't mentioned her the entire time they'd been traveling. But he must have been thinking of her the entire time.

"There's got to be people you can rely on to help," said Deepta. "The entire planet wants these scum out of here. You can use that to your advantage."

"Wish we could," said Kinkaid. "But if the last day has taught us anything, it's that we can't trust people too much. I appreciate the thought. Truly I do."

"You gotta be kidding me," Deepta said, leaning toward

the commander. "You're here about to die, and you won't take help from other people."

"It's not that," said Kinkaid. "Like I said—"

A woman rushed over. "Commander, we've got a problem. A transmission is coming from the planet."

"So?" Kinkaid raised an eyebrow.

"It's from a Samsara Fleet away team. From a Colonel Chin to the fleet."

"What the hell?" asked Ishmael, jumping up.

They made their way to the console the rebel had been manning. After a few quick gestures, the synthesized voice from an implant rang out, clear as day.

"Samsara Fleet, this is Colonel Alexander Chin on behalf of Colonel Nicole Bergeron. All assault teams are in position, and the plasma lances have been disabled. You are clear to attack." His message was followed by a string of authentication tones.

Colonel Chin was commander of Assault Team Charlie. There's no way he would have contacted the relay without Nicole's permission or at least trying to contact her. Either Alexander had made the announcement under coercion, or the Nasi had compromised their communications.

"Can you transmit out?" asked Nicole.

Kinkaid shook his head. "We'd lead the Nasi to us, and even if we didn't, they've blocked the entire net." He pointed to a section of the console that was a mass or red lights.

"How long until the fleet's here?" asked Ishmael.

"A day, maybe a few hours more," said Nicole. "Not long

enough to disable the lances."

"Well, we'd better damn well find a way," said Ishmael. "If we fail, then half your fleet will be destroyed in minutes."

Nicole turned away from the console and paced between it and the wall, her hands behind her back and her head down. In the corner of her mind, she realized it was her "officer's position," something she'd at first unconsciously mimicked from Kal. It helped her to think, especially in situations like this.

"You think you can help?" Nicole asked, wheeling to face Deepta.

The woman returned her look, fire in her eyes. "Damn straight. I can't get ships or armored transports, but I can get people. The leaders and politicians on Patagonia are sycophants, sucking up to those bastards, while us common folk are left holding the sack. We're ready for a change."

"They'll lead the Nasi right back to us," protested Kinkaid.

"So what?" asked Nicole. "We've got a day or two until the fleet gets here. If we don't have those lances disabled, we'll risk losing the entire war."

"Just tell me when or where you need people and I'll find them," Deepta said. "We can tell them to meet up at a set time and place with whatever weapons they can find."

"You're resigning them to death."

"Maybe," Deepta admitted, "but I'm willing to do it. I know others will be as well. There're millions of people out there that are just waiting for the word. Waiting to be told how they can help. We do it the old-fashioned way; go to the cities and let people know they're needed. Tell them to tell others. One person turns into five which turns into twenty-five and so on."

"You'll need a way to get around quickly," Nicole said.

"And discreetly," added Ishmael.

"Having someone zoom around the planet is going to raise a lot of flags," said Kinkaid. "You'll need protection of some sort."

"What are we gonna do?" asked Ishmael. "I'm not sayin' no. Just skeptical."

"I don't know yet," said Nicole. "But it's an idea at least. We know that there aren't that many Nasi on the planet. If we can overwhelm them and take down those sites even for an hour, we give the fleet a chance."

"You're suggesting we mob them?" asked Kinkaid. "Throw people at them?"

"Is it so crazy?" asked Deepta with her hands raised. "There's billions of people on Patagonia and only thousands of Nasi."

Ishmael tilted his head. "I mean, I've heard worse ideas."

"I've *had* much worse ideas," said Nicole. "You'll need support though. It can't just be one woman, no matter how capable, traveling around the planet asking for help."

"It won't be," Deepta said passionately. "It starts with us and spreads—"

"Like a virus?" asked Ishmael.

Deepta shot him a look of warning. "Like an idea. We can spread the word around each major city on the continent and tell others to keep spreading it. This planet's an explosive that's just waiting for someone for press its detonator."

"You'll need some way to get around the planet," said Kinkaid. "We've still got a few ships and transports but nothing that's fast enough to get everywhere in time."

"What about your ship?" Ishmael asked Nicole. "It should still be there."

Nicole didn't have any reason to believe the *Chester* wouldn't still be in the same location. But the way everything had come crashing down, she wouldn't bet a credit on it. Still, with the battle suits stashed outside of Foyleton, they had the means to carry Deepta's insane idea out.

Nicole studied the woman. She knew that Deepta was not the type of person to put her faith in a flight of fancy. Still, the plan put a lot of responsibility on a woman that Nicole had met just that day. How could a mission that had been planned out for months now rely on a woman who was clearly hiding from something?

Can we trust her? Nicole asked Ishmael through her implant. He met her eyes and nodded.

"Fine," said Nicole resignedly. "Let's see how popular you are. We'll take you to where you need to go."

"We'll need weapons at the sites," said Ishmael. "Even with every Human on the planet helping us, we'll be dead before we start unless we have enough firepower."

"The Front has caches scattered throughout the planet," said Kinkaid with an edge of excitement. "We can collect them and bring them to the rendezvous sites."

"It'd be a gutsy move," said Nicole. "The Nasi are sure to notice at least some of it."

"Remind me, what's the difference between gutsy and stupid?" asked Ishmael.

"If it works, it's gutsy." Nicole smiled sweetly.

"You're gonna do this with these sad sacks?" the Alliance leader asked, motioning at the people milling about the room. Nicole hadn't seen a group so defeated since the war began and the Nasi had destroyed Earth.

"Watch yourself," Kinkaid shot out. "They're still in shock and mourning. We lost a lot of good people today."

"They can do that later. We've all lost people."

"They'll fight," said Kinkaid. "They always do."

Deepta needed an hour to plan out their route, explaining she needed to figure out how to cover the most ground in the least amount of time. Kinkaid gave her access to one of the Front's consoles and the woman immediately sat down and began plotting, clearly at home using the technology.

"How do you know her again?" Nicole whispered to Ishmael.

"Ah, that's her story not mine." He made the motion of closing a zipper over his mouth. "Besides, Alliance rules, we don't talk about our customers' business."

While Deepta worked, Commander Kinkaid allowed Nicole to use one of their ships and detailed a few of his best rebels to aid her. Their goals were to see if they could contact any of the other assault teams and retrieve their battle suits and the *Chester*. After flying to the large mountain range that split the continent of Pangea, Nicole tried making several calls to the other teams but received nothing in response. She checked with the Front soldiers, and they confirmed that her signal had never made it onto the net. Somehow the Nasi were blocking long-range communications across the planet.

They lifted off and flew to the edge of Foyleton. The suits were untouched. Nicole deactivated the security protocols, activated her suit, and linked the other ones to the Front fighters. All three of the rebels were former EDF soldiers and had battle-suit experience, so they were quickly able to get into the suits and get them working. As she watched the suits close, it struck her how quickly things were moving. It had only been a few hours since Nicole, along with Sergeant Peng's team, had left the suits to enter Foyleton.

They took off, jetting toward the *Chester*. Nicole felt a measure of apprehension as they neared where the ship *should* be. She had no longer had any idea of what the Nasi were capable of. Days ago, she would have thought it impossible that they could round up the entire resistance force on the planet in fell swoop.

As they neared the location of the ship, an icon on her suit's heads-up display indicated the *Chester* hadn't moved. Since it was camouflaged, it was impossible for her to tell the ship's condition. What would they find when they broke the veil of the ship's optical projectors? A dozen battle-suit clad

Nasi waiting with weapons ready?

Hold your positions, Nicole instructed over the net. She touched down on the loose soil and strode towards the ship. As she crossed the veil created by the optical projectors, the *Chester* appeared as if out of nowhere. The ship's ramp was already down, and Chief Ramos and Captain Uhaa stood at the bottom, worried expressions on their faces.

"What the hell is going on?" asked Ramos.

"We haven't been able to reach *anyone*," said Uhaa, his eyebrows bunched in concern. "We heard Colonel Chin's message, but that's it."

You can come on in, Nicole said over the net.

"Everything's been compromised," said Nicole as she strode up the ramp. She stepped into a dock and pulled off her helmet as her suit unwrapped itself from her body. "When I was inside the Alliance Front, they attacked and captured everyone in Sergeant Peng's team."

Chief Ramos grew pale. "The entire squad? Captured?"

Nicole nodded grimly. "Not just the Bones, all the assault teams have been taken out—at least I think so."

"Who are they?" asked Uhaa as the three Front rebels tromped up the ramp and started docking their suits.

"What remains of the Front," said Nicole. "There's a few dozen of 'em left. We've got a day to somehow take those plasma lances offline before the fleet arrives."

"This has all been one big setup?" asked Ramos, flopping onto a jump seat. She stared at Nicole as if beseeching her to say it wasn't true.

Nicole nodded reluctantly. "Seems like it. Looks like the Nasi knew a helluva lot more than they were letting on. We sprung the trap and we've got a day to unspring it."

"How are we gonna do that?" Ramos studied the three Front soldiers. "There's, like, six of us."

"There's more than that," said one of the rebels.

"Let's get airborne and I'll fill you in on what I know," said Nicole. "We've got a lot of work ahead of us."

"So we're basically going to go around and ask strangers for help, ma'am?" asked Uhaa. "We're recruiters now?"

"We're whatever we need to be," replied Nicole. "So, yeah, we're recruiters today so we can be soldiers tomorrow."

They had returned to the small command room at the PF base. Kinkaid had ordered several teams to collect weapons from the caches scattered across the planet. Ishmael was conferring with some of the remaining fighters, providing location information for additional Alliance caches that dotted the area. The Alliance leader had decided to stay with Kinkaid to assist, while Nicole and Deepta led the effort to recruit personnel. Deepta had finalized her route. It would take them to every corner of the continent, including the major cities of Kasongo, Foyleton, and Chengdu.

"We're all that's left?" asked Uhaa, rubbing his hands together.

"Not *all*," said Ramos. "You heard the colonel. There are

others."

"Civilians that *might* come." Uhaa absentmindedly bit the nail of his index finger. "Ma'am, are you sure this is the best plan? We could fly back to the fleet and warn them."

"We could find the others and free them," said Ramos excitedly.

"I've thought about it," Nicole said. In fact, she'd thought about it several times since she'd realized her friends and comrades had likely been captured. "But there's no chance of recovering them in time. We don't know where they are or even—" She couldn't finish the sentence.

"We can't warn the fleet either," Nicole continued after a moment. "They'll have already left before we can reach them. And you know as well as I do, they're going to fold close to the planet." The tactic prevented the Nasi fleet in orbit from retreating. Unfortunately, it also prevented Samsara Fleet from retreating as well.

"What about getting through on the net?" asked Uhaa. "I mean there's got to be a way to get around whatever the Nasi did to it."

This time it was Chief Ramos who shook her head. "I was looking at it while we were waiting for the rest of the team. Whatever's blocking the planetary net is coming from the Nasi Foothold. There's no way around it. Unfortunately, life isn't like some holo where a genius hacker can come along and make everything right."

"It's gonna be like a holo where the team flies around and recruits people?" asked Uhaa with a smirk.

"Guess so." Ramos shrugged.

Kinkaid strode toward them from across the room. He'd been supervising the crews preparing the small fleet of transports to fly across the planet gathering weapons and supplies. They would have to move slowly and in small groups to avoid notice. Even then Nicole was sure several would get stopped or destroyed by the Nasi forces. She just hoped enough made it so that Deepta's recruits had weapons to use.

"We're almost ready," said the Front leader. "This is the last chance for us to back out. With the comms grid down, there'll be no way to call it off."

"Well, we all know the when, where, and why," said Nicole. A strange thought occurred to her—there was a good chance she'd never see Kinkaid again. If everything went according to plan, Patagonia would be liberated. She found it hard to believe that they both would survive through the next day. She held out a hand. "It's been a pleasure seeing you again."

"You too," Kinkaid smiled and pulled Nicole in for a hug, surprising her. "Whatever happens, we've put up one helluva fight."

"Indeed." Nicole returned the smile. "We just need to fight for one more day."

Chapter Ten
Nicole | Patagonia

The *Chester* soared above the Patagonian forest near the continent's eastern coastline. So far, Deepta had had them land in several mid-sized villages and cities. It was shocking how quickly the woman was able to gather a crowd and enthrall them by her every word. She somehow possessed an intimate understanding of each area and a natural ability to rally people to her cause. Nicole wondered if the woman had been a politician in an earlier life.

Thankfully, the Nasi hadn't been present at any of the towns they'd visited, only local security patrollers. It was as if the war wasn't even happening. *How much had the Nasi attacks on the Patagonian government affected the people in these cities and towns?* Nicole wondered. *Did they even know?* From what she could see, they either didn't know or just didn't care. Most people on the former Human colonies believed the new Human governments were puppets of the Nasi, and Nicole couldn't disagree. If the Nasi disbanded the government and created a new one, did it matter for the average citizen?

At each stop, Deepta would stride through the town and stop at gathering points—the town center, the largest restaurant, markets—and start speaking in a loud voice. She'd lay it out, not embellishing or diluting the details. As she spoke, people stopped what they were doing to listen. At first, it'd be the children, then their parents would follow.

Soon, after a couple of minutes, a crowd would gather, watching Deepta with rapt attention. It reminded Nicole of the books she'd read on ancient Humans when the only way to spread news was through a town crier.

After telling the citizens what had happened, Deepta would beseech the crowd for help. Her eyes wide and full of determination, she'd tell them that Samsara Fleet needed their help. Needed them to join the cause and spread the word. By the time she finished, it was always deathly quiet. Then Deepta would finish by saying, in a voice so faint the crowd was forced to lean in to hear, that if anyone was interested in helping to come and let her know now.

Then she would clap her hands to signal her speech was over, and one by one people would rush forward, their faces lit with passion, asking what they could do. Deepta would give each person coordinates and a time to meet and ask that they pass along the word to everyone they knew.

After traveling along the eastern coast, they had a long stretch without any stops as they made their way toward the center of the continent. Deepta sat in a corner of the cargo bay, reading something on her implant. Nicole sat down next to her, a small tablet in her hand.

"Reading up on the next stop?" asked Nicole quietly.

Deepta smiled. "Gotta scout out the terrain to be as efficient as possible. The Front had some information on the cities we're going to. Helps when you've got a few extra minutes to inspire people to risk their lives."

"You're so motivated," said Nicole earnestly. "Why

weren't you in the Front before?"

"I don't know." The smile disappeared. "I could've joined. Maybe I should've. But when the call came, I just couldn't answer."

"Why?" Nicole couldn't imagine the woman next to her letting these things happen without trying to fight back. Deepta was clearly a soldier—perhaps not an EDF or Samsara Fleet soldier, but someone who was disciplined and fought for what she believed in.

"It's complex," said Deepta. "And I've known you for a few hours. If we all live, then maybe we can talk."

"Fair enough," said Nicole. Everyone was entitled to their secrets. Lord knew she had her own. She cleared her throat. "How do you get them to listen to you?" It was something she'd been wondering as she watched person after person leave conversations with Deepta, a look of righteous determination on their face.

"It's not me," Deepta said. "I'm just the messenger. I'm offering something that people can't resist. A way to fight back and have some sort of control. A way to finally change all the crap they've been watching go on around them. They just need a way to get involved."

Nicole didn't doubt what the woman said, but she also knew it was more than that. Deepta was much more than a messenger. What had the woman done? Who'd she been before and why had she needed the Alliance's help? All questions that would have sat at the top of her mind if it wasn't for the fact that they were going to be landing soon and risking being discovered by the Nasi.

That was another thing that surprised Nicole, the complete absence of Nasi in the places they visited. She'd figured they would be skulking through the towns. Instead, they were walking down major roads in broad daylight and attracting huge crowds. Much of the apprehension she'd had at the beginning of their recruiting trip had vanished.

"We're getting close to Chengdu and this next stop's a pretty big town," said Deepta. "We should split up. I've seen you talk with your soldiers. You know what to say and they listen to you. It's no different with these folks. Military types always seem to think civilians are some sort of strange foreign creature."

Nicole had never thought of herself as a "military type." She hadn't been an officer in Samsara Fleet very long at all. She felt a strange sense of pride that Deepta saw her that way.

"Sure," Nicole said. "That works." She realized she felt a strange sense of apprehension over speaking to large groups of people. How could she be in the middle of a war and feel nervous about public speaking?

The *Chester* was slowing; they must be close to landing. Nicole stood up and made eye contact with the four Front soldiers in battle suits. They nodded at her and three of them put their helmets back on.

"We're gonna split into two groups this time," Nicole said to Sergeant Gruppenhiem, known to everyone as Grupp. "Two with me and two with Deepta."

The sergeant nodded curtly and placed his helmet on with a click.

Seconds later, the cargo bay door opened, revealing a dense network of vines and trees. A wall of humid tropic air washed into the bay, bringing a floral scent with it. In general, Patagonia was a relatively tropical climate, but this area of the planet was even more so. The ship barely fit into the green and blue walled clearing they'd landed in. Due to the size of the town, they'd decided to land just outside and make their way on foot. Although they hadn't seen any Nasi so far, it didn't mean they weren't out there.

"Let's go," said Nicole. She turned to the Front Team leader. "Battle suits take lead, we'll split up once we get onto a road. Until then, you need to clear the path for us."

"Yes, ma'am."

They started out with Grupp in the lead. He cleared the brush ahead of them using the serrated machete that popped out from the forearm of his suit, cutting away wide swathes of hanging vines and creepers. The other soldiers used their boots to kick away the debris, allowing Nicole and Deepta to keep pace behind them. It was slow going.

"When we get to town, we'll split up," said Deepta. "I'll take left, you take right."

"Sounds good." Nicole pulled off a piece of vine that had fallen from above. "Remember to stay close together so we can maintain direct comms link."

Deepta nodded. "Will do, boss."

After a few more minutes of hacking through the forest,

they reached a gravel-covered utility road and followed it toward the town. The trees towered above them, blocking out the light and creating the sensation they were walking through a tunnel. Above them, the canopy was alive with the chirps and screeches of animals. Nicole tried to remain calm, but her hand remained close to her side where she had her pistol holstered.

"Town should be ahead in any second," said Deepta. "This one's too big for us. We stop at a few places, five minutes each, and then head back."

"Sound good," said Nicole. She looked ahead, trying to spy anything other than the multihued forest. For a moment, she caught the decidedly unnatural profile of a building. They were close.

"What's that?" asked one of the Front soldiers.

They all stopped. A rustling, like wind through the leaves, came from the side of the trail. Nicole couldn't place the noise—a ship flying low or a battle suit heading through the branches perhaps. She checked the tacmap using her implant. There was *something* organic rushing toward them. It moved in a kind of swirling pattern, coasting from left to right as it traveled. The movement didn't seem Nasi or Human. It wasn't direct enough.

"Get under cover," Nicole hissed to Deepta, pulling the woman toward the edge of the trail.

The four Front rebels knelt, raising their weapons towards the wood line. It wouldn't be long until whatever was rushing at them would be breaking through.

Hold fire, Grupp ordered. Get visual first.

They'll be dangerously close before we see them, said one of the other fighters.

I know and I don't care. We're not going to fire at something when we don't know what the hell it is. Sergeant Grupp raised a smidge in Nicole's estimation.

The noise grew into a thunder of cracking limbs and shivering leaves. The plants near the trail started to sway lightly, dropping branches, and causing the native birds to scatter into the air with alarmed buzzes. Then Nicole saw it; a shape, something enormous, perhaps half the size of the *Chester*, came swinging through the canopy, using its tentacles to grab onto the limbs and propel itself forward, creating a vortex of destruction as it moved.

"What is that thing?" hissed Nicole, her pistol out.

"A Shu Dragon," whispered Deepta. "I've never seen one before. Only heard about 'em."

Holy.... The voice on their net trailed off.

The dragon had paused at the edge of the trail. It balanced between two large trees, thick tentacles wrapped around the trunks with three other tentacles floating in the air. What Nicole would have thought of as its face was angled downwards, studying them with its cluster of eyes.

Keep still, Grupp said. It'll move on in a second.

Nicole felt drawn to the creature above them. She admired the iridescent scales and sleek mass of the creature. It opened its mouth, revealing several rows of a glistening metal teeth. Without warning, the dragon leapt across the path and continued onwards, the cacophony of its travel quickly fading into the distance.

Deepta sighed, falling backwards with a thump. "I *never* want to see one of those again."

"It was amazing," said Nicole, still in awe. The creature was burned into her memory. "Just amazing."

"They used to roam the planet but were hunted down," said one of the soldiers. "They'll attack almost anything. Livestock. Humans. Doesn't matter."

"Why do we have a right to live more than they do?" asked Nicole.

"Right, wrong. These are the concepts of children," scolded Deepta. "Ultimately, no creature has more of a right to live than another. We live because that's what we're supposed to do."

"Good philosophy lesson," said Grupp. "Ready?" He and his soldiers had put away their weapons and stood near the center of the road, looking at the two women.

"Let's move," Nicole said.

The edge of the town was just around the corner. As opposed to larger cities, like Kasongo or Foyleton, Xardi was built inside of the forest. The buildings melded into the trees, even using them as support sometimes. A paved perimeter road and fence encircled the city with local security stationed at the entrance. Two men sat back in chairs, their weapons leaning against the small railing that encircled the defensive platform they were on.

They barely seemed to notice as the four Front soldiers,

Nicole, and Deepta walked toward them.

"What're ya doin' in Xardi?" asked a guard casually as they approached.

"Recruiting," shouted Deepta. "You've heard of Samsara Fleet, right?"

"Bunch of delusional vets flyin' around? Yeah, we've heard of 'em."

"Well, they're about to liberate Patagonia," said Deepta. "See her?" She pointed at Nicole, who tried to look the part of a heroic military leader. "She's part of their initial assault team. They've got a fleet comin'."

"Against the Nasi," chuckled one of the men. "Good luck."

"Haven't you noticed how the Nasi factories have stopped? How they're not building ships anymore?" asked Deepta. "Why do you think that is?"

"They got everythin' they want already."

"You really think the Nasi will ever be satisfied?" asked Nicole. "That they won't just take more and more? I mean, how much have they taken from Xardi?"

The men looked at each other. "Bastards took over all the mine output," admitted one of them.

"And they keep taking a little bit more of everything you make, don't they?" asked Deepta. "Perhaps even made examples out of a few people you knew."

The men were quiet, and Nicole could tell Deepta had their full attention.

"All that can end," she said. "We can actually be

independent—from the Nasi and the UEG. But we'll need your help. The only people left fighting are winning. It doesn't seem like it, but they are. That's why the Nasi bumped up the tributes a year ago. That's why it's been so hard to find things."

"So what? You're looking for people to die?"

"No," Deepta shouted. "To fight. There's a battle coming tomorrow—"

"Tomorrow?" the smaller man asked, his eyes wide.

Nicole nodded. "Yeah, tomorrow. And we need every person that can shoot to be a part of it. I can guarantee that if we stop the planetary defenses, the Nasi fleet doesn't stand a chance."

The two men looked at each other, unspoken words flying between them. "We'll think about it," said the taller one. "You can come on in though. We haven't seen Nasi around here for a long time."

"Doesn't mean they're not around though," warned Grupp. "You mind us stayin' in our battle suits?" It was normally illegal or at least heavily frowned upon to wear battle suits in urban areas.

"Nah, probably smart." The taller man waved them through.

"Come and see us," offered Deepta. "We're not going to be long. We need people to fight *and* to spread the word."

After entering the city, they split into their groups and walked through the wide paths that wound under and through the trees. Nicole could feel the eyes of the locals on her—

143

more specifically on the two battle-suited Front rebels behind her—as she scanned for crowds of people.

Several trees surrounded a large clearing, filled with tables and stalls. Although the stalls looked like they were intended to be mobile, the market had a sense of permanence about it. Perhaps the locals had originally meant for the area to be used for occasional events, but over time, it had become a permanent fixture of their town. The trunks of the surrounding trees extended upwards and merged together, forming a spire that reached to the top of the forest.

Nicole spied a group of families eating and playing in a corner of the square. Adults talked with each other as children zoomed between their legs, giggling and shouting at one another. As Nicole approached, the talk died down. One by one, everyone stopped to stare at her and the two rebels behind her.

"Hey!" shouted Nicole, waving her hands above her head. "I'm from Samsara Fleet."

"Hello," giggled a small girl, running up to her and then veering back to her agitated father.

"I wanted to tell you what's *really* going on. Our fleet, which has been fighting the Nasi, is on its way to liberate Patagonia from Nasi control." A murmur moved through the crowd. "They're afraid, which is why they shut down the long-range nets across the planet. They're afraid because they know we can win."

She'd been hoping for some smiles, a small cheer perhaps. Instead, she got stone-faced stares.

"We need your help," said Nicole. "The Nasi have created several defensive sites to protect their fleet. If those sites are operational when the fleet gets here, we'll lose everything. We're asking for every able-bodied man and woman to join us in taking these sites down. The Nasi can't destroy us all. If—"

"You sure about that?" asked a large man near the front of the crowd. "They did it once already. They leveled half the planet."

"Look, we're not asking you to fight their fleet," Nicole said. "We just need help to take out these sites. Once they're destroyed, Samsara Fleet can protect you."

"How can you protect us if you can't protect yourselves?"

"Shut up, Klem," a woman shouted from the other side of the group. "Let the woman speak."

"It's simple," said Nicole. "These sites are plasma lances. They're underground. Deep enough that orbital weapons can't hit them. Over the last year, we've had agents scouting out their locations and how to destroy them."

"We're just ordinary citizens," said a middle-aged woman. "All the fighters have died or left." A murmur of agreement.

"No!" Nicole's shout quieted the crowd. "I refuse to believe that. I refuse to believe that you won't fight for your planet and your families."

"We just want to live in peace," said the woman. "Nasi. Human. It doesn't matter who's pulling the strings. We get up and do the same thing every day anyway."

Nicole had heard that argument, or some version of it, on every planet under the Nasi control. In truth, she could understand it. She'd grown up in the communes of Earth, barely surviving under a regime that didn't seem to care whether she lived or died. When the planet had been destroyed, she hadn't felt much of anything except for her family; she'd almost died from the pain of losing them. But for the planet, the most she could feel was indifference. After years fighting the Nasi, she'd seen enough to realize it *did* matter. They would let these people have their markets and their lives. But they would ask more and more of them, and impose stricter and stricter rules, until they suffocated them.

"I want to live in peace as well," said Nicole, holding her weapon out. "I want nothing more than to set aside my weapons." She forced a smile. "But they'll never let me. They took my family already and they'll continue to take, just a little more each time, until I've forgotten what freedom truly is."

She noticed the two guards were watching at the back of the crowd.

"I've got to leave soon. But I'll stay here for a few minutes to talk with whoever wants to help. Spread the word then head to fight. Other fighters and weapons will be waiting for you."

Nicole backed up and waited at the edge of the square with the two Front rebels flanking her. Most of the crowd turned and went back to what they were doing. Shopping. Talking with one another. Shouting for kids to be careful.

After a few seconds, the same man who'd interrupted her speech—Klem—sheepishly walked forward. "Hey," he said, "I...I don't know what I'm gonna do but figured it wouldn't hurt to get those coordinates from you."

"Thank you," said Nicole. She used her implant to transmit a small bundle that contained rendezvous coordinates, time, and an encrypted certificate that authenticated she actually was with Samsara Fleet.

"Aren't you worried about this getting to the Nasi?" asked Klem.

"No, not really," said Nicole. "I trust people. I believe even if you don't help, you won't actively try and betray us."

That wasn't true. They'd talked it over quite a few times and knew it was a very real risk that some idiot might attempt to curry favor with the Nasi and hand over the coordinates and times. When the Humans arrived, there'd be bots there to take them to the *real* rendezvous coordinates. There would also be some hidden surprises for any Nasi assault force that showed up.

Klem raised in his eyebrows doubtfully. "I'll think about it."

"Do that." Nicole smiled. "But don't too long."

"I hope you're right." He stepped away, letting the woman behind him move forward.

"About what?" Nicole asked.

"All of it."

Kal frantically searched the Nasi motor pool for a place to hide. Despite the chaotic parking, the area was otherwise clean and orderly with no piles of parts or opened storage containers to use as cover. The transports were flush against the ground, resting on their bottom thrusters, which meant there was no room to crawl under.

"In here," whispered Bo, motioning from the open cabin of a vehicle. Kal followed the Jadid and Sergeant Kimathi into the hauler and activated the door, which closed without a sound.

He peeked over the console and watched as a transport glided into the bay. Its sleek profile was interrupted by plasma cannons mounted to the front and a missile turret perched on top. It was a vehicle built for war.

As two Nasi soldiers stepped from the vehicle, Duke glided toward them. "How may I be of assistance today, soldiers?"

"We need to repair our assault transport," said one of the soldiers. "Our maintenance techs are at capacity. You have been ordered by the station command to provide us with assistance."

Duke nodded and walked around the vehicle, scanning it with a handheld device. After he'd finished, he whispered some words to the other members of Delta Unit, and they climbed onto the transport and started pulling panels off. At first, the two Nasi soldiers stood watching. But as Duke's team continued to work, the soldiers grew bored and sat down in the very same place where the Skulls had been minutes before.

Being a soldier for the Nasi isn't much different than being a Human one, thought Kal sardonically. A lot of sitting and waiting.

He scanned the bay, trying to figure out where the rest of his team was. The only possible place was in the transport that the Nasi were leaning against.

"How much longer?" asked one of the soldiers.

It was a question that would have engendered a sarcastic retort from a Human maintenance technician. Daggs simply replied, "Approximately fifteen more minutes," and continued back to her work.

The soldier gave a small grunt of annoyance and stood. She gracefully strolled through the vehicles in the bay, cocking her head to the side as she looked them over.

"What is your primary mission?" asked the woman.

"Logistics and supply," said Duke, not looking up from his work.

"Specifically what type?" The soldier opened the rear door of one of the vehicles and stuck her head in. "These look to be armament transports."

"They are. One of our functions is to transport ammunition and weapons to field units."

The woman hummed and closed the door. "These are sensor resistant containers," she observed, still walking around the haulers.

"Yes," Duke responded. "Per standard operating procedures all the vehicles' cargo beds are sensor resistant and hermetically sealed during transport."

"You could sneak anything into the Foothold then," she said. "And no one would notice."

Where's she going with this? wondered Kal.

Kal ducked down as the woman made her way to the front of their vehicle. He pulled out his pistol, waiting for her to open the door and discover them. A slender violet hand traced along the window directly above his head, making a small squeak against the glass.

"I've got a proposition for you." The woman's hand disappeared.

Kal couldn't hear Duke's response.

"Well, you could say that it is not *completely* within the regulations," the soldier said. Her voice grew fainter as she walked away from Kal. "But I think there's an opportunity for both of us."

Again, an unintelligible reply from Duke.

"Yes, we have thought of that," said the woman with a trace of annoyance. "There is an establishment in the city. A place that is friendly to us. Because of the increased security and high operational tempo, it's getting more difficult to get there. But the Human owner has agreed to supply us, provided we can pick up the goods."

Kal slowly peaked over the console again. The woman was next to her ship facing Duke, who'd stopped working and was perched on the hood of the transport, facing her.

"We might be able to come to an arrangement," he said. "What're you offering in return?"

"How about a hundred thousand credits?"

Duke laughed. "What would I do with credits? What about something I *need*? You have access to the perimeter security, right?" The soldier nodded. "Well, I'll need your help to get in and out of the Foothold to do this. I want that same access all the time. Add me and my unit to the unrestricted list."

Now it was the woman's turn to laugh. "I don't have that kind of access. Even if I did, you'd be found out in a moment. However, I know people in the Security Access Center that can help."

"That's a serious security violation." The male soldier's head jerked up. Kal hadn't been sure he'd been paying attention.

"So what?" The woman asked. "You want Scaff, right?"

Kal studied the man and realized he was a junkie; Kal knew the signs. His hands, which were resting on his knees, had slight tremors. And the natural purple of his skin had a faint hue of sickly yellow. The Nasi reluctantly nodded his head at his partner's question.

As the other members of Delta Unit worked over the assault transport, the deal was done. Duke was given *almost* unfettered access in and out of the Foothold. Kal couldn't believe their luck; it was almost too simple. They would be able to get out of the Foothold, find a ship, and return to the fleet to let them know what happened. Finally, their luck was changing.

The members of Delta Unit finished their work and crawled off the ship. Duke went over the repairs with the soldiers in excruciating detail, outlining everything his team had done while the woman nodded appreciatively.

"This will be satisfactory," the woman announced when he was done. "We'll let our supervisors know of your performance. You can expect more of us to come for assistance."

"Why?" asked Daggs.

The question surprised the other Nasi—including the other members of Delta Unit—who swiveled their heads to look at her. "Why" was not a question that Nasi asked, especially ones without any Shishen tattoos of rank.

"The Grand Ancient is realizing her plan," said the woman after a pause. "The enemy fleet will be here in days. We need to prepare our equipment for the battle. And when we win"—she smiled—"we'll need your help for the celebrations."

The Skulls waited for the all clear from Duke before emerging from their hiding places. Kal's mind raced. He kept thinking of the soldier's parting comment. How could she be so sure the fleet was coming? If it was true, the fleet wouldn't stand a chance against the plasma lances on the planet's surface.

With Delta Unit's new security access, they could get the

Skulls out of the Foothold, but Kal still wasn't sure where they should go. The Nasi soldier had seemed so certain Samsara Fleet was on its way. He reached a decision, one that he was sure the others wouldn't like, and pulled Duke to a corner of the room.

"We're going to need more than you to help us," said Kal.

"How many more?"

"A *lot* more," Kal said. "How many of the Nasi on New America are like you?"

Duke considered. "We have about a thousand civilian logistics specialists in the Foothold. And there are—"

"No, I mean who would be willing to help us."

Duke's eyes widened. "I don't know. I haven't even thought to ask. Questions like that are dangerous."

"You heard that soldier. Our fleet is going to be here. There must be a reason why they know that, and I'm sure they're not planning on welcoming them with confetti and gifts."

"Yes, I would also doubt that." Duke looked confused.

"What I'm saying is, is that if we don't figure out a way to complete our mission, then thousands of people—Human and Jadid—will die."

"You need Nasi who are willing to fight against Grand Ancient Baykara."

"Exactly."

Duke cleared his throat and his eyes darted around the room nervously. It still amazed Kal how much the Nasi had changed since they'd first entered the universe. They'd become so…Human for lack of a better word.

"What are you talking about?" Daggs asked as she walked toward them with Fry and Trip following.

"He is asking our help to find people willing to fight against the Grand Ancient," said Duke.

"This isn't what we'd discussed," said Fry, looking at Duke. "Helping the Humans escape is one thing. This is treason."

"Helping the Humans is treason too," Daggs said. "This is worse, yes. But make no mistake, we are already in violation."

"We don't agree with what the Grand Ancient has done." Fry pointed his finger angrily. "But an open rebellion?"

Bowen cleared his throat. "I can understand your reluctance. This is not something to be taken on lightly. But if I may, I think there's another way to look at the situation. Do you consider yourself Jadid or Nasi?"

"We're both," said Trip, putting his tablet on a nearby maintenance cart. "The Nasi are but a part of the Jadid. One dedicated to leading the whole toward a better future."

"That's what your Grand Ancient has said, but is it true?" Bo tilted his head. "Your people are going against the will of the other Ancients. The Nasi have attacked and killed Jadid. They've killed countless Humans. The Nasi have betrayed and are in open rebellion against the Jadid."

"Only for the greater benefit," said Fry.

"Perhaps," Bo's tone clearly indicated he didn't think so. "But if that's the case, then the same logic would apply here. Would helping the Humans not be going *with* the will of the

Ancients and be a sign of loyalty to the Jadid?"

The conversation drifted into a mishmash of Logos, ethos, and other rhetorical concepts that would have bored Kal silly had not there been so much riding on it. He almost dove to the ground when Bo abruptly brought his sidearm out and fired a single bolt at a nearby transport. The plasma left a small ring of char on the side of the vehicle, and the metal bowed in slightly where the heat from the blast had warped it.

"You can't have it every way." Bo's voice, while low, still seemed to thunder through the chamber. "You've seen what's happened, and you know what's right. To hide behind your byzantine concepts of loyalty and morality while allowing billions to suffer and die is rank cowardice. You need to decide, here and now, what side you are on."

No one spoke. The Humans were too shocked to say anything, and the Nasi seemed to be too invested in their own thoughts. Kal had never seen Bo so emotional. As a Jadid, he was naturally, inhumanly, taciturn.

Duke exchanged glances with the other Nasi. "We need a moment."

As the Skulls walked toward the other end of the room Duke called out, "Bo, can you stay here?"

Bo looked at Kal, who nodded, then turned around and joined the Nasi. The Skulls went to the far end of the motor pool and sat against the wall made from prefabricated Nasi weaves. Kal could hear the hushed tones of the Nasi on the other side but was unable to make out any words.

"What're you thinkin', sir?" asked Corporal Sato.

"Just about how weird this all is."

"I mean what's your plan, sir?"

"No idea," Kal replied flatly. "But the Nasi knew our plan. We have to assume they've somehow called the fleet using Colonel Roberts. If Samsara Fleet gets here, they'll ambush them and blow 'em apart with the plasma lances. Add on the fact that every asset we've got has been neutralized and we're looking at a very difficult situation."

"How did we end up relying on our enemy to save us from our enemy?" asked the corporal.

Kal shrugged. "The cards have been stacked against us from the start. We're still breathing. Hell, we're even winning this war. We just have to see it through." He only half meant the words. The darkness that he'd tried so long to keep at bay was always there on the edges, whispering quietly.

"We've decided to help you," announced Duke after they'd called the Humans back. "We're Jadid and we have a loyalty to our own people. But"—he held up a finger—"you must make two promises."

"What?" asked Kal.

"That there will be a place for the Jadid in your universe when this is all through," said Duke. "Some of us may wish to return to Altterra, but many will not. There needs to be a place for those who wish to stay."

"You know I can't guarantee that." Kal was a general,

156

sure. But something like that would have to come from the Fleet's commander, General Samaha herself. Even then, it might not be enough. Kal was sure there would be many people out there who'd want vengeance on every single Nasi.

"The promise that you'll work toward it is enough," said Bo.

"Then, yes, I promise I'll do what I can."

"The other thing is that Bowen must stay here with us," said Duke. "He's the only one who can lead us."

The scientist's face had a decidedly sour expression. Clearly this was not what he wanted. However, in Kal's experience, often the best leaders were the ones who had leadership thrust upon them by circumstance rather than those who sought it out. Besides, Bo was a Jadid who had been captured by the Nasi and then joined the Humans. There was no other person in the galaxy who knew all three groups as well as he did.

"You okay with this?" Kal asked Bo.

The Jadid nodded. "Yes, I've accepted it." He didn't exactly seem thrilled, but it would have to do.

"It's fine by me in that case."

"Excellent," Duke smiled and clapped his hands in a very Human expression of eagerness. "Then we will get you out of the Foothold and into Kasongo. Bowen will stay here to help us."

"What'll we do?" Sergeant Popov asked Kal.

"We're going to find out exactly how many of our people are left," Kal replied. "I doubt the Nasi got every single rebel force on the planet. And maybe some of the assault teams are still out there. As long as their objectives are the same, we can find them."

"We can set up a regular rendezvous outside the Foothold, sir," suggested Bo. "Similar to the bar on Mariga. While you rally the Human forces, I will work inside the Foothold to get intel."

"As I recall, The Flying Snow Worm was rooted out by the Nasi and we almost died," said Sergeant Kimathi wryly.

"It took months for them to ferret it out," said Bo. "Based on what they've told me"—he motioned toward the four Nasi—"the security on New America is even more lax."

"We've got what, a few days to put together a plan to destroy the lances?" asked Sergeant Kimathi.

"Then I'd suggest we get to work." Bo raised an eyebrow.

Chapter Twelve
Kal | Nasi Foothold, New America

Before Delta Unit could leave the Foothold, they needed to receive a resupply request. Without one, they would immediately be flagged as suspicious, security access or not.

While they waited for the call, Kal tried not to think about what Sergeant Kimathi had told him earlier. If the Nasi had somehow gained access to Humans' implants, they were even more screwed than he originally had thought; any captured soldier captured could involuntarily become a collaborator. It also meant that any communication could be intercepted or faked. Kal hoped the Nasi weren't able to access the more advanced functions of the implant like memory storage.

Finally, a request for resupply came in, and Duke called for the Skulls to climb into the back of the transports—Delta Unit needed two of them. Kal reluctantly climbed back into a weapons tube and waited for the hauler to be loaded, listening to the pings of missiles and ordinance being loaded around him.

The cargo door shut, and he was surrounded by darkness again. He could feel the gentle sensation of lifting from the ground and moving forward as they left the bay. The fact that they were traveling through the most secure perimeter in the known galaxy while surrounded by explosives was not something he wanted to think about. Thankfully, he wouldn't have much time to feel any pain if they were caught.

It wasn't long before the vehicle stopped. Kal guessed

they were at the enormous wall that surrounded the Foothold. Had the security guards noticed something? Was it a trap?

He breathed a sigh of relief when the vehicle lifted off again and continued its progress.

Perhaps a half hour later, Kal blinked as the door slid open and light streamed inside. The sun was close to setting but still bright enough to blind someone who'd been immersed in darkness for the better part of an hour.

"If you go around that corner, you'll find the Banker's Deposit," said Daggs. "It's a Nasi friendly chembar."

"How do you get in there?" asked Kal. "Doesn't everyone see you?" The Nasi bar he'd been to on Mariga had a secret entrance that allowed the Nasi to enter without being seen.

She smiled. "Sure, Humans see us, but they don't care." A pause and the smile disappeared. "'Cept for the ones who hate us. They've thrown some rocks and even a grenade in there before."

"Sounds dangerous," said Kanumba.

"Ever since that happened, there's always been a lookout," said Fry. He shrugged. "Besides, the Human who threw that grenade isn't around to cause trouble anymore."

"Good to know," muttered Private Ma.

After agreeing to meet Duke later that day, the Skulls split into small groups and entered the establishment. Sergeant Kimathi gave strict orders for the soldiers to only observe and record anything they heard or saw that might be important with their implant. They were there on a simple recon mission—listen to what the Nasi were talking to each about

160

and don't engage.

The Banker's Deposit was a posh establishment, but one which had clearly fallen on hard times. The thick red runner that led from the entrance to the rear seating area was worn and stained. The gold fixtures that adorned the walls twisted at odd angles. The clientele was a mix of Humans and Nasi, most of them clearly under the influence.

As Kal stepped over a Nasi passed out on the floor, he thought back to his life before Samsara Fleet. He'd been no better than the poor bastard. Drugs had a way of taking over your life. Unfortunately for many of the Nasi, they were not ready for it. In the past year, it had gotten much worse, and Kal had seen more and more Nasi with signs of addiction.

"What are we doing here anyways?" whispered Sergeant Chedjou. "We're a bunch of fugitives—essentially—that are hanging out in a bar full of our enemy."

"Look at them," Kanumba hissed back. "They aren't going to report anything. Even if they were coherent to notice us, I'm guessing they'd rather not have to explain how they found us."

The Banker's Deposit had several floors, each dedicated to a different activity—drinking, chems, entertainment, and more. It wasn't the type of establishment Kal was used to. Simple spacer bars were more his speed. Places to get a quick drink, get high, and maybe have a bite to eat.

Kal and Chedjou sidled up to the first-floor bar and sat down while the others moved up the dim staircase in the back. A Nasi was passed out next to them, her face planted on the bar, a small pool of drool under her head.

"Whadya want?" asked a man behind the bar in a threadbare scarlet vest.

"Whatever's handy," said Kal. "And a water."

The man snorted. "Do we look like the kind of place that's got water?"

"I mean you look like you used to be." Kal looked around the room.

"Yeah, well, that's long gone," the man said. "It left when these purple bastards came." He smacked the Nasi draped on the bar on the head, eliciting a faint groan. "They can't hold their chems worth a damn."

The barkeep grabbed two glasses from the shelf behind him and filled them with a greenish liquid. He placed the glasses in front of Kal and Chedjou with a small thump.

"Drink up. Nothin' else to do around here."

"What happened to this place?" asked Chedjou. "Looks like it used to be something special."

"Yeah, *used* to. When the Nasi came, all our business dried up. Eventually they came looking for a place of their own, and the boss had no choice." The bartender shook his head. "Who would've thought they'd be the biggest deadbeats in the galaxy."

"But this is the financial district," protested Chedjou. "This is where all the credits are."

The barkeep snorted. "Again, used to be. The Nasi skim half of everything we got. Not much to finance when every bit of surplus goes to the Nasi." He leaned in conspiratorially.

"Not a lot of people realize, but the worst is yet to come. They're gonna raise their tribute again. A lotta mouths are gonna go empty."

"Why're you here then?" asked Kal. "If you hate them so much."

"You'll think I'm crazy for sayin' this but, I don't. Sounds funny I know. I just don't…care for 'em." He shrugged. "But I need to feed my family, same as the next guy. Jobs are gettin' scarce. They're not bad customers except lately."

"Lately?" Chedjou asked.

He nodded. "They're gettin' into fights more and more. At first, they were scared. Like a kid out on town for the first time. Wanted to try some forbidden stuff but didn't want to get caught. Now it's like they don't care anymore." He whistled. "And if they get into a fight, forget about trying to break it up. We had a bouncer who ended up in the hospital. Now we just let them go at it. At least it's been light the last couple of days."

"Well, hopefully, Samsara Fleet will be here soon." Kal tried to make the comment as offhand as possible to see if the man bit. Still, he felt like the words burned in the air after he said them.

The barkeep eyed him up and down. "I wouldn't be talkin' 'bout them too much around here." He sniffed and leaned toward Kal. "I don't think they realize who they're dealin' with. I hear the customers talkin', and they're gonna unleash a world of hurt on those guys when they get here."

"Like?"

The man's eyes narrowed. "Why're you askin' so many questions?" He leaned back and forth between Kal and Chedjou. "We don't get that many Humans anymore. What're you doing here?"

Kal's mind froze. Why hadn't he thought of a cover story? Anything? It felt like an eternity but could have only been a second or less before Chedjou replied.

"I grew up here," she said. "Dad worked for Unified Capital. Live out in the country now but thought I'd stop in since it used to be home. You know, for old times' sake."

"Which streets?" The man narrowed his eyes.

"Hyperion and Avenue 451," she replied innocently. "Just round the corner."

The barkeep continued to look at them skeptically. At that moment, the Nasi next to them jolted upright and demanded another drink in a loud voice.

"Well, welcome home." The barkeep shook his head. "Bet its nothin' like you remember."

After Chedjou finished both their drinks, she and Kal walked around the Banker's Deposit's first floor. It was split into two areas. One section, with a bar at one end and booths scattered throughout, was for alcohol. The other—containing a different kind of bar and low-slung plush chairs—was for the hard stuff. The latter was what really made Kal's skin crawl.

It was mostly filled with Nasi though there was the

occasional Human. All of them were sprawled across the comfortable-looking cushions and chairs, their limbs splayed out and eyes open, staring unblinkingly as they felt the effect of the drugs.

"Gotta say, this actually makes me feel sorry for the poor bastards," said Chedjou quietly.

Kal nodded back. His heart wept for them. He wasn't far enough removed—nor would he ever be—from his own addiction to not feel every single sensation that they were going through. He could remember the hunger and shame between fixes along with the pure bliss that came along with the hit of Kuaile, his drug of choice.

"Just listen," instructed Kal. "Some drugs'll make you talk to the wall. We just need to keep our ears open."

They made their way around the room and found places on a worn velvet settee. Human servers distributing small ampules and vials slowly made their way around the room, tending to their customers. Kal sensed a dark pallor of death and suffering filling the room, punctuated by sharp intakes of breath when customers took a hit.

A Nasi brushed by them in a sweep of air and roughly pulled someone off the floor by the front of their shirt.

"Get off," grumbled the addict as he staggered backwards. He looked like a wild animal with his bloodshot eyes and disheveled hair forming a nest around his head.

"You need to get back to the Foothold," said the other Nasi wearing the skintight uniform of a security patroller. "Questions are being asked."

"Let them be asked. Who cares?"

The drug-addled Nasi suddenly lunged and was easily tossed to the ground. The two grabbed at each other and wrestled in the dim green light. Their movements were quick, faster than any Human, and sharp as a knife. For a Human, many of the blows would have broken bones, but the Nasi simply shrugged them off.

"You're pathetic," shouted the patroller. "You've got a unit waiting for you."

"I'll be there."

"You're already late." The patroller suddenly lashed out and struck the Nasi across the face, sending him back to the floor. "You're the only engineer left who can divert the plasma. If you don't get yourself right, then we'll both pay the price."

"I'll be there, damn it. It's not like the fleet's coming today."

The patroller looked around the room. Kal quickly turned his head down and studied the floor.

"They might," the patroller said. "We don't know when they'll come—except that it's gonna be soon." Kal carefully raised his head and watched the two Nasi headed toward the door. "We need to get out there. If the changes aren't made in time—"

The patroller stopped talking as he noticed Kal and Chedjou looking at him. He paused for a moment then continued pulling the other Nasi towards the door without finishing the sentence.

Kal desperately wished he could follow them. Instead, he and Chedjou continued to sit quietly, waiting to see if anything else happened. No one in the room moved except to occasionally raise a hand to call for the "waiter." Kal wondered if any of them even realized an argument had happened in front of them. They were gone, lost to a world only they could see.

Nothing happened for the rest of the time Kal and Chedjou sat in the room. Less than a half hour later, the other members of the Skulls drifted past them and out the front door. They waited a few minutes and then followed.

"Find out anything?" Kal asked once they'd regrouped in a nearby alley.

"Something's happening," said Kimathi. "But I guess we already knew that. Heard a lot of them talking about how busy they were. Got the impression that up until now, New America's been a vacation for the bastards."

Kal relayed the conversation that he'd overheard in the chembar.

"Diverting plasma," said Ekon. "I'm not an engineer but sounds like something you'd need to do with a *plasma* lance."

"And I thought you said you weren't an engineer," said Corporal Sato, earning a nasty look from the squad leader.

"They're clearly getting ready for the fleet," said Kal. "There's an urgency to everything."

"They expect to win," said Sergeant Popov. "They're not worried about the fleet, they're hunting it."

The Skulls made their way through Tiradentes' streets in small groups, close enough they could still use their implants to communicate without using the planet's net, but far enough away they couldn't see each other. They had an hour to kill before meeting Duke and decided to investigate what had happened to the Tiradentes Liberation Front.

Although the TLF preferred to remain in the countryside, they had several safehouses and operation centers in the cities. Over the past year, Kal had been to a few of them. There was a risk in trying to contact whatever remained of the TLF, but it'd be worth it if they were successful; being dependent solely on the Nasi was not a great feeling.

We've got eyes on the objective, said Sergeant Kimathi. *No signs of activity, enemy or otherwise.* They were outside the third, and final, safehouse Kal knew of. The previous two had both been ripped apart; nothing remaining except jagged craters in the sides of buildings.

The squad leader and Private Ma had gone ahead of the group to take a position overlooking the TLF safehouse. The building was an abandoned store near the center of the city, the kind of store that sold junk and odds and ends that no one seemed to want. On New America, they called them bricbracs, but Kal had called them pawn shops back on Mariga.

Heading inside, Kal said as he stood up and walked down the narrow street with Chief Kanumba at his side. They tried to appear casual but kept a firm grip on their sidearms, which were hidden in their waistbands beneath their untucked blouses.

While Kimathi and Ma watched from above, the other Skulls took positions around the building so they had eyes on any avenue of approach.

Okay, we're entering the building, Kal said as the door in front of them slid open with a screech. *See you on the other side.*

"What the hell does that mean?" asked Kanumba.

"I don't know. Sounded cool. I think." Kal gave a sheepish grin.

Kanumba's eyes widened in surprise. "Think again."

The interior of the store was surprisingly clean and orderly. White shelves lined the walls and were arranged in even rows down the center of the store. Goods were arranged neatly on the shelves, either in their original packaging or in small transparent containers.

"Welcome!" A mechanical voice boomed through the store. Kal barely stopped himself from shooting his own leg in surprise. "We don't get many people lately."

A low-end shopbot rolled from behind a row of shelves and came to a stop in front of them. Like the store, the bot was cheap but well maintained. Its face was a crude mechanical reproduction of a Human's, permanently fixed in a pleasant if somewhat vacuous grin.

"Just browsing," said Kal. "Anyone else around?"

"The owner is currently away," answered the bot. "But I

am here to help with any issues you may have. You can rest assured that I am fully capable of handling any customer inquiries."

It seemed like a canned response, so Kal decided to try again, rephrasing his question. "I'm not really interested in purchasing anything. I just want to speak with the owner. I know them personally."

"The owner is currently away. But I am here to help with any issues you may have. You can rest assured that I am fully capable of handling any customer inquiries."

"This is getting us nowhere," said Kanumba. "Clearly this bottom-rung bot is not programmed to facilitate clandestine meetings between underground fighters."

"Any attempt to steal from this establishment will be met with the highest level of force allowed by law."

"We got it," said Kal to the bot. "We're just browsing."

"Please take all the time you need."

They walked through the store, looking for any sign of a way into the safehouse. When Kal had been there before, a doorway behind the counter had been open. Now there was nothing to even suggest it existed.

"You think you can hack that thing?" Kal asked, pointing at the bot with his thumb.

Kanumba snorted. "Considering it's basically a child's toy? Yeah, I think I can."

"See if you can access the store's security feed through it."

Kanumba nodded and pulled a tablet and two cables from

her pocket. She marched to the back of the bot and plugged the tablet into a port on the back of the machine's head. Less than a minute later, they were watching the store's security feed on the tablet.

"Keep going back," instructed Kal. He hoped to find something that would let them know how to enter. Most places tied their security to the neural implants. When he'd visited earlier, Kal remembered one of the TLF rebels mentioning how this safehouse was one of the only ones that had a mechanical entry system. It allowed them to use it with assets that didn't want to be seen by Human eyes. Now they just needed to find how to get in.

"Jackpot," Kanumba cried.

A grainy video showed a group of people walking into the shop and doing something to the bot. A second later the entrance slid open, and they walked through.

Kal examined the shopbot. There were no obvious buttons or panels on the outside. He began pulling and pushing at every screw and wire he could find.

They both jumped as the door to the safehouse slid open with a thunk. They'd barely recovered from their surprise when plasma fire erupted from the opening. Kal and Kanumba dove to the side as one of the bolts hit the bot, melting a chunk from its torso, and filling the room with the smell of ozone and burning plastic.

Plasma sizzled above their heads, flying across the store and hitting the front wall in multiple places. Whoever the shooter was, they had horrible aim. The firing stopped, and

Kal peaked over the wall, trying to get a visual on their assailant.

He was shocked to see a small girl with shoulder-length blonde hair standing in the open doorway. She looked to be young, about ten years old—the same age his daughter Lan Fen had been when she died. The girl was shaking a small plasma pistol in her hand clearly trying to get it to work.

"Hey, kid," Kal shouted. "We're not here to hurt you."

A plasma bolt hit the shelf below his head, and he ducked back down. Guess she wasn't *that* bad of a shot.

"We're looking for the TLF," Kal said. "We're trying to find out what happened."

"How do I know you're not one of them? A collaborator?"

"Besides the fact we could've blown you away?" Kanumba asked rhetorically. Kal shot her a warning look and she shrugged.

"We need your help," said Kal. "The Nasi have captured most of the TLF and our friends from Samsara Fleet. We—"

"Samsara Fleet?" asked the girl cautiously.

"Yes. We're from the fleet. We're here on a mission and need your help to find out what's happened."

Silence.

The girl's small pistol clattered down the aisle between the shelves, stopping between Kal and Chief Kanumba.

Chapter Thirteen
Nicole | Patagonia

Chengdu was a fan of white next to the sparkling blue of the ocean. Nicole almost felt at peace as she watched the city from the air. White-crested waves lapped against sandy beaches crowded with people. She imagined the cool tang of the ocean air against her skin as she looked through the galley's viewscreen.

The *Chester* flew parallel to the edge of the city and touched down in a small field surrounded by trees. There was no way they could enter a city as large as Chengdu wearing their battle suits. There were sure to be Nasi patrollers, and the last thing they wanted was a fire fight. According to Deepta's schedule, they had an hour to get in, talk to as many people as possible, and get out. Getting shot at would certainly get in the way.

Thankfully, the foliage wasn't too dense, and they were able to easily reach the city despite only having hand tools to make their way through the countryside.

"You got this," Deepta said encouragingly to Nicole. "You did pretty well back there in Xardi."

"I got half as many people as you."

"We'll only know how successful we are at the end. Remember, one person can tell three more who tell three more, and so on. Who knows how many will really show up?"

They tromped through a culvert that carried wastewater from the town. A thin trickle of water coursed beneath their feet. Small moss and lichen attached to the bottom danced in the currents and eddies. As buildings grew larger around them, the culvert dove beneath the streets and became a sewer. The rhythmic echoes of their boots splashing in the water had an almost hypnotic quality to Nicole.

"This is us," said Deepta, pointing at a placard on the wall. A narrow metal ladder disappeared above their heads. "We'll meet you back at the ship?"

"Sounds good," Nicole said. "Just be careful. Remember we can't wait, so don't miss the time cut off."

"We'll be there," said one of the rebels behind Deepta.

"Good luck."

Their mission in Chengdu was different. Deepta had contacts from her previous life that she was going to meet. She was rather vague on details, only volunteering that in a city as large as Chengdu she knew people, and if they were going to get the message out, she needed to use them.

Nicole continued walking through the sewer with Grupp and the other Front rebel trailing behind. They were heading toward the city center. Although not as large as Kasongo or Foyleton, Chengdu was still enormous. She'd have to be careful and stay strictly to the schedule.

Nicole watched their progress on the map superimposed over her vision by her implant, supplementing the information with periodic checks of the location placards on the walls. The dim aura of her light and the sound of the water trickling around them began to weigh on her. What was she doing? Tramping underneath a city on her way to try and recruit people? It was ridiculous and futile.

She stopped underneath a ladder and looked up. According to her implant, they were in the center of the city in what was called the financial district though many of the businesses there had nothing to do with finance. Wordlessly she started to climb the rungs of the ladder until she was in a small passageway between two ornate white stone buildings.

"Where to now, ma'am?" asked Grupp.

"No idea," said Nicole. "Deepta's instructions weren't that specific. We need to walk around and just find people."

"This plan isn't much of a plan," observed the rebel.

Nicole shrugged and started walking toward the sound of people and vehicles.

Chengdu was a planned city, and its streets formed an almost perfect grid with tiny squares at every few intersections. A salty ocean breeze swept around them, carrying the occasional whiff of street foods and the sound of conversation. Nicole led them from square to square, giving her speech about the fleet and how they needed help from the citizens.

She'd learned to expect the same questions every time she spoke. What can we do? How do we know it's not a trap? Why should we care? She'd developed a standard answer for each. Each time a small crowd of people formed, and many would stay to meet with her after. Grupp and the other rebel, Tak, stood behind her, their hands hovering near the quick release holsters on their thighs.

"We don't have much time to get back to the ship," said

175

Grupp after Nicole finished her fourth session.

Nicole checked her implant. He was right. They'd need to head back to the *Chester* soon. She wanted to speak to at least one more group though. Despite Deepta's speech about how their message would spread, Nicole worried they'd never have enough people to make a difference. How many of these unassuming people would show up when they were needed?

"There's a square a few streets down that way," said Nicole, pointing in the opposite direction from where the ship was waiting. "Let's hit that up real quick and then we'll go back to the *Chester*."

"That's gonna be cuttin' it very close," observed Tak, licking his lips nervously.

"Every single person we talk to can make a difference," said Nicole. "I don't wanna finish this mission feeling like we didn't use *every* opportunity."

"Lead on then," Grupp said, cracking his knuckles.

Nicole led them the few blocks to a square that overlooked the ocean. The humid wind coming off the water smacked her in the face while children ran to and fro, holding the strings of kites that soared above their heads. Recreation drones zoomed above the waves, their pilots controlling them using implants or small tablets while sitting on benches overlooking the ocean. It looked like a tourism ad, the perfect vacation spot for the weary.

"Hello! I'm here from Samsara Fleet!" Nicole shouted over the wind. She'd found mentioning the fleet was the easiest way to grab attention. And it worked. A small murmur of alarm rippled through the crowd.

Soon she had a throng of people around her, pressing in to hear her words over the crashing of the waves. The kids continued to fly their drones—adult things could wait—but their parents stood around her and listened as she explained what was happening.

After Nicole was done with her speech, she waited for the standard trickle of people to circle around her. This crowd was no different than the rest. A mix of the uninterested, skeptics, and one or two people who hinted that they might help. She thought of Deepta's words and hoped the woman was right.

"Down!" Tak shouted, tackling Nicole to the ground. She hit hard on her left shoulder as a hail of plasma fire streamed through the area where she'd been standing. Wincing slightly, Nicole crawled behind a nearby stone wall for cover.

"We've got at least three Nasi soldiers," shouted Grupp.

The crowd screamed as the Nasi continued to fire, their bolts tracing the top of the wall. The sounds of playing and laughing children had instantly been replaced with the whistling of plasma fire.

Nicole looked around, her training taking over. It was about as bad of a position as they could be in. The ocean was to their back, meaning limited avenues of escape. Without their battle suits, they were severely outgunned by Nasi. The potential for collateral damage was high with the civilians scattered throughout the area. And to top it off, they needed to get back to their ship as soon as possible. Their only option was to run. She checked her implant, looking for an escape route while Grupp and Tak returned fire.

Pressed against the ocean, every escape route required them to go through or past the Nasi attacking them. She cursed herself for not thinking of that earlier. She'd been lulled into thinking the Nasi were too busy preparing for Samsara Fleet. Obviously, they weren't.

"How good are you two at swimming?" asked Nicole. She spotted a sewage pipe directly beneath them on the map.

"Good enough," shouted Grupp as he ducked beneath the wall as plasma bolts rained overhead.

"You got anything to distract them?" asked Nicole.

"We both got some grenades," said the rebel. "One each."

Nicole pointed to a small square cover in the center of the park, about fifty meters from their location. "That leads to a sewer line. On my mark, use everything you got and take off. I'll cover you and then be right behind."

"You should take the lead," said Tak.

"No." Nicole grabbed the man's sleeve. "And I don't have time to argue. On my mark, you go."

She counted down from three and then popped up, firing quick bursts in the general direction of the Nasi. Grupp and Tak jumped up, throwing their grenades, and took off. Seconds later, a greenish-orange explosion shook the cluster of bushes where the Nasi had taken cover.

Nicole quickly backed up, holding her pistol in front of her as she looked for a sign of the enemy. Plasma bolts streaked out from behind two fountains on either side of the bushes, missing her by centimeters. Nicole cracked off several shots at the fountains, still unable to see the Nasi, and still back-pedaling as fast as her legs would go. She tripped and landed on her back as a missile streaked above her head, exploding behind her.

"Damn it!" Nicole swore. She estimated she was only halfway to the sewer entrance. She wouldn't make it this way. Flipping over onto her front, Nicole jumped back up and sprinted away from the Nasi. She saw a body facedown on the ground in front of her—either Grupp or Tak. The Nasi unleashed their full fire, plasma rounds sizzling through the air around her.

As she passed the body, Nicole realized it was Tak. The man's empty expression stared at her as she ran past. There would be time to think about him later. Compartmentalize as Kal always said.

The grate was already off the sewer entrance and Grupp must have made it inside. Nicole dove into the opening, feeling a blossom of pain in her side. She went over the lip and dropped in as plasma fire streaked above her. She landed on a small ledge, directly underneath the opening. Grupp was already there, his weapon pointed up towards the opening.

"Time to dive," said Nicole, peering into the inky water several meters beneath them. She took out her only grenade, set it to a time fuse, and attached it to the side of the small shaft they were in. She hoped it would do enough damage to seal the entrance and prevent the Nasi from following them.

Grupp nodded then jumped from the edge into the churning waters beneath. Nicole hesitated for a second and then followed suit, jumping feet first.

She tried to calm the sudden sense of panic as she splashed into the chilly water. She heard the dull thump of her grenade going off above and heard splashes from debris falling into the water around her.

Nicole surfaced and opened her eyes, feeling the sting of salt water. She pulled out her light and flashed it around. Grupp was right next to her, his face red from exertion. He tugged at Nicole's sleeve and pointed to a dark opening just under the surface on one side of the chamber. Nicole had never been much of a swimmer though she'd at least had more practice in the past year. Hopefully it would pay off.

She dove and then kicked forward, using her free hand to pull at anything she could find. She followed Grupp into the opening and made her way through a pipe with her light barely illuminating a small slice of the area in front of her. Once they reached the small chamber on the other side, Nicole stood up and gasped for air as her head broke the surface of the water.

"Damn! That's cold!" shouted Grupp as his head popped up next to her.

Nicole nodded back, her teeth already starting to chatter. She checked her implant. The sewers formed a complex maze underneath the city. This seemed strange to her considering how orderly and evenly laid out the streets above were.

"I'm gonna...take us on a bit of a strange path," said

Nicole, trying to control the chattering of her teeth. "We can't go...straight back to the ship."

Grupp nodded. "Okay...I'm ready."

They zigzagged through the pipe maze, making their way in the general direction of the *Chester*. Although the water wasn't deep, the trip was exhausting and slow since they had to swim through the pipes connecting the chambers. The farther they went from the ocean, the worse the smell got. When they'd entered, the sewers had smelled like salt water. After a half hour, they were filled with the noxious fumes of Human waste.

"Finally," groaned Grupp as he pulled himself out of the water and onto the damp ultracrete floor. They'd finally reached a section where they could stand and wouldn't need to swim through the frigid waters anymore.

"You can say...that again," said Nicole as she lay down on the surprisingly warm ground. She struggled not to gag from the smell.

Now that they could walk, Nicole figured they should be able to make relatively fast progress through the tunnels. They had already missed their rendezvous time with the *Chester*. Perhaps Deepta and the crew had waited for them, but she doubted it.

"Poor Tak," said Grupp, looking back the way they'd come.

"You knew him well?" asked Nicole.

The sergeant nodded and wiped his face against his soaked sleeve. "Yeah, we grew up in the same neighborhood.

He was a few years younger than me. Good kid."

"We've lost a lot of good kids." Nicole pictured several in her mind.

Grupp nodded, then stood up. There was a time to talk about the people they'd lost. Now wasn't one of them.

As they ran through tunnels, Nicole's soaked clothing rubbed uncomfortably against her body. She kept her pistol out, ready for the Nasi to come crashing down on them at any moment. The tunnels led to an open culvert and then an open canal as they exited the city. The warmth of Patagonia's sun felt amazing, and the shivers that had been racking Nicole's body gradually ceased as her clothing warmed.

"Ship should be close by if they stayed," said Nicole, checking her implant. She crawled out of the culvert and was amazed to find that somehow, she'd led them right to where they'd blazed a trail through the underbrush on their way into the city.

"Think they've left already?" asked Grupp as he ran behind her through the woods.

Nicole said nothing. The truth was she doubted it. They *should* have, but maybe they hadn't follow orders and were still waiting.

They entered the small field where the *Chester* had touched down. Nicole's implant didn't detect anything, but she still ran to where it should be, hoping to cross through the optical camouflage and find the ship waiting for them. Nothing was there; the *Chester* had left. They'd done exactly as they were supposed to. Still, Nicole felt a surge of anger.

"Well, this sucks," said Grupp, flopping down onto the matted ground where the ship had been.

"Yeah," Nicole said, sitting down next to him.

They idly looked around the clearing for a moment. Nicole knew they should move, get out of the open but for just a second, she didn't care.

"Guess we need to find a ride," she said lightly. After everything, she couldn't help but see the humor in the situation.

"Guess so," agreed Grupp. He stood up and held out his hand to help her up.

Chapter Fourteen
Nicole | Patagonia

Under normal conditions, Patagonia had a dense network of public transports and ships that allowed citizens to easily travel across the Pangean continent. Unfortunately, things hadn't been normal for a while. The public transports had been shut down the previous day, and the ships hadn't flown since the Nasi had taken over the planet.

Grupp and Nicole trudged back towards the culvert using the same path they'd taken two times before. Nicole felt a wave of exhaustion as they padded through the underbrush. The past half an hour had taken its toll. Only now as the adrenaline wore off and the reality of their situation hit home, did she feel the weight of everything that had happened.

"You know anyone from around here?" asked Nicole.

Grupp grunted. "Nah. I'm from Kasongo. Don't really know anyone there either. People I did know are dead and buried."

"Nasi?"

"Who else?"

They crept down into the culvert and made their way to the edge of Chengdu. Nicole's only objective was to find a way out of the area. If they went too far into the city, they were likely to be found by the Nasi. If they tried to hitch a ride in the countryside, they'd stick out like a sore thumb. Their only option was to follow the sewers and stay near the edge of town.

"Let's try here," said Nicole, putting a hand on one of the metal rungs leading up.

"Good a place as any," agreed Grupp.

Nicole did a double take as she looked at the wasted landscape around her. They appeared to be in the center of a demolished building. Rubble littered the ground around them, and jagged rebar stuck out from ultracrete floors that had been sheared away from the blast. Rays of sunlight streamed through enormous openings in the ceiling above, glimmering off cans and refuse someone had hastily pushed into piles.

"What is this place?" asked Nicole. Most of the debris and wreckage from the initial Nasi attack had long been cleaned up.

Grupp shrugged and bent down to pick up a sad stuffed animal that had been thrown on top of a heap of garbage.

Nicole checked her implant. The building showed up on the map, but there wasn't anything identifying it. No name. No address. Then it clicked. Only one type of building was this large and didn't appear on a map.

"This is a commune," said Nicole. Communes were on every Human-occupied planet. The large buildings—really clusters of buildings—were where the poor and forgotten were forced to live. She'd lived in one herself before joining the United Earth Government and traveling the stars.

"Why's it like this?" asked Grupp. "No one cares enough about a commune to destroy it."

"Samsara Fleet," said a small voice from the shadows,

causing them both to jump. "The Nasi destroyed it trying to get to one of their squads. Then I guess they just liked doing it because they didn't stop and just leveled most of it."

Something clicked in Nicole's mind. Kal and the Skulls had been in Chengdu before and hid out in a commune. This must be the same one. It amazed her how no matter what they did, innocents always got hurt.

"Can you help us?" asked Nicole, trying to make out who she was talking to. "We need to find a way to Foyleton."

A boy, in his early teens, stepped out from beneath a demolished floor. He was so coated in dust and grime it was impossible to tell what he looked like underneath. His large dark eyes studied the two of them and a small grin dashed across his face.

"You think if I could get to Foyleton I'd stay here?"

"I think you may know people who can help us get there," said Grupp impatiently. "It's important."

"Why's it important to *me*?" asked the boy.

It was a good question. For the people she'd talked to in the squares, it had been easier to answer. They had homes and careers. They had opportunities for the future. What did this kid have? His life had been written before he'd been born. She stopped herself. That wasn't completely true. She'd made it out of the communes of Earth. There was at least a *chance* for him to have a better life.

"There's a buncha credits in it if you help us out," said Grupp. He wagged his finger. "But they'll be delivered *after* you help us. Don't think you can take us to your friends and rob us." He lifted his shirt to reveal the holstered weapon tucked into his waistband.

"We'll give you a hundred credits now and a thousand when you get us to someone who can help us," added Nicole.

The boy cupped his hand in his chin as if he was considering their offer, but Nicole knew he was already hooked. They were offering a fortune—an almost unfathomable amount—for a kid in the communes.

"You can call me Zip," said the boy. "Whadd'ya called?"

"I'm Nicole and this is Grupp," Nicole said. "I take it that's a yes. You got a chit?"

Since the kid was obviously under eighteen, the only way for him to get or spend credits was through a chit, a small card that he'd carry with him. Adults normally used their implants. Though some, like Nicole, still used a chit so they couldn't be traced.

Zip nodded and pulled his out from somewhere inside his baggy clothing. He held it toward Nicole, and she transferred a hundred credits. After verifying the transaction with a small smile, Zip started walking farther into the dilapidated structure.

There were parts of the building that had survived the Nasi attack. The hallways they walked through still had their walls and roof. The inhabitants had piled furniture and scraps to section off areas, which made it almost impossible for Nicole to see farther than a few meters in front of her.

"Where're your parents, Zip?" asked Nicole as they

followed the boy through the halls. Zip clearly was at home in the twisting run-down hallways of the commune. Nicole imagined he'd probably never known anything else. The clean open streets of downtown Chengdu were probably as alien to him as Altterra, the Nasi home world, was to her.

"They're busy," said Zip, scrambling over a support that had fallen in the middle of the hallway. "It's just me now."

"Sounds lonely," said Grupp.

Zip only grunted as he pulled himself through a hole in the ceiling that led to the floor above. "Careful," he said, pointing to a piece of rebar that stuck out from the ceiling, ready to catch people unaware.

Nicole gingerly followed with Grupp straining to keep up. Although the commune she'd lived in had been more orderly than this, her body still remembered how to scamper over obstacles and crawl through holes.

"Much farther?" asked Grupp, a tinge of suspicion in his voice.

"We're here," said Zip, knocking on a flimsy metal door.

A man, barely in his twenties, opened it. He looked at Zip with a smile then noticed Nicole and Grupp and pulled out a pistol.

"Who're they?"

"They're lost," said Zip. "They need a ride and have *lots* of credits."

The man raised his eyebrows. "Well then. Come on in, your majesties." He held the door open and made a deep theatrical bow at the waist.

Nicole casually tapped her thigh, checking to see that her weapon was still holstered, and walked in. On the other side of the door was an enormous room with small makeshift tents against the walls. Small fires were burning in front of them.

"We got visitors," yelled the man who'd opened the door. "They got credits. Zip brought 'em in."

A large woman glided from one of the campfires and stood in front of Nicole and Grupp. A jagged scar bisected her face from chin to forehead making her otherwise pleasant smile appear intimidating. Despite her size, the woman moved like a dancer, effortlessly gliding through the firelit chamber.

"Good girl," said the woman to Zip with an affectionate pat on the head. "Go get seconds. You earned 'em."

Zip turned to Nicole. Now she could see the feminine features in the young girl's face. *How had she thought Zip was a boy?* "Remember, you owe me a thousand credits," Zip said quietly before running off to one of the tents. "I'll collect later."

"We need a ride to Foyleton," said Nicole, "and we're willing to pay."

The woman twisted her mouth. "If you got credits, why can't we just take 'em?"

"We've got 'em secured," said Grupp, holding up his chit. "Military-grade encryption."

"More importantly, we're here to *help* Patagonia," said Nicole. She explained that Samsara Fleet was on its way to liberate the planet, and they needed help to take out the plasma lances. The other woman listened without interrupting, holding up a large hand to shush anyone else who started to speak.

After Nicole was done, the woman held out her hand. "Name's Mother Ju. I'll help you, but it's gonna cost more than just credits."

Nicole wasn't sure what General Samaha would say about the deal she'd just made. It certainly wasn't one she could enforce herself. In the end though, they needed to get to Foyleton, and what Mother Ju was asking in return was pretty reasonable in her opinion.

Mother Ju's demand was simple, a seat on whatever government Patagonia had after the war. She said she wanted to be "the one givin' the orders rather than takin' them." Specifically, she wanted her and people like her—those who "lived outside of civilized society" as she put it—to have a say in what went on. It was both an enormous ask and a naive one. Nicole explained she didn't have the authority to control what Patagonia did after the war. Mother Ju looked her up and down and said, "A promise'll be enough."

Nicole promised. And she meant it. If she survived long enough, she'd record the deal she made in the mission logs and pass it along to General Samaha. If she lived to the end of the war, she'd personally fight to make sure that *everyone* on Patagonia—and all the planets—had a say. She owed that to them. She owed it to her family, who'd died penniless in a commune back on Earth.

Minutes later, Nicole sat in the back of a farm transport with bales of dried plants around her. Ju had explained to her and Grupp that if the Nasi came close, they needed to lie flat and the transport would cover them with the bales, hiding them from sight and covering their heat signature with the natural biological heat of the plants. Mother Ju and Zip sat across from them, the latter demanding to be included since she'd been the one to find them.

"How do you have access to a vehicle like this?" asked Nicole.

Ju smiled and gave a small wink. "Just some tricks of the trade. When you're the boss, you gotta have a few transports up your sleeve."

"Probably stolen," said Grupp dismissively. "People who live in the communes'll steal anything they can get their hands on."

Nicole leaned towards the Front rebel and positioned her face in front of his. "*I* used to live in a commune on Earth ya know."

Grupp didn't flinch. "I didn't know. But it doesn't change anything. You got out. Everyone knows that anyone who stays in the communes are too lazy to leave. They like living there. No job. No rules. Just take whatever you can."

Nicole bit her tongue. She'd heard it all before. Her parents had both had jobs and still hadn't been able to escape the communes. The truth was the United Earth

Government had had winners and losers, and the system was designed to reinforce this relationship. But she wasn't about to argue with the man, at least not there. At any moment she could be relying on him to keep her alive. Let him hold on to his misconceptions and prejudices for now.

"People like you are why we need representation in the government," said Ju with a wag of her finger. "People who don't even *see* the problem can't begin to help us solve it. Sitting in your comfy home, ignoring the problems of your fellow Humans. This is why so many people don't have a problem with the Nasi." She growled. "But I see things differently. There's hope with Humanity. A hope that we don't have with the Nasi. Things can get better, and I believe over time, in broad sweeps, it does."

"You think people will help?" Nicole asked. She didn't know why she asked the question. Was she looking for affirmation or support from the woman? But it was the question that had been plaguing her since they set out from the PF base.

Mother Ju nodded with a small smile. "I do. I'm here helping after all. I'm risking me and my little Zip to help."

"We're gonna tell everyone about you and what you're trying to do," said Zip. "After you give us our money of course."

"Wait," Nicole smiled at the girl. "I thought the deal had changed."

Zip frowned and shook her head. "*Our* deal didn't change. You still owe me a thousand credits." She pulled her chit from her pocket and held it out toward Nicole.

As they approached Foyleton, the driver turned around in his seat and motioned for them to get down through the cab's back window. Nicole lay on the metal floor bed and turned her head as the bales rotated to cover them with a hum. She fought her immediate instinct to panic as everything grew dark and an earthy smell filled her nostrils. She felt the transport slow and touch down with a small thump. They must be at an inspection station.

Mother Ju had warned them about this. The largest cities had periodic checkpoints that the Nasi used to inspect commercial vehicles coming in and out. She'd said it'd be nothing to worry about, but Nicole couldn't help wondering if the Nasi's protocols had changed in the past few hours.

Muffled voices came from above. It was impossible for Nicole to tell what they were talking about, only that there were questions being asked. She could hear the two voices go back and forth then a third joined in. The intensity and pitch grew until one of the voices shouted, and she heard the whine of a plasma rifle being fired. Several shots in quick succession.

Nicole jumped with each shot and tried to reach at her sidearm. Unfortunately, the bales had trapped her hand to her side and her weapon lay just out of reach. As she struggled, she heard voices around the vehicle, talking in a detached monotone. There was a sudden small thump that she couldn't place. She heard the sound again, closer. Nicole gasped as a metal blade or rod burst from the bale above her heard, embedding itself in the metal subfloor, only inches from her face. She heard the blade retract and several more thumps before everything went quiet. She shivered as she waited for something to happen. It was still. No voices. No sounds.

Then there was the thunk of a door closing and the sensation of being lifted from the ground and moving again. Nicole tried to feel around her, but all her limbs were pinned down. She thought about calling out but had no idea if there was a Nasi sitting above her at that moment. She wondered how the others were doing; Zip's large black eyes swam in her face. Nicole tried to take solace in the fact that she hadn't heard a scream or shout from any of her companions. Most likely, they all were fine.

She hoped.

The vehicle touched down a few minutes later and the engine whined to a halt. Nicole waited, picturing herself trapped and starving to death underneath the false bottom of the transport bed.

"Everyone okay?" hissed Mother Ju.

"Good," Grupp whispered back.

"Good," said Nicole.

A silence seemed to hang menacingly in the air. "G— good," said Zip in a wavering voice. "I got hit though. In the leg." The words hit Nicole in the gut.

The bales rotated upward, letting in a harsh, unnatural

white light. Nicole pushed herself up, her joints protesting, and looked for Zip. Before she was fully up, Mother Ju had already jumped from her spot and was hovering over the girl. Nicole glanced at Grupp, who was shaking his head ruefully, and then pulled herself up to sit next to Ju.

Zip lay on the transport bed, blood staining her patchwork pants and forming puddles around her legs.

"Goddamn it," cursed Ju as she examined the girl. "Goddamn Nasi. Goddamn pieces of crap."

Nicole reach through her pockets and found a bandage which she handed to Mother Ju. The woman shot Nicole a grateful look and gently wrapped it around the child's leg. Zip let out a small gasp as the pain-relieving drugs began to work.

"Better?" asked Ju.

Zip nodded weakly. "A little. What's in that? I mean, it's gold."

Nicole laughed. "Everything a growing girl needs."

Mother Ju picked up Zip and got her out of the transport with Nicole and Grupp's help.

Nicole looked around. They were inside some sort of storage facility with other commercial transports parked around them. She guessed they had all been seized in the same violent manner at checkpoints entering the city. There were charred plasma burns and slashes on several of them.

"We seem to be in an old EDF facility," said Nicole after checking her implant.

"Looks like the Nasi have been busy," observed Grupp, kicking the side of the vehicle parked next to them.

Ju looked at the front cabin of the transport they'd been in. "They were good kids," she said quietly. "Didn't deserve that."

"The Nasi don't care," said Grupp. "We're not people to them, not sentient. We're just obstacles to be overcome or resources to be harvested."

Mother Ju nodded in agreement.

Nicole looked around for a way out. A three-meter high wall, which had seen better days, surrounded the impound lot. Several hundred civilian transports sat scattered across the crumbling tarmac under bright lights atop poles every few meters. She could make out a dilapidated building on the other side of the yard with a light glaring above it, the faint sound of a holo projector at full volume emanating from inside.

"Can you walk, Zip?" asked Nicole. The girl took a few tentative steps and nodded.

They crept towards the perimeter, using the vehicles as cover. When Nicole got close, she realized the wall was in even worse condition than it had first appeared. It looked like no one had done maintenance on it in decades. Several holes, *almost* large enough for them to crawl through, dotted the side.

They scurried along the wall away from the shack, looking for a place to crawl out and finally found a small opening that led outside to a field. The lights from above the lot cast long shadows across the open space, making Nicole worry she could be shot from behind at any moment as they rushed away from the facility. Looking back, she was glad to see Zip was able to keep up. The drug-laden bandage was doing its job, but they needed to get the girl to somewhere she could rest soon.

They found a small hiding place amongst a cluster of bushes and took cover. "Okay, so we got to Foyleton—barely," said Nicole after they'd made it a safe distance from the facility. "Is there somewhere we can go?"

"There's only one person I trust in this city anymore," Mother Ju said with a wave of her hand. "Follow me."

Chapter Fifteen
Kal | Tiradentes, New America

The girl's name was Asha.

She led them to the safehouse hidden at the back of the store. Asha explained that she'd come to the safehouse looking for her father, a TLF member. He'd left their home a couple of days earlier, saying he had to go out on a mission but hadn't returned.

"My dad said that if I get lost to sit down and wait and someone will come and find me," explained Asha.

"Good advice," said Kal.

The TLF's safehouse was a small affair: two bedrooms with a small common room connecting them. A large multiscreen console filled one of the room's walls, its screens showing live feeds of areas around the building.

"How long have you been waiting?" asked Kanumba gently.

"'Bout a day." The girl's large eyes welled up.

"Well, you're safe now. We'll get you out of here." Kanumba tried to put her arm around the girl, but Asha shied away.

"Any idea where everyone went?" asked Kal.

Asha shook her head.

Kal pressed his hand against the bioscanner on the console unlocking the controls—the TLF had granted him access to their systems months earlier. He searched through the general announcement board, looking for any sign of where everyone in the safehouse had gone to or what had happened to the TLF and the other resistance groups on the planet.

"Looks like the TLF wasn't the only one hit." Kal pointed to a message begging for help in the general inbox from the HLL, Human Liberation League, another resistance group that operated on the western continent of New America.

"Not surprising," said Kanumba. "The Nasi are nothing if not thorough."

Kal continued to look through the system, looking for any sign of where the others might have gone. The base might have been compromised, but Kal doubted it. If that was the case, the Nasi would have either destroyed the safehouse or at least had a team waiting for stragglers. *No,* thought Kal, *the people here went somewhere.* Though why one of them would leave their daughter with no notice, he didn't know.

"Do you have an inbox?" asked Kal, looking down at Asha.

"Oh, yeah," she said smiling. "I forgot about that. My dad set one up for me a while back."

"Can you access it?"

Asha walked up to the console and placed her hand on the sensor and logged into the machine. An icon appeared in the corner of the screen, indicating an unread message.

```
Pea, I hope you find this message. If you
are reading it, I wasn't able to get to you
in time. We went to the place where you said
```

you were super cold. If you can find any of
our friends, come meet us. But don't travel
alone. Love, Dad.

"The place where you were super cold?" asked Kal. "Do
you know where that is?"

Asha screwed up her face in thought, then shook her
head. "No."

"Think real hard," said Kanumba. "Any idea at all?"

Asha sniffed. "No."

"Don't worry, it will come to you," said Kal. "I always
remember things the most when I'm not trying to remember
them."

Asha cocked her head to the side. "That doesn't make any
sense."

"Oh, it does. You'll see." Kal placed a hand on her
shoulder and turned to Kanumba. "Let's go. We need to take
her with us."

It was time for them to meet up with Delta Unit. The
rendezvous point was a small alley in the city's financial
center, close to the Banker's Deposit. The sun was setting, but
the street was as dark as night since the tall buildings around
them blocked its orange glow.

Kal watched as the Nasi logistics transport set down at the
alley's mouth, blocking it. Asha stood at his side, her small

hand gripping his own nervously. Kimathi had his squad in positions about the area, staying out of sight.

"You've found a recruit?" asked Daggs as she strode from the vehicle.

From a Human, it would obviously be a sarcastic comment. From a Nasi or Jadid, Kal wasn't sure. Children were rare, almost unheard of in their society. Their low fertility rate, combined with their infinite lifespan, meant they almost never procreated.

Asha gave a quick nervous inhale. "Not quite," said Kal, giving her hand a reassuring squeeze. "More like a friend."

Daggs looked the small girl over as Asha buried herself behind Kal. "Well, I would make sure she knows how to shoot at least. Everyone should know how to use a weapon."

"We may have found some pockets of resistance still around," said Kal.

"Excellent. Bowen has been even more effective than we expected." Daggs frowned. "I know it's according to our plan, but I'm still disheartened by how quickly our people will turn against their leader."

It was this kind of convoluted Jadid logic Kal couldn't understand.

"We heard some Nasi talking about diverting plasma," said Kal. "I think they may be doing something to the plasma lances before the fleet arrives. Have you heard anything like that?"

"That's disheartening you were able to overhear that. The standards really have gone downhill." Daggs shook her head sadly. "Most of the engineers in the Foothold have been reassigned to field duty, so that would seem to corroborate your theory. With Bowen's work, we have a growing number of allies within the Foothold and should be able to find out more. We were able to confirm that your relay ship was contacted by Nasi posing as Humans and departed to signal the fleet to attack."

"Which means we have about four days to figure out what's going on," said Kal.

"And to gain enough support to win," added Daggs.

Asha gasped and squeezed Kal's hand.

"What is it?" he asked gently.

"I know where my dad is," she said. "You were right, I just needed to not *try* and remember, and I remembered."

"Where is he, child?" asked Daggs. "And why should we care?"

Asha narrowed her eyes defiantly. "I'm not telling you. You might use the information to betray us."

"I could easily kill you all right now," Daggs said matter-of-factly. "But I will not," she added hastily.

"I'd like to see you try," said Asha taking a step forward, her hands balled at her waist.

"Okay, okay." Kal gently pulled the girl back by her shoulder. "You can tell Daggs. She's a friend. Not all Nasi are bad and not all Humans are good."

"Well, yeah, of course." Asha looked at him skeptically and Kal gave an encouraging nod.

"Up north," Asha said. "There's a place on the western

continent he took me to. But that's all I'll say with *her* around." She pointed at Daggs, who regarded the girl coolly.

"You are right not to trust me," said the Nasi. "I may betray you at any moment."

Kal rolled his eyes at Daggs then turned to Asha. "We'll talk more in private." He turned to the Nasi. "Any chance we can get a ride?"

"No. That's completely outside of our unit's operating area. We'd be flagged for further investigation immediately."

"Guess we're going to have to do this the old-fashioned way."

"What way is that?" asked Asha.

"We're gonna have to steal a transport," said Kal.

Asha broke out into a wide grin.

Kal and Daggs agreed that while Bowen and Delta Unit scouted the Foothold for more information and tried to recruit more Nasi to their side, the Skulls would try and find out what remained of the Human resistance on planet. Kal and half the squad would head to wherever Asha's father was, and the other half would remain in Tiradentes with Sergeant Kimathi to see if they could find more evidence of the TLF in the city and maintain comms with Delta Unit.

Asha's mood had picked up now that she was going to see her father again—and steal a transport. She pestered Kal with questions as they walked through the streets, looking for a model that was old enough for Kanumba to hack and was in an area where there wouldn't be a lot of witnesses. They finally found what they were looking for, and Kanumba quickly overrode the vehicle's security system using her small tablet. Asha sighed with disappointment when she saw how simple the entire process was.

The trip across New America would take the better part of the night and most of the next morning. They left the city and headed northwest, crossing through an industrial zone and into the countryside filled with agricultural zones. Other than the occasional light of a field drone in the distance, there was little to look at.

Asha began talking to Kal, telling him about her life. She'd grown up on the streets of Tiradentes and had been alone for a long time. As she talked, Kal realized that the father she'd been referring to was actually an adoptive father. Her biological parents had disappeared before the Nasi had come. She'd been through a lot.

After finishing her story, Asha gave a long sigh. "I'm bored," she announced. "How much longer?"

"We got about ten minutes less than last time you asked, kid," Kanumba responded. Kal could tell the otherwise stolid engineer was on her last nerve.

"Tell me, Asha, what's this place we're going to?" Kal had a pretty good idea. He'd reconned the map on his implant and knew the planet pretty well after countless missions. Still, anything to distract the girl—and himself.

Asha sat up in her seat and faced Kal with an earnest

expression. "Well, it's this top-secret training facility. My dad took me there just once. It's where his soldiers got to train with some of their friends." Kal knew that it was a base near the planet's pole on the western continent that belonged to another rebel group called the People's Army. The TLF had probably been there for joint training exercises. He hadn't been there before, but he'd heard TLF leaders refer to it as the Fridge.

They'd decided to stop by the closest town, Hope, before heading to the base. It was one of the few towns on New America that wasn't in an urban zone, built out of the need to support the industries near the north pole. Kal wanted to scout out the area and make sure there hadn't been Nasi activity before entering the base.

"What was it like there?" Kal asked.

"Well, super cold," Asha replied. "My dad made me wear *two* coats the entire time I was there. On the bright side, I was able to get all the warm cocoa I wanted."

"Sounds like it was fun."

Asha screwed up her face in what Kal had come to recognize was annoyance. "Well, boring mostly. Dad wouldn't let me watch what they were doing."

"Well, I'm sure he had his reasons." *Like not getting you killed.*

"I can't wait to see him again," Asha said, turning to look out the pitch-black window.

"I'm sure he feels the same way," said Kal. The girl now acted like she wanted to be left alone. He was pretty sure he saw her wipe away a tear in the reflection and didn't want him to see her cry. Kal could understand that.

Asha snuggled into Kal's shoulder but kept her face pointed away. For a moment, Kal was reminded of when his children had still been living. Stephen and Lan Fen would do the same thing before bedtime, burying their small bodies into him as they wound down from the day.

Kal didn't say a word and tried not to move a muscle as they both fell asleep.

❖

"This is Hope?" asked Kanumba. "I guess that's why I'm a pessimist."

Kal had to admit the town of Hope did not live up to its name. It sat in the center of a vast expanse of tundra with purple mountains in the far distance. Unpaved roads skirted between the thrown-together metal buildings and shacks of the small frontier settlement. Kal guessed the entire population could have lived in one of the sky-high towers in Tiradentes.

Kanumba parked the transport in a lot near the town center. As Kal exited the vehicle, the wind immediately cut through the thin fabric of his free merchant outfit.

"Damn," cursed Corporal Sato. "This place is freezing."

"I can see why your dad wanted you to have two coats," Kal said to Asha.

The girl nodded, shivering slightly and keeping her arms

tightly around her torso.

Private Chadha pointed to the bright holosign of a general provisions store. "Sir, perhaps we should get outfitted."

A half hour later they stood outside the store, dressed in an array of civilian cold weather gear that Kal's father would have described as "gently used."

"I love this," said Asha, twirling a small braid of fabric that draped down from her cap.

Kal felt a small pang of happiness and then a flash of embarrassment. They were trying to save Humanity, and he was smiling like an idiot because a girl liked her hat.

"Now that we're all snug, let's get down to business," said Corporal Sato. Since Sergeant Kimathi was back in Tiradentes, she was the ranking NCO and responsible for the mission on the ground. "Sir, anything we're looking for specifically?"

"Evidence of Nasi or rebel activity," Kal replied. "I don't want to head to the training area without seeing if anything's gone down here."

The corporal nodded and began barking out orders. Kal could tell she was overcompensating, trying to assert her authority rather than wearing it naturally around herself like a mantle. It was a trick that took a while for leaders to be comfortable with. Sergeant Jones had been a master and Sergeant Kimathi was rapidly approaching his level. Kal made a note to talk to Sato later about it.

Sato split them into pairs and assigned them areas to patrol. Kal grabbed Asha and told the corporal he'd go with her. He couldn't trust anyone else to take care of the girl. For her part, Asha seemed ecstatic to be paired up with him.

Conducting a recon in a large city like Tiradentes was simple. They could blend in with the crowds and hide among the normal traffic and bustle of city life. In Hope, that wasn't possible; they would stick out like a sore thumb wherever they went. Kal just wanted to quickly investigate and get to the Fridge.

The air grew warmer as the sun crested above the distant mountains. As he walked through the increasingly busy streets, Kal reexamined his initial impression of Hope. It had seemed dour and depressing at first. But with the light sparkling off the thin film of snow on the ground and the hum of common people going about their day, it now reminded him of the quaint towns he'd seen on holos, the kind that had only *really* existed on Earth.

Asha walked circles around him, stopping to examine everything in their path while spouting a nonending narrative.

"Dad never let me go out into the town. Always said I needed to stay out of sight. He would go in though. Sometimes it's just not fair."

Kal gave a hum of agreement.

"That store's sooo cool. What is it about mining equipment that's so interesting? I wanted to dig all the way to the center of the planet until I found out it wasn't possible. Still would be cool though. Maybe I'll figure out a way to do it."

Hope was a town built on mining. Minerals were the only thing in the frozen tundra around them. Kal had expected the citizens to be like the ones on Mariga, hard-faced and dirt-covered. Instead, they smiled as they walked past in their simple but immaculate work clothes. Occasionally someone would stop to compliment him on what an adorable daughter he had or wave at Asha, who'd shyly wave back.

"What's a constable?" Asha asked. She pointed at a small building made from ultracrete blocks.

"Our next destination."

Asha ran ahead, forcing Kal to shout for her to wait. He didn't want to alarm her, but who knew what the allegiances of the local security force were or what they'd been told. Kal doubted the Nasi knew they were there, but he couldn't guarantee it. A day ago, he would have said it was impossible to hack into a neural implant.

A young woman looked up from between long curtains of silver hair as Kal and Asha walked through the door. She had clearly been watching something on the console in front of her and quickly tapped on the screen to stop it.

"What do ya need?" asked the woman.

Kal had been furiously working out a cover story on his way inside the building.

"I'm looking for a friend," said Kal. "Well, not a friend, an acquaintance is more like it."

The clerk watched him coolly, waiting for him to continue.

"And, well, me and my daughter wanted to see if he's here."

"Name?"

"Me or the person I'm looking for?" Kal asked. He could

feel the heat rising in his face. Despite being the commander of a scout team, he was horrible at lying.

"Let's start with the person you're looking for." She tilted her head. "You're not from Hope, are ya?"

"No, just visiting," said Kal.

She laughed. "You thought you'd come see the sites? Maybe take in a show?"

"No." Kal felt a blush creep up his face. "We're visiting family. My friend's name is Ade Yang." It was the name of Kal's first small arms instructor.

The woman shook her head. "We got one person in detention, and his name's not Ade."

"What are we gonna do, Dad?" asked Asha as she pulled at his sleeve. "I know Uncle Ade is kinda crazy, but I can't believe he got mixed up with those people."

We are officially off script, thought Kal.

"Aren't you the cutest?" The woman gave Asha a concerned look, but Kal could see the hint of a smile behind it. "What happened to your uncle?"

"He got mixed up with some people. They were called the Freedom Army or something like that."

"People's Army?"

"Yeah," Asha smiled, "that's it. He got mixed up with them. Something about taking back our planet. Now's he's gone."

The woman's look of concern had turned genuine. She looked up at Kal. "What are you—"

The door slid open, letting in a blast of cold air and two

210

Nasi soldiers—a woman and a man. They held their daton rifles casually at their sides as they scanned the room. Kal couldn't help but feel a pang of envy as they glided up to the desk, their movements a perfect combination of power and grace.

"We're looking for collaborators," said the man without preamble. "Let us into the holding cell at once."

The clerk simply nodded and the door behind her slid open with a click. The man glided through the opening while the woman stood at a corner of the room, watching the three Humans carefully. Nasi had evolved from Humans, but sometimes it could be hard to tell from their features. Except for her lithe, powerful body, the woman could have passed as a Human if she applied a coat of makeup to cover her skin's violet hue.

"Why are you here?" asked the woman.

Kal tried to gently nudge Asha behind him. "We were just looking for a friend."

"He's not here," added the clerk quickly. "They were just leaving."

"Stay." The woman's tone left no room for argument.

Kal let his hand drift towards his waist, closer to his pistol. He'd learned a long time ago to always position it so he could fire without pulling it out when facing a Nasi. The accuracy was a bit off, but there was no way that he could outdraw them.

A minute later, the sound of several plasma bolts came from the holding cell, and the male Nasi strode back out.

"This one looks familiar," said the woman, motioning at Kal with her daton.

"We'll take him in then," replied the man.

"No," Asha screamed, running in front of Kal and outstretching her hands to block the Nasi.

Kal pressed his pistol's trigger stud while pushing Asha to the floor. The bolt miraculously hit the Nasi man in the center of his chest. The woman raised her daton and fired, but the bolt sizzled past Kal. She spun to the floor as a kinetic round hit her in the head, dead before she landed.

Kal turned around to find the clerk with a pistol raised, a small whiff of smoke still emanating from the barrel.

"You okay?" asked Kal. Her left arm ended in a charred stump from the Nasi blast. "We can get you help."

"Don't worry about it," said the woman. She raised her arm, revealing that it was a cybernetic augmentation—melted wires and tubes poked out from her elbow. "We've got to get out of here. What are you? TLF, Eastern Dawn, Darkside?"

"Samsara Fleet," Kal said.

The woman raised her eyebrows. "Really?"

Asha was curled in a ball, hands covering her face, whimpering softly. Kal bent down and gently touched her shoulder. "You okay, Asha? I know that was scary."

The girl sniffed. "I'm…I'm okay." She moved her hands from her face and looked at him with red-tinged eyes. "I've seen worse."

Kal helped the girl up, hoping what she said wasn't true. She was way too young to have seen worse than that.

"So it's true?" asked the clerk. "The fleet is here?"

"Not yet," said Kal, "but soon. The Nasi knew we were coming. We're looking to rally whatever remains of the resistance."

"Well, you're pretty much screwed then, spaceman." The clerk walked around the counter and to the door. "Let's get out of here before more arrive." She kicked the woman's body. "They always do."

Chapter Sixteen
Kal | Hope, New America

The woman—who went by name Cinder—rushed through the streets of Hope with Kal and Asha in tow, looking for the other Skulls. The town was small enough that they could find them by walking around, and Kal didn't dare use his implant to communicate.

They kept to the sides of the streets, quickly ducking into doors as they looked for the other members of their team. Kal kept expecting a squad of battle-suited Nasi soldiers to appear at any moment, but it was calm and no one seemed aware that a firefight had just occurred.

After they found the other four Skulls, Cinder led them to her apartment in a block-sized building on the edge of town. They barely fit in the cramped confines of the front room. As soon as the last person was in, Cinder slammed the door shut and wheeled around to look at Kal.

"Over a year of work, gone," she said accusingly. "We need to make this quick. Why are you here?"

"Did you know what was going on?" Kal asked.

"I knew *something* was happening," said the woman. "Field agents like me don't get to know the whole plan, just our small piece. I was told to operate as normal. When I joined the People's Army, they sent me here as their plant in Hope."

"Plant?" asked Private Chadha.

"Yeah, I stay here and keep an eye out on the town. Keep

my head down and watch comings and goings and the like. As I'm guessing you know, we've got a base nearby."

"A training area, right?" asked Kal.

She nodded. "Yeah, mainly. We occasionally run missions out of it, but there's not much up here. Which leads me back to my question, what are *you* doing here?"

Kal explained their mission and Samsara Fleet's imminent arrival in system. He kept it strictly need to know. Despite the holes in his story, Cinder didn't ask questions; she was experienced enough to understand that he wasn't going to tell her everything.

As Kal spoke, Cinder's face grew darker and darker until she dropped back in a chair and let out a deep groan as he finished. "Everything we've been working on, gone in a day."

"There may still be hope," said Kal.

"At least you're in the right town—Hope," said Cinder bitterly. "You actually think there may be TLF survivors in the area?"

"Yeah," said Kal.

"If what's you're saying is true, I can't believe it." Cinder sighed. "Though I haven't been up to the base in a few days. If there were any, they'd head there."

"Anything different with the Nasi activity?" asked Sato.

"Nothing out of the ordinary." Cinder pushed herself from the chair. "I'd love to chat more, but we need to get out of town. Soon as the Nasi find out what's happened, they'll come down *hard*. I can help you get to the training area."

"The Nasi have captured or destroyed several TLF bases,"

said Corporal Sato. "Going to that training site could be walking into the enemies' hands."

"I would've heard something if the Nasi had captured the base," said Cinder. "And trust me, it's not easy to find."

"Then can you take us there?" asked Kal.

Cinder nodded. "Give me one second." She walked into another room and returned a minute later with a small bag slung across her shoulder and gave a thumbs-up. "Ready to go, General."

Corporal Sato ducked his head out the door and then motioned for the rest of the team to follow. As they exited the apartment, they fanned out and headed toward their transport. Halfway through the town, Kal felt a tight squeeze on his hand and looked down to see Asha staring at something in the distance. It was a ship coasting gently over the mountains and heading straight toward the town. From this distance, Kal had no idea if it was friendly or not, but the twist in his gut meant he didn't want to find out.

He saw the others had noticed it as well and picked up their paces, practically running between locals toward the lot in the center of town. As Kal rounded a corner, he let out a small breath of relief as he saw the transport sitting among the other vehicles in the packed lot without a Nasi in sight.

With several grunts of surprise and muttered apologies, they climbed inside the cabin. With Cinder, they now had seven people to cram into the two rows of seats. Kanumba and Kal sat in front, with Asha wedged between them while the rest piled into the back seat.

"Make friends, everyone," Sato said.

The doors weren't even fully closed when Kanumba lifted off. As they made their way out of the small town, Kal scanned the skies, fruitlessly trying to locate the ship Asha had pointed out.

"See anything?" asked Cinder from the backseat.

"Nothing," Kal replied, "I don't know where it went. Anyone tell what kind of ship that was?"

"Nasi," said Kanumba. "One of their security craft. You can tell by the wings."

"There," shouted Asha, squeezing Kal's hand again. She pointed to their right. Sure enough, a Nasi patrol ship had landed near the edge of the town, and two soldiers in battle suits were stepping off the ramp.

"Don't do anything out of the ordinary," warned Cinder in a low voice. "We don't know they're here for us. The Nasi send patrollers out here to check up on us sometimes."

Kal hoped she was right but doubted it. He felt his heart beating in his chest as they continued through the town, keeping pace with traffic. Buildings blocked his view of the Nasi soldiers and their ship.

"Okay, now you can punch the accelerator," ordered Kal as they cleared the last building. "Get as much distance between us and that town as possible."

Kanumba obliged, and soon they were soaring over the barren polar landscape, kicking up a small trail of snow as they sped toward the distant mountains. Kal continued to glance backwards, looking for the Nasi or their ship, but he

217

didn't see anything leave Hope.

The flat tundra began to rise, and the light dusting of snow turned into a deep blanket that covered everything except for the brown and gray daggers of stone that jutted out from the hillsides around them. Cinder programmed a destination into the transport's nav computer and Kanumba followed the calculated path as it led upwards, winding through the valleys of the mountain range.

"The Fridge is built into the mountains," explained Cinder. "You're not going to be able to see it before we get there, but I know of a place where we can at least get a visual on it before we enter."

Kanumba followed Cinder's instructions as she guided them through the narrow ravines that winded and climbed up the mountainside. The bare stone walls were a relief, providing Kal with some sense of protection. It would be difficult for a Nasi ship to attack them while they were surrounded by the ice and stone of the mountains. The ravine they were flying through leveled off onto a small plateau that looked out over a network of crevices with sparkling blue glaciers draped across them.

"Everyone out," Kal said as Kanumba brought the transport to a stop.

It took a few moments for everyone in the back of the vehicle to untangle themselves. But after a few curses and apologies, all seven of them were crouched at the edge of the plateau. Mountains reached around them, their peaks lost in clouds. Below them, the ravines and glaciers twisted and doubled back, creating a seemingly endless maze of stone and ice. Kal could see several large birds, easily twice as large as a person, soaring above, looking for prey. He could only describe the scenery as breathtaking. He'd never seen anything like it even on Mariga, his ice-covered home world.

"Amazing," said Sato. "Just, amazing."

"See that?" Cinder pointed at the chasm directly beneath them. "That metal structure is the entrance."

It took Kal a moment to figure out what she was pointing at. A gray structure, no larger than a single-family home in Tiradentes, jutted out from the rocky wall below them.

"That's the entrance, the *only* entrance, to the Fridge."

"Chief, you got goggles?" asked Kal.

Kanumba nodded—he could always trust her to come prepared. She pulled them from a pocket in her loose cargo pants and put them on. After a few minutes of the chief humming softly to herself, she pulled the goggles off and handed them to Cinder, who had her arm outstretched.

"There's no sign of…anything really. No tracks or markings that would indicate anyone's been there for ages. No heat signatures either."

"Not surprising," said Cinder, looking through the goggles. "The winds come through the ravine and blow everything away. The good news is I don't see any signs of charring or attack on the entrance."

The hum of an engine sounded over the wind.

They dove to the ground as a Nasi assault ship crested over the hill behind them and flew directly over. The plasma bolts and hiss of missiles that Kal anticipated failed to materialize. Instead, the ship continued forward, sailing over the chasms and disappearing as it soared over the peak opposite them and dropped down the other side.

"Get back in the vehicle," Kal hissed.

They scrambled in a mad rush to the transport, piling in on top of each other. Kanumba had the vehicle turned around and was racing down the way they'd come before everyone was in their seat.

"Do you think they saw us?" asked Private Ma.

"Doubt it," said Cinder. "If they had, they would've engaged."

"Nasi assault ship sensors face outwards," added Kanumba. "There's a hole in their coverage directly below the ship. I think we just happened to be at the exact right location."

"Or else they want us to think that so we'll lead them to the base." Cinder's tone indicated which one she thought was true.

"All the more reason to get there quickly," said Kal. "You got a way in?"

"I do." The People's Army rebel tapped her head. "It's coded to my implant."

"Get us there as fast as possible," Kal said to Kanumba. She nodded and continued to navigate down the gravel-covered ravine. She pulled the yoke left, slamming the passengers into the side of the vehicle, then doubled back onto another branch, which headed back upwards.

"Get your elbow off my—" The rest of Private Chadha's statement was drowned out by the roar of the transport's thrusters as they rounded a corner.

After one more rise and a sharp turn, the Fridge's metal door was before them. As they approached, it slid open, triggered by Cinder's implant. Kal glanced around, searching for any Nasi watching them. All he could see was the blue sky above and the gray of the cliff faces surrounding them.

After they'd entered, the door slammed shut, surrounding them in darkness. Kanumba flicked on the headlights, illuminating an ice-lined tunnel that led downward through the rock. They traveled for several hundred meters and then began to ascend. The soft eerie light in front of them grew brighter until the tunnel abruptly ended, opening into an enormous room filled with a bluish glow.

"What *is* this place?" asked Sato.

"I told you, the Fridge," said Cinder. She leaned forward, eliciting a grunt from someone else in the back seat, and pointed to their right. "You can park there."

Kanumba brought the transport to rest, and the Skulls slowly crawled out, craning their heads to study the enormous chamber. The ceiling and many of the walls glowed in an uneven blue light. At first Kal had thought it was sunlight filtering through glacial ice, but as he looked closer, he realized it was something else instead. The light pulsed; it was coming from multiple slowly moving *things* in the ice. Small pieces of maintenance equipment and consoles were clustered together on the patchwork metal floor, dwarfed by the enormity of the room around them.

Asha smiled. "Isn't this place so cool?" she asked Kal. He nodded back to her with a forced smile and turned to Cinder.

"Did the People's Army build this place?"

"Yes and no," said Cinder with some pride. "We found it mostly like this. But we created the entrance and added a few touches."

"What's the light?" asked Corporal Sato, her mouth slightly open.

"Fish."

"Correct me if I'm wrong," said Kal. "But don't fish live in water?"

Cinder shrugged. "What's ice 'cept frozen water?"

Kal pushed aside the hundred other questions that popped to mind and walked toward the nearest cluster of consoles. The gigantic room amplified the sound of the Skulls' heavy boots tromping on the metal flooring.

"Where is everyone?" asked Kal. "Is it always this empty?" Had they come too late? Had the PA moved to another location or been killed?

"There was a lot more people and stuff here last time," said Asha.

"Asha's right; It's strange that there's no one out here," Cinder said. "This is the landing bay and training area. The command center, living quarters, and everything else is in a small series of caves over there." She pointed to a dark alcove. "If anyone was here, they should have come out by now though."

As if on cue, a figure, silhouetted by the light above, ran from the alcove. It was tall and slender, the movements graceful and fast. It wasn't Human. It was a Nasi.

"Get under cover," Kal shouted. He ran around the other side of the bank of consoles, dragging Asha with him and pulling his pistol from its holster.

"Asha! Asha!"

The girl managed to pull her hand from Kal's grasp and ran towards the Nasi. "Dad!"

They reached each other and the Nasi picked up the small girl, twirling her around as she giggled happily. His smiled broadly enough that Kal could see the light reflecting from his teeth from where he crouched.

"Hold fire," shouted Kal. *What the hell?*

Sato looked at him in astonishment. "Sir. Respectfully. What the—"

Asha shouted from the Nasi's arms, "Everyone, come meet my dad."

Chapter Seventeen
Nicole | Foyleton, Patagonia

Nicole studied the enormous dilapidated structure with crude graffiti scrawled on the side in front of them. They were clearly in one of the less than desirable neighborhoods of Foyleton. The buildings were run-down, their previously vibrant facades cracked and faded from years of neglect.

"Another commune. Of course," sneered Grupp as he looked at the building.

"We don't travel in your rarified circles, Sergeant Grupp," said Mother Ju with a condescending pat on the back. "We deal with the regular folk who do most of the workin' and livin' on the planet."

The rebel stepped away from the woman and looked at Nicole. "What're we doin' here anyways? How's this help us get back to the *Chester*?"

Nicole tried to keep the annoyance out of her voice. "We need to get her"—she motioned towards Zip—"somewhere where she can get help. Then we'll rejoin the *Chester*." Grupp was a good person and lord knew she needed him, but she didn't appreciate his condescending attitude towards Mother Ju and Zip. She'd still be living in a commune herself if it hadn't been for a few lucky breaks.

"They can handle it on their own," said the sergeant. "Zip's a tough girl; she'll be fine." He looked downward for a moment, uncertain.

"Well, you're right about that," said Ju with an

affectionate smile at the girl.

"The ship's not here yet and they won't leave for another two hours according to Deepta's schedule," said Nicole. "This is part of our mission. Getting the citizens in the commune on our side will be a help."

Grupp rolled his eyes but kept his mouth shut as they walked through the half-open door that served as an entrance to the building. Like every other commune, it was a maze of hallways and rooms created by inhabitants erecting barriers, breaking through walls, and adding rickety stairwells. The air was rank, a mixture of mold and body odor. Mother Ju led them through the building, passing by people huddled against the walls, until they reached a solid-looking metal door—one of the few they'd seen in the building.

An advanced security system of sensors and automated weapons surrounded the door. Ju pressed her large hand against a bioscanner, and the door cracked open with a small click.

"Momma Ju!" shouted a small man as they walked through.

"Scrapper!" Ju rushed over and enveloped the man in a bear hug.

The room was large and similar to where they'd first met Mother Ju. It had been carved out of the building by removing pieces of the walls and ceiling. Makeshift structures lined the perimeter and people sat about or milled around the area. Stars shined through the glass ceiling above their heads, giving the impression they were outside. It reminded Nicole of a small country village.

"What're you doin' here?" asked Scrapper, twirling his wiry mustache and looking them over.

"Desperate times call for desperate measures, my friend," said Ju. "You got some aid? The Nasi bastards got Zip." She motioned to the girl.

Scrapper's eyes widened when he saw the bandage around Zip's leg. "Medic, now!" he shouted behind his shoulder. Two people scrambled over and helped Zip to one of the shacks and set her down on a cot with Nicole and the others following behind. A balding man walked over and pulled off the bandage, inspecting the wound. He pulled a small device from a chipped cabinet in the corner and ran it over her leg. After a few minutes of inspection, he gave a satisfied nod. "It's not too bad. The cut was clean, and the bandage has already started the healing process. Give it a day or two and she'll be back to normal."

"Where'd you get an EDF bandage?" asked Scrapper. "That's expensive stuff right there."

Ju pointed at Nicole. "Courtesy of our new friend here. She's some sort of hoity-toity person with Samsara Fleet."

"Really?" Scrapper studied her for a moment. "I met a few of your people before. Runnin' around tryin' to save us all. Didn't care much about what we thought though."

"I'm from the communes on Earth," said Nicole. "I get it. I'm here to help."

"Here to help," Scrapper chuckled, shaking his head.

"The fleet's gonna try and take back Patagonia

tomorrow," said Ju. "They're lookin' for help."

Nicole noticed a few of the faces that had crowded around the shack looking at each other in the firelight. "Keeps gettin' more interestin'," said Scrapper. "Why do you need our help? You got battle suits, ships, and all that."

"The Nasi knew about our plan," said Nicole. "We're lookin' for every hand we can get." She explained how the Nasi had captured the Front bases and taken over the government. After she was done, Nicole braced herself for a barrage of questions and demands. She had her answers and protests ready in her head.

"I'll help," said Scrapper simply. "And I know more than a few others that will too."

Nicole just looked at him in surprise.

Mother Ju saw Nicole's expression and laughed. "That's why I brought you here. I knew ole' Scrapper would help. He's former EDF. What do they say? You can take the soldier outta the military, but you can't take the military outta the soldier?"

"If you're former EDF, why are you here?" Nicole asked. "Surely you should be on a pension or something."

Scrapper shook his head. "Nah, I got out a long time ago. Right after the Torgham War. Wish I'd stayed though." She could hear the regret in his voice. "Instead, I came back home and well, one thing led to another, and here I am. Seems like the EDF doesn't care too much about *former* soldiers." He cleared his throat. "But that doesn't matter anymore. I'll help. I can get you people, and I can get the word out."

"Thanks," Nicole didn't know what else to say. She'd

expected anything but immediate agreement.

"Gonna be tough getting to some of these places," observed Scrapper after Nicole had sent him the coordinates of the lances.

Nicole nodded in agreement. The Nasi plasma lances were either in the middle of nowhere or buried beneath the ocean in a network of caves. "The lances are in remote locations. There're ways to get to them though."

"You're gonna lose a lot of people before they even reach the sites." Scrapper rubbed his dark beard thoughtfully. "I know some people who owe me favors. We can help distract the Nasi."

"What do you mean?" asked Nicole.

"You might need to take out the plasma lances, but you'll also need help all over the planet," said Scrapper. "You'll need to pull as many of their forces away from the lances as you can. My people can do that."

Grupp patted the man on the back. "Thanks. Glad to hear some fellow Patagonians give a crap about the planet."

Mother Ju pushed the sergeant. "We *all* care. But I haven't heard you act like you give one crap about *us*. All I've heard out of your mouth is how people who live in the communes are lazy or greedy. The same people who saved your ass I might add."

Grupp's eyes flashed, and he raised his right arm for a moment before putting it back down. *Probably a good idea,* thought Nicole. Mother Ju did not seem like a woman to be messed with.

"We've still got to get back to our ship," said Nicole. "We got separated from the rest of our team in Chengdu."

"I can help you," said Zip, sitting up in the cot with surprising speed.

"Didn't you hear a word that the medic said?" asked Scrapper. "You need to rest."

Zip crossed her arms across her chest. "I found 'em. I'm gonna make sure they get back."

Mother Ju gently rested her hand on the girl's shoulder. "You need to stay in bed. Your leg may feel okay, but it's still healing."

"But—"

"No." Ju looked down at the girl, seeming more imposing than ever. "You'll stay and that's it."

"No worries, little one," said Scrapper soothingly. "I can take them." He smiled. "Besides, you don't know where you're going."

Zip screwed up her mouth and flopped back onto the cot.

Nicole checked her implant. According to Deepta's schedule, the *Chester* should be just outside the city, near the mountains to the west. She transmitted the coordinates to Scrapper. "Can you get us there?"

He nodded. "Let's go."

Walking through Foyleton with Scrapper was a completely different experience than when Karl Garcia had led them through the city over a year earlier. Garcia had grown up in a life of luxury—paid for by drugs and crime—but still luxury. Scrapper lived in the shadows and knew every back alley, sewer, and rooftop path. More than once, they were forced to duck down at the sight of distant Nasi patrols. But none of them noticed the four Humans scurrying above or below them.

They reached a small tarp-covered transport parked in a small alcove on one of the roofs. Scrapper yanked off the cloth and told them to jump in. Soon, they were zig-zagging through the city at a speed Nicole could only describe as "irresponsible." The combination of high speeds, winding roads, and eccentric buildings gave her the feeling she was in a simulator.

As they neared the edge of the city, the skyscrapers and narrow streets gave way to lower profile buildings—still in a mix of architectural styles—and wide vacant roads. The sun was rising on the horizon and the city was waking. Public transports floated above the roads, carrying workers, while cleaning drones patrolled the streets, washing away the dirt and debris from the previous day.

Scrapper set their vehicle down in a small passageway between two squat buildings at the very edge of the city proper. The rusty off-colored vehicle looked at home in the dirty, weed-choked passageway.

"We're close," said the man. Nicole checked her implant. He was right, they were no more than a few hundred meters from where the *Chester* should be.

The passageway led to a field of tall grasses that rippled in the gentle breezes. The distant mountains glowed orange from the rising sun. The picturesque scene was the stark opposite of the factories and run-down buildings Nicole saw when she turned to look back at the city. On colony planets, the line between the city and countryside was stark. Back on Earth, the cities had blended into the landscape around them due to millennia of Human expansion leaving no land untouched.

"Spread out," instructed Nicole. "You won't be able to see the ship. Hopefully, they'll see us though."

They got into a line, each a few meters apart, and walked through the shoulder-height grass. Nicole scanned the area, searching for any sign of an optical cloak but only saw the craggy foothills and waving grass.

A low-throated hum sounded from behind them, and Nicole barely had time to dive down before an assault ship passed only meters overhead. The ship's thruster wash parted the grass and sent dust and small pieces of dried plant into Nicole's eyes. She kept her body to the ground and tried to locate the ship with her blurred vision. She could hear it somewhere in front of her, moving to her left. It was searching. Whether for the *Chester* or them, she could not be sure. She looked to either side but couldn't see the others over the bent stalks of the grass. Thankfully, she didn't think the assault ship could see them either since she could hear it hovering in circles.

After a few seconds of waiting to hear the telltale hiss of

plasma or an explosion, Nicole picked up her head and raised the upper half of her body from the ground. She could see the steel gray assault ship in front of her. It was a model she'd never seen before, clearly only atmospheric with stubby wings and side doors that had been lifted open so the passengers could fire their weapons.

There was three, perhaps four, Nasi in the back. Their stick-like daton plasma rifles oriented outside the vehicle. She could tell they weren't in battle suits by their profiles. It meant her team had a chance if the *Chester* was nearby. A Human in a battle suit was more than a match for a Nasi without one.

Nicole barely had time to register the sounds of rockets before two explosions rocked the craft, sending it spiraling into the field. Two Humans in battle suits materialized fifty meters in front of them and flew upwards before dropping onto the wrecked Nasi ship. As they dropped, they fired into the ship with their kinetic machine guns.

"Get up!" Nicole shouted. She jumped up and was relieved to see the other three looking at her. "Get to the ship."

Nicole took off at a run toward where the Humans had appeared. She didn't spare a moment to look at the Nasi wreck as she ran. There was nothing she could do if the Nasi were still alive, and her comrades seemed to have the upper hand.

Nicole saw something move out of the corner of her eye and turned her head in time to see a Nasi's lithe body leap from the grass and tackle Mother Ju. Nicole stopped, shocked, then turned and started running towards where the woman had landed.

Grupp was already past her and dove toward where the woman had landed, a knife in his hand. She heard grunts of fighting and then stumbled into a writhing mass of Human and Nasi bodies. Grupp straddled a Nasi, stabbing down with his knife, which was already streaked with blood. Mother Ju lay to the side, a gash across her side.

With a grunt, Grupp fell to the side and lay on his back.

Nicole ran to Mother Ju's side and bent down to examine the injury. She had a hand-width gash on the side of her abdomen. The torn fabric was already stained red, and the stain was growing.

"It's okay," said Ju, waving away Nicole. "It's just a minor wound. The bastard missed by centimeters. There's some blood, but I doubt I'll even have a scar. Him on the other hand"—she pointed at Grupp—"he needs some help. That purple son of a bitch got a few good ones in before going down."

Nicole looked at Grupp and realized bloody roses were blossoming on his abdomen and thigh. She scurried over to him, conscious of the dying sounds of gunfire from the Nasi wreckage.

"Hero move, Grupp," said Nicole. She smiled and tried to keep the worry from her face.

He smiled back at her.

"And you saved a worthless commune dweller," added Mother Ju, placing her hand on his arm. There was genuine

233

warmth in the words.

"Don't remind...me," said Grupp, coughing slightly as he got the words out.

Nicole felt in the sergeant's pocket and found a bandage. She quickly pulled it apart, lifted up the Front rebel's blouse, and placed it on the wound. The wound wasn't big but it looked deep.

"Wasn't sure we'd see you again." The voice came from the battle suit behind them. It was Chief Ramos.

"Yeah, we had to take a detour," Nicole said. "Can you get him in the ship?"

"Sure." Ramos picked up Grupp. The delicate nature with which she was able to lift him was a testament to her skill with the suit.

Nicole offered a hand to Mother Ju, who just waved her away and pushed herself up. The woman looked up at Sergeant Grupp, cradled in the arms of Ramos' battle suit. "You're okay, Grupp. Ya know that?"

Grupp didn't have time to respond before Ramos lifted off and flew just above the grass toward the *Chester*, which had appeared before them.

"Never thought I'd see the day," Ju said, trudging next to Nicole. Nicole had to agree. She never ceased to be surprised by the choices people made—both good and bad.

Scrapper was already at the ship by the time they arrived. His previous well-groomed facial hair was plastered around his face, making it look like he'd sustained a jolt of high energy.

"Get in the ship," came Captain Uhaa's voice from an external speaker. "We've got incoming."

Nicole ran up the ramp with Scrapper and Ju beside her. It was already halfway closed by the time they stepped foot in the ship's cargo bay. Ramos stepped out of her armor and looked back at Nicole. "Can you get him attached to the medbot, ma'am?" she asked. "We've got more incoming. Looks like Deepta and the others are on their way as well."

Nicole nodded and rushed to the small compartment where the medbot was kept. Normally, she'd move Grupp onto a bunk but there wasn't time, and Scrapper and Ju didn't have a clue where anything was. She used the restraints that came with the bot to secure Grupp to the floor then attached the tubes and sensors from the machine to his body. If he wasn't too far gone, the nanobots and drugs in the machine would be able to repair the wounds. He was bleeding out fast though, and she didn't know if he'd be able to make it.

Nicole was knocked to the ground as the *Chester* took off and swung to the side. The enemy had found them, and they were in combat. There wasn't any attempt to hide the ship's location anymore.

"Ma'am," came Uhaa's voice over the intercom, "can you man the side gun?"

"Yes," Nicole shouted. As she ran towards the hull, a panel opened and a large fully automatic kinetic weapon dropped from a compartment in the ceiling and pointed outside the ship. Nicole slid onto the small bench affixed to the side of the weapon and scanned the area in front of her using the small screen on the weapon's trunk-like barrel.

A transport barreled down a gravel road, heading toward them while weaving around parked vehicles. She would've wagered her next paycheck—if she'd had one—that Deepta and the others were inside. On the tacmap, three red dots trailed closely behind the transport. Nicole could see the Nasi in full battle suits coasting over the tops of buildings, trying to catch up with the vehicle. From what she could tell, they would easily reach it before it reached the *Chester*.

She didn't wait. She pressed her finger on the firing square and sent a stream of metal at one of the Nasi. As soon as they dodged to the side, she went onto the next target, causing them to change direction as well. At this distance, her chances of killing them were slim to none; all she was trying to do was buy her friends time.

The *Chester* hovered above the grassy field and slowly headed toward the transport. It looked like all three of them—the *Chester*, the transport, and the Nasi—were going to meet up at the same point at the edge of the city.

The buildings provided decent cover for Deepta's transport, blocking the plasma fire and missiles from its Nasi pursuers. Nicole's cover fire helped as well, forcing the Nasi to dodge and preventing them from getting a good lock on the transport. She tried to anticipate their movements and led them as they got closer, hoping to score a lucky shot and take at least one of them down.

The *Chester's* plasma cannon joined in with Nicole, sending several volleys of greenish-blue fire at the attackers.

Nicole gave a small cheer as one of the Nasi dropped from the sky, their suit emitting a small gout of flame. They'd gotten at least one of them. However, the remaining two were getting perilously close to the speeding transport, and the buildings were about to run out.

The back ramp opened, causing the wash from the thrusters to whistle through the cargo area. As the transport reached the edge of the city, the *Chester* turned ninety degrees and dropped, allowing the vehicle to soar into the cargo hold. It launched up the ramp, bounced off the ceiling, and crashed into the far wall before coming to rest on the floor. A whiff of sulfur and metal filled the cabin as tendrils of smoke rose from the vehicle.

The *Chester* launched into the air as missiles pounded the hull. Thankfully, the battle-suit-launched projectiles were too small to pierce the armor of the advanced scout corvette.

Nicole jumped off her seat and stepped back as the gun retracted back into the ceiling and the opening in the hull slid shut. She had to grab onto a handhold to keep herself steady as they gained altitude and accelerated away from Foyleton.

Nicole looked at the smoking transport and felt a pang of fear as she realized Sergeant Grupp had been restrained against the floor of the cargo bay when it had come flying in. Somehow the vehicle had missed the sergeant—whether by going over or to the side Nicole couldn't be sure. He was still in one piece though, lying on the floor with the medbot next to him.

The orange transport's door opened, and Deepta stuck

her head out.

"How's that for an entrance?" she asked with a grin.

Chapter Eighteen
Nicole | Patagonia

After moving Sergeant Grupp to one of the staterooms and securing the transport, Nicole sat down with Chief Ramos and Deepta in the galley. As the adrenaline subsided, she realized she hadn't eaten anything in a day and grabbed a snack from the food fabricator.

"Glad to see you back," said Deepta as she took a large gulp of water. Her hair was piled in a nest on her head and her skin had the glow of someone who'd been sweating profusely.

Nicole nodded. "Thanks. I see you've been busy."

"I've been talking with some associates. It's good to see I still have *some* influence with people." Nicole wondered what people Deepta knew that would be awake or at least willing to talk to her in the middle of the night.

"We've made some friends as well." Nicole took a bite of her food. "Talked with several people in the communes."

"That's good. I never was able to make much headway with those folk. They're not the most trusting of outsiders."

"Can you blame them?"

"Never said I did." Deepta shrugged. "Still, it doesn't make it easy for me."

"Do you think the Nasi know what we're doing?" asked Chief Ramos.

"Oh, I'm sure of it," Nicole said. "When we assault those plasma lances, every single Nasi soldier on the planet will be waiting."

The chief digested her comment for a moment, her finger on her lips. "Are we sending these people to die?"

Nicole bit down some of the retorts that came to mind. It was a serious question, one that deserved a real answer. "Perhaps. But we're not *sending* anyone. Everyone on this planet knows exactly how deadly the Nasi are. We're giving them a chance to fight for once. A chance that they know can make a difference. Is it dangerous? Perhaps. But you know exactly how dangerous what we're doing is, and you're still here."

"Still. This'll be a bloodbath; we're counting on numbers to overwhelm superior firepower."

"Perhaps I can tip the scales a bit more," said Deepta. "We've still got enough time to make it to Kasongo before the assault. I've got connections there. *Good* connections. I might be able to get some things to even the odds."

"The Nasi ferreted out all of the civilian weapons caches a long time ago," said Nicole.

Deepta scoffed. "The ones they knew about. My associates have been hiding weapons for a long time, and I know they weren't discovered. Also, I know they're not exactly friends of the Nasi."

A year ago, before Nicole had spent a significant amount of time on Patagonia, she would have taken the last point for granted. Since then, she'd come to appreciate the attitude of people like Mother Ju who saw the Nasi as bad but not much worse than the Human government they had previously.

"We haven't got much time left," Nicole said doubtfully.

"There's still just enough," Deepta replied. "Trust me. This'll be worth it."

"The Nasi know what we're doing but don't know where we are," Ramos said. "We start going off mission and we're inviting trouble."

Nicole bit her lip as she considered Deepta's offer. The woman was right; they needed something more than just people. They needed the weapons to help them fight. "We're heading to Kasongo anyways, right?" she asked.

The two other women nodded.

"What's one more stop?"

Despite Ramos' assurances the Nasi didn't know where they were, Nicole felt a sense of dread when Captain Uhaa announced they were approaching the city. She'd spent most of the short flight next to Grupp and was pleased to see his vitals were improving. Mother Ju also spent the entire flight next to the sergeant, watching him quietly. Nicole wondered what was going through the woman's head as she stared at the man who represented everyone she'd loathed only days earlier.

The *Chester* touched down in an abandoned factory outside the city. Nicole would've liked to place it in a more remote spot, but they needed to be able to get in and out of the city quickly. Besides, there were only hours before the attack on the Nasi lances was to begin. Miraculously, the transport that Deepta had crashed into the cargo bay still ran, which saved them the trouble of finding a way to get around the city.

Although there was some worry that using the same vehicle they had in Foyleton might give them away, Nicole overrode any protest. There wasn't time to try and find another way around the city. Nicole drove while Deepta sat next to her, and Scrapper and Mother Ju whispered in increasingly loud tones to one another in the back seat.

The city was less chaotic than Nicole thought it would be. Whether it was because of the early morning or the Nasi crackdown, she didn't know. But she remembered there being many more transports and people on the streets even on the outskirts of the city. Now only automated utility transports flew past them, carrying finished goods and raw materials.

"Strange," said Deepta, echoing Nicole's own thoughts. "No one's around."

Nicole nodded and continued heading toward the rendezvous point Deepta had entered into the ship's nav computer. The argument between Scrapper and Mother Ju in the back seat reached a crescendo, and then there was silence.

"Fine," Scrapper said exasperatedly from the back seat. He slapped the back of Nicole's chair. "Mother Ju and I need to be dropped off. I'll give you the coordinates where you can let us out."

"There's something we need to do," added Mother Ju. "We're going for a long shot."

"What do you mean?" asked Nicole. "What long shot?"

"You'll find out if it works," replied Ju. "Besides, probably best if I don't tell you now. You ever heard of plausible deniability?"

"I'm familiar with the concept." Curiosity and annoyance battled in Nicole's head. Why was the woman being so damn cryptic? "But in this case, I'm not sure it applies."

"No one—Nasi or Human—is going to be thrilled with what we're planning."

"Which is why it's a bad idea," said Scrapper.

"I just sent a coordinate to the nav computer," Ju said. "Pretty please. Drop us off there."

"Fine," Nicole sighed. "At least it's on the way."

As they went farther into the center of the city, the relative uniformity of the warehouses and factories gave way to the eccentric architecture and winding streets that the city was known for. Buildings of almost every color and material jostled against streets that wound through them, snaking left and right then splitting and joining back together at random locations.

"Something happened," said Deepta, staring out the window. "They're all armed. Like very visibly armed."

Nicole studied the people on the sidewalks. The woman was right. Every person on the street had a pistol holstered to their side or a rifle slung across their shoulders. She also started to see signs of fighting—plasma marks on buildings, spent ammo boxes, and burned-out vehicles.

"There was a battle here," Nicole said, alarmed. "This all must have happened last night."

"The Nasi removed the government," Scrapper said. "I'm guessing some of the factions decided it was their chance to take control."

It hadn't been that long since Patagonia had been embroiled in a civil war caused by the Nasi invasion. It had been a brutal affair from everything Nicole had heard from Kal. Thanks to the Skulls, Foyleton had eventually emerged triumphant. It was sad for her to see how quickly the citizens had returned to violence with Karl Garcia no longer in power.

Nicole brought the transport to a gentle stop next to a large inverted pyramid that looked ready to fall over at any moment. Its shiny metallic surface mirrored the surrounding buildings, creating a disorienting effect.

Mother Ju and Scrapper stepped out of the vehicle and walked next to the driver's side window.

"We won't see you again until this is all over," said Ju. "Don't wait for us to get the hell out of the city. We'll see you later."

"Maybe," added Scrapper.

"You gotta have faith, man." Ju slapped the man gently on the back.

"I *don't* have faith. I have plans. That's what's kept me alive this long."

"I've got faith in you both," Nicole said.

A group of four people, dressed in black with green rags

tied around their arms, appeared at the corner of the building. Their rifles were out and pointed at the transport. Nicole hadn't seen them before, but it was clear by the way they were moving to encircle the vehicle that they were not there just to talk.

"Get out of here," Nicole ordered as she pulled her weapon from its holster. Deepta had also pulled her pistol free and lowered the passenger-side window. "We'll give you cover."

"Thanks." Ju and Scrapper moved behind the transport and began to back away

"In the name of the Nasi Protectorate, stop what you're doing," shouted the woman at the front of the group.

"Nasi Protectorate?" asked Deepta incredulously. "What a bunch of pricks."

"Back off," Nicole shouted in reply.

One of the vigilantes shot a plasma bolt that sailed above the vehicle, splashing against the side of the pyramid.

"Guess they're done talking," said Deepta.

"Good, 'cause so am I."

Nicole pressed the accelerator forward and fired through the open window at the group. Her shots hit the ground near the four Protectorate members, and they hastily jumped back to avoid the speeding transport. As Nicole spun the vehicle around, the attackers ran to the side of the building. Nicole pressed their advantage, speeding around the corner and stopping at the entrance to a narrow street filled with refuse containers. She hastily slammed on the reverse thrusters as she realized there was no way they could fit into the narrow passageway. As she backed up, several shots came from the alley, sailing past their vehicle.

"Well, they can't shoot worth a damn," said Nicole.

"Just point me toward them and keep in one place," ordered Deepta as she leaned out the passenger-side window with her pistol at the ready.

Nicole turned the vehicle so Deepta was facing the four attackers head on. A bolt sailed from behind a refuse bin, and Deepta almost instantly fired back, her bolt hitting a woman square in the chest. As another bolt hit the side of the transport, Deepta fired, hitting another Protectorate member in the upper torso. A few seconds later Deepta fired two bolts into the alley in quick succession, hitting two people in the back as they ran away. Nicole shuddered slightly; it was a cold-blooded move.

Deepta gave a satisfied grunt and turned to face the front of the vehicle. "Okay, let's move."

Nicole took off, still thinking about what she'd just seen. She considered herself a pretty good shot, but Deepta was on another level. Kal was the only person she knew with that level of accuracy, and he'd been a small arms instructor for years. But even he wouldn't have had the cold-blooded nonchalance that the woman sitting next to her had. Nicole had seen Deepta's face as she turned away from the alley after killing four people. Her expression had been...satisfied; Nicole could think of no other word than that.

Whatever else Deepta was, she was a killer.

❖

The plasma from the firefight had fatally damaged their transport. Nicole had hoped they could at least make it to the rendezvous location, but the vehicle sputtered to a stop less than a kilometer away.

"Guess we're walking," said Deepta as she pulled herself out of the cabin.

Nicole opened her door and stepped out of the vehicle, eying the passersby. The sight of a plasma-damaged transport stopping in the middle of the street didn't seem to faze them. "We'll need to keep an eye out." She wished Scrapper or Mother Ju was with them; they seemed to know every hidden nook and cranny on the planet.

As Nicole and Deepta strode along the sidewalk, the locals kept their heads down and hands close to their weapons. Thankfully they didn't see anyone with an armband. They did pass several more signs of fighting, including more than one hastily erected barricade. Whatever had occurred the previous night seemed to have blanketed the entire city. It left Nicole wondering how long it would be until violence broke out again. She just hoped that the fleet would arrive— and win—before it did.

"In here," whispered Deepta, pulling at Nicole's sleeve.

They entered a tall glass skyscraper that would have been normal on Earth or New America but was too conventional for Kasongo. It was built in what Nicole would have called the standard Human style. Cold and efficient, it was a mass of straight lines that seemed to signal dominance over the planet and buildings around it.

At the base of the tower was an enormous open entrance, easily big enough to fit three ships side by side. On the other side was an enormous open-air atrium with a smattering of people walking through. A large pane of standalone consoles faced the entrance. A clerk stood just behind them, watching nervously as the few people nearby interacted with the machines. He walked toward Nicole and Deepta as they stepped to the bank of consoles with an uneasy smile.

"We got it," Deepta said with a raised hand and a tone that left no room for discussion. "No need."

The kid closed his mouth and stepped back as she sauntered to one of the screens. After a few swipes and taps, a door opened in the bank of lifts behind the consoles and Nicole followed the woman into a glass-lined car. A couple of hundred floors later, the doors opened, revealing a brightly lit reception area. A woman sat behind a semicircular desk and looked up with a smile as they approached.

"You're new here," stated Deepta. "Tell your boss Whisper's here to see him."

The receptionist's eyes opened in surprise and then she squared her shoulders as if preparing to do battle. "Mr. Matisse is very busy, ma'am. I can't disturb him right now. However, I can take—"

Deepta slammed a hand down on the desk, causing the woman to jump. "If you don't disturb him, I will. He *will* see me, and if you don't get him right now, this *will* be your last day."

"Fine." The woman's perfunctory smile had been wiped from her face. Her lips moved slightly, and her eyes grew distant as she spoke to someone through her implant. Nicole noticed her eyebrows twitch in surprise; she clearly hadn't expected whatever answer she'd received. The secretary motioned to the door behind her. "Please enter."

Deepta brushed past the desk and through the now unlocked glass door. Nicole had to jog slightly to keep up with the woman as she paced down the wood-paneled hallway. She was starting to think they were lost when a deep voice boomed from behind them.

"Whisper!"

Nicole turned around to see a large man dressed in slacks and a formal shirt. His fine clothes couldn't hide his enormous bulk or the tattoos that ran across his face, slightly reminiscent of the Nasi Shishen tattoos. The man wasn't tall, but he was wide and looked to be almost completely muscle. As he approached, Nicole did a double take. His eyes were a solid shade of black.

"We've got to talk," said Deepta.

"Always cutting to the chase." The man grinned. "That's what we always liked about you. Follow me."

He led them into a large office with floor-to-ceiling windows covering one wall and sat down in the large formfitting chair behind an enormous desk. After quickly inspecting the room—a habit she'd learned in the past year—

Nicole sat in one of the chairs across from him while Deepta idly walked near the windows, looking at the city beneath.

"Nice digs, *Matisse*," said Deepta as she her hand slid along the window with a small squeak.

"I can see about getting you an office," the man said. When Deepta didn't respond, he continued to speak. "I'm honored you've been keeping up with us. We knew you didn't *really* die, but it's nice to know you care enough to keep track."

"I thought about sending a note on Discovery Day," Deepta said lightly. "But with how you're always changing your location it *almost* seemed like you didn't want to be found." She wheeled around to face the man. "But you know how I *always* keep track of my friends."

"Probably for the best." Matisse folded his hands on the desk. "Why are you here?"

"I've got a deal for you. A big one."

"I thought we were done making deals."

Deepta pressed her lips together. "So did I. But things change."

"Listening."

"I want everything you have. Every single piece of equipment. All of it delivered to six specific locations across the planet. And I want operators there with it, ready to teach people how to use it."

Matisse exhaled and shook his head. "That's a big ask. A *huge* one. What do we get out of this deal?"

"The chance to keep operating."

"Not like you to come at me with threats, Whisper." Matisse seemed disappointed. "You used to be more subtle. Besides, it's a completely useless one at that. What you're asking will take everything our organization has. It'll wipe us out for years. Decades maybe." He stood up and circled around the desk. "It's always nice to revisit the past. But sometimes, it may be better to leave it buried."

Deepta rushed over and stood in front of the man—who topped her by at least a head. "This is no idle threat. The fact that I'm here should tell you that. I was gone. Out." She pushed the man's chest with a finger. "Samsara Fleet is inbound and you're going to help them out. They've got the people, but they need more weapons. Weapons that can kill Nasi. You're the only game in town with the Alliance gone."

Matisse stood still, Deepta's finger still planted in his chest, and looked down at her. "You know we're not some sort of humanitarian organization. And frankly, I'm not too pleased with your tone. You come at me with threats." He delicately grabbed her finger and pushed it down. "Very unprofessional."

"You know I'm no longer a professional. I'm retired, baby." Deepta smiled.

"Then take up golf," Matisse said with an edge of annoyance. "And get out of my office and my building."

"How long can you last if the Nasi controls the galaxy?" asked Nicole. "What happens when they discover you?"

"The UEG didn't find us in centuries," said Matisse. "And the Nasi won't find us either."

251

"*Yet,*" said Nicole. "But they found the Alliance and almost wiped them out. How lucky do you think you can be?"

"Luck doesn't have a part in it."

"Someone's gonna make a mistake, Matisse," said Deepta. "You know it. The Nasi are gonna capture the wrong person and then your whole organization will go down. They can't be bribed like Humans."

Nicole wasn't so sure that was true anymore. But she wasn't about to correct Deepta when she was on a roll.

"And I'm guessing that if I don't help you now, you'll provide the information to them." Matisse arched an eyebrow.

"Look," Deepta held out her hands, "I don't want to threaten you. I respect you and the Organization. We've always had a good relationship. But this is beyond you and me. I mean, in the end, you're Human too." She paused. "You are, right?"

"Close enough." A smile cracked Matisse's chiseled face. "Fine. I'll look into it. You should know enough to understand this isn't a decision I can make on my own. Give me the locations and I'll see what I can do."

"We don't have much time," said Nicole.

"And remember. If you betray us, I have safeguards in place to make sure the information I know gets into the right hands." Deepta stood up. "It's not a threat, just a promise."

"You and your promises, Whisper." Matisse chuckled, but his eyes remained as dark as night.

Chapter Nineteen
Kal | The Fridge, New America

Kal eyed the Nasi sitting across from him. This wasn't some worker; it was an officer. Sinuous black tattoos—the Nasi Shishen—wrapped themselves around every centimeter of his body. For the Nasi, they were a symbol of rank. Kal knew enough to estimate the Nasi sitting across from him was their equivalent of a colonel or general in Samsara Fleet—high up there. His imperious face and sharp features reminded Kal of a bird of prey. The effect was spoiled by the bright smile and beaming eyes looking down on Asha, who sat in his lap.

After a confusing but heartwarming reunion between Yonder and Asha, the Nasi led them through a small cluster of naturally occurring caverns to the base's living quarters. Bunk beds lined the walls with a mishmash of furniture in the center. Although functional, it was a spartan environment with a sheet serving as the door and a single string of lights hung from the ceiling providing the only light.

"*He's* your father?" asked Kal, looking at Asha.

She screwed up her mouth. "Well, not really. But he's the closest thing I've ever had." She noticed Kal's expression. "I'm sorry I didn't tell you before. But I knew if I did, you wouldn't understand. Yonder saved me."

The Nasi looked at Kal earnestly. "My unit found her hiding when we were on a raid. I…I just couldn't leave her."

"What did you do to everyone here?" asked Cinder, her

voice almost frantic. Kal remembered the first time he'd been forced to view the Nasi as people rather than monsters. It was a hard adjustment.

"I didn't do anything to them," said Yonder. "When I found out the Nasi were looking for this base, I came here to warn them. They were already gone though."

"He's one of them," said Asha proudly. "He's a member of the People's Army."

"A high-ranking Nasi is a member of the People's Army?" Kal asked in disbelief.

"Asha helped me gain clarity," explained Yonder. "I had believed everything I'd been told when I first came here. Seeing her so alone and frightened…it changed things." He gave the girl's hand a squeeze. "At first, I just wanted to help her. But then I realized that the only way to help her and to realize the vision that we—the Nasi—had, was to fight against Grand Ancient Baykara."

"You spied for the People's Army?" asked Kal.

Yonder nodded. "Yes. And the TLF. Until I was found out a few days ago. I barely escaped the soldiers sent to kill me."

"Then you went to the TLF's base in Tiradentes?"

"And I found it empty. But the Nasi were still looking for me. So I left a message for Asha and came here."

"You're the only one here?" asked Corporal Sato.

"I am. The others left to attack the nearby plasma lance."

"Which explains why it's so empty," said Asha, clapping her hands together as if solving a mystery.

"Why would they do that?" asked Kal. "How do they even

know about it?" The location of the lances was a closely held secret.

"I don't always understand why you Humans do what you do," said Yonder regretfully. "My guess is because it was something they *could* do. I've found Humans love the illusion of control. When faced with a problem, you choose to do something—anything—rather than face the idea that some things can't be changed."

"I don't like this at all," said Cinder, her eyes still locked on the Nasi.

"Those people are walking into a trap," said Kal. "The Nasi are *expecting* an attack."

"I told them this," said Yonder. "They didn't listen. Although they've given me access to their bases, they still don't fully trust me."

"Fancy that," Cinder snarled. "I mean, why are they so close-minded?"

"I realize *why*," Yonder said. "But it still means a full company—some two-hundred soldiers—just left to an almost certain doom."

"Do you know what the Nasi are doing to the lances?" asked Kal.

"The lances weren't my responsibility. I only know that my unit had been told to expect a Samsara Fleet attack. That's when I found out the command knew of the Fridge and tried to warn them."

"And that's how you got caught," Kal finished.

Yonder nodded gravely.

"How long since they left?" asked Cinder.

"An hour perhaps," said Yonder.

Kal pulled up the battle plan in his implant. Which lance would this unit have attacked? The plans detailed where the Samsara Fleet assault teams would attack but didn't provide any information on where the various rebel factions would.

"You know where they went?" Kal asked.

Yonder pulled out a tablet. Its screen consisted of small particles, almost like grains of sand, which moved and changed color as he tapped on its surface. The screen morphed and extended out into a three-dimensional representation of the area.

Yonder tapped on a large mountain that rose from the center of the screen. "Here," he said. "Not far from where we are."

Kal cross-referenced the location with the map in his implant. It was about an hour flight from their location.

"Are there any tactical vehicles left?" asked Kal. "Or did they take all of them?"

"There's one left," Yonder said.

"Then let's go. We need to get to them before the Nasi do."

Kal could understand why the People's Army had left the run-down ship. It was old even for the relatively lax standards of the PA, predating even Kal's military career. Chief

Kanumba had looked over the assault ship and declared it barely able to fly. "Barely able" was enough for Kal.

He was grateful that at least the ship's interior was clean. Two pilot's chairs were at the front with several rows for passengers behind them. Kanumba and Cinder took the front chairs and began to spin up the engines while Kal and the rest of the Skulls buckled themselves into the passengers' seats.

Kal had wanted Asha to stay at the Fridge, but both she and Yonder had refused. He tried to ignore a small pang of jealousy as she plopped down next to her father and grabbed his hand. After he'd gotten her restraints on, the girl leaned into him and whispered insistently. Yonder looked at her fondly, a smile playing at his lips as he listened.

"How do we get out of here?" asked Kal once Kanumba had powered on the creaky old ship. "There's no way we're fitting through the tunnel we came in through." There was no obvious way for the ship to exit, and there were Nasi patrols in the area looking for the base. Kal imagined them trying to save the People's Army only to lead the Nasi right to them.

"There's another entrance for ships," explained Cinder. She pressed one of the buttons on the pilot's console, and the metal floor in front of them split apart, revealing a square-shaped hole big enough for the ship to fit through.

"We've got to go through there?" asked Corporal Sato nervously.

Cinder nodded. "Yup. It's a bit tricky to navigate, but is completely invisible from the air."

Kanumba grumbled as she inched them forward and then

lowered the ship into the shaft. Proximity alarms blared as they followed the exit tunnel down and away from the cavern. A metal door beneath them dilated open, and they exited the underside of an outcropping of rock and dropped into a ravine. Kanumba followed it away from the mountains and any potential Nasi observers. As the ravine grew shallower, she pulled up the nose of the ship, and they coasted over the peaks that dotted New America's pole.

"They were going to land here"—Yonder pointed to the tacmap—"and then move ahead. I estimate it's about forty-five minutes between the landing zone and the objective."

"Can we reach out to them via neural net?" asked Kal. It'd be nice if they could just call the assault team and tell them to turn around. He turned to Cinder. "You have access to their net, right?"

She shook her head. "No. They go radio silent when they go out on a mission. Maybe their assault ships can reach them."

With Yonder's help, Kanumba found the People's Army landing site on a plateau that jutted out over an enormous canyon. She brought the ship down at the edge of the formation of ships. They were an eclectic mix of surplus military vessels, merchant ships, and even a few barges.

As soon as their ship had touched down, the Skulls were out and establishing a perimeter. The plateau would have given them great fields of fire if it hadn't been for the mass of ships blocking their view of the canyon.

"Check out the area," Kal ordered. "They're not

responding to any calls." He tried to hail anyone in the area with his neural implant again, but there still was no response.

The Skulls fanned out to inspect the ships, looking for any sign of pilots left behind. After a few minutes, Corporal Sato made her way back to Kal.

"They sent everyone out on the mission," reported the corporal.

"Not a wise move," said Kal. "They've got no air support or backup plan." He noticed that Yonder nodded in agreement.

"We need to reach them before they enter the mountain," said Sato. "If they go inside, there's no way for us to reach them."

The Nasi plasma lances were underground, which protected them from orbital attack and allowed them to use geothermal energy. The land above the weapon didn't matter since the beam vaporized anything from water to solid rock. The Nasi had a small city's worth of personnel in each lance compound so they could protect and maintain the weapon indefinitely. Any patrol that went into the caves unprepared would almost certainly never get close to making it out.

"This is about as close as we can get by ship without tipping them off," warned Chief Kanumba.

Kal turned to Yonder. "Can you run ahead and try and catch up with the PA fighters? You're a helluva lot faster than us."

"No," Asha shouted, wrapping herself around the Nasi's leg. "We're not splitting up. I'm staying with him."

"You're stayin' with the ship, Pea," Yonder said gently as he gently patted the girl's head. "You're what's important to me. Anything happens to you, and I'll die. Besides, Kal is right. I'm the only one who can reach our friends in time."

"I don't want to lose you again." Asha sniffled.

"I know it may be hard to understand right now, but this is something I have to do." Yonder continued to slowly pet the girl's head as he peeled her from his leg. "I used to think the only thing that mattered was the outcome, what happens at the end. Now I've come to realize how you get there matters even more." He pulled the girl close. "You taught me that. Now I have to do the right thing even if it means putting myself at risk. You understand?"

Asha nodded glumly and buried herself into the Nasi's lanky body, turning her head so that all Kal could see was her golden mane of hair. He felt another surge of jealousy rise in his chest and tamped it down.

"Go," Kal mouthed to the Nasi.

Yonder bent down and gave Asha a final hug then turned and sprinted in the direction of the entrance to the Nasi plasma lance. In a second, he was gone.

"Let's follow," Corporal Sato said.

Asha started to break out in a run and Kal jumped forward, barely catching her by the shirt. "You're staying here, Asha. Chief Kanumba will stay by the ship, and she'll need someone as a copilot."

"But, Kal, Yonder needs me." Tears streamed down Asha's cheeks. Kal felt a surge of sorrow and jealousy as he remembered his two children, now long dead.

"He needs you to stay here, safe, where he won't worry about you." Kal felt a spike of physical pain as he stared at her wide blue eyes. "So do I."

She watched him for a moment without moving and then finally nodded and wordlessly walked back to the ship and climbed inside.

"We're not going radio silent," Kal said to Kanumba, breaking the silence. "If something happens, let us know."

"Good luck, sir." Kanumba gave a loose salute.

"Thanks." Kal turned to Sato. "Lead the way."

Corporal Sato led them toward the entrance to the Nasi plasma lance at a brisk jog. The ground was uneven and scattered with stones, forcing Kal to look down so he didn't sprain an ankle. The wind, which had roared through the area earlier, had died down. The only sound was the rhythmic crunching of their steps as they made their way through the terrain.

Kal wondered what they'd find when they arrived at the entrance to the plasma lance. Would there just be the bodies of the People's Army cut down by the Nasi? Perhaps there would be nothing. Hopefully, Yonder would catch up with them before they reached the site. If he didn't, then the Tac-I team would be forced to turn around; entering would be a pointless act of suicide.

Yonder appeared at a bend in front of them as if out of nowhere. Somehow his steps barely made a noise against the loose stone.

"I reached the assault team," the Nasi said. "They're on the way back."

"Excellent." Kal felt relief wash over him. He turned to Corporal Sato. "Let's hold here and we'll return to the ships with them." They might actually get out of this situation alive.

The Skulls took positions against the side of the canyon and waited with their weapons drawn. It wasn't long before the first rebels appeared. A column of fighters followed close behind, armed with a hodgepodge of weapons: rifles, pistols, rocket launchers, and even a few plasma blades. As he watched them trudge towards his position, not even watching the tops of the canyon for ambush, Kal shuddered to think what would have happened if they'd managed to reach the Nasi base.

"Hey," Kal called out. He remained under cover in case a spooked PA fighter let off a round.

"General Norman, is that you?" asked a voice from the column.

Kal stood up and walked to the front of the column. "Yes, it's me."

A man, wearing an assortment of military and police issued body armor and carrying a decades-old plasma rifle walked towards Kal. A gray armband indicating his rank—first lieutenant—was wrapped around his left arm. "The Nasi told us you had ordered us to head back based on new intel," said the lieutenant, clearly disappointed.

"You were walking into a trap. They've done something to the plasma lances."

"But the fleet is coming," said the PA officer. "We—"

A rocket shot through the canyon and exploded against the wall, showering the people underneath with shrapnel. Cries echoed through the area and the PA soldiers frantically ran to find cover.

Kanumba, we've got company, Kal shouted through his implant. Get your ass over here now.

The PA soldiers were scrambling across the rocks and boulders, still trying to find a place to take cover. Kal ran to the side of canyon and crouched behind a boulder next to Private Chadha. The young private had his weapon out and took calm, measured breaths as he surveilled the situation. Kal couldn't help noticing the difference between the deliberate actions of the well-trained Tac-I soldier and the chaotic return fire from the People's Army.

"Get behind cover," the lieutenant shouted from the small depression in the center of the canyon where he'd dove. Kal wished the young officer would follow his own orders.

Four Nasi in full battle suits appeared in the air at the end of the canyon, flying low and slow over the hardscrabble ground, their heads swiveling as they studied the area. They reminded Kal of the birds of prey he'd seen earlier. They weren't concerned with being attacked; they were the hunters.

A sudden flurry of small antipersonnel missiles launched

from each of their suits, striking the top of the canyon walls. The explosions tore pieces of rock, some as large as a person, from the canyon and sent them raining down on the Humans underneath. Kal gasped as several rock shards stabbed into his back. A group of PA fighters, shaken by the onslaught, stood and ran from their positions. The Nasi unleashed a barrage of well-placed plasma fire, cutting them down before they were able to take more than a couple of steps.

The Nasi continued to float down the gorge and methodically fire at the exposed Humans. The PA fighters fired back, but their small arms couldn't pierce the energy shields and armor of the battle suits. The Skulls knew well enough to not even try.

"Sir!" Chadha pointed to a body, not more than a few meters from their location. A missile launcher was still clutched in the dead woman's hands.

"I'll distract them. You get the launcher," said Kal. "Don't miss!"

Kal noticed the Nasi were moving laterally away from his and Chadha's position and were focusing on the far side of the canyon. He grabbed his only grenade from his pants, primed it for a proximity detonation, then stood and sprinted across the ground, hurtling over a fallen PA fighter. As he ran, he threw the grenade with his cybernetic right arm, launching it across the canyon toward the Nasi. They turned and fired back at him, their rounds seeming to hit hitting the ground around his feet.

The grenade exploded in front of one of the Nasi, sending

them backwards several meters. The blast distracted the other Nasi, and the plasma fire died down long enough for Kal to make it behind cover. He took a deep gulp. Somehow, he was still alive. The question was, for how long. He stole a glance back into the canyon and ducked as plasma bolts saturated his position. Well, he'd definitely gotten their attention.

Kal didn't dare to look again; the Nasi knew where he was and any attempt to run or fire on them would almost certainly mean his death. Instead, he leaned back against the boulder and waited for them to come. They'd already be moving to encircle his position, and once in position, one of them would attack from above.

He heard the hiss of a rocket at the same time it exploded impossibly close to him. A Nasi battle suit flew over the boulder and crashed to the ground in front of him. The bottom half of the armor was gone, torn off by the force of the explosion. Chadha hadn't missed.

The sound of a fresh burst of plasma fire came from the other side of the boulder. The Nasi were firing without stopping. They were angry or maybe even scared. Not a response they would have had a year ago, but the Human's universe had changed them. Kal peeked into the clearing and saw the three remaining Nasi soldiers, hovering in a line, training their fire on what he guessed was Chadha's position.

There was no warning when the Skull's ancient assault ship barreled through the canyon and slammed into the line of Nasi, tossing them against the canyon walls like dolls, and continued out of sight. The remaining PA soldiers scrambled from their positions and encircled the unmoving Nasi, shooting with everything they had.

The ship returned moments later, a small whiff of smoke trailing from its front, and came to a stuttering rest on the canyon floor. The pilot's door slid open, and Kanumba leaned out and looked around for a few seconds before finding Kal.

"Let's go," the chief shouted.

Kal ran to the ship but was cut off by a crowd of PA soldiers trying to clamber into the back as well. They reached the door and began pushing and pulling at each other to enter the craft. Kal shouted for the fighters to calm down, but his words were lost or ignored by the men and women desperate to escape.

I thought these people were supposed to be trained, Kal thought to himself.

He pointed his plasma pistol at the side of the ship and shot a bolt at the lowest setting. It had the intended effect; the crowd instantly dove to the ground, allowing Kal to rush forward and block the door.

"Pilots only," Kal shouted. "There's not enough room for everyone. They'll come back with the ships and pick us up. The rest of you get back under cover."

An angry hum met his words, but Kal stood firm, and the other Skulls joined him in blocking the frightened PA rebels. There was a painful minute of arguing between the soldiers as to who was a pilot or not—a fight even broke out, which Kal had to stop with another shot above the assailants' heads— but they were able to fill the back and lift off, heading back to retrieve the other ships.

After they'd left, Kal ordered the PA fighters back to their positions and told them to be ready. He could only imagine what the Nasi would attack with next. Orbital fire was not out of the question.

"I hate this so much, sir," confided Corporal Sato.

Kal knew she meant. It was excruciating to be a sitting duck. Even worse was the feeling that they couldn't count on any of the PA fighters around them.

The wait was tense but thankfully uneventful. The small fleet of People's Army ships arrived led by the Skulls' battered assault ship.

Kal got up from his position and began to jog towards the cluster of ships as they touched down on the canyon floor. One of them exploded in a ball of flame and metal, throwing him back. Another ship on the far side of the formation exploded a second later, sending a cluster of nearby PA fighters to the ground. Four more Nasi dropped from the edge of the canyon, missiles and plasma fire streaming from their pitch-black suits. Screams rang through the area as men and women rushed to the ships or writhed on the ground, wounded by the blasts.

Compartmentalize, Kal said slowly to himself. It's time to work.

Kal blocked out the screams and images of death around him and stood up. Needles of pain stabbed his torso, evidence that shrapnel from the blast had hit him. The other Skulls had taken positions near him, and they ran together toward their ship, which Kanumba was moving towards them.

"Help."

The word had been shouted, but Kal had barely registered it. He looked down to find the People's Army lieutenant that he'd talked to minutes before. The man's arm was gone, and his face fixed in an expression of pain. Kal motioned for the others to keep going and picked the man up, putting his remaining arm around his shoulder.

"I'll get him," Yonder said, appearing next to Kal. The Nasi lifted the wounded man and cradled him like a child as he bounded toward the ship.

Explosions and weapons fire continued to fly across the area. To their credit, the PA fighters didn't give up. They covered each other and fired back at the Nasi with whatever weapons they had. It was a losing battle though; several more ships exploded from the Nasi onslaught. By the time Kal reached the Skulls' assault ship, over half the small fleet had been destroyed.

"Let's go," Kal shouted as he jumped through the ship's rear door. When his body hit the metal deck, they were already shooting upwards out of the canyon.

Chapter Twenty
Kal | New America

Only three ships and twenty-three people, not including the Skulls, survived the Nasi ambush. Worse than that, they still had no idea what the Nasi had done to the plasma lances. The loss had been because of overconfidence and lack of training on the People's Army's part, not on any significant change in Nasi tactics.

There was nowhere to go except the Fridge. Kal had concerns they might lead the Nasi back to the base, but with the amount and severity of injured, there was no other choice. They desperately needed medical supplies and a place to regroup.

They landed inside the enormous main cavern, and Yonder sprinted to retrieve medical supplies from the back area. Unfortunately, the base didn't have a medbot; the medicated bandages would be the best they could do.

The other two ships arrived shortly after, and a stream of wounded fighters trailed out and fell to the ground exhausted. The least injured ones circulated through the crowd applying bandages and what little medicine they had.

Asha watched the entire procession without word, her eyes wide and mouth slightly open. Chief Kanumba had made her sit in the far back of the assault ship, so Kal wasn't sure how much she'd actually seen of the battle. He wondered what this would do to her. How could a child recover from the sights that she'd seen? Could he do anything to protect her from it? Take her away from it? It would mean leaving her with strangers or on the street, something he couldn't imagine doing and something he doubted Yonder would accept either.

The People's Army officer, First Lieutenant Evan Tetlow, hobbled through his wounded fighters and provided reassuring words. Kal admired the man for his good intentions though not for the execution of them. After he'd given the lieutenant a chance to see to his fighters, Kal pulled him aside.

"Tough loss, today," Kal said, placing a hand on Tetlow's shoulder. A loss that could have been prevented if the man had listened to the intel Yonder was giving him. But Kal wasn't about to assign blame then. Not with almost all the young officer's soldiers gone.

Tetlow looked past Kal, his face vacant. "I was a fool. I should've listened to Yonder."

"Why didn't you?"

"Honestly, I don't know… For one, he's a Nasi." Tetlow shuffled his feet. "And the fleet is on its way and heading into a trap. There's not much time."

If you knew there was a trap, why did you rush in? Kal bit the question off and regarded Tetlow coolly. The man was at the edge of breaking. It was a place that Kal was very familiar with; he lived at that edge.

"Have you heard from any of the other People's Army bases? Any of the other rebel factions?"

"The TLF is almost completely decimated," said Tetlow,

shaking his head sadly. "They were the worst hit. The other factions took losses of some sort or another, but they're mostly still operational."

"I haven't been able to get a hold of any of the other Samsara Fleet assault teams," said Kal. "Our net has been compromised by the Nasi."

Tetlow looked at him askance. "Compromised? I didn't think that was possible."

"I didn't either, but they figured out a way." Kimathi's description of the severed head popped into Kal's mind, causing him to shudder slightly.

"What do we do?" Tetlow asked, looking past Kal at the wounded laying on the metal floor.

"We build a new force with whatever we can find. Half my team is working on contacting our allies around the planet, and we need to rejoin them. Can your soldiers find the other factions and have them come here?"

Kal established a new neural link between himself and the commander, allowing them to communicate over the planetary net without the Nasi intercepting the comms. With the new encryption keys Kal generated for the direct link, no one except him and Tetlow could decrypt the traffic.

"We're gathering our forces for a final assault and need to get whatever's left out there. Have them meet us back here at the Fridge."

Tetlow looked at his fighters and then back at Kal. "I don't know. My soldiers have been through a meat grinder."

Kal nodded. "True. But this is what we're here for. It's

what you're all fighting for. This war isn't going to be won by valiant assaults. It's going to be won by men and women getting knocked down, time and time again, dusting themselves off, and continuing with the mission."

"You're a lot more optimistic than I am." Tetlow shifted on his feet.

"Not optimistic, realistic. There's no glory to be had. It's a grind. I've lost almost every person I care about. But my team and I keep going out and accomplishing our missions. No matter the cost. No matter how we're feeling." *And the cost has been almost too much to bear*, Kal thought to himself.

The PA commander turned and looked Kal in the eyes. Whatever he'd been about to say died on his lips. Instead, he took a deep gulp. "Okay, we're in."

"You've got two days," said Kal. "Then we'll meet back here. Hopefully we'll know exactly what trap the Nasi have laid for us inside their plasma lances."

"And if we don't?"

"Then we still attack."

The trip back to Tiradentes was as uneventful as their trip from it. The Tac-I team kept to themselves, looking out the windows as the late afternoon sun dropped beneath the horizon. Both of New America's moons were in the sky, and their glow illuminated the large swathes of forest.

Kal tried to feign confidence, trying to reassure himself

that despite being ambushed by the Nasi, the Skulls hadn't lost a single soldier. But he continued to wonder what the enemy had in store for them.

His mood wasn't helped by Asha. On the flight to the Fridge, she'd held his hand and talked away. Now she sat next to Yonder, chatting happily to the quietly nodding Nasi. It was childish, but Kal couldn't help feeling jealous.

Once they were near the city, Kanumba merged onto one of the main arteries into the city, allowing them to blend in with the mass of vehicles. Kal's anxiety, always bad even on the best day, was going to overdrive. He forced himself to remember that there was no reason the Nasi or local forces would have to suspect they were affiliated with any rebel group.

Chief Kanumba cursed. "Domespat blockade coming up."

Several patrol transports were parked on the road, their turrets facing up to prevent anyone from trying to fly over the checkpoint. Two patrollers, dressed in the black and green uniforms of the Domespat stood on the side, inspecting the transports before waving them through.

"Could we look any more suspicious?" asked Private Chadha.

"A bunch of people with bloodstained clothes, a Nasi, and a small girl? What's to see?" Private Ma asked.

"I'll handle this," Yonder said confidently.

"Aren't you a wanted man?" asked Kanumba.

Yonder smiled. "They're Humans. They don't know that."

After waiting in the line of vehicles, Kanumba brought

them to a rest and a Domespat patroller walked up to the driver's side. Kanumba opened the door, and before the patroller was able to ask a question, Yonder had darted to the front of the vehicle and was centimeters from her face. The woman stepped back, obviously alarmed.

"What's the meaning of this?" bellowed the Nasi.

"I—It's a routine traffic stop," the woman responded weakly.

"If you want to stop your fellow filthy Humans, then fine. But don't you *dare* assume you have any authority over me."

"Yes, sir."

"It's not sir. It's Chief Subordinate Agent Trokar to you. Now let us pass." Yonder pointed towards the city on the other side of the checkpoint.

The woman jumped back and motioned to the other patrollers to let them through. With a smile and a wink, Kanumba lifted off and proceeded through the checkpoint.

"Chief Subordinate Agent Trokar?" asked Kal.

Yonder laughed. "I made that up."

They found a dark alley not far from their prearranged rendezvous with Kimathi and the other Tac-I team. One thing Kal appreciated about Tiradentes and its enormous buildings was that there was no lack of dark secluded spots to stash people or vehicles.

Their meeting place was at the back of a chembar known as the Sticky Wicket. Sergeant Kimathi had selected the spot, saying wistfully that he'd always wanted to go there as a kid. It was dark and cramped. Bottles and empty drug ampules littered the ground, reminding Kal of Nicole's story about the alley where she'd almost been assassinated.

For a recovering addict, a chembar wasn't the best place to be. Unfortunately, they made perfect places to meet. Kal figured he'd been in twice as many chembars since he'd gotten clean than when he'd been on Kuaile.

He cautiously walked into the narrow passageway. The rest of the team was nearby, close enough that they could talk through a direct link but far enough that they could run if need be. As he passed out of sight of the pedestrians on the nearby street, two people appeared from a doorway. Kal felt a pleasant shock when he saw Cell Chief Rafaela Pham standing next to Sergeant Kimathi. She smiled when she saw Kal's expression.

"Never thought you'd see me again, huh?"

"Honestly? No," Kal said. "But glad I was wrong."

Pham's smile vanished. "Neither did I. I was lucky though; most didn't make it out."

"But some did," said Kimathi. "And we're getting the band back together."

"No idea what that means," said Kal. He still hadn't gotten used to the sergeant's affinity for ancient expressions and memorabilia.

"It's an expression—never mind." Kimathi rolled his eyes. "Bottom line, there's still some fight left in the TLF."

"We were able to make contact with the People's Army at the Fridge, their base near the Northern Pole," said Kal. "Seems like there are more rebel groups still operating than we initially thought. The TLF seems like it was the hardest hit."

"The Domespat might have helped us out," said Kimathi. "They forces used to remain split up. Made it harder for the Nasi to infiltrate all of the groups."

"The PA are glory hounds," said Pham derisively. "You're going to need more than them to win."

"They've got contacts," said Kal. "Almost every rebel group on the planet comes to the Fridge to train."

"We'll see."

"Any word from Bo?" asked Kal.

"Oh, yeah." Pham smiled. "He's been busy."

Kal let the other members of the team know it was safe to come out. Yonder appeared out the shadows a few seconds later and wrapped Pham in his arms, picking her up off the ground.

"Good to see you again Yonder," the cell chief laughed.

After Yonder put her back down, she knelt and gave Asha a warm embrace, pulling her head into her chest. Kal was shocked; he'd assumed Pham had a heart but hadn't seen a shred of evidence up to that point.

If the Nasi surprised Sergeant Kimathi, he didn't show it. Instead, he waited for the warm greetings to finish then turned around and strode down the passageway and onto the streets.

Kal and the others followed Kimathi and Pham through Tiradentes' crowded streets. It was morning, and commuters rushed past while jam-packed public transports glided over the streets. Kal couldn't be sure, but he felt like there were significantly more Domespat around than even a day before. They huddled in small groups on the street corners, scanning the citizens as they strode past.

Kimathi stopped at a vibrant green door caked with what appeared to be hundreds of layers of paint. The paint-laden door creaked as he opened it and he then waved for them to enter.

A blast of smoke, bumping music, and the stench of too many bodies in too small a place hit Kal like a wall. Faux brick walls lined either side of an empty hallway lined with holos of Tiradentes. In another life it was the kind of hallway Kal had sought out when the drugs turned on him—relatively clean and away from the eyes of others.

"Owner's a friend of mine from way back," said Pham, leading the way. "He converted his place into a Nasi bar at my request."

"At your request?" asked Yonder, surprised.

"Yeah." Pham turned back to look at her friend. "You know what they say. Keep your friends close and your enemies closer."

"Why are you looking at me like that?" asked Yonder playfully.

The cell chief laughed. "Don't worry. Anyone who takes in a daughter as wonderful as yours can't be all bad."

"Damn right," said Asha. She blushed. "I mean, darn right."

"I knew hanging around a bunch of soldiers would be a

bad influence," said Yonder lightly.

Although it was now a bar, the building had clearly been built for another purpose. They wound through a maze of hallways with doorways leading to small featureless rooms at irregular intervals; it appeared to have been designed to confuse. Kal continued to hear the sounds of music and people but never saw another person. He'd hear the sound grow louder and expect them to enter a large room filled to brim with people, but they would turn a corner and find another long, barely furnished hallway.

Pham opened the door at the end of a hallway, leading to a room with a bare metal table in the center. Bo and two Nasi sat across from each other, clearly in the middle of an intense conversation. Bo stood up with a smile as they entered while the Nasi jumped to the side and crouched down facing the doorway, clearly ready for a fight.

Bo held out his arms. "Stand down. These are friends."

"Allies perhaps," muttered one of the Nasi, relaxing slightly.

"They are friends of *mine*," said Bo. "But yes, allies to our cause. I think you already know the general."

"Oh, yes," said one of the Nasi, a tone of respect entering their voice. "We know of the general. Never have seen what he looks like though. I thought…"

"I'd be taller?" Kal asked.

The Nasi nodded. "Yes. You Humans are so short. And weak. It's amazing that you've been able to stand against the Grand Ancient for so long."

278

"Thanks for the compliment. I guess."

"Humans are rather embarrassed about their physical shortcomings," Bo explained to the Nasi. "What you said would be considered rude to them."

The Nasi blushed. "A year in this universe and still learning," he said to himself. He turned to Kal. "Apologies for my words."

Kal waved his apology away. "Don't worry about it. If you help us, then you can call me whatever you like."

Nasi paused for a moment. "No revenge? No justice for what has happened?"

"Justice will be peace," Kal said. "Yes, there are lives, billions of them, gone. But there are still billions out there. We need to find a peace where your Grand Ancient is not ruling Humanity's colonies, one where Humans and Jadid live as equals."

"And the Nasi?"

"The Nasi ideology is toxic and deadly," Kal said. "It comes from a woman who is bent on vengeance for a crime that happened hundreds of years ago."

The Nasi looked shocked. Kal doubted they'd ever someone speak about the Nasi and Grand Ancient Esma Bayaka in that manner. He wasn't sure if he'd hurt or helped Bo's efforts. But he wasn't going to pussyfoot around the truth; it had to be said.

"Hm. You've given us a lot to think about," the Nasi woman said gravely to Bowen. She looked to the man, and he gave a small nod. "We'll do what you ask."

279

Bo bowed his head. "Thank you."

"We'll be back soon," said the man to Bo. He turned to face Kal again. "Thank you. It's been an honor to meet you."

The Nasi glided out of the room, and the door clanged shut behind them.

"Who were they?" asked Kal.

"They lead a security team that patrols outside the Foothold," Bo said, sitting back down.

The Nasi scientist-turned-revolutionary detailed exactly what he'd been up to in the past day and a half. He had been able to meet with several Nasi teams inside the Foothold.

Despite having captured all four Human colonies and rewriting the history of a portion of the galaxy, the Nasi were few in numbers. Kal guessed it was a big reason why they let the Human governments on their colonies exist and why they were so quick to resort to lethal force and surprise. Those were the tactics of an outnumbered opponent. Even now, years into the war, Humans outnumbered the Nasi hundreds-to-one. With only a few converts, Bo could make a big difference in the success of their upcoming mission.

With some help from Delta Unit, he had spoken to several suspected Human sympathizers within the Nasi ranks. Despite knowing that many of the Nasi were demoralized, he confided that he was still surprised by how many were receptive to his message. Many Nasi simply wanted the war to end. They had left their home planet of Altterra and come to the Human's universe to live a new life. They'd been told that they would be greeted as liberators and long-lost brothers and sisters.

Instead, they'd found only hate and resentment.

"It was shocking," confided Bo, shaking his head. "The amount of resentment and dissatisfaction that has grown right under the Grand Ancient's nose."

Bo described how many Nasi were looking for a way out of Esma's plans. They felt trapped, wanting nothing more than to end the battle and live a life in the Human's universe. There were also some who wanted to return to Altterra and the lives they had known. Unfortunately for them, Esma would not allow it.

Although adept at warfare and subterfuge, the Nasi were infants when it came to politics and influence. The Ancients had maintained a tight grip on their "children," and the Jadid and Nasi had never experienced a situation where their personal interests so completely diverged from their leader's. Bo had been able to take advantage of it to a degree he'd never expected, making inroads into several key units in a short amount of time.

"Guess all that talkin' you did during our missions finally came in handy," said Sergeant Kimathi with a wink. "But what about soldiers? Will any of them fight with us?"

"We won't have time for that," said Bo. "To ask people to pass information and help is one thing. For them to take up arms against their fellow Nasi is another."

"Did you find out what they're doing to the plasma lances?" asked Kal.

Bo nodded. "As we guessed, they knew exactly when we were going to arrive and what our plan was. They had trouble

281

infiltrating all the rebel groups on New America, so they created traps and diversions within the plasma lances as a backup."

"What kind of traps?" asked Ekon.

"Rerouting plasma conduits. Creating fake nexuses for us attack. The plans that we have are essentially useless."

"Any luck getting the new ones?" asked Kal.

"Not yet," Bo replied. "But we're working on it."

"Bo, you gotta step on it my man," Kimathi said, patting the Jadid's back. "Time is one thing we don't have."

"What *do* we have?" Pham asked.

They exchanged looks with one another—it was a difficult question.

"You've got me," Asha said cautiously. "And you've got Yonder." She pulled him forward.

"You also have surprise on your side," Yonder added. "And it sounds like you've got the cooperation of a lot of people within the Nasi." He scowled. "Damn Esma Baykara for turning us into this. When we were Jadid, we were better than all of this."

"Actually, I think our original plan can still work," Kal said. "To your point, we've regained an element of surprise. And an enemy is most complacent when they think they already won."

"So what? We just go in and attack, sir?" asked Kimathi incredulously. "We *still* don't have the weapons to fight, not to mention we lost our ship and the explosives to take out the nexus."

"We have to." Kal looked at Yonder. He had an idea that was so audacious it might just work. "You know the Nasi protocols and organization better than anyone. With what Bo has told us, is there a way to get inside the armory?"

"Get inside the *armory*?" Yonder's eyes widened in surprise. When he realized Kal was serious, he rubbed his chin thoughtfully. "There's no single armory. There are many of them. But maybe, with a lot of help, you could get in there."

"We get everything we can from the armories, get those plans, and get whatever competent—and I *mean* competent—fighters we can." Kal looked around at the others. "We do all that, then we got a chance. It'll be game changing as Kimathi says."

Kimathi shook his head. "Game *on*, sir. But what you're talking about is a suicide mission."

"No, it isn't," Kal said, tilting his head towards Asha. The little girl's eyes had gone wide. She didn't need to know that.

"Oh," Kimathi stuttered. "Yeah, you're right. This is *totally* survivable."

In truth, of course it wasn't. But that was where they were. It was their best shot at saving the fleet and overcoming the Grand Ancient Esma Baykara. If they had to die in order to do it, so be it.

Chapter Twenty-One
Nicole | Kasongo, Patagonia

After leaving Matisse's office, Deepta and Nicole walked through the streets looking for a transport to take them back to the *Chester*. Despite not seeing a single Nasi patroller or ship, Nicole felt like the threat of attack was omnipresent.

"Just stay here and keep a look out," said Deepta, stopping in front of an old transport they'd found at the mouth of a small passageway. "I can override the controls on this thing."

Nicole nodded and pulled her pistol out, keeping it out of sight at her side. Deepta crouched near the driver's side of the decades-old transport and pulled out a small tablet. A minute later the door creaked open, and Nicole slid across to the passenger's seat.

The sun was overhead, and the streets were growing more crowded. Nicole couldn't place her finger on why, but she felt like she was on a ship about to fold. There was an anticipation in the air, a sense of action to come. Armed groups wearing different colored armbands patrolled the street, looking like they were itching for a fight. They scanned the streets as they walked, stopping people and stepping right in their faces while screaming questions at them. Several groups were in the process of erecting new barricades, stacking whatever they could find to provide cover.

"This city's about to explode," said Deepta as she watched a patroller drag a screaming woman across the street. "People are going to die today."

A lot of people, Nicole thought to herself. *Not just here in Kasongo, but across the planet.* Patagonia was about to be engulfed in civil war once again. And she was largely responsible.

The Nasi were nowhere to be found. They'd had a hands-off attitude toward the planet; letting the Humans kill each other so long as the resources they needed were provided. Despite that, after what had happened the previous day, Nicole had expected to see Nasi fighters looking for rebels. After reflecting for a moment, she realized the Nasi probably couldn't be happier with what was happening. The more the Humans killed each other, the easier they were to control.

After only one close call, they were able to reach the *Chester* without being harassed by any of the roving bands. Stepping through the veil created by the ship's optical cloak, Nicole was grateful to find Chief Ramos sitting on the cargo ramp, her arms wrapped around her legs.

"Welcome back," Ramos said as she stood up. "Where are the others?"

"They had business to take care of," said Nicole. "They're not returning, at least not here."

They parked the stolen transport in the ship's cargo bay and headed to *Chester's* galley—it served as an operations room of sorts during missions. Nicole grabbed food and drink and sat down at the table that filled most of the room. Captain Uhaa, Chief Ramos, Deepta, and the Patagonian Front rebels had filed in after her, eager to hear what they would do next. Nicole was surprised to see Sergeant Grupp shuffle into the room as well, his medbot trailing behind him. He continually clenched and released his jaw in pain, and he was as pale as snow, but she considered it a small miracle that he was even standing so soon after his injury.

Nicole took a long sip of tea. "We've run out of time," she said quietly. "We've done everything we can. It's time to begin the offensive."

She brought up a map of the planet on one of the viewscreens and went over what they already knew. The six Nasi plasma lances were spread across the continent. Five of them were along the edge of the continent, underneath the water. The sixth was in the very center, located in the mountains that between Kasongo and Foyleton. As they'd recruited citizens across the planet, they'd given only one of the six coordinates to each person they talked with, hoping to ensure their forces were split evenly. The only question remained was where should they head to?

The group went back and forth; no location seemed better than the other. Finally, as Nicole went through their options for the third time, Captain Uhaa interrupted.

"Ma'am, the long-distance net just cleared," he said excitedly. "We're being hailed."

"Patch it through the speakers." Nicole felt a sense of elation. Who had cleared the net?

There was a click, and then a familiar voice rang throughout the room. It was Captain Federov, commander of one of the other Samsara Fleet assault teams on Patagonia.

"Assault Team Alpha, this is Echo."

Nicole wanted to jump and cheer. At least one other assault team was still out there. They weren't the only ones who'd survived the Nasi purge.

"Echo, what's your status?" Nicole asked breathlessly.

"We're in position. We sustained heavy casualties but have all our equipment." Which meant they still had the explosives needed to take down the nexus. "Do you have any knowledge of the other teams?"

"No," said Nicole. "Do you?"

"We believe that Charlie Team is still active—we heard some reports of attacks in their area. I don't know how effective they are any more."

Nicole wondered why the Nasi had opened the planetary net. Was it part of some grand strategy? Had they broken through Samsara Fleet's new encryption protocols? The less that was said, the better.

"As you heard, the fleet is on its way." She felt saying it over the net since the Nasi were the ones who called them. "You can expect local assistance at your location." She assumed the Nasi would have already known that as well.

"Roger that." Federov paused. "What kind of assistance should we expect?"

"I can't tell you that." Nicole hoped he understood why. "But hopefully you can use them."

"Thank you," Federov said. "And ma'am? Good luck."

"You too."

Nicole closed the connection. It was good to know that at

least one of the other teams was still out there. Should they try and reach out to the others? What did they have to lose at that point? As the commanding officer of the operation, she had a responsibility to at least try and see if she could regain some aspect of command and control.

Nicole had Uhaa attempt to hail the other teams. Major Chen, commander of Charlie Team, was the only one to reply. Like Echo, they were at their objective, having heard the call that came from Sergeant Bhatt and realizing they'd need to attack the lances sooner rather than later. Nicole gave Chen the same advice she gave the Echo Team leader and then closed the line.

At least fifty percent of their teams remained somewhat operationally capable. It wasn't great, but it was a hell of a lot better than she'd thought an hour ago. She wondered why the Nasi would open up the net. Either they felt it gave them some advantage…or someone else had done it.

Hey Nicole, said a voice in Nicole's implant.

Mother Ju? Nicole was confused.

Like what we did with the net? Nicole could imagine the tones of satisfaction that must be dripping off the words. Had to get some people to help us out. I'm racking up some debts, but it'll be worth it. Also, got a bit of information.

Where did you go? asked Nicole.

We had some friends who'd been put away for a while in the Kasongo detention center. Decided to let them all out on the promise of good behavior.

You broke into a prison? asked Nicole. She could

understand why they didn't tell her.

Yup, Ju replied. More than one in fact. You got some very angry people heading to those lances to help you.

How did you break into a Nasi prison? Nicole asked.

I didn't. These are people put away by the Human authorities.

"What's going on?" asked Sergeant Grupp. Nicole had been silent for a while and she realized that everyone else around the table was staring at her.

"Talking with Mother Ju. She and Scrapper orchestrated several jailbreaks." The others' expressions ranged from amused—Deepta—to scandalized—Grupp.

Deepta whistled. "Man, that woman definitely wants to see the planet burn."

Grupp screwed up his mouth thoughtfully. "Well. I mean anything that causes chaos probably helps us."

—That's why you need to get to the lance in the northwest corner.

Wait, what? Nicole motioned for everyone else in the room to shut up. She'd just missed something important over her implant.

We just took down a planetary communications jammer to talk. You think you'd pay more attention. Nicole could imagine the annoyance in Ju's tone. You need to get to the Nasi lance at the northwest edge of Pangea. The Nasi have been moving a significant amount of heavy equipment there.

Why? asked Nicole.

Hell if I know, Ju replied. I'm just telling you what we

found out. The other sites are obviously guarded as well. But that one has some serious firepower.

Thanks, said Nicole. Again, she wondered how much of the conversation was being monitored by the Nasi. *Will I see you again?*

Maybe. You never know in this galaxy. We're continuing to send everyone we can find toward the sites. Just a warning, they're not all...civilized.

Ju cut the line leaving Nicole wondering what she meant. She wished she had more time to care.

"Head to target three," Nicole ordered. "The Nasi have extra reinforcements at the site, and we're going to need everything we can get."

There was no way to detect a plasma lance from the air. That was one of the reasons it had taken Samsara Fleet a year to find them all. The entire weapon was below ground and almost completely self-sufficient. A small city's worth of power and plasma generation equipment were required to make the things work, and all of it was contained hundreds or thousands of meters below the planet's surface.

As the *Chester* skimmed across an orange and brown tinged forest with a sparkling blue ocean in the far distance, Nicole kept an eye out. The Nasi knew they were coming and would have defenses to prevent any ship from getting too close. She was in the ship's cockpit, sitting in the command console behind Uhaa and Ramos. The small viewscreen next to her seat showed nothing—no friendlies or enemies to be found. But they were getting close, and Nicole had expected to see something by now.

"Can you believe it?" asked Captain Uhaa.

"Believe what?" Ramos turned to look at her co-pilot.

"This is it. We're in a ship with a bunch of rebels flying toward a highly guarded weapon we barely understand. And we're relying on a group of—let's be honest—hardened criminals for help." He smiled. "I just thought it'd be more…heroic."

"I don't know," said Nicole. "It's kinda heroic if you think about it. People—of all kinds—coming together to overthrow an oppressor."

"That sounds nice and all—"

An alarm blared and the consoles flashed red. Three anti-air missiles had suddenly appeared on the tacmap.

"Well, there we go," said Uhaa calmly as they descended low enough to the ground that they were below the tops of the broad-leafed trees. "Was wondering when that would happen."

The missiles had fanned out from the same origin in front of the *Chester* but quickly altered their courses to head directly towards them. There was no mistake about it, the Nasi had pierced their optical cloak.

Uhaa bit his lip as he continued to fly forward, skimming the treetops and weaving around large clumps of trees that jutted out from the rest. The ship's AI helped the pilot, but

Nicole knew that the precision he was flying with came solely from a career spent training for situations just like this one—situations that most pilots would never face.

The missiles came at them from three directions. Nicole wasn't worried about the one that was approaching from the front; the speeds that the ship and missile were heading toward each other allowed little room for error or correction on the missile's part. But the two approaching from their flanks would be able to maneuver to take them out.

"How close are we to the rendezvous point?" asked Nicole.

"Still about twenty kilometers out," Ramos replied.

Nicole called back to the cargo bay and instructed everyone to get into battle suits; if the ship went down, the suits gave them a better chance of survival.

Uhaa maintained the same trajectory toward the entrance to the Nasi cannon site as the first missile approached. At the last second as the missile was about to impact, he flicked the yoke, causing them to skid sideways for just a second and skirt the speeding missile, causing it to detonate into the forest canopy.

"Nice," said Ramos. "Still got two left. They're coming in fast."

On the ship's main viewscreen a large rock-faced peak jutted from the forest in front of them. Nicole could feel the sweat pouring down her face as she watched the two red dots on the map grow closer. Several gray icons appeared on the tacmap as they crossed over a clearing.

"We've got ground-launched countermeasures in flight." Ramos' tone was between glee and disbelief.

Seconds later, the two missiles disappeared from Nicole's screen.

"Set us down," instructed Nicole, trying to control her tone. She would take a firefight over the feeling of helplessness she experienced when the ship was under attack.

"We're over the rendezvous point."

"And it seems like there's at least some friendlies down there," Uhaa said happily.

The *Chester* touched down next a small river that wound through the forest. They were still a few kilometers from the entrance to the Nasi's plasma cannon but getting any closer would have been suicide. Surely they'd have heavy anti-aircraft systems.

As soon as the engines had come to a stop, Nicole and the two pilots headed to the cargo bay. The others were already in their battle suits, waiting. Nicole stepped into her suit and swallowed as it closed itself around her body. As she put the helmet on, she felt a sense a finality. One way or another, nothing would be the same after this mission.

The Triple-A, which had been designed to pierce the hard armor around the Nasi nexus, was already loaded on a small skiff. Just being around the device made Nicole nervous.

"Everyone ready?" she asked.

"Ready as I'll ever be," said Sergeant Grupp. The man had somehow gotten himself into one of the battle suits.

"Grupp, you're practically dead already," said Deepta.

"The only thing you're ready for is a medbot."

"I'm not sitting on a ship while you get the glory," said the sergeant.

"Let's move out." Nicole appreciated the banter—it helped dull the edge. But they still had to locate whoever had shown up to help. The countermeasures had been fired from near their landing spot. At least there were *some* allies nearby.

She stepped down the cargo ramp and scanned the area with her suit's sensors. Nothing came up; the area appeared deserted except for small creatures scurrying through the trees above. There was almost nothing underneath the broad canopy of the forest, allowing Nicole to see much farther than she had expected.

"We'll move out on foot," said Nicole. "Thrusters will give us away."

They ran in a loose line between the enormous trunks. Despite the lack of undergrowth, there were still plenty of places to hide. Nicole didn't trust her suit's sensors one bit, she knew there were people nearby, both friend and enemy.

As she crested a small knoll, Nicole's sensor lit up, highlighting several Nasi lying in wait on the relatively level ground in front. She dropped to the ground and reflexively fired her railgun, managing to pierce one of the Nasi's helmets. Neither they nor the other two Nasi lying in the area moved.

We've got contact, Ramos called out over the net. The rest of the team moved laterally, trying to get into flanking positions around the three Nasi.

Nicole reassessed the situation and noticed pools of blood around the three bodies. Then she noticed the bodies of Humans lying on the outskirts of the clearing—at least ten of them. There'd already been a firefight here. It was hard to say who'd won, but the fact that three battle-suited Nasi lay on the ground had to be considered some sort of a victory.

"Looks like we've got at least some enemy here," Deepta knelt by one of the Nasi bodies. "And they're armed with missiles."

"Nasi took out three of ours for every one of theirs," said one of the Front rebels. "Not a good exchange."

"I'll take that any day of the week," said Nicole. "That's better than I expected."

She'd learned that sometimes brutal honesty was the key to success. The Nasi were genetically enhanced, well-armed, and well trained. If her team won this battle, it would be due to numbers and luck. Pretending anything else would be a grave mistake.

"Let's keep going." Nicole pointed forward. "That's the rendezvous point."

They continued moving toward the ocean until they reached the coordinates Nicole had been giving out over the past day when asking for help. The clearing was littered with bodies. She didn't dare count how many lives had been lost in the place. All she knew was that it numbered in the hundreds. Scarring from explosives and plasma littered the area. As expected, the Nasi had known they were coming and had lain in wait. Nicole could see small sparkles of light between the trees; the ocean was only a few hundred meters away.

"Damn!" Grupp somehow managed to pour everything that Nicole felt into that single word.

Identify yourself.

The command came over an unencrypted open net. Nicole couldn't place the voice except to say that it was Human. She felt a wave of relief. At least there were some survivors.

This is Lieutenant Colonel Nicole Bergeron, commander of Samsara Fleet Assault Team Echo. Where are you and who am I talking to?

You made it. Meet us here. She received coordinates for a location further down the coastline.

When they reached the location, Nicole noticed a small cave in the ground, covered with a small tent of leaves so it was almost impossible to see from above. She stepped underneath the orange canopy and found the opening led to a large cavern.

The cave was filled with people of all types. All of them were armed. The weaponry was as varied as the people who held them. From ancient kinetic pistols to heavily armed assault craft, and everything in between. She thought about how the same thing was playing out in five other places across the planet. It was the most beautiful thing Nicole had seen in a long time.

"Welcome to the revolution," said a man, stepping forward. It took Nicole a moment to recognize him. It was

Commander Kinkaid. The old man smiled. "We're ready."

"Where did all this come from?"

Kinkaid winked. "I told you we had weapons caches." He looked back. "Though I have to admit, there's a lot more here than I expected. Apparently, the Nasi weren't nearly as good at demilitarizing Patagonia as we all thought."

A small alarm sounded in Nicole's suit. It was a relay from the *Chester.* Samsara Fleet had just entered the space around the planet. She felt a bolt of worry surge through her body. They weren't ready. They lances were still active.

"Listen up everyone," Nicole shouted through her suit's external speaker. "Samsara Fleet has entered the space around Patagonia. They can destroy the Nasi fleet orbiting the planet; but only if we disable the plasma lances. I am sending you all the information I have on the facility. We need to get inside and destroy the nexus. If we fail, Samsara Fleet, our only hope, will be destroyed. Will you fight with me?"

Several people around her nodded, and a few even shouted their agreement or waved their weapons in the air. Disappointingly many people in the cave were too far away to hear her and continued checking equipment or talking amongst themselves, unaware of Nicole's attempt at a rousing speech.

She fired her weapon in the air and the crowd quieted down. Nicole said the same speech again, and this time, the entire cave was listening. There wasn't a burst of applause or cheers, but every face in the cave seemed to have the same look of determination as she finished.

The Patagonians had had enough and were ready. More than that, they were eager. Already, people were climbing onto the heavy weapons on the perimeter and firing up their engines while others checked their weapons and tightened their tattered ballistic armor. It wasn't the inspirational scene she'd seen in the holos, but it'd have to do.

They had a mission.

Chapter Twenty-Two
Nicole | Patagonia

Although they had numbers, Nicole quickly realized they didn't have any organization. The people there had come in small groups, making their way to the cavern by whatever means necessary. They were nothing more than an armed mob.

She called out, asking for the leaders of each group to step forward. Sometimes they surprised her. A boy, no more than eighteen, was leading a group from Kasongo while an elderly woman had become the spokesperson for a group from a small town in the west of the continent. Nicole quickly assigned them positions for the assault and then told them to relay it to their teams.

The heavy weapons and transports were the first to move out of the cave. The dismounted soldiers—for now they were all soldiers—followed, clumped together in groups and trudged through the trees. Nicole and the others in battle suits took the rear, corralling anyone who seemed confused or were injured from the earlier fighting. The Triple-A was loaded onto a transport which hovered next to them.

Stay out of site of the entrance, Nicole instructed to the heavy weapons teams at the front. When we get close, we'll conduct a recon before moving further.

According to Nicole's tacmap, the plasma lance's entrance was on a small hillock only meters from the ocean with about a hundred meters of cleared land between it and forest.

Unfortunately, there was no way for them to avoid a frontal assault on the position.

They reached the edge of the forest and halted behind the last line of massive trunks. Nicole and Ramos used their thrusters to move to the front and scanned the area ahead. The entrance to the plasma lance had been carved out of the hill. She wasn't clear what defenses there were, but Nicole knew it would be heavily guarded. Meanwhile, the equipment and people behind her were fanning out, getting ready to assault from all sides.

Her display beeped as it bracketed several areas around the square opening in the hillside—potential heavy weapons emplacements. She didn't see any Nasi in the area but knew they would be nearby as well.

Move forward with the heavy weapons, Nicole called out over the net. Target these locations. Remember, as soon as the fighting starts, you keep going no matter what. She forwarded the suspected weapons emplacements to the entire group.

The weapons moved forward to fire on the base entrance. They were a strange mix, just like the people piloting them. Some were surplus EDF, still with the telltale markings. Others were clearly civilian transports that had been modified with armor and cannons. Still others seemed to be custom weapons systems, built from the ground up. Nicole even saw a few Zzyr and Kurz weapons in the mix.

We've got movement. The call came across the net as plasma streamed from around the lance's entrance. Nasi seemingly appeared from nowhere, jetting from behind the hill and streaking towards their formation, firing as they went.

We've got the air, Nicole called to the others in battle suits. *I want this area cleared.*

With pleasure, Grupp replied.

Nicole activated her thrusters and shot over the people and machines below, heading directly towards the swarm of Nasi. They dove toward the Human forces, strafing them with plasma fire and missiles. The Humans fired back, and despite their poor aim, they knocked several Nasi from the sky due to the sheer numbers. For every shot that disabled a Nasi, many more simply bounced off the battle-suits' armor or were absorbed by their energy shields.

Split into two and take them from the sides, Nicole ordered. They had to avoid getting between the Nasi and the Human formations. The last thing she wanted was for one of them to be taken down by friendly fire.

Nicole lined up several shots with her railgun, missing each time. The Nasi were moving too fast for either her or her targeting computer to compensate. She switched to her plasma rifle and her suit's built-in missile system.

Thankfully it was a target-rich environment. She picked the closest Nasi and launched a salvo of three missiles at them. The projectiles streaked forward and connected. Her target had been focused on the vehicle-mounted plasma cannon below and hadn't even tried to evade her attack.

An enormous plasma blast seared past Nicole, almost taking her out. She looked to her left and was greeted by the sight of a fleet of Nasi fighters heading toward them over the choppy ocean water.

Of course they would have air support, thought Nicole. They knew we were coming.

The Nasi fighters unleashed a hail of death and destruction as they approached. The pilots didn't seem to care if they hit their own people; they fired indiscriminately, taking out Human and Nasi alike.

One of the fighters abruptly exploded in a ball of fire, sending bits of its fuselage onto the battlefield below.

Colonel Bergeron, said a voice over the net. Matisse sends his regards.

A swarm of fighters flew overhead, firing their weapons at the Nasi. The enemy clearly hadn't expected the attack and hastily scattered. Fortunately, several reacted too late and ended up either hurtling into the ocean or crashing into the trees, smoke trailing behind them.

Thank Matisse for me, said Nicole.

And tell him Whisper sends her thanks as well, Deepta added.

With Matisse's gift, the Humans ground down the Nasi defenders. They took heavy casualties, but from what Nicole could tell, so did the Nasi. While the battle raged on the ground, the two groups of fighters flew above, trading fire.

After several minutes, the final Nasi soldier was down. Nicole estimated the assault team had already lost half their heavy weapons and a third of their people. Things would only get more difficult once they entered the caverns that housed the plasma lance. She hoped they still had enough people to accomplish the mission.

"Well, they know we're here," Deepta said as she landed next to Nicole.

"They don't seem to be pleased to see us though," Grupp said.

The sergeant had proven to be a formidable force in the battle suit. Outside of the suit, Nicole doubted he would have been able to walk to the entrance due to the extent of his injuries, but in a suit, none of that mattered. She'd seen him easily handle the Nasi two on one.

"Get inside," Nicole ordered. "Matisse's fighters aren't going to be able to hold on much longer." The Human aircraft had had the element of surprise, but the superior Nasi technology was starting to turn the tide of the air battle.

It took the heavy weapons several minutes to get through the heavy blast door that blocked the entrance. Finally, the doors were reduced to a puddle of metal, and the group entered the caverns.

Nicole ordered the remaining weapon transports to lead the procession but not outpace the dismounted soldiers. One lesson Kal had imparted on her was that mounted and dismounted troops had to work in unison. Despite her orders, they sped ahead of the main formation, disappearing in the dark mouth of the cave.

"At least they'll serve as an early warning system for us," Deepta said coolly as she watched a makeshift assault craft speed through the entrance and into the cave, leaving the rest of the formation behind.

Nicole grunted. She couldn't match Deepta's flippant attitude. The people in that transport would likely get themselves killed because of their ignorance or stubbornness.

As she waited for the last of their forces to enter the base, her viewscreen suddenly turned black and she felt herself knocked forward as a shockwave enveloped the area. Small bits of dust and stone pinged against her armor. Nicole looked up and saw a beam made of solid white light streaming into the heavens. It was so bright it almost overwhelmed her suit's display, making it impossible for her to see anything until several seconds later when the beam disappeared.

"What happened?" gasped Grupp.

"They just took out one of our ships," said Ramos. "That's the plasma lance in action."

"Holy hell."

After they'd recovered from their shock, the group sped through the melted doors, following the detailed map that Nicole had distributed earlier. Over the past year, agents working for Samsara Fleet and the Patagonia Front had risked their lives to get the information to build that map. Now she just hoped that their sacrifices would be worth it.

Below them was a complex that included the plasma lance, an energy plant, and a plasma generator. The three components themselves were almost impossible to destroy, but the connections between them were vulnerable. Or at least slightly more vulnerable. The nexus—the device where the various streams of plasma were joined together to be piped directly to the cannon—was in the center of the facility. As they continued to descend, Nicole thought back to what Samsara Fleet's engineers and planners had told her—they had no idea what would happen when the nexus was destroyed.

The dense network of tunnels would have been impossible to navigate without the map. The assorted hand- and headlights of the group bathed the ceiling and walls in light and banished the darkness to the small offshoots. Passages veered off and joined back together. Some doubled back and forth before ending in a dead end or fading into an impossibly small passageway. Their motley army continued to weave through the caverns, slowly making their way down, underneath the ocean bed, toward the center of the Nasi cannon.

Nicole and the others in battle suits used their thrusters to fly up and down the formation, checking on the soldiers and using their sensors to scan the area around them. In some places the caverns became so narrow they were forced to walk alongside the others. Nicole was shocked to see the transports and heavy weapons somehow make it through the constricted passageways.

"You think we'll make it?" asked a man walking next to Nicole.

"Of course," she lied. "We're already in."

"They've got to have more surprises waiting for us." The man looked around wildly. "I think we're all a little bit crazy doing this, ya know? I mean, I'm a machinist, and now, here I am crawling through a cave. I mean, what do we even do if we make it there?"

"You gotta be a little crazy, for sure," Nicole said. "But you must be a little crazy to do anything. Think of the first people who folded or flew in an aircraft. Nothing great is accomplished by thinkin' straight. Every once and a while you gotta just say, screw it, let's see what happens."

The man laughed. "You're alright. Who are you?"

"I'm the person leading this mission," said Nicole.

He regarded her with renewed interest. "Well, I gotta say I like your attitude. Though I have a feeling that things are probably not going according to whatever your plan was."

Nicole slapped him gently on the back, careful not to send him flying across the cavern with her battle-suit's augmented strength. "The key part to remember when planning is that chance and the enemy always get a say. Honestly, I know we can do this." This time, she meant it.

An explosion rocked through the cavern sending large pieces of rock cascading down. Nicole's suit's status screen shone red as a large boulder landed on her shoulder, sending her to the ground. She could hear screams and cries of pain but couldn't see a thing through the thick smoke and dust.

She stood up and quickly checked her battle-suit's self-diagnostics, which was already starting to repair most of the damage the large boulder had done. However, her missile launcher, which had sustained a direct hit, was offline.

Miraculously, the man she'd been talking to was already

up and dusting himself off. "A little crazy, huh?" he asked with a cocked eyebrow.

"Maybe a lot crazy," Nicole admitted.

Another boom rocked through the cavern, sending down more dust. It took Nicole a moment to realize the second blast had been the cannon firing again. *Another Samsara Fleet ship destroyed.* She wondered how long they would be able to hold out.

She ran toward the front of the group, where most of the cries of pain were coming from. The explosion had brought an avalanche of rock down from the ceiling and split their group in two. Enormous boulders, easily as large as a ship, blocked their progress. It would have taken hours for them to go through, hours they didn't have.

Kinkaid? The commander had been at the front of the formation with the heavy weapons the last time Nicole had seen him.

I'm here, he responded. We've sustained casualties from the blast.

Keep going forward, said Nicole. We'll figure out a way to get back to you. We don't have time to stop.

Will do.

She knew it was harsh, but Nicole didn't have time to think about the injured and dying. They'd have to leave them there. She tried not to look at the bodies that littered the ground near her and instead studied the map in her suit's display.

There hadn't been time or opportunity for the fleet's agents to record every tunnel in the network of caves. In many places the map simply ended, disappearing into nothingness. Nicole hoped that one of those unmapped areas could lead them back to the rest of their group and the nexus.

She contacted the leads through her implant and directed them to get their people moving to one of the unmapped tunnels. Several said they couldn't leave the injured, but she overrode their protests despite empathizing with them. She hovered as close to the ceiling as possible and watched as the mass of people doubled back, away from the wall of rubble, and moved down one of the side tunnels.

Nicole made her way to the head of the formation and turned on every external light her suit had to light the way ahead. The crowd seemed more than happy to let her lead them through the pitch-black caves.

How's it going back there? Nicole asked Grupp. The sergeant was providing security at the rear of the formation.

I don't know. The words came through toneless due to the limitations of their neural connection, but Nicole could tell he was having difficulty speaking. *There's...just a lot of bodies here.*

Focus on what we need to get accomplished, Nicole said. We'll come back to get them.

If we live, Nicole thought.

Nicole was relieved to discover that the uncharted tunnel continued to descend toward the nexus. Other paths branched off but came looping back, joining the rest of the tunnel and creating a weave that headed in the right direction.

Nicole tried to reach Kinkaid and the other half of their formation, but the mountain blocked the signal; they were truly on their own. She continued to hear the periodic firing of the plasma lance, and every time she couldn't help picturing a Human or Jadid ship being destroyed in orbit. The soundless explosion, pieces of the ship cleaving in two, and people dying as they were cast into the voice of space. She had to continually resist the urge to fly ahead of the group to reach the nexus before the weapon could fire again.

Nicole continued to use her tacmap to track where they were in relation to the other parts of the plasma lance. As they reached a point where they were directly at the center of the facility, she stopped. If they went any farther, they would completely bypass the plasma lance. Unfortunately, there was no way to reach the nexus from where they were—or any of the other components for that matter.

"Hold up," Nicole called out as she stopped. Like a coiling spring, the rest of the formation gradually ground to a halt behind them.

If we keep going, we're just going to pass the objective, Nicole called out over the command net.

We don't have time to go back, said Chief Ramos. They're slaughtering the fleet.

You don't know that, said Captain Uhaa.

I damn well do, sir, Ramos shot back. I've seen what these

cannons can do.

Stop talking and start looking, said Nicole. We're so close. Use your deep scanners to see if there's some way to get out of here.

She ordered the soldiers around her to maintain their position and walked back toward the section of tunnel that was closest to the nexus. Using her suit's deep scanners, she peered through the walls to see if there were any nearby tunnels or caverns they could blast their way to. She needed to find some way to get closer to their objective that didn't require them to make the arduous journey back up.

I've found something, Uhaa called out. I'm detecting an open area a couple of meters from here.

Nicole rushed to the pilot's location. He was about two-thirds down the formation, almost parallel to where the Nasi plasma cannon started inside the ground. Nicole confirmed his findings; there was some large void in the stone. It was impossible for her to say exactly how large, or whether it was a cavern or tunnel, but it was at least the size of the space they were in.

"Can we make it through this?" asked Nicole.

"All our heavy weapons were at the front of the formation with Commander Kinkaid," said Grupp. "We don't have anything to get through stone this thick."

Nicole fired her plasma rifle at the wall in frustration. The bolt hit the wall harmlessly without even leaving a mark. They were so close.

She ordered the soldiers in battle suits to look for another way to get through, but she was starting to accept the fact they would have to circle back and try a different way. It would take time, time the fleet did not have.

The rest of the soldiers began to make their way back, jogging down the gravel-strewn tunnel floor as the plasma lance boomed again—another Samsara Fleet ship lost.

There's one more option, said Deepta. What about the explosives?

Nicole paused mid-scan. Could they do that? What other choice did they have?

Bring up the Triple A, she ordered.

The transport was at her location less than a minute later. Nicole picked up the explosive charge and affixed it to the wall. The shape charge was designed to pierce the armored plating of a nexus, so it should make short work of the relatively brittle stone wall. Still, she remembered Kal's warning about how volatile and destructive Triple-A was. Was she about to blow them all up?

After starting the timer, Nicole joined the other soldiers who had taken positions farther down the tunnel. When the charge went off, Nicole was surprised by how small the blast was. It was nothing compared to the explosion that had split their group in two earlier. Even the plasma lance produced a larger shockwave.

Nicole reassessed her opinion of the weapon once she saw its handiwork. A hole, easily big enough to drive two transports through, had been blasted through two meters of solid stone.

"There's something on the other side," shouted Grupp.

Nicole realized the man was right. A faint glow was coming from the other side of the hole. They tunnel on the other side *must* connect to the Nasi plasma lance. Nicole ordered the soldiers in battle suits to the front; they would go through first.

Ramos, come with me, ordered Nicole. Rest of you stay here.

They entered a tunnel that was roughly the same size as the one they'd come from. A sickly yellow light was coming from one end, illuminating the cracks and imperfections of the tunnel walls. Nicole smiled as she looked at the map. The tunnel almost certainly led to the nexus; it was literally a hundred meters away from their position.

Tunnel's clear, Nicole called out. Come on through.

Finally, something goes right, said Grupp. We're sending through the rest. I'll cover the rear until everyone's through.

Nicole and Ramos took up defensive positions on either side of the passageway as the rest of their team poured through the hole, their weapons held in a ready position as if they expected to be attacked at any moment.

Another blast vibrated through the mountain—another ship lost. Nicole thought of the fleet in space, wondering which ship had been destroyed.

Hurry up, Nicole shouted over the open net. *They're still firing.*

That wasn't the cannon, someone shouted. One of the—

The transmission cut out and an explosion lit up the cave

in front of Nicole. They were under attack.

They're at the front of our formation, Uhaa called out. We've got Nasi weapons systems and dismounts attacking.

They're also behind us, Grupp said. We've got at least a hundred of them.

We're surrounded, Nicole realized.

Chapter Twenty-Three
Kal | Tiradentes, New America

After their meeting with Bo, Cell Chief Pham left the building saying that there were several groups out east who were active and left to track them down. Before going, she confided to Kal that her opinion of the People's Army was less than stellar—"polar hillbillies" is what she'd called them—and she wanted to find people she could trust. He wasn't sure what a hillbilly was, but from the tone of her voice, it wasn't good. He couldn't say he disagreed with her assessment of the PA.

By Kal's reckoning they had approximately twenty-four hours until Samsara Fleet folded into orbit around New America. If the plasma lances were still online, the fleet wouldn't stand a chance. The Skulls had to find weapons, get the updated schematics for the plasma lances, and collect whatever fighters they could at Alpha North before then.

After Cell Chief Pham left, Kal called the group together to figure out how to get the Skulls into the Nasi Foothold and plunder the weapons caches. Yonder explained they were some of the most heavily guarded areas in the base; simply walking in and taking what they wanted wasn't an option.

"There's only one way for us to get in and out without dying," said Yonder. "And that's by having a permit. Occasionally, we have need to move weapons outside the Foothold for a major offensive. But the order to move them would need to come directly from the planetary governor."

"There's got to be some way around that," said Kimathi.

"Not a good one." Yonder tapped the table idly. "One thought. Bowen, have you made any contacts within the central security office?"

"Yes." Bo nodded.

"We'll need them to give me access to the Foothold's central tower. I can get into the Governor's office and create the permits."

"Aren't you a wanted man?" asked Kal.

"I am," Yonder admitted. "But I doubt anyone has memorized my face. I'm not the only traitor to the Nasi cause. If I use different access codes than my own, no one should be the wiser. I know my way around the tower and can get in and out quickly."

"You sure about this?" asked Kal.

Yonder looked at him quizzically. "No, I'm not sure that this will work. But I think it's the best course of action."

"Good enough," Kal said.

"We can bring the weapons back to Transport and Storage Unit Forty-One Delta. You'll need to use their haulers to get the materials out."

"Can't someone else do it?" asked Asha. "What about you, Kal? You're super crafty, right? Everyone seems to think so."

Kal pushed aside the sting of her words and looked down at her. "I'm sorry, Asha. Only your dad can do this. I won't make it three meters in the tower."

Yonder put an arm around his daughter. "He's right. It has

315

to be done, and it has to be me who does it."

❖

Kal sat in the cab of Delta Unit's hauler, idly tapping on the console. He'd set it up so he could watch feeds from the cameras mounted inside the bay. The Skulls were in Delta Unit's bay, sitting in separate haulers, waiting for Yonder to return. Trip sat motionless next to Kal, her hands at her side. He'd tried to make idle conversation with the woman, but she wouldn't respond beyond single word answers. Either Jadid didn't make small talk, or she had other things on her mind.

"What'll it look like?" asked Trip abruptly, causing Kal to jump.

"What will what look like?" he asked, confused.

"If you win and Grand Ancient Baykara is gone, what does that look like?"

"A lot less people will die for one."

Trip waved his words away and looked at him. "Death doesn't concern me. I think you know a bit about our history, so you realize that death has become like a friend to the Jadid. I care more about the living, what will our quality of life be like." She cleared her throat. "I've heard about Human history. You sent people to camps or exterminated them, even those you called friends."

"They're *your* ancestors too," Kal said. "You came from Humanity." He looked away. "Even if it doesn't seem like it sometimes."

"I can't imagine your people letting us live in peace. Not after everything that's happened."

"I don't see what other options they have," Kal said. "Remember that more than three quarters of Samsara Fleet is Jadid. Your people will be just as responsible for our victory as any Human. And your leaders will be part of that peace."

Kal caught movement on one the viewscreens and zoomed in. Yonder had run through the bay doors and was rushing to each vehicle, stopping to talk with the passengers. Kal opened the cab door as the Nasi approached, and Yonder glided in to sit next to him. He handed a small cylinder to Trip, who inserted it into the small computer—a comeca, the Nasi equivalent of a neural implant—which was strapped around her wrist.

They would arrive at the weapons caches scattered around the Foothold simultaneously, load the vehicles, then immediately depart for Alpha North. If it all went to plan, the Skulls would be gone before the Nasi security teams noticed that someone had cleared them out of a substantial portion of their weapons. Chief Kanumba and Asha had already left for the base and would be there waiting for them. Bo said he had some final stops to make in the Foothold but promised he'd find a way to the Fridge with the plasma lance plans.

"Let's roll," Kal ordered.

Trip looked at him with a puzzled expression.

"It means let's go," explained Yonder.

"Ahhh." Trip nodded and started the engine.

They glided through the bay doors into one of the

317

Foothold's main thoroughfares. Despite Yonder explaining there was no need, Kal slunk in his seat. For the Nasi, Human labor was cheap, and they often used people for mundane activities like transporting cargo. It might raise a few eyebrows after they picked up the weapons at the cache but still not so out of the ordinary as to attract much attention.

Kal had only *really* been in a Foothold once before, and he'd been raiding it at the time. The compound's low slung oval buildings appeared almost organic in nature with their irregular and multihued sides. They were built using prefabricated Nasi weaves, panels of an ultralight and strong fabric, that was stretched across metal frames. The areas between the buildings—they weren't streets as much as empty space—were mostly empty except for the occasional Nasi or vehicle.

"The Foothold was meant to hold many more Nasi than this," said Yonder. "Samsara Fleet—*you*—ended up putting a stop to that plan." Yonder gave Kal a crooked and very Human smile. "Ya know, if it wasn't for you and your soldiers, I think things would have ended up very differently."

"Right place at the right time."

"Maybe." Yonder seemed content to leave it there.

"Remember. Do not speak," instructed Trip as the hauler glided into the Nasi armory and brought them to a rest in the center of the large building. The interior was lined with a honeycomb of bays while several mechanical arms hung from the middle of the ceiling, dangling like the tentacles of a deep-sea creature.

Two Nasi, dressed in loose coveralls, approached the from the other side of the building and one made a gesture which Kal took as "sit there and wait." They walked to a nearby console and soon two of the arms on the ceiling swung to life, pulling several containers from the ground, and placing them within the storage bays. It was the type of activity that Humans had long since delegated to automated drones and bots.

After they'd secured the storage bay door, the workers strode across the open floor and stepped next to the hauler.

"Access card."

Trip held out her comeca to be scanned. "This is a lot," said the worker. It was a statement and a question.

"Yes," agreed Trip. "We have been tasked with bringing it in anticipation of a major offensive."

"You have a Human with you." The Nasi looked down at Kal. "Hey."

"Hey." He was surprised at the informal greeting.

"What do you think of all this?" asked the Nasi woman.

"The Foothold is amazing," Kal said, trying to muster as much excitement as possible. "Just a marvel that us Humans could have only dreamt about a couple of years ago."

"I've been into your city and talked with other Humans," the woman said skeptically. "I know you're lying. Stop saying what you *think* I want to hear."

Kal debated dropping the act for a moment, then decided to double down. The truth was too risky a proposition. "Not at all. Just the technology behind this hauler is amazing."

The woman noticed Yonder sitting next to Kal—specifically the Shishen tattoos encircling his hands and face—and stiffened.

"Apologies, Officer. I did not see you in the vehicle."

"Just fulfill the ordinance request," replied Yonder. "We need to get to my unit."

The woman spun around and moved back to the control console. Several of the appendages on the ceiling swung into action, plucking ammunition and weapons boxes from the bays and placing them into the hauler with a clink and scrape of metal on metal.

Once they were loaded, the hauler's back bay clicked shut, and the woman returned to the front of the vehicle.

"Everything is loaded, Officer. We'll just need your acknowledgment of receipt." The women held out a slate for Yonder.

"I am not on the document," said Yonder. "Have the driver sign."

The loader shook her head. "We cannot do that. Orders from the planetary command is that the most senior officer present must sign."

Yonder sighed and started to step out of the vehicle. As he slid out of his seat, he looked at Kal and Trip with a raised eyebrow and tapped his holster with his free hand.

Trip nodded and turned on the engine.

Yonder stepped around the front of the vehicle and pressed his hand against the tablet the loader held out. The woman turned the tablet around to study the screen and immediately jumped backwards. Before she could make another move, Yonder pulled out his pistol and fired directly into her torso. At the same time, Trip slammed the transport forward, hitting the other loader and sending him flying across the room, into the wall of storage containers. He fell to the ground with a thud and lay still.

Yonder ran to the building's entrance and slammed his hand on the entry panel. As the door dilated open, he jumped back to the vehicle and slid into the cab next to Kal. Trip accelerated forward, exiting the armory before the door had finished opening.

"Any idea if they triggered an alarm of some sort?" asked Kal.

"Probably was triggered as soon as I touched the tablet," said Yonder.

"Then why'd you do it?" asked Kal.

"I don't know." A note of exasperation touched the Nasi's words. "Probably because I don't like the idea of having to kill others. I thought maybe my biometrics wouldn't set it off." He slumped down in the seat. "Stupid, I know. But all this killing. It's been enough for me."

It was a very un-Nasi like sentiment. Yonder seemed to realize that as soon as he'd finished speaking because he looked down for a moment, wringing his hands.

It was also a sentiment Kal could fully understand. The faces of the people he'd killed swam before Kal's eyes. They were the ghosts that would haunt him the rest of his life. A silent army—led by his family—of people he'd let down. He hadn't had any choice, just like Yonder, but it didn't make him any less responsible.

"We're not going to be able to leave via the main gate," said Trip.

"What about the others?" Kal asked.

"They should be fine," said Yonder. "Security will be looking for me. Drop me off; I'm a liability."

"How'll you reach us?"

"I'll find a way," said Yonder. "I still have allies within the Foothold."

Trip pulled into a narrow space between two of the buildings, and Yonder jumped out of the vehicle while it was still in motion. A second later, he'd vanished.

"Neat trick, that," Kal said to himself.

Trip nodded, then headed to one of the gates. Each team had been assigned a specific gate to depart the Foothold. Having a line of them go through one would have likely raised alarms.

The Foothold's enormous wall loomed above them as they waited to exit. Kal couldn't help noticing the plasma cannons and missile launchers perched on top of the wall pointed their direction. A single press on the guards' wrist-mounted comecas would send Kal and Trip into oblivion.

"Access?"

The guards couldn't possibly have seemed less interested as they scanned Trip's comeca. Their attitude was a far cry from what Kal had first seen when the Nasi arrived. It was the kind of attitude he would have expected from a young Human soldier manning a guard post in some backwater planet. Clearly if there was an alert raised, this guard either hadn't received it or didn't care.

"Okay, you're free—"

"Stop!" A Nasi officer—based on the narrow band of Shishen tattoos across her face and arms—came running up to the vehicle. She had her sidearm out, pointed at directly at Kal's head. "Step out of the hauler, Human."

Fear shot through Kal, and he looked at Trip. She returned the look blankly. If he was looking for help, she couldn't, or wouldn't, be able to provide it.

"I said, get out!" The officer turned to the guards, who were now fully alert. "Watch this one. I've seen his face before."

As he stared down the barrel of the officer's pistol, Kal idly noted that it was a Human-built one. It didn't have the irregular shape and strange tones of a Nasi-built device. He noticed the depth of blue in the Nasi's eyes as she pointed it at him, her finger just touching the trigger stud.

"Yes, ma'am. I'm getting out." Kal opened the hauler's door and slowly slid out of his seat, his hands raised in the air. As his feet touched the ground, a blast erupted behind the Nasi officer, knocking them both down. Kal lay still for a moment, dazed from the blast. He could hear explosions and the sound of plasma fire around him. Then he heard another sound—shouting. Someone was shouting his name.

"Get up!"

Kal pushed himself up. Trip was leaning over the front seat

323

of the transport, shouting with her arm extended. "Get into the cab, Human."

Kal's instincts took over and he jumped forward, grabbed the Nasi's outstretched hand, and leapt into the vehicle. The guards had taken cover around them and were directing their fire at the top of a building inside the Foothold.

None of them seemed to pay any attention as the hauler sped through the gate. Kal adjusted a viewscreen so he could see the battle raging behind them. As the image shifted, he saw a body fall off a tall oblong building onto the ground. Plasma rounds hit it as it fell. Whoever it was, was dead. No doubt about it.

Yonder.

The Nasi officer had been trying to get out and saved them instead. Kal felt a pain in his gut and thought of Asha. She had lost both parents and now her adoptive father. He could almost picture her face crumbling when she heard the news.

Trip sped through the gridded streets of Tiradentes, weaving in and out of traffic and taking sharp turns and doubling back. All the while, she progressed farther and farther away from the Foothold. Finally, near the edge of the city, she merged in with other traffic and followed it as it left the city proper and headed out into the countryside.

Chapter Twenty-Four

Kal | New America

It was the middle of the night by the time Kal and Trip reached the Fridge. There was nothing outside the hauler's windows but inky blackness. Neither of them said a word during the hours long trip. Kal spent the time replaying the scene of Yonder falling from the building over and over in his head. What would he tell Asha?

The Fridge was completely filled; ships and transports of all makes and models were scattered throughout the enormous central cavern. There was barely enough room for Trip to set the hauler down on the metal-plate-clad floor.

The hum of conversation and maintenance greeted Kal as he opened the cab door. Men and women sporting the uniforms of different rebel groups filled the area, preparing for the upcoming assault. Pilots performed checks on ships and transports, while others practiced tactics in the small section of the cave that wasn't covered with vehicles.

It took Kal several minutes to find anyone he knew. After talking with several people, he located the Skulls and Cell Chief Pham sitting in a small circle near a wall, talking. They had pulled together several crates as makeshift benches and had the easy relaxed air of soldiers between missions.

"Good to see you, General Norman," said Chief Kanumba, waving her hand in greeting.

Kal nodded to her and looked for Asha. He hated to have to tell the young girl that she'd lost a parent. Again. At the sound of Kal's name, Asha appeared from behind Sergeant Kimathi, her hair half done up in braids.

"Dad? Dad?"

Asha ran up to Kal and looked up at him. "Where's my dad?"

Kal's mouth froze. What could he say? He'd been dreading this moment the entire trip from Tiradentes, and he still didn't know what to say to the girl.

"He's still coming," Kal said lamely. "We got split up." Trip's head swiveled to look at him, but she didn't say a word.

Asha frowned. "You sure?"

No not at all. "Yes, I'm sure. He's on his way."

Seemingly satisfied with Kal's answer, Asha walked back to Sergeant Kimathi, who returned to braiding her hair while talking with Private Ma.

The sergeant noticed Kal's look of astonishment. "What? I do this for my younger sister."

"He's the best," Asha said, smiling.

"I try. I try." Kimathi patted her on the shoulder and continued to work.

Kal pulled Cell Chief Pham to the side. "How are we coming along?"

"Well, better than expected," said Pham. "As you can see, we've basically filled the base. A few of these outfits are untested. But there's also a lot of *real* fighters in here. We've started to go through the Nasi equipment we procured, and it should make a pretty big difference."

Pham led him to one of the haulers. The back had been

opened and the crates inside had been stacked in three neat piles nearby. She pressed a small bump on the top of one of the crates and it dilated open. Pham reached in and pulled out a daton, the Nasi plasma rifle.

"These are better than anything we have," Pham said. "Maybe your fleet has something better, but us rebels are used to getting the dregs." She twirled the weapon with a small flourish. "But the real prize is in the next two piles."

Pham walked to the second stack of square-shaped crates, opened one of them, and motioned to Kal. "Take a look."

Inside were grenades of all shapes and sizes. Kal couldn't tell what all of them were, but he did see a few he recognized from having them thrown at him.

"Explosives like these are forbidden on New America," said Pham. "We've got some, but it's hard to have a huge supply with the Domespat."

Kal nodded and made what he hoped was an appreciative grunt.

"And these," said Pham, walking slowly to the third pile. "Well, they *could* be the difference between victory and defeat if we can get them working."

She reached into a case and pulled out a crumpled pile of black fabric.

"What is it?" asked Kal.

"Nasi battle suit." Pham said it almost reverently. "I've been on the other side of these things for so long. Never thought I might have one of my own." She smiled. "Only question is whether we can get it to work."

327

Kal picked up one of the suits and studied it; it was surprisingly light and flexible. Human battle suits were controlled through the wearer's neural implant. Since the Nasi didn't have them, it meant there had to be some sort of mechanical control inside the suits. He studied the folds of fabric, fruitlessly looking for some sort of pad or console. They'd need Bowen's help; he was the only one who had enough understanding of Nasi technology to even *attempt* to make the suits work.

"I figure Yonder must be familiar with them. When he gets back, he can give a quick class." Pham set the suit back in the crate.

"Uh, about that..."

Pham shot Kal a glance. "You couldn't tell her." A statement, not a question.

Kal shook his head.

"I don't blame you. After all that girl's been through, I wouldn't want to be the one to break the bad news either."

"I'll tell her when this is all over," Kal said.

"If you survive," Pham said, closing the case.

Kal was overseeing a training exercise with several rebel groups when Bo arrived in a banged-up transport that had clearly gone through several rounds of aftermarket modifications. Kal was relieved to hear that he had been able to find the updated plans for the Nasi plasma lances. But when he told Kal exactly what the Nasi had done, the relief quickly faded.

"Bo, you're telling me they've purposely rigged the entire place to blow?" asked Kimathi.

"Afraid so," said Bo. "More than that, they've rerouted the plasma so that there are also several false nexuses at each site. Essentially, they've built these plasma lances into bombs."

"Snip the wrong wire and boom," said Pham bitterly.

"Well, bombs haven't contained wires in hundreds of years—even here—but yes." Bo nodded his head gravely.

Kal studied the plans that Bo had downloaded to his tablet. It was not a pretty picture. The plasma lances were relatively simple in design: plasma flowing from a generation plant meets energy produced by a reactor and then funnels to the barrel. There were a lot of added complexities that he didn't fully understand, but that had been the main idea. With the new design, the Nasi had added false conduits and lined the entire system with anti-tamper defenses, making it next to impossible to take out. Add to that, the fact that the Triple-A charges for the missions had been destroyed with the *Cumae*, and it was downright depressing.

Kal sat the tablet down next to him and placed his head between his knees. Every time they thought they were getting somewhere, it all went to hell.

"Does this really change anything?" asked Kimathi. "I mean, we always knew this was a one in a million shot."

"If by always, you mean in the past two days by always,

then yes," said Chief Kanumba.

"Look, we got several thousand heavily motivated fighters, and the weaponry to arm them," said Pham. "To include Nasi battle suits."

Bo looked at her. "*Nasi* battle suits?"

Pham nodded.

"Perhaps there's something we can do in that case," said Bo. "The fail-safes can be turned off at the lances' central control rooms. A squad wearing full battle suits would likely be permitted to enter. They'd just need to bluster past the guards."

"What about overriding these fail-safes?" asked Kal. We'll need someone who knows their systems."

Bo bit his lower lip. "True. I can probably provide some help, but we'll need people who know the system. We'll need Nasi to join in the mission."

"All we've got is Delta Unit," said Kal. He turned to Duke. "Would your people be willing to help?"

The Delta Unit leader had already said they wouldn't take part in the fighting, that they didn't want to be part in an attack on their own people. Now he looked as if he was at least reconsidering that stance.

"I don't know," said Duke. He took a deep breath. "It's a lot to ask. More than we had originally agreed to."

"Well, one way or another we're going ahead with this mission," said Kal. "Your unit can decide whether we have a chance of surviving it."

❖

While Duke met with the other Nasi, Bo stood on top of one of the rebel ships, yelling out instructions on how to use the battle suits. It had been surprisingly easy to convert them for Human use. A small issue was that only the taller Humans were able to fit inside them.

Kal felt strange wearing the Nasi suit. He'd expected it to be the same or at least relatively similar to a Human battle suit. Instead, it felt like putting on a bathrobe as compared to wearing a suit of armor with the Human one. The suits were made from a thick fabric with several rigid containers affixed to the outside where the weaponry and other systems were stored. Rather than stepping into it, Kal pulled it one like a set of coveralls. Once inside, he pressed a small control in the interior of the hands and the fabric turned into a hard shell.

Controlling the suit was difficult: the suite of sensors that lined the interior amplified every move Kal made, and he found himself crashing into the walls of the cavern more than once as he tried to master it. After an hour of embarrassing failure, he was able to leap over the ships and fly through the room in a relatively controlled manner.

Thankfully he wasn't the only one having difficulty. Rebel fighters crashed against the ceiling, walls, ships, and each other as they tried to master the Nasi battle suits. Kal was having a great time; it was impossible not to laugh as hardened soldiers flew into cavern walls with a string of curses.

Satisfied that he'd learned enough to not immediately die, he deactivated his suit and placed it into the ship the Skulls' had commandeered. Duke was waiting for him as he turned around.

"General, we've had a chance to think it over," said the Nasi formally.

"And?"

"We're willing to help," said Duke. "All of the members of Transport and Storage Unit Forty-One Delta are in."

"Thank you," said Kal. "You're giving us a chance."

"We felt it is what we owe," responded the Nasi solemnly. "Our people brought this war here. We have been complicit in it even if we did not personally destroy Earth or kill anyone."

"Do you know how to use a battle suit?" Kal asked.

Duke chuckled. "Of course. All Nasi do."

When he felt the fighters were fully trained on the suits, or at least as trained as they could be, Kal called the command group together. They huddled off to one side of the bay along with the Nasi who had volunteered to be a part of the mission.

By their estimates Samsara fleet was approximately twelve hours out, just enough time to get to the lances and mount their assault. He went through the plan with each assault team commander, ensuring that they knew it forward and back and that their Nasi counterpart understood their part as well.

They'd have to enter the lance sites at their main entrances. The cover story was that they were rooting out potential insider threats and needed to see the security logs. Bo and the other Nasi felt like none of the Nasi would immediately question their story for fear of being labeled a traitor themselves. Once inside the control room, they'd have to take out the Nasi and inject a script that would disable the self-destruct protocols, at least for a time, and signal for the others to commence their attack.

"You sure they're not going to question us?" asked Kimathi. "That they'll let us in?"

"Well, *sure* is a strong word," replied Kal. "But Bo seems pretty confident."

"You'll need to each act your part," said Bo, facing the Nasi. "Do not let them question you. Ensure you tell them anyone who does so is immediately assumed to be a traitor." They nodded back at him.

"The good news is that we can use the planetary net once the mission starts," said Kal. "At that point, it won't matter whether the Nasi know we're attacking or not."

"I got one more idea," said Pham. "We've got fighters who aren't here. Citizens in Tiradentes and elsewhere that want to help. Let's put them to use."

"How?" asked Kal.

"The Nasi probably expect us. They know we're going to attack and will send everything they have to repel it," said the cell chief. "But what if they're being attacked everywhere?"

"We have enough people to do that?" asked Kal.

Pham laughed. "Of course not. But we have enough to *seem* like it."

❖

Kal completed another round of training with the Nasi suit. It still wasn't a second skin like the Human version, but he was getting there. The teams attacking lances on the far side of the planet had already left, leaving the Skulls and the three remaining assault teams. Kal felt a renewed sense of purpose now that they had committed to the mission.

Asha walked up to him as he stripped off the Nasi battle suit and placed it on the ground. Her sky-blue eyes were rimmed with red, and he already knew what she was going to ask.

"Where's my dad?"

He didn't want to have this conversation, especially now. Asha didn't like to talk about her life, especially before she met Yonder, but Kal had an idea of what is must have been like. Would she ever have a chance at happiness or a future?

Kal went to one knee. "I'm sorry, Asha. I don't think he's returning."

He reached toward her, but she stepped back, wrapped her arms around her body, and turned away.

"He was very brave," said Kal softly. "And he loved you very much."

"I know." The girl's voice came out stilted as her body shook softly.

Kal touched her small boney shoulder. "I had a little girl who was brave and smart like you. Her name was Lan Fen. I loved her very much, but I lost her, just like you lost Yonder." Asha sniffed.

"We have one mission left, then this will all be over, and you can stay with me." He regretted the words as soon as they were out of his mouth. What was he going to do with a kid? Bring her on the *Ofira*? Take her on missions?

Asha turned and looked at him, tears streaming from her eyes.

"I have a friend I'd like you to meet," Kal continued. "Her name is Nicole. She's super nice. And brave like you."

Maybe it could work, thought Kal. Maybe she could live on the ship.

"I'm alone again," said Asha.

"No, you're not," Kal said emphatically. "You've got me. You've got everyone here. You will *never* be alone again." As Kal said the words, he was surprised to realize he meant them. If there was one good thing he could do, it was to make sure Asha's future would not be the same as her past. He'd make every single person in the Fridge promise to take care of the girl if he had to.

"Thank you." Asha turned and gave him a small hug, then darted away, scrambling between the ships.

Chapter Twenty-Five
Nicole | Patagonia

Nicole froze. What were their options? They were under attack from the front and the rear. Their forces were split, and their heavy weapons were gone.

Fire back with everything you have, she shouted over the net. Keep moving forward. We just need to get to that nexus.

Kinkaid and the other half of their force were in some other part of the nest of tunnels. There was no calvary coming to save them. Nicole remembered something Kal told her once. She'd asked him why they continued to train in close quarters combat when their enemy had missiles and plasma rounds.

"If you're fighting hand-to-hand, haven't you already lost?" Nicole had asked.

He'd looked at her with a trademark Kal expression, a mixture of humor and determination. "Maybe," he admitted. "But you've never really lost until you stop fighting. Sometimes—almost never—but sometimes, you can win through sheer force of will. You might not be able to outthink or outshoot your enemy, but you can refuse to go down and throw every last thing you've got at 'em."

This was one of those times, Nicole realized.

She ran toward the front of the formation as flashes of explosions and plasma danced on the walls of the cavern. The other fighters saw what she was doing and started to shout and run behind her, pushing toward the front of the column and the enemy.

"Keep going," Nicole called out. "Don't stop until we've run over those bastards."

She wished she had something more inspirational to say, but even though she'd been a diplomat, speeches didn't come naturally. Still, the people around her screamed in determination and redoubled their pace, running toward the increasingly loud sounds of fighting. When Nicole reached the front of the formation, a carpet of bodies littered the ground in front of her. Nasi crouched behind barriers lining the tunnel ahead, firing indiscriminately into the mass of people.

Nicole launched in the air and flew at a battle-suited Nasi standing in the center of the tunnel. She twisted in midair, using the lateral thruster while keeping her railgun pointed directly at her target. The high-velocity slug went through the creature's head, and they dropped to the ground before she landed.

She immediately moved to the side, evading a rocket, and slammed into a Nasi that had taken cover against the wall, crushing them. She flew to the other side of the tunnel, unsheathing the meter-long sword from her gauntlet and impaled another soldier against the stone.

Let's go, Ramos called out. Follow the commander.

The mass of people behind Nicole surged forward, and the tunnel grew bright as day from the green and blue plasma fire crisscrossing through the area.

Nicole continued to stalk forward, methodically choosing her next target and locking onto them before she had time to think. Her mind filled with images of the people she'd lost because of the Nasi. She was no longer Nicole Bergeron. She was vengeance.

We're not going to make it.

Nicole snapped out of her trance-like state and looked around. She was far ahead of the main body. So far ahead she couldn't see any other Human. Nasi bodies were strewn across the ground around her.

An assault ship flew down the tunnel in front of her and eight battle-suit-clad Nasi jumped off and streaked towards her with fluid grace. The ship's gunner fired an explosive charge at her, barely missing and hitting the tunnel wall.

They fired another shot which hit at her feet and sent her flying across the tunnel and into the far wall. Her suit's diagnostic panel flashed red and then died. The helmet's viewscreen blinked and then faded to black. She was entombed in the battle suit, unable to move or even see what was going on around her.

Nicole waited for the inevitable. Her breathing was deafening in the lifeless helmet, and she could feel the vibrations of battle going on around her. Hopefully, the others would be able to reach the nexus. Hopefully the sacrifices that she'd made were not for nothing.

Someone ripped off her helmet, and she felt a rush of cool smoky air across her face. A featureless head loomed above her.

"Miss us?" the strange creature asked.

Nicole couldn't speak. What was going on?

The person standing over her pulled their helmet up, revealing a small beard and a smile that gleamed in the darkness of the cave. Scrapper.

"Cat got your tongue?" he asked.

"I thought I was dead."

He laughed. "You almost were. But you can't die yet. Not when we're so close. You got us all together, so you need to finish it."

Scrapper turned Nicole's suit over and activated the emergency release. The seam along the back and limbs popped open and Nicole gingerly pushed herself up and out. The tunnel around them was strewn with bodies, both Human and Nasi.

An army of people stood in front of her. Their patched fabric clothing had metal plates and spikes weaved into it. They wore masks with horns or grotesque faces edged into them and brandished weapons that appeared to have been made at home from spare parts.

"Where the hell did you come from?"

Scrapper helped Nicole up. "We followed the trail of bodies."

Nicole realized what she was looking at; these were the citizens of the communes, the outcasts of Patagonia. There were hundreds—maybe thousands—of them and they'd come to fight.

"Thank you," Nicole said. "Your people have certainly earned a seat at the table in whatever government Patagonia has in the future."

"Oh, we'll hold you to that," snapped Mother Ju. The woman was wearing a plate-mail dress that was fashioned from transport body panels. Nicole could hear the whine of motors as she moved closer and saw the glint from a metallic exoskeleton underneath the plates. "But let's focus on the Nasi for now."

She tossed a weapon to Nicole. It took Nicole a moment to realize it was a railgun. From everything she knew, the weapon shouldn't exist; railguns were only able to be used with battle suits due to the recoil and energy consumption.

"The thing has a kick, so be ready," Ju advised.

"I think we've got every Nasi on the planet up ahead," said Scrapper.

"The nexus is there," said Nicole. It had to be based on what she'd seen on the tacmap.

Nicole reflexively dropped to the ground as a cascade of explosions thundered in the tunnel ahead of them. She flushed as she realized she was the only one that had. The others had simply turned and brought their weapons to the ready. The people of the communes were not about to be intimidated by a few loud noises.

She heard heavy footsteps and turned around to see two battle-suited fighters running toward them. The rest of her assault team was following not far behind. Nicole stood up and gave a small salute with her weapon.

"The other group," said Sergeant Grupp through his suit's external speaker. "They must have reached the nexus."

"Then what the hell are we waiting for?" Nicole hefted the

railgun onto her shoulder. "Remember the mission isn't to kill Nasi; it's to destroy the plasma lance. Do whatever you need to make it happen."

Nicole turned and ran toward the sound of fighting in the tunnel ahead. The others joined her, their metal armor clanging and creaking as they sprinted. The few people in battle suits took off and flew ahead, their plasma fire preceding them.

Nicole crested a small rise in the tunnel to find an enormous cavern filled with chaos. Nasi and Humans fought in groups, trading fire or engaged in hand-to-hand combat. Despite their superior numbers, the Humans were losing. The Nasi moved from position to position with a fluid grace, their datons seemingly a part of their bodies. The area was too crowded and filled with smoke for Nicole see the nexus, but she *knew* it was beyond the sea of Nasi in front of her.

Bergeron, is that you? It was Kinkaid.

Yes, we came with some friends.

'Bout time. The Nasi are slicing us apart. Our heavy weapons are gone.

The battle was steadily turning in favor of the Nasi defenders. Despite their numbers and grit, the Human forces were outmatched. They could have outnumbered the Nasi a hundred to one and would still lose in the long run.

"We can't wait for the long run," Nicole whispered to herself. That was the key. Their one chance. The battle had to end now. The longer the Nasi dragged it out, the greater their chance of victory.

We're losing, Nicole said to her small cadre of leaders, and the longer this goes on, the less chance we have of winning.

You may need to brush up on your pep talks, ma'am, Captain Uhaa replied.

We have a single chance to get past the Nasi, Nicole said. Which means we have to work together. It's all or nothing. We need to be—she thought back to the ancient game Sergeant Kimathi liked to play—a wildcard. On my signal, battle suits and heavy weapons teams, ignore everything else go directly at the nexus with everything you've got. Everyone else, cover them.

Sounds suicidal, said Grupp. I like it.

Wait for my mark, Nicole instructed.

She adjusted her implant to broadcast over the wide net so that every Human in the area could hear her. *In three we make our push*, Nicole said. She was shouting, which wouldn't translate over the net, but it didn't matter to her. *Either we destroy the nexus now or we all die trying. I want you to put everything you can into getting there. Cover the battle suits and the heavy weapons. This is it.*

Nicole counted down from three. When she reached zero, every Human in the cavern let loose a withering barrage of fire. The plasma rounds bounced off Nasi shields and sizzled into the cave walls and ceilings. Missiles streaked into groups of Nasi, and grenades exploded all around. The battle suits and transports flew over the crowd, straight at the nexus' location. Whenever a Nasi attempted to fire at them or get in their way, missiles and plasma coated them, taking them out.

After a quick assessment of her life decisions, Nicole ran forward into the center of the battle. She saw many other people had the same idea. Mother Ju ran toward a group of Nasi while firing at them with a railgun in each hand. Several people dressed in the homespun outfits of farmers formed into a wedge and charged towards the nexus, lobbing grenades in front of them. Two merchants stood back-to-back and deliberately fired at the Nasi surrounding them, ignoring the return fire that came so close it singed their hair.

Initially, the Nasi were taken aback by the ferocity of the Human attack. But they recovered quickly and started to use their opponents' aggression against them. The Nasi would fall back, allowing a group of attackers forward, then encircle them and wipe them out from behind.

Nicole heard a series of loud explosions from the direction of the nexus. She ran towards them, expecting to be cut down at any time.

As she pressed forward, Nicole realized that she was surrounded by friends and the common people of Patagonia. They pressed bravely forward against the meat grinder of the Nasi. Each time someone fell, another one rushed forward to take their place.

They broke through the enemy formation, destroying everything in their path, until Nicole saw a glint of light reflected off a large box partially embedded in the cave wall. As she got closer, she could see dents and charring on the outside. It'd been hit by something for sure. One thing she didn't see were any battle suits overhead. Had they all been taken down?

As if in answer to her question, a battle suit flew across the room and crashed into the nexus with its meter-long blade extended and then dropped to the ground, rolling several times before coming to a stop. She could see a ragged gash in the armor of the nexus.

Nicole tried to reach whoever was in the battle suit over the net. There was no answer. She looked around and realized that there were only a handful of Humans around her from their initial assault. Mother Ju was meters away, a vicious gash across her cheek and several of the panels of her armor missing. She looked at Nicole and shook her head slightly. Their plan had failed.

"Look," Ju shouted, her voice barely audible over the din of the fighting around them.

A pulsing glow emanated from the tear in the side of the nexus. The blade had gotten through the armor. Now they needed to plant the explosives inside. Nicole would have killed for a grenade or missile.

She looked around for something to use, but her small group was surround by Nasi who were quickly and methodically killing every Human left. Nicole's eyes lit on the battle suit, and she ran toward it with Ju on her heels.

She was about to reach the suit when a Nasi jumped in front of them and swung out with his daton, barely missing Nicole's head.

Thankfully he was not wearing battle armor. But even

without it, the violet creature was more than a match for two Humans. Nicole was already jumping to the side when he pointed his daton at her. The shot passed centimeters from her face. As she fell, she fired her railgun wildly from the hip, but the shot sailed wide, pinging off the armored nexus.

The Nasi already had her sighted in, their weapon pointed directly at Nicole's center of mass. Nasi occasionally missed but never twice.

A blade burst through his chest, coated in blood. As the creature fell forward, the person in the battle suit behind it fell to their knees.

"Get out of here," Grupp's voice said from the external speaker. "I've got to finish this." His suit made a grinding noise as he stood up.

"Nah," Ju said. "You don't get to play the hero again. I'm going with you."

Grupp paused then pulled two grenades from a thigh pocket in the suit and handed one to Ju. "Fine. I've got two left. Let's go."

"I'll cover you," said Nicole. She hadn't come that far to just walk away. She would see this to the end. When the war started, she'd betrayed everything. She'd at least finish it honorably.

Grupp ran forward, his blade still extended from his left arm and his railgun held in his right, and Nicole and Ju followed. The handful of Humans remaining around them saw what was happening and put everything into holding off the Nasi.

They reached the nexus, and Nicole and Ju took positions on either side of Grupp. A small trail of plasma had leaked from the side and started dripping on the ground, hissing and smoking where it made contact with the cave floor. The Front rebel reached into the tear, placing several grenades in the lining between the Nexus' outer armor and whatever was holding in the plasma.

"Let's go," Grupp shouted as he roughly grabbed Nicole and Ju around the waist. He launched into the air with the two women pressed tightly against his suit as plasma fire continued to streak around them. Nicole was barely able to breathe with Grupp's metallic arm pressing her chest into the suit.

She wasn't sure what she expected. In fact, they hadn't talked about what would happen if they were successful in destroying the nexus. A blinding light perhaps. Perhaps a sudden feeling of peace as the explosion disintegrated everything inside the cavern. Instead she felt a painfully intense pressure in her ears as a shockwave followed them across the room. It overwhelmed Grupp's thrusters and sent them spinning head over heels through the air. An enormous ball of white and blue plasma mushroomed from the nexus, overwhelming the Nasi surrounding it. It almost filled the entire cavern, coursing along the ceilings and walls like a living thing and swallowing anything in its path.

They crashed to the ground near one of the cavern's entrances; close to where the remains of Kinkaid's forces were. The impact ripped Nicole and Ju from the suit's grasp and sent them across the ground and into a nearby wall.

Nicole pushed herself up and looked around. The ground around her was littered with Human and Nasi bodies alike. The living streamed out of the chamber, running from the ball of plasma that was filling it. Humans and Nasi ran in different directions as if by unspoken agreement.

Nicole got to her knees and then willed herself to stand, her mind barely registering the stabs of pain. She looked at Mother Ju, who'd stood up next to her and had a nasty gash near her hairline. The woman was shouting something, but Nicole couldn't hear a thing over the high-pitched tone that filled her head.

They looked back toward Grupp. He lay motionless on the ground. Ju rushed over shouting something, and he slowly pulled himself up.

Nicole, Ju, and Grupp followed the crowd of Humans running through the caves toward the entrance. The growing mass of plasma behind them lit the way, casting long shadows in front of them. Occasionally, someone in front of Nicole looked back, their eyes wide with fright. Nicole would study their face to see if it was someone she knew, but the tunnel was too dark for her to tell. Based on the light and a growing sense of heat on her back, she could tell the plasma blob was catching up with them.

Ju grabbed Nicole's sleeve and pulled her toward a tunnel that led upwards. Nicole followed, trusting that the woman knew where she was going. Nicole looked back. The plasma had filled the entire tunnel behind them and continued to pulse forward. As they raced through the winding tunnels, the plasma grew ever closer. Nicole's nose was filled with a metal-tinged sulfur odor that caused her to gag. She could see from Mother Ju's tearstained eyes and open mouth that she was having the same issue.

They spilled out of the tunnel, and Nicole almost ran off a narrow ledge that traced the top of a cliff the dropped to the ocean. Grupp reached out, snatched the back of her blouse, and pulled her against the side of the mountain as the plasma oozed from the opening they'd just exited and landed in the water with a gout of steam.

Nicole's implant suddenly burst to life. *Attention citizens of Patagonia, this is General Frederick Zhou of Samsara Fleet. We have destroyed the Nasi fleet orbiting your planet.*

They'd done it. Nicole couldn't believe it. *They'd done it! The plasma lance had been destroyed.* She dropped down onto the ground and looked across the canyon. Had anything ever looked so beautiful?

Chapter Twenty-Six

Nicole | Patagonia

It took an hour for Nicole and the others to reach the
Chester. Out of the thousands that had participated in the
assault, there were only twelve in Nicole's group—including
Grupp and Mother Ju. She had to believe that there were
more survivors, but she didn't see another person on their
way to the ship. Her joy at their success had faded with the
awareness that the others who'd fought beside them were
most likely dead. Chief Ramos and Captain Uhaa were
nowhere to be found when they reached the ship.

She climbed up the rear cargo ramp to find a priority
message from General Zhou already waiting for her on the
ship's computer. The ringing in Nicole's ears had subsided to
a constant faint tone, and she was able to hear again.

"Colonel Bergeron, we need you to report back to the
Resolution"—General Zhou's flagship—"as soon as possible.
We've got additional information to discuss. I understand that
the mission was compromised, and you may not have all your
forces. Once we've disabled all Nasi installations on the
planet's surface, we'll be sending out rescue teams to look for
them. Despite that, I need you to report back now."

It wasn't like Zhou to be so curt—or to have such an
imperious tone to his message. However, the Nasi had shown
they could block long-range transmissions. It made sense that
he wouldn't want to talk specifics over a net even if it *was*
encrypted. Nicole didn't like the general's orders, but she

wasn't completely surprised. They'd always known that the destruction of the Nasi fleet would only be the beginning of their work on Patagonia. Still, she'd thought she'd have at least a *few* minutes to relax.

After tending to their wounds with the medbot, Nicole, Ju, and Grupp left the planet's surface aboard the *Chester*. Nicole was overjoyed to see the smattering of green icons on the ship's tacmap. Samsara Fleet truly had arrived; there wasn't a Nasi ship left in orbit. Unfortunately, the plasma lances had clearly had an effect before being destroyed. Only a third of the fleet remained, and all of them were Jadid.

"What happens now?" asked Ju, staring out the cockpit viewscreen, captivated by the blue orb that was Patagonia. It dawned on Nicole that the woman had never left her home planet before.

"It's going to be a long road," said Nicole. "But with the Nasi gone, Samsara Fleet can stabilize the planet and end the fighting."

"And this time, you'll be a part of that," Grupp added from the copilot's chair.

"I'll keep my promise," Nicole said. "General Zhou, who's leading this fleet, will know exactly what you've done."

Ju touched the planet on the cockpit's viewscreen. "We just want a say. That's all."

"You'll get it," Grupp said gruffly.

As they neared the *Resolution*, Nicole could see scarring on the hull and a large portion of the ship had been ripped out, leaving a cloud of debris hovering in the area. The crew was lucky to be alive.

They touched down in one of the enormous landing bays and Nicole, flanked by Grupp and Ju, stepped down the cargo ramp. She wasn't sure what to expect when the ramp dropped, but it certainly wasn't Jadid walking around stone-faced, going about their jobs as if nothing had happened. They'd just won a major victory. They'd liberated a planet. She would've thought she'd see at least a smile or two.

The Nasi would have smiled, Nicole thought to herself.

"Colonel Bergeron." General Zhou stood smiling at the base of the *Chester's* ramp.

"General Zhou." Nicole saluted. If it had been anyone else, she would've expected a hug. But the general had always been distant and had become even more so since joining Ancient Wang's personal staff.

Zhou turned on his heel and beckoned Nicole. "Follow me," he said. "We need to talk."

"What about the soldiers?" Nicole asked, gesturing behind her.

A small twist of his mouth indicated Zhou's annoyance. "No worries. We'll take care of them." He turned back around and continued walking.

Nicole followed the general through the twisted alien corridors of the ship. Jadid may have evolved from Humanity, but they often seemed to be a completely different species. The dim, winding hallways were at testament to that.

Zhou led Nicole to a small office and the general took a seat behind the desk, the smile on his face gone. Most

351

Humans who had quarters or offices aboard an alien vessel did something to make them less foreign. However, Zhou's office looked identical to any other Nasi room Nicole had been in, featureless and dim with a minimum complement of furniture.

"Colonel Bergeron, congratulations on your victory," said Zhou. "You called us to the planet a bit too early. But in the end, you came through."

"It was a setup—"

Zhou waved her protests away. "I look forward to reading your report. I called you here to discuss something else."

Nicole didn't like the sound of that. She leaned forward. What else could there be to discuss? The liberation of the last two colonies, Wudexingqiu and Mariga?

"I have a lot of respect for you as an officer." Zhou tented his hands on his desk. "What you've done with barely any training—or at least only on-the-job training is amazing." He took a deep breath. "I am telling you this because I'm concerned. We are so close to victory, but what does that victory mean?"

He's talking like the Jadid, Nicole realized.

"Freedom, sir." Nicole didn't know where he was going but she didn't like it.

Zhou waved her comment away again. "Yes. But more than that, freedom to do what? You've seen what the UEG was. Do we want to go back to that? Or do we take this opportunity to evolve, to become more?" His voice rose with excitement. "I've been talking with Ancient Wang, and he has

352

a vision for Humanity. A vision for peaceful coexistence between us and the Jadid. They are our long-lost brethren and can teach us so much."

"What does General Samaha say about this?" Nicole asked.

"When I've talked to her about it, she's been"—he shifted in his chair—"uncomfortable with it." He frowned then continued speaking. "But we don't have time to wait for her to come around. Ancient Wang has a plan, and with the Jadid, we can accomplish it. Without the Jadid, what do we have? Leave these planets to their own devices once again? Let the rest of the galaxy swallow them up whole?"

Nicole hated to admit it, but the general had a point there. The Nasi had essentially blasted away the military might in this part of the galaxy. But the rest of the species were rebuilding. What was to say that they wouldn't decide to take over the Human colonies with the Nasi gone? They needed the Jadid.

"Who'd lead this group, sir? You? Wang?"

"For now, Ancient Wang. But in the future, once we're stable and secure, we can open elections. We can rebuild and create something even more powerful than the UEG."

Was this why he wanted to speak with me? Nicole wondered. It wasn't something that was time-sensitive. It wasn't even something that she would normally be involved in; she was just a scout commander after all. She felt a sense of dread as she understood the subtext of Zhou's words. Either she got on board or she wasn't leaving the *Resolution* anytime soon.

Nicole shook her head vehemently. "It's something, but for now, we need to reinstall the Patagonian government. *They* need to decide the next steps for their planet." There were so many people who'd been lost. She wondered if Garcia and the rest of the government—or the rest of her team—were still alive on the planet. The Nasi weren't known to be merciful. Also, she expected that the fleet had already obliterated many of the Nasi facilities from orbit, places where they might have held prisoners.

Zhou shook his head. "No, I will be the planetary governor for now. The Jadid will carry out the administrative functions of the planet with Human officers that I've handpicked from the fleet as their seconds."

"This sounds like a dictatorship, not a democracy."

Zhou slammed his hand down on the table. "So what? Was democracy that great? It already failed us. The politics and infighting? This is what we need for now. We'll rebuild and become stronger than any force in the galaxy. Humans *will* become the dominant species. Then after a few years, Ancient Wang will relinquish power and open free elections for a new interstellar Human government."

Nicole snorted. "That's what they all say." She'd studied the great dictatorships of the past. They always started the same way; an emergency—sometimes manufactured, sometimes not—and a promise to give up power when things are better. Only they *never* do get better. There's always a new enemy, a new problem.

"I won't be a part of this," said Nicole finally. She knew what that meant. She also knew that Zhou had expected her decision and that his own twisted code of ethics meant he felt he had to at least ask.

Zhou's eyes flashed and he reflexively clenched his hands into fists, but his voice remained as calm as deep space. "When the Nasi first attacked, General Norman allowed me the time to understand how I needed to change my point of view." Nicole knew what he really meant was that Kal locked him in his stateroom until he realized that the EDF had ceased to exist. "I am going to extend you the same courtesy."

Two Jadid guards strode into the room and grabbed Nicole by the arms before she could put up much of a fight.

"Take her to the brig," Zhou commanded. He looked at Nicole with a trace of sorrow. "I understand your hesitation. Eventually, you will see that this is the right thing, the only thing, for Humanity."

The two guards firmly escorted Nicole through the winding corridors. The Jadid they passed looked through her and didn't seem to find anything suspicious or particularly interesting about a Human prisoner being shoved past them.

She tried to protest, to say something to the guards, but they refused to acknowledge her. *How had this happened?* Nicole thought in despair. After everything they'd done to overthrow the Nasi, their only reward was a new dictatorship.

As the guards shoved her through the hallways, she felt a soul-crushing weight of despair and thought of her friends. Mother Ju. Scrapper. Grupp. They were all in danger. Ancient Wang must already be heading to New America. If Kal and the Skulls were successful, all they'd get was imprisonment— or worse. She doubted that Ancient Wang would be as hesitant to kill as General Zhou.

As they turned a corner, a violet streak lashed out. Before Nicole could register what was happening, the two guards were down, their bodies twitching slightly. A small—for a Jadid—woman stood in front of Nicole. It took Nicole a moment to register who she was looking at. Ai Martinez, a Jadid scientist who'd been captured by the Nasi and then rescued by the Skulls.

"Come on," Ai hissed, grabbing Nicole roughly by the arm. "Just act normal."

Although they weren't close, Nicole knew Ai decently well. She'd wondered for a while if there might be a romantic relationship between her and Bo. She hadn't been able to confirm her theory, but Bo's affinity for Humans had certainly rubbed off on the woman after months together on the Ofira.

Ai pulled a shocked and stumbling Nicole through the ship's hallways. When they arrived outside the flattened circular door of a landing bay, she shoved Nicole against the wall and peeked through the opening. Nicole could hear the ships inside taking off and landing at an almost constant pace. The Jadid were busy; they must still be hunting down the remnants of the Nasi on the planet's surface.

And any Human resistors, Nicole thought dismally.

Ai crept toward the door, clearly getting ready to run through. Nicole pulled at her arm.

"Wait! What about the others?"

Ai looked back, a wistful frown on her gaunt face. "I'm sorry. They're all in holding cells. I barely got to you in time."

"We can't just leave them."

Ai turned and grabbed Nicole by the shoulders.

"We've got to get out of here. You're all I can save. Perhaps we can make it to Bo and the Skulls in time." She paused and took a deep breath. "I've heard things about Ancient Wang. I don't think he'll be as lenient to dissenters as your General Zhou has been. The Skulls—and everyone else on New America —are in danger."

Nicole ran a hand through her hair. What could she do? Leaving felt like an act of cowardice, but Ai was right. She didn't have any way to help the others if she stayed. If they left, she *might* be able to warn Kal in time. Despite that, she remembered the mantra of the Tac-I: leave no soldier behind.

"There are more of us," Ai hissed. "We had our suspicions about Wang. There are others who will free as many people free as possible when the time is right. If we stay, we risk exposing them."

The choice was clear. The Bones and everyone else on Patagonia would have to fight without Nicole. "Let's go."

Ai nodded and grabbed Nicole's arm, twisting it until Nicole thought it might break. "I'll try to be gentle with you," the Jadid whispered in her ear.

Nicole nodded, unable to speak from the pain.

As they stepped into the landing bay, a guard, dressed in the form-fitting Jadid uniform, stopped them with a raised hand.

"What are you doing here?"

"I am taking this prisoner to the surface," Ai said evenly.

"Documents?"

Ai held onto Nicole with one hand and stuck the other arm—the one with her comeca—towards the guard. After a scan, he nodded and then motioned for them to proceed.

She led them to a small shuttle and pushed Nicole up the side ramp. The interior was cramped, only a single chamber with benches lining the side and a pilot's console up front. It was a style of ship that Nicole had never seen before, a strange hybrid of Nasi and Human technology.

"What is this ship?" asked Nicole.

"Ah," Ai said with a small smirk. "There's only one ship in the fleet that I can requisition without approval from higher." She raised her eyebrow, clearly waiting for Nicole to figure out what she was saying.

After a moment Ai let out an exasperated sigh. "It's a skip ship."

Skip ships were the only vessels that could make the journey between the Human's Universe and the Jadid's. There were only a handful of them in existence and they were almost priceless. Due to difference in the concept of space between the two universes, a skip ship could make the journey between New America and Patagonia in hours instead of days.

Nicole hugged the scientist. "You're a genius."

"Well, yes, I am one of the foremost experts in inter-universal travel in the two known universes," said Ai with a confused tone. "Of course I'm a genius. Now we need to leave."

She strode to the front of the ship, and in seconds, the engine was spinning up. The gentle hum was the most reassuring thing Nicole had heard in months. She just hoped they would reach Kal in time to warn him.

"Scientist Ai," General Zhou's voice boomed from a speaker. "We know you are harboring the prisoner Nicole Bergeron. You will stand down now."

"Damn it," Nicole swore.

Ai continued the warm-up procedure, seemingly unfazed.

"The landing bay energy shields are activated," said Zhou. "There is no escape."

As Zhou was speaking, a ring of Jadid soldiers encircled the small ship. There was no way out. In order to fold and escape, they needed to be free of gravitational interference. If they folded in the landing bay, they would almost certainly implode.

Despite that, Ai continued to work. The ships systems were now fully online, and Nicole could see a panel of green in front of the Jadid.

"What are you doing?" Nicole asked. "We can't fold out of here. Are you gonna blast your way out?"

"Sorry," said Ai as she looked back at Nicole. "We don't

have any weapons, but we do have one thing that Zhou doesn't know about. I've been working on trying to overcome Rodriguez's paradox. I was looking at the pattern of gravitation interference against fold drive emissions and realized that there's potential to cancel out the waves and—"

"You figured out a way to fold from inside a ship," finished Nicole.

"Yup," chirped Ai happily.

"How certain are you that this will work?" asked Nicole as she eyed the Jadid outside, rolling a large bot toward the ship.

"About fifty percent," said Ai. "Much better odds than if we stay."

"Since you're not leaving the ship, we will have to take additional steps," said Zhou. As he spoke, an arm at the top of the bot began to spin. As it picked up speed, the arm started to glow brighter and brighter until it was almost painful to look at. A plasma cutter. The Jadid were going to slice through the ship's hull.

"I guess so," Nicole couldn't hide the uncertainty in her voice.

"Oh, it's certainly better," Ai said. "Even if you add in an unreasonably high margin of error."

The plasma cutter was slowly gliding towards their ship. It would be seconds before it started cutting through the hull.

"Are you ready?" asked Ai eagerly. "Although unplanned, this will be a great test of the new drive." She frowned. "Though I would have liked to have sensors to record it."

"Just do it." Nicole closed her eyes and waited.

A second later Ai's shout caused Nicole to jump. "We've arrived!"

"You ready for this?" asked Sergeant Kimathi.

"Ready as I'll ever be," said Kal.

Kal, Kimathi, Private Ma, and Private Chadha stood behind Bo in their vehicle's cargo bay. All five were wearing Nasi battle suits but hadn't placed their helmets on yet. The other Skulls and rebel fighters were in position at the bottom of the mountain, ready to enter through a service entrance.

"Let's go then," said Kimathi. He motioned to Bo. "After you."

The Humans placed on their helmets and followed Bo down the transport's ramp. They were only meters from the large oval entrance to the plasma lance. Two guards stood on either side and stiffened to attention as they approached with their datons still slung casually on their backs.

"Open the door," commanded Bo, "and take us to the central control room. I need to speak with this bases' security officer." His voice was distorted through his suit's external speaker.

Please work, Kal thought to himself.

One of the guards jumped to a panel near the door and the entrance dilated open without making a sound.

So far, so good, thought Kal. Maybe this plan will actually work.

They followed the Nasi guard through the warren of tunnels until they came to a heavy-set door. The guard placed a hand on the security panel and the door slid open, revealing a large circular room lined with consoles.

The four Nasi in the room turned to study them as they entered. Their faces betrayed no hint of emotion except a detached curiosity. One of them, clearly the senior officer based on the multiple lines of Shishen tattoos swirling around his body, stepped toward them.

"What are you doing here?" The question was delivered without malice or curiosity.

"We've been sent by Governor Fermott," Bo said. "You will allow us access to your security feeds. There have been multiple reports of leaks from this facility, and they must have come from one of your soldiers."

The officer shook his head, his face betraying a hint of anger. "That's impossible. There is no way for information to leave this facility." He held out a small tablet. "I want to see some sort of authorization."

"Move aside and contact the governor," said Bo. "Your traitor could be trying to escape right now."

"No." The word was final. Kal felt his stomach sink. Apparently, the Nasi weren't as easily cowed as they had hoped.

The officer turned to the men in the room. "Cover these soldiers and order all personnel to their stations." He turned back to Bo. "Take off your helmet and wait there. I *will* contact the governor's office to verify you."

One of the Nasi technicians began to tap away at his screen when all hell broke loose. Kimathi fired a plasma bolt, hitting the technician in the back and into his console. As the other Nasi jumped to cover, Bo fired a bolt into the officer's midsection.

Kal wasn't sure what security protocols were in the room and didn't want to allow the two remaining technicians time to activate them. They'd taken cover behind a large bank of consoles in the center of the room and started firing intermittent shots toward the Humans.

Kal motioned for the others to split and take the Nasi position from either side.

The two groups moved around the perimeter of the room, firing their datons at the top of the consoles to keep the enemy's heads down. As they grew parallel to the consoles, Kal and Kimathi lunged forward, firing at the two Nasi before they had a chance to react.

"Get the system's defenses down," Kal shouted after checking the room to make sure all the Nasi guards were down.

Bo ran over to one of the consoles, pulling out the small device that he had created from a pocket in his suit. It was what Chief Kanumba called a skeleton key—a device preprogrammed with intrusion algorithms designed to break the Nasi security protocols.

While Bo inserted the key into the system and began tapping on the screen, the others took positions to cover the main entrance to the room. Kal bent over the bodies of the technicians, looking for any sign they'd called for assistance. As he crouched down, a softly blinking light on the underside of the console caught his eye. Damn.

"They activated some sort of security system," Kal called out. He turned to Bo who was bent over the nearby console. "How's it coming?"

"I am not sure," the Jadid responded.

Kal wanted to tell him to hurry up. Unfortunately, there wasn't a thing the scientist could do; the key worked automatically, and no one in that room would be able to make it go faster. There wasn't even a timer or status indicator to tell them how long it would take.

"Should we tell the assault team to start?" asked Kimathi.

"Why not?" asked Kal. "Looks like things are going to crap anyways."

Kal sent the signal for the other team to breach the service entrance over the local net. Then he sent a signal over the wider planetary net, letting the other five assault teams know they'd begun their assault.

Just as Kal finished the second transmission, the door to the control room slammed open and two battle-suit clad Nasi rushed through the doorway. Before they were fully in the room, a rocket exploded between the two, sending them flying out of the room.

"Get that door sealed," shouted Kimathi.

"It's not possible," said Bo, still studying the console. "The alarm overrides the door control, preventing anyone from locking it."

"Well then, I want charges set around it. Anything comes through there gets vaporized."

Ma and Chadha ran to the door and began setting directional proximity mines on the surrounding walls.

"System's deactivated," shouted Bo.

A blast ripped through the front of the room. Kal dove to side of the console, his daton poised, and tried to make out anything in the smoke. Finally, he gave up and unleashed a nearly constant barrage of plasma fire towards the entrance of the room. Bolts from the other members of the Skulls flew through the dark toward the door as well. As the smoke cleared, Kal could see enough to make out two Nasi in battle suits slouched against the wall.

We're taking heavy resistance, reported Corporal Sato. Not even halfway to the nexus. We need you down here.

The Nasi have us pinned inside the security room, Kal said.

Damn it. We'll try and keep going. Sato cut the line.

Kal reviewed the layout of the plasma lance compound on his implant. The only way out of the control room was through the door they'd entered. The Nasi would have set up a kill zone outside the door to ensure they didn't get out—at least that what's Kal would have done. The good news was the hallway outside quickly branched a few hundred meters after they entered. If they could get past the initial defenses, they would have a chance to get away.

Kal scrambled across the room to Sergeant Kimathi, keeping his daton trained on the opening. "We need to get to the others."

"No shit, sir." Kal could picture Kimathi's expression

behind the Nasi helmet.

"Helpful," said Kal. "But any other thoughts? Like how to get past the Nasi soldiers that are surely waiting for us on the other side of the door?"

"Sometimes brute force is the only thing that works," Kimathi said. He motioned to the nearby fighters. "Count of three, we go through that door and destroy everything in the hallway outside. Use everything you got. Understand?"

Chadha and Ma nodded.

"Sir, you cover the door." Kal nodded.

Kimathi counted down and then jumped forward, using his suits thrusters to aid him as he swept to the door with the two fighters trailing behind. Before he'd reached the threshold, he'd launched a volley of antipersonnel missiles ahead of him, followed by a continuous stream of plasma from his daton. Chadha and Ma were right behind, running through the door with their rifles on full auto.

Return fire from the Nasi poured past them, melting the control room's bank of consoles. Most of the shots missed; but a few hit the energy shields built into the suits, which absorbed the shot in small arcs of white.

Kal jumped up and ran after the other three, motioning for Bo to come with him. The battle in the hallway was already over by the time he reached the threshold. Two Nasi battle suits lay against the wall, and three more were scattered on the ground ahead. Kal realized he had no way of telling if the corpses were of friends or enemies. He could see two figures standing in the corridor ahead of him. They weren't firing, which was a good sign.

We lost Chadha, Kimathi said over the local net.

Kal looked at the corpses scattered across the hallway; their identities hidden by the black battle suits. Which one was the private? He desperately wanted to know. It was silly, but he hated the idea that someone who he'd fought beside laying anonymous among the enemy.

Sato, we're on our way, Kal reported over the local net.

Hurry up. We're taking heavy casualties. The Nasi have heavy weapons down here.

They ran through the twisting tunnels of the base toward the rest of their team. The scars along the walls were evidence that the Nasi had carved them out of the rock, yet their strange paths made them seems like they were naturally occurring caverns. As they made their way downward, the planetary net started to fill with the chatter of status reports as the other five teams began their assaults around New America.

The nervousness and uncertainty that Kal had felt at the beginning of the mission had disappeared. They were committed. There was only one way forward and they were on it. At this point, there was nothing he could do except focus on the task at hand. This was how he liked it. No gray areas, no confusion. Just shoot and move.

Kal could hear the sounds of battle growing in front of them as increasingly brighter flashes of light reflected from dull walls.

The others are ahead, said Kimathi. We're approaching

from the enemy's rear. When I fire, light them up with everything you have.

The tunnel widened into a large circular room. Plasma scars and charring covered nearly every centimeter of the walls and ceiling. Shrapnel and pieces of destroyed equipment lay scattered across the floor. The Nasi forces had taken cover behind several large rock barriers in the center of the room. Most of them were unarmored, but Kal saw at least a few battle suits among the explosions that rocked through the area.

As soon as he was clear of the tunnel, Kimathi fired his daton at the Nasi while launching several missiles at them. Kal and the others were right behind, unleashing a maelstrom of destruction. The Nasi were fast, but not fast enough to avoid the wall of plasma and explosives that were hurled at them from behind. They either fell in place or dove from their cover, exposing themselves to the withering fire from the other side of the cavern.

The enemy in battle suits turned and flew toward Kal's forces. Nasi were quick; Nasi in battle suits were almost like lightning itself. They dodged through the plasma fire and explosions and straight toward Kal and the others. Soon they were among the Humans, firing their datons or swinging them in a furious weave of strikes.

One of the Nasi locked onto Kal, swinging their daton at him as they streaked past. Kal dodged out of the way of one of the strikes then brought his own daton to the side to block the next blow. They flew across the dark cavern, swirling around one another as Kal deflected blow after blow. The others were also caught up in the same aerial dance, facing off against the Nasi. The Humans on the other side of the room continued to rain fire down on the few Nasi that were still behind cover.

His opponent landed a viscous blow on Kal's helmet, sending him to the ground. His suit's shield flared as the Nasi fired a round at his prostrate body. Even with a battle suit, Kal was no match for the Nasi. It was a battle he couldn't win. At least not by conventional means.

He remembered Sergeant Jones, the Skulls' former Squad Leader.

"Sometimes you know you're licked," Jones had said, pacing in front of the squad. "When that happens ya got three choices. Go down swinging, run away, or"—he held up a finger for emphasis—"ya do somethin' so crazy it just might work."

It was time for option three.

The Nasi landed and rushed toward him, daton across his body, ready to swing. Kal started to fly back as if to avoid the blast, then reversed course, slamming into his opponent. He wrapped him up and pulled him close as they streaked across the room. As soon as Kal was body to body with the Nasi, he pressed the detonation button on the grenade in his left hand.

The blast sent them both flying to the ground. Kal's suit immediately lost power, and he couldn't see a thing as he hit the ground. Hard.

Kal couldn't move. The impact had knocked the air from his lungs, and he felt a wave of fire across his back. In the silent cocoon of the disabled suit his only companion was the pain that coursed through his body. Finally, he managed to pull his helmet off with his right hand and look around the cave. Without the enhanced optics of the suit, it was almost pitch-black. He could see the silhouettes of bodies in front of the small fires that flickered across the ground. The fighting was over. All Kal could hear were the groans of the wounded.

Kal stood up, almost crying out as his back protested. His cybernetic right arm was completely gone, and his left arm was bleeding through small gashes in the Nasi battle suit. Kal began to peel off the heavy armor, wincing as it pulled at the slashes across his body. A Nasi battle suit streaked across the room and landed next to him.

"You okay, sir?"

It was Sergeant Kimathi.

"I'll be fine," Kal replied. "Now help me get this damn thing off."

Kimathi gingerly helped Kal pull himself out of the Nasi suit—something that would have been impossible in a Human one.

"Sir, you sure?" asked Kimathi as he gently tugged the suit from the ruined stump of Kal's cybernetic arm. Kal noted the genuine tone of concern in the sergeant's voice. He never could understand Kimathi. Sometimes it seemed like the man hated him, other times it seemed like he revered Kal.

"I'm sure," Kal replied. He looked at Kimathi. "Thanks."

The sergeant gave a quick nod and flew across the room.

As Kal followed Kimathi on foot, Cell Chief Pham and a small cluster of fighters appeared in the dim light in front of him. After looking over Kal, she had one of her people wrap a bandage over his injured left arm. The nanobots and pain killers immediately went to work. By the time he reached the rest of the group, he could barely feel anything at all.

"Sergeant Kimathi has already started moving forward," reported Corporal Sato. "He said he couldn't wait any longer for your ancient ass to get here."

"Sounds like him," Kal replied.

They trudged forward, heading down one of the tunnels that branched from the room. Kal found himself surrounded by the other injured. Two fighters in Nasi battle suits trailed behind them, acting as guards. Small strings of light embedded in the walls guided their way as they continued to descend the mountain.

Get ready, Kimathi said over the local net. We're about to destroy the nexus.

"Time to see how good those plans Bo retrieved are," said Pham.

A second later, an enormous blast reverberated through the hallway in front of them. The energy seemed to ripple through the walls themselves, causing small pieces of rock to patter along the floor and raising a musty cloud of dust.

Did we do it? Kal wondered. Did we actually destroy the nexus?

"Well, we're alive," the Pham remarked philosophically as

she pulled herself from the ground.

As soon as the words were out of her mouth, a plasma bolt flew through the tunnel from behind them. Kal turned around and spotted the feline movements of several Nasi moving toward them. The two fighters in battle suits returned fire, causing the Nasi to scatter against the wall.

Pham cursed and tackled Kal to the ground as an antipersonnel missile flew over their heads and detonated against the tunnel wall, sending fragments of shattered rock through the mass of already injured Humans.

"You were saying?" Kal asked.

"Shut up." Pham aimed her daton at the far end of the tunnel and fired.

Kal had given up his rifle since he was down a limb and unable to use it. He pulled Pham's pistol from her holster and rolled over to aim down the tunnel. He could see shapes and shadows skittering just out of sight. It was impossible for him to tell how many there were. Whether thirty or three hundred, he didn't know. What he did know was that they were outgunned. The only people in their group who weren't injured were the two people in battle suits. The rest of them were like Kal, the walking wounded. They could put up a fight, but if the Nasi got much closer, they'd easily finish them off.

Sergeant Kimathi, we're under attack, Kal called out over the net. Get your ass over here, now.

Nexus has been destroyed, Kimathi replied. We're on our way back. Get ready to run.

373

Kal would have felt overjoyed if he wasn't trying to dodge plasma fire.

The Nasi continued to move closer. One of them ran ahead of the others, their body profiled against the wall lights. Plasma poured from their rifle as they smoothly ran toward the group of casualties. Kal took a calming breath, aimed, and pulled the trigger stud. His shot hit the Nasi in the torso, sending them to the ground.

Two—then three more—Nasi ran towards them. Their movements were not the coordinated attack Kal was used to. These were not soldiers; they were the workers and scientists that maintained the lance.

Why don't they leave? Kal wondered to himself. It's already over. We destroyed the nexus.

In truth, he realized he wouldn't ever know, and even if he did, he probably wouldn't understand. The Nasi thought differently than Humans. It was the same twisted logic that caused them to destroy the Earth as a way to *help* Humanity. The Jadid didn't understand the Nasi fully, and they were the same species. What hope did a Human have of grasping why they did what they did?

A grenade exploded in near a cluster of already wounded people, eliciting shrieks of pain. The Nasi's attack was close enough that they were picking off those that were too wounded to take proper cover against the tunnel sides or those that were too far to the rear of the formation.

Follow me. It was Kimathi. We've got a wall of plasma heading your way.

What?

No time to explain. Just be ready to run.

A battle suit roared past Kal and the others, landing near the Nasi. As it landed, it spun in place and plasma blossomed from its rifle. Several Nasi fell backwards, crying out in pain. The soldier swung their daton across their body, taking out two more Nasi that were rushing toward them.

Five more battle suits flew through the scattered wounded directly at the Nasi attackers. They pushed the Nasi back toward where they'd come from until all Kal could see was the bluish-green flashes of plasma.

Get up and run, Kimathi called out over the net. Kal could sense the urgency in the words even if they came through his implant as a mechanical monotone. He noticed a glow emanating from where the nexus had been. It was growing brighter.

Kal jumped to his feet and rushed to help people up, sending them to follow Kimathi and the others. As he helped the last wounded up, the rest of the assault team ran past, hundreds of Humans with looks of terror on their face. The tunnel was now almost as bright as day from the glow behind them. A wall of plasma, extending from floor to ceiling, moved toward them, vaporizing everything in its path.

Kal took off the other way, sprinting as fast as he could. The glow from behind him continued to grow and he could feel the heat and smell ozone. He didn't dare look back; the last thing he wanted to do was trip on the uneven tunnel floor. Instead, he focused on the people in front of him and on the sound his feet made on the ground and his deep ragged breaths.

Kal arrived in the circular room that had been the center of the earlier fighting and weaved through the corpses, following the stream of people into another tunnel that sloped upwards, towards the surface. Kal's lungs screamed in pain as he ran, complementing the stabs of pain in his back.

The light from the plasma slowly faded. When Kal looked back, he couldn't see anything but darkness; they'd outrun the plasma. He slowed his pace but continued to move at a brisk jog.

Kal cheered in his head as he ran through the oval utility door of the base. Around him was more evidence of fighting: craters, bodies, and destroyed equipment. The polar wind sheared through him and the sunlight streaming from above caused him to blink rapidly. Despite the carnage, there was no battle going on anymore.

Somehow, he'd survived.

Kimathi reported that Sergeant Popov and Corporal Diaz were both dead and Bo was missing. Half the Tac-I squad was gone. The news wasn't a surprise but still hurt worse than anything the Nasi had done to him.

Kal cut the connection and joined the other survivors as they slowly made their way to the assault ships.

On their way back to the Fridge, the ship's pilot announced that Samsara Fleet had folded into the space around New America, and a weak cheer broke out inside the cabin. For Kal and the other survivors of the plasma lance, there was nothing for them to do but wait. Their part was done.

They listened on the open net for any news of what was happening above. As expected, it was completely silent. The ships touched down inside the Fridge and Kal rushed as fast as his damaged body would let him to the base's control room. He found a small crowd already there, listening to the fleet's net and watching the tacmap.

"You're back," Asha cried, running to him. Her face fell as she saw his missing arm.

"Don't worry," Kal said. "I lost it awhile back." The girl looked at him, confused. "It was a cybernetic arm. I just need to get a new one." He faked a smile.

Four of the other five other teams had successfully destroyed their targets but had sustained extremely heavy losses. The other team was a full loss; their last transmission had been their cries of pain as a plasma lance took down a Samsara Fleet ship. The lance destroyed another two ships before the fleet was able to maneuver from its field of fire.

Without five of their six plasma lances, the Nasi weren't able to hold against the superior firepower of Samsara Fleet.

Before long, only two Nasi ships were left in orbit. They attempted to use the space above the remaining plasma lance as a safe haven. But after an hour, the fleet were able to wipe them out and fully secure the space above the planet. The fleet made a planet-wide announcement declaring New America liberated and calling on the remaining Nasi to surrender.

It was as if a switch had been flipped. The mood inside the Fridge transformed from mourning into a jubilant celebration. As the news spread that the Nasi fleet had been eradicated, people ran through the caverns, darting between ships and shouting at the top of their lungs. Several had been optimistic enough to bring drinks and cracked open bottles of liquor to celebrate their victory. Kal and what remained of the Skulls joined in, but they remained a drink behind and a step back from the others. There were still two planets left to liberate. Their mission was not done.

As he walked through the cave, a smile plastered on his face, patting people on the back with his remaining arm, Kal noticed the Nasi sitting off to the side. What could they be feeling? They'd been instrumental in bringing down their own people.

Kal took a seat on the front of a transport and watched the celebrations continue. He noticed the people who stood by themselves, watching, and wondered what they had lost. What could make them not want to join in the revelry that was going on around them? Were they like him, wondering if the cost had been worth it?

"What'll we do next?" asked Asha as she sat on a metal crate next to Kal.

"I dunno," he replied. "We've won, but it will take years for New America to really recover. The Domespat still rule the planet." He couldn't imagine the fascist government would last long now that their Nasi enablers had disappeared. But he also couldn't imagine they wouldn't fight to remain in power with everything they had.

"You remember your promise, right?"

Kal nodded and turned his head to meet her gaze. "Of course. I can't wait to introduce you to Nicole." He didn't dare add—couldn't add—if she's still alive.

Asha smiled, her entire face lighting up. "Me neither."

"We still have to do one thing though."

Asha's smile vanished. "What?"

"Well, there are still two planets left," Kal said. "They need our help too, and we can't let them down. I'll need to go for just a bit to help them."

"But—"

"You won't be alone, ever again," Kal said emphatically. "I promise. You have all of these people"—he waved his hand around the chamber—"to look after you."

"I don't want to go with just *anyone*," Asha protested.

"I will come back," Kal promised.

Kal's implant beeped. He'd received a priority transmission from the fleet. It was Ancient Bao Wang.

Kal, you came through, the Ancient said.

We always do.

We need to talk with you. There're some elements of the transition of New America back to Human control that we need to discuss. I'm afraid it can't wait.

Kal sighed. Of course. There was always another thing. Always the next mission. The next problem to solve.

I need a ride. Our ship was destroyed. The ships that remained in the Fridge were too old for him to even *try* and leave the atmosphere with.

Again? How many ships is that? Bao asked with what Kal could only guess was amusement.

Kal had lost count. *It's enough.*

I'll get you a new ride, said the Ancient. Just you. Leave your team there. He cut the connection.

The Ancient clearly wasn't letting their victory on New America get to his head. Nicole had told Kal he acted as if he was being charged by the word when he spoke. Ancient Wang was the opposite.

"Who was that?" asked Asha.

"Ancient Wang. He's the leader of the Jadid fleet that came to help us."

Asha screwed up her mouth. "Dad told me the Jadid never helped anyone but themselves."

Interesting Yonder would tell her that, thought Kal.

"Well, maybe in the past," he said. "They've changed."

Asha shrugged. "I guess anyone can."

The Jadid tender arrived shortly after. Whatever Ancient Wang wanted, he wasn't wasting any time. When the Jadid stepped out of the ship, there was a brief moment of panic. Some of the people hadn't heard they were coming and thought the base was under attack.

"Get back soon, sir." Sergeant Kimathi said, raising his glass towards Kal. "We still got work to do."

Kal raised his good arm in response and crouched into the small Jadid ship. The three Jadid soldiers gracefully followed behind, and the door closed with small hiss. As they lifted off from the planet, no one spoke. The passengers looked across the two benches of seats at each other.

Kal thought how strange it was that the Jadid were the ones who were the least changed by this universe. The Nasi had spent several years among Humans and had unconsciously adopted their mannerisms, taking on many aspects of their culture, and had generally become more Human themselves. The Jadid, on the other hand, had remained aloof and separated despite having been a part of Samsara Fleet for over a year.

They left the atmosphere and Kal looked down at New America. The patchwork of zones and blue oceans appeared pristine. It was if the past two years had never happened. Billions of people below had been liberated, and there was no way to know. He wasn't sure what he expected or why that bothered him. But it did.

Surprisingly, the tender landed on Ancient Wang's flagship, the *Galaxy's Edge* rather than the *Gedorhan's*

Return, General Samaha's flagship.

The landing bay was a hive of activity as Kal had expected. Jadid pilots and crews glided purposely between ships as maintenance techs conducted checks. A steady stream of fighters and assault ships flew through the bay's energy shield, heading towards the planet.

Ship Chief Kevin Yoshida, the commander of the *Galaxy's Edge*, stood waiting as Kal exited the tender. He was enormous even for a Jadid, standing at least a head taller than those around him. Kal was surprised to see him, having expected to find Wang waiting for him with a smile and a hand extended.

"Congratulations on the victory, General." Yoshida gave a curt nod of his head and then turned, clearly expecting Kal to follow—which he did with some hesitation. Something felt off.

"I see you're already landing forces on the planet," said Kal.

"Yes." Yoshida slowed, realizing his normal pace was forcing Kal to jog behind him. "We must take advantage of the situation. The Nasi forces are scattered, and Ancient Baykara is still at large."

"I'm sure she'll show up," said Kal. "I mean, it's not like she's got a lot of allies down there. At least not anymore."

"You'd be surprised," said Yoshida, stepping into a lift. "She's exceptionally skilled at manipulation. Look what she's done already."

"She did create the Nasi," Kal admitted. He followed the Jadid officer into the lift, the door silently closing behind them.

"That she did."

"What will happen to the Nasi on the planet?" Kal asked.

"I believe that Ancient Wang wants to speak to you about that." Yoshida shifted his giant frame slightly, a rare sign of discomfort from the normally stoic officer.

The question seemed to shake Yoshida enough that he disengaged from the conversation. Instead, he made a show of concentrating on tapping instructions into his comeca to forestall any further conversation.

"Kal Norman," Ancient Bao Wang's voice seemed to almost boom off the walls of his office as Kal entered. Kal noticed a few new items in the room, splashes of colorful artwork on the walls, a small statue—poorly made—of a man with his arms extended on the desk. The Ancient wrapped Kal in a hug, almost lifting him off the floor.

"Kal," said Bao, setting him down, "we've achieved an amazing victory today. You've achieved an amazing victory. I've already been briefed on what you were up against. Somehow you did it. Amazing."

It was the kind of cloying speech that Kal was used to from the man. He was the opposite of his "children," the Jadid. Bao was a man who led with his emotions and seemed to put everything out there, even if much of what he put out was BS.

"Sit down, Kal," Bao said, motioning to the chairs set up in the corner of his office. "I'd offer you some whisky, but I know you'll just decline."

"Water would be just fine right about now." Kal walked

with the Ancient to the corner where several chairs were arranged around a small table topped with two decanters. Bao poured two drinks: one clear, one a deep ochre.

He held up his glass in a quick toast and then took a deep swallow. "You don't know how long I've waited for this drink. To finally get Esma. Well, suffice it to say it's been decades in coming. Centuries even."

"It's amazing," Kal agreed, taking a moment to study the intricate crystal glass in his hand. "But Esma is only a part of it."

"No," Bao said, almost shouting. Kal's head popped up to look at the man. Something was different. "She's the sickness, the disease. The Nasi are but a symptom."

"Perhaps. But we still need to handle them. They'll need to be relocated and somehow repatriated back into Jadid society. Have you discussed it at all with the other Ancients?"

Bao scoffed. "Musa and Kingsley will do what I say at this point." He swirled his glass, causing the whisky to creep up the side, perilously close to the lip. "You know, I've come to realize that the centuries did something to us. Perhaps it was Altterra. I don't know. But it made us complacent. At first, we just had to survive. Then we built a goddamn society. It's insane."

Kal just studied the man. What had happened to him?

"Somewhere along the line, the others became content with what they had. Don't rock the boat. Don't make any waves. Just sit in our palace and watch our children"—he made air quotes—"do everything. When I got here, I realized exactly what we had been missing…"

"What?"

"This!" Wang raised his glass in the air. "Happiness. A sense of enjoyment out of life." He leaned forward toward Kal. "Esma is twisted by her own issues. Her sense of revenge. Her inability to see the bigger picture. But she was right about one thing. We had to make a change." Bao poured whisky into his glass until it dribbled over the rim.

Kal's eyes darted through the room. The Ancient must be drunk. But there was something more—a mask had been dropped. This was the real Bao Wang. Kal pondered his situation. He was helpless, there was no way to get off the *Galaxy's Edge*.

"I don't necessarily disagree with anything you're saying, but what exactly does this all mean?" asked Kal. "What are you saying?"

Bao leaned forward. "We burn it all to the ground, Kal." He laughed. "Wipe out the Nasi and their fascist leader. Take out these corrupt governments and build a new Humanity. Take over the goddamn galaxy. Do what Esma *said* she wanted to do and do it right."

"I'm guessing you'd be the leader of this new Human empire?" asked Kal. He wished he'd brought a pistol with him.

Bao touched his nose with an index finger. "At first, sure. But one day I'll pass away. The curse of living in this wonderful universe." He finished his glass and slammed it on a table. "Then we'll see about a new way to govern, one that's fair and equitable. One that ensures Humanity progresses and rules the galaxy rather than being the pathetic bootlicks they were before we got here."

"What about Samaha?" asked Kal. "What did she think about all this?"

Bao shook his head sadly. How had Kal been fooled so long by this man? How had he not realized exactly what he was? Samaha was gone. It was a hard blow. He'd never been friends with the woman, but he'd respected her. She'd been a rock in a position where most people would have folded.

"General Zhou?" asked Kal. "What about the other fleet?"

"General Norman, he orchestrated this entire operation. How could he not agree?"

Despair washed over Kal. The entire operation had been a setup from the start. They'd never had a chance. They'd been fighting Esma Baykara so that Bao Wang would twist the entire thing to his advantage. It also meant that even if Nicole liberated Patagonia, she'd end up in the same situation Kal was in now.

"I see you realize what this means," said Bao, placing his hand over Kal's. "But listen. I came here to see what you thought of my real plan—"

Kal started to speak, but the Ancient held up a hand. "Don't bother. You've already told me everything I need to know." He pulled a kinetic pistol from his robes, an old model Kal hadn't seen before. "I want you to know I appreciate everything you've done for the cause. We never would have made it without you."

A circle of light from the corridor appeared on the floor. Someone had entered the room. Kal didn't dare turn around. He wanted to see the round coming. Bao looked past him, his lips twisted in annoyance.

"What the hell? I told you—"

He dropped to the ground in a heap. Kal turned to see Ship Chief Yoshida with a pistol in his hand. The Jadid leapt to Kal and pulled him out of his seat by his arm.

"General Norman, we need to get out of here now!"

"Do not run. Do not look around. Do not do anything that would attract attention," Yoshida hissed. "The order for your capture has not reached the crew yet."

"Wha—"

"There will be time to explain everything later."

"Did you kill Ancient Wang?" Kal asked.

"No." Yoshida sounded scandalized. "I could never do that." A pause. "Even if it might be better for all."

The ship chief paid no attention to the other Nasi officers they passed in the hallway. Nasi rank did not directly correlate to the ranks of the Earth Defense Force or Samsara Fleet, but Yoshida was the ship's commander and outranked almost everyone aboard.

They ended up in one of the capital ship's gigantic landing bays, this one filled with Human ships organized in no decipherable manner. A few Jadid technicians wandered through the area, stopping occasionally to inspect a bulkhead or tap something on their comeca.

Yoshida grabbed his arm and rushed him through the ships. "Pick a ship."

As Kal scanned the room, the implications of what Ancient Wang had told him fully sunk in. The fleet that he had been a part of had been twisted to become the very thing they were fighting against. Samsara Fleet had been overtaken and General Samaha overthrown. What had happened to his friends in the fleet? Colonel Petrov, commander of the *Ofira*? Chief Kanumba's son, Jae-Ho, what would happen to him?

"We're running out of time." Yoshida kept glancing at his comeca. "Pick something now."

Kal walked towards a sleek Shreen brand privateer vessel with the name *Paycheck* emblazoned on its front. Its design was somewhere between a merchantman and fighter. It had enough room for long voyages but also had some speed and more than a few weapons. Kal stepped up the ramp and quickly inspected the interior. When he'd been a merchant, he would have loved having a ship like this. In his current situation, he wasn't sure it mattered what ship he used.

"Get out of here," Yoshida said, tapping on his comeca. "And I should warn you, the other half of the fleet, commanded by your General Zhou left for Patagonia already." And that meant he already had a chance to kill Nicole.

"I'll—"

"Do not tell me what you're planning," said Yoshida. "I doubt we'll see each other again." He wrung his hands then held one out to Kal. "Best of luck."

Kal shook the ship chief's hand and watched numbly as he walked down the ramp. "You're already cleared to depart," said Yoshida, looking back. "Get out before the Ancient regains consciousness."

"What to do next?" Kal asked himself.

He rushed to the bridge and activated the ship's engine. It was difficult to go through the preflight sequences with one arm, so he had to rely on using voice commands with the ship's AI. It was something a professional pilot like himself hated doing since AI tended to be overly cautious.

As soon as the console was green, Kal lifted off and shot through the bay's energy shield, joining the stream of Jadid ships heading toward the planet's surface.

His first mission was to check on his soldiers. The Jadid knew about the Fridge, and he was certain that Ancient Wang would order the Skulls to be captured or killed.

The breath left Kal's body as the *Paycheck's* sensors swept the site of the base. It had been obliterated. The giant cavern was a smoking ruin, destroyed by orbital fire. Multiple fires burned in the area and several Jadid ships were on the ground, their soldiers sweeping through the area for survivors.

The darkness that Kal always fought to keep at bay took over. All had been lost. There was no chance of saving the people he called friends.

A sensor pinged; the Jadid fighters in the area were lighting him up with their scanners. Kal immediately pulled the yoke up and gained altitude, trying to create enough separation between him and what had become his enemy. Thankfully, the Jadid didn't give chase, and Kal was able to exit the planet's atmosphere.

As New America faded behind him, Kal tried to find some ray of hope. He cut the ship's engines, letting the *Paycheck* speed through the vacuum as he tried to decide what to do next. Everything they'd worked through had been lost. Everything he'd done had been a waste.

Kal let the ship speed away from the planet for hours before finally making his decision. He input the coordinates to his destination and slapped the fold button with a small sob. The *Paycheck* disappeared.

Nicole | New America

New America appeared on the viewscreen in front of Nicole and Ai. Their ship's sensors immediately picked up the large Jadid fleet as well as several clouds of debris scattered in orbit. The battle had already happened, and Ancient Wang and his Liberation Fleet had won. It should have been a time for celebration, but Humanity had only traded one overlord for another.

Nicole eyed the tacmap, wondering what was happening aboard the Jadid fleet orbiting the planet.

"I can't believe all of these ships would turn their back on the fleet," said Nicole.

"There were rumors that Ancient Wang was performing loyalty tests on his crews for the past year," said Ai as she started to maneuver them toward the planet. "He'd remove anyone who questioned his orders."

"What about the *Ofira* and the *Merrimack*?" Nicole asked. They were the only two remaining Human ships. Would Wang just destroy them?

Ai shrugged. "I imagine they'll fall in line. I would guess

that the Ancient has Humans in place to take command. Or perhaps he'll just have them destroyed."

Colonel Petrov. Nicole wondered what would happen to her friend. Unfortunately, Petrov was back in Patagonia, and Nicole was light-years away. She wished she'd spent more time paying attention to what was going on around her rather than just focusing on the next mission.

"We're being hailed," reported Ai.

"Audio only," said Nicole. "I have to imagine Wang has triggers to make my image set off every alarm his security team has. When he finds out what you did, you'll be in the database too."

"I'm looking forward to that," Ai replied dryly. She activated the ship's comms.

"Jadid ship *McCullough*, report intended destination."

"Tiradentes," Ai replied.

A moment later, a different voice came on the line. "*McCullough*, you are assigned to the Liberation Fleet around Patagonia. What are you doing here?"

"We were ordered here by General Zhou to retrieve a Human prisoner."

"Head to these coordinates." A series of coordinates flashed on the viewscreen. "We will have soldiers there to confirm your orders. Any deviation will be met with lethal force."

"Well, I definitely know *not* to go to those coordinates," Nicole said when the line had clicked off. Ai nodded in agreement.

"Was this ship designed to be a skip ship?" asked Nicole. It wasn't like any skip ship she'd been in before.

"Well, it was originally built to study irregularities in deep space," said Ai.

"Explains why it's built like a rock."

The *McCullough's* hull was at least twice the thickness of similarly sized vessels. Metal supports stretched underneath the flooring providing additional support as well. It looked to be nothing if not solid.

"I think we'll need to test exactly how durable it is," Nicole said.

Ai raised an eyebrow. "Even if we were to crash into one the Jadid ships, they'd still be able to destroy us. Additionally, we'd almost certainly not reach them before being incinerated by plasma."

"What if we crashed into the ocean?" Nicole asked. "Made it look like an accident."

"We'd need to escape the wreckage before they came to recover us." Ai paused. "It would also be a waste of a priceless experimental ship as well."

Nicole nodded. "True, but the Jadid just captured the planet from the looks of the tacmap. They have forces scattered all over. There's a good chance they might not even see where we crashed. If we enter the atmosphere fast enough, they'll have a hard time following our trajectory."

Ai looked skeptical.

"Any other suggestions and I'm all ears. Absent that, let's go smash into the ocean."

The Jadid scientist finally sighed and gave a small shake of her head. "Fine."

Nicole studied New America. Where could they go? At first, she'd wanted it to be somewhere near Tiradentes. The city was the location of the Nasi Foothold, which she assumed the Jadid were already in the process of occupying. If Kal and the Skulls were still alive, they would most likely be imprisoned there.

Unfortunately, half the sensor platforms on the planet were concentrated in the area. The Jadid would be able to locate them almost instantly. She studied the northern portion of the planet. There were a few small towns near the poles and not a sensor platform in sight according to the tacmap.

"There," said Nicole, pointing to a small town named Hope. The ocean was only a few kilometers from the town. "We can land in the ocean near there and then make our way to the town."

"Through the tundra?" asked Ai. "I may survive, but you almost certainly will not."

"We've got thermal blankets and an emergency kit," said Nicole, pointing to a small box affixed to the inside of the hull.

Ai sighed again but began tapping on the console, entering in their new destination. As they reached the edge of the exosphere, she adjusted the ship's flight path, turning them almost ninety degrees. Nicole hoped that would throw off the Jadid and allow them to escape.

They strapped on their restraints, placing the webs of

padded straps across their torsos and waists. They were much thicker than the ones that Nicole was used to, clearly designed for severe impacts.

The ship's thrusters fired at their maximum output, sending a deep thrum reverberating through the reinforced hull. The Jadid fleet continued to hail them, clearly realizing they were not following instructions. A phalanx of missiles shot from one of the capital ships and flew toward them. Nicole estimated they would reach the *McCullough* right as it entered New America's atmosphere, giving them a fifty-fifty chance as to whether the ship would be destroyed in mid-flight. She liked the odds.

"Well, we're definitely committed now," remarked Ai. "At max velocity and beginning our entry."

Seconds later, they were buffeted by a series of small thumps as the Jadid missiles exploded from the atmospheric friction of reentry. Nicole looked at the fast-approaching planet and wondered if they'd live through the crash. She'd faced death many times before and found that the more often she did, the more philosophical she became. Was landing on New America even worth it? Was Kal still alive? Her heart said there was still her a chance, but her head said that it was insane.

"Firing lateral thrusters," Ai said. The *McCullough's* trajectory changed again, and they began moving diagonally while still dropping like a rock.

As the ice-capped polar mountains grew to dominate the viewscreen, the ship's reverse thrusters fired, and Nicole routed all available power to the inertial dampeners. Her vision still grew hazy and faded out from the pressure of their sudden change in momentum.

Nicole woke to the sound of them screeching on metal and the groaning of the sturdy ship being subjected to forces that would destroy any other one. The small air bags built into the restraints had inflated to further cushion Nicole and Ai from the impact. Nicole could see the eerie red glow of the emergency lighting through her blurred vision.

"We've successfully landed," said Ai cheerfully.

They unstrapped themselves and unsteadily made their way to the back of the ship. Nicole grabbed the survival kit and quickly checked the contents. A few ration bars, some thermal blankets, an emergency transponder, bandages, and some other small items. Thankfully, there were several breathers inside to allow them to swim under the icy water.

She handed one to Ai and pulled another over her own head, then strapped the kit onto her back.

"Ready?" asked Nicole.

Ai nodded.

Nicole slammed the emergency open switch on the side hatch, and it sprang open, immediately letting in a gout of water. Her body went into shock and she could barely breath as the water instantly reached her waist. Once the flow of water had subsided, they swam out of the vehicle and made their way toward shore.

The breather not only allowed Nicole to breath underwater, it let her see as well. She made out small schools of fish swimming around them as well as the dark shadows of larger creatures below. They kept under the surface, swimming slowly but steadily toward the shore. What must have been a couple of minutes felt like a lifetime to Nicole. Her body numb, she straggled onto the pebble-strewn shore and looked back. Small chunks of ice floated on the ocean surface, but the *McCullough* was nowhere to be seen.

Ai flopped down onto the ground next to Nicole. "This was… an incredibly dumb idea."

"It. Was. The. Best I could. Come up with," Nicole said through chattering teeth.

After some fumbling, she managed to pull out two thermal blankets and activate them. She lay on the ground next to Ai waiting for her body to recover enough that she could actually move.

"That ship was priceless," said Ai wistfully.

"So's our lives."

"If the Nasi don't capture it, we should try and recover it," said Ai.

Nicole nodded. That was way too far into the future for her to think about right then. Her main focus was not dying from exposure.

"You ready?" asked the Jadid, the purple color in her face having returned.

Nicole swore under her breath and cursed her frail Human body. It was so unfair the Jadid had so many genetic advantages. After a couple more minutes of recovery, she staggered to her feet.

"Let's go."

They trudged along the coarse sand, heading towards Hope. From there, Nicole wasn't sure what they'd do. But she knew she wouldn't stop until she'd found Kal.

Esma | New America

Esma Baykara cursed as New America disappeared from the viewscreen. She'd been forced to run like a coward from Bao's loathsome Samsara Fleet. She'd thought her plan was perfect. Lure them in and then destroy them.

This universe is a curse, thought Esma.

It was this universe that had cast her out, destroyed everything she'd loved. Now that she'd returned, it felt like it was one failure after another. But she'd already gone in with everything she had. There was no returning to Altterra now. Patagonia and New America had fallen. Her scout had told her that before Esma had executed her for her failure. With only two of the Human planets under her control, she knew it was but a matter of time before Bao came calling.

She idly twisted a strand of her graying hair around her finger. Just a couple of years ago, it had been a sandy brown. She hadn't expected the discomfort she'd started to feel as her body aged. Her time running short and Bao would consolidate his control on the two planets he'd captured and then come for the other two. She didn't have much hope of stopping him.

"Grand Ancient, where to?" asked the ship's pilot.

"Mariga," she replied.

She had a little bit of time before Bao would come after her. The ice-covered planet was her favorite Human colony. She'd never liked the cold, but she did love the dark and twisting confines of the network of caves under the planet's surface. It would be there that she would destroy Bao. She'd make him pay for his betrayal.

In the end, Esma knew she couldn't win. But she also knew she could make Bao bleed.

Aamina | Patagonia

"That piece of crap," General Aamina Samaha muttered as she watched the Jadid assault ships sweep over her head.

She'd never fully trusted the Ancient, and she thanked her lucky stars she hadn't. He'd always seemed like he was playing a different game. Now that his plan had been revealed, Samaha wished she'd been better prepared. But at least she'd done what she could.

She was glad that she'd seen the signs in General Zhou and realized he'd been brainwashed by Ancient Wang. It had given her the chance to escape once the battle around Patagonia had finished. General Frederick Zhou had been a good officer, but he'd been corrupted by Wang, and she could only guess what the snake had told him.

Hopefully, the *Ofira* and the *Merrimack* would be long gone from Patagonia, heading toward a secret rendezvous spot. Before the fleet had folded, she'd warned their commanders, Colonels Petrov and Richards, that something may happen and to be ready to leave if it did. Her spies within the Jadid had warned her that the Ancient had something planned and knew to hold their tongues and wait for further instructions.

"What do we do, ma'am?" asked her aide, Private Bolin Ricci.

"We get the hell out of here," said Samaha. "Then we find the Skulls."

"Do you really think they're alive?" asked the private.

"You know as well as I do they are," Samaha said. "And I'm sure they're pretty pissed."

Aamina Samaha had had a long and somewhat illustrious military career. She'd fought in the Torgham War as an officer in the EDF and against the Nasi as the commander of Samsara Fleet. She'd seen her fair share of the galaxy and had learned a thing or two. She'd learned that allies and enemies could change at any moment and to always understand people's motivation. Ancient Wang had won the day. He'd captured Patagonia and she had to assume his forces had done the same at New America. But he was at the mercy of forces beyond his control or understanding.

The Nasi had started to learn that holding onto a planet and a people were *much* more difficult than capturing them.

Bao clearly hadn't figured that out yet. The other thing he hadn't learned was to never—*never*—piss off Aamina Samaha.

It was a lesson she was going to enjoy teaching.

If you enjoyed this book and want to receive additional stories for free then please consider subscribing to my newsletter. You can find a link at my website: www.rileycollins.info. You will get free books and short stories and occasionally be notified of new releases and offers. You will not be spammed or have your information shared with anyone else.

Author's Note

Thank you for reading the fifth book in the Samsara Fleet series. Originally, I had planned on making the series five books, but as the story unfolded, I realized it just wasn't going to be able to be wrapped up in five books. That said, I expect the next book to be the last in the series and plan on making it as long as it takes to get done. I hope that you will stay around for this final chapter.

In this novel, my intention was to compare the reactions and responses of Kal and Nicole when facing a very similar situation. Their journeys are intended to be very similar but diverge due to choices they make and the unique nature of each planet. I've heard from some readers that they like it better when they are together (and I'm sure they would agree) but sometimes life just doesn't work out that way. :)

Being a self-published author has been an adventure. Continuing to try and tell a good story while learning the ins and out of finding new readers is a challenge, an incredibly rewarding one.

Thanks,

Riley

Glossary

Organizations / Species

Council of Ancients - The ruling council of the Jadid. Consists of the Humans who have survived since the original experiment stranded them in a new universe.

Domespat - The Domestic Patrol is a repressive police force on New America.

Earth Defense Force (EDF) - Former military force for the UEG. Ended shortly after the destruction of Earth and capture of the four Human colonies by the Nasi.

Jadid - A race descended from Humans who were unwillingly used as test subjects in the development of the fold drive. When the Humans, now called the Ancients, arrived in a new universe, their offspring had mutated due to the unique properties of their universe. The mutations changed their appearance and greatly increased their physical strength, dexterity, and endurance. The Jadid also were found to cease aging within their universe once they reached adulthood.

Nasi - A sect within the Jadid. Let by Ancient Esma Baykara. They are dedicated to returning the Jadid to the Human universe and leading Humanity against the other species of the galaxy.

Not Bergeron's Boneheads (aka the Bones) - An elite scout team formed from members of the Skulls. Led by Lieutenant Colonel Nicole Bergeron.

Not Norman's Numbskulls (aka the Skulls) - An elite scout team formed immediately after the initial Nasi attack. Led by Brigadier General Kal Norman.

Patagonia Front - Rebel group on the planet of Patagonia that's led by Frederick Kinawadi, a former member of the Skulls.

Samsara Fleet - A multispecies fleet dedicated to the defeat of the Nasi forces. Originally made up of the surviving species of the Nasi attack, it was greatly supplemented by the inclusion of the Jadid Liberation Fleet under Ancient Bao Wang.

Tac-I - Tactical Insertion. Soldiers that are trained for clandestine missions, such as capturing bases and stations.

Tiradentes Liberation Front (TLF).- One of several rebel groups on New America. Located in the area around the planetary capital and split into distinct operational cells.

Unified Earth Government (UEG) - Former interstellar government of Humanity. Ended when the Nasi destroyed Earth.

Planets

Altterra - Home planet of the Jadid. First discovered by the Ancients when the experiment they were part of failed, sending them into another universe.

Earth – Home planet of Humanity. Destroyed by the Nasi in their initial invasion.

Mariga - Human colony. Extremely cold surface

temperatures has forced all Human settlements below ground into large subterranean cities. Controlled by the Nasi.

New America - Human colony. Centrally planned with large zones for various activities, such as industry, mining, housing. Capital is Tiradentes. Controlled by the Nasi with the New American Empire as their puppet government.

Patagonia - Human colony. Has one large continent, Pangea. Capital is Kasongo. Controlled by the Nasi with Foyleton, led by Karl Garcia, as the Human Government.

Wudexingqiu - Human colony. Planet is almost completely water with isolated islands. Most cities and development occur under the oceans. Controlled by the Nasi.

Key Characters

General Aamina Samaha - Former EDF General. Highest ranking member of the EDF who survived the Nasi invasion. Current commander of Samsara Fleet.

Ancient Bao Wang - One of the original Ancients stranded on Altterra. Commander of the Jadid Liberation Fleet forces.

Bowen Nguyen - One of the Jadid's foremost experts in fold drive technology. Originally captured by the Nasi to assist them with the development of skip ships, he was rescued by the Skulls and joined their team.

Staff Sergeant Ekon Kimathi - Tac-I squad leader for the Bones. Originally from New America, he joined the EDF shortly after the Nasi invasion.

Grand Ancient Esma Baykara - One of the original

Ancients who was stranded on Altterra and founded the Jadid. Esma harbors a deep grudge against Humanity for being stranded and created the Nasi.

Brigadier General Kal Norman - Former EDF Colonel who retired when his family died in a tragic accident. Spent a decade as a free merchant, transporting cargo across the galaxy. When the Nasi attacked, he returned to the EDF and then helped lead the initial resistance against the occupiers.

Lieutenant Colonel Nicole Bergeron - Former diplomat for the UEG. Initially held as a prisoner for unknowingly trading secrets to the Nasi. Given a direct commission into Samsara Fleet by General Samaha.

Cell Chief Rafaela Pham – Commander of the largest operational cell within the Tiradentes Liberation Front.